VIRIDIA

<u>BOOKS BY TIM FRANKOVICH</u>

<u>Heart of Fire</u>
Until All Curses Are Lifted
Until All Bonds Are Broken
Until All the Gods Return *(coming soon)*

<u>Dragontek Lore</u>
Viridia

VIRIDIA

DRAGONTEK LORE, BOOK 1

by Tim Frankovich

To the McMillan family,
heroes all,
fighting against a more insidious dragon
for far too long.

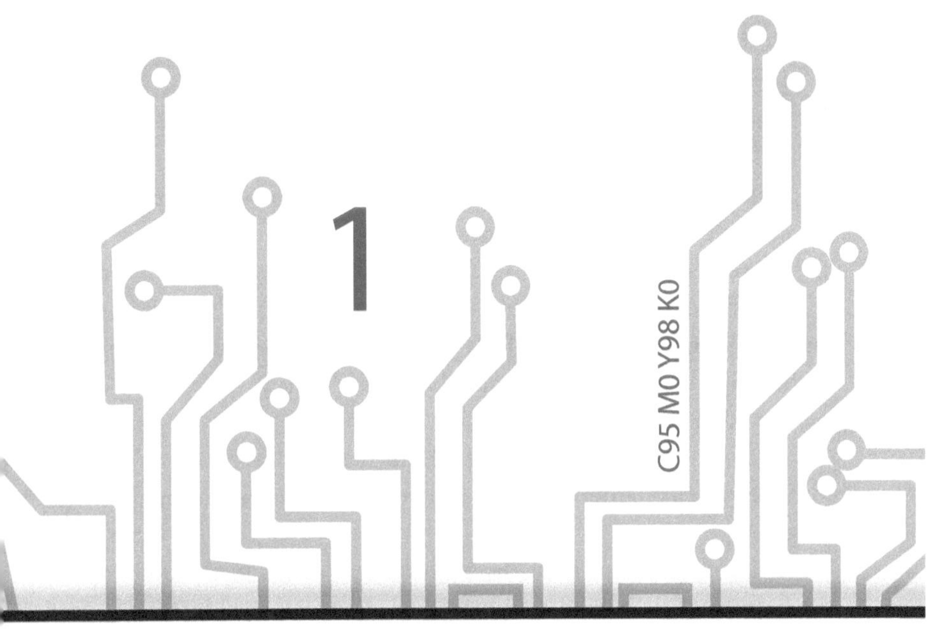

"What's it like to share a birthday with the dragon?"

I almost dropped the bicycle I was carrying to the repair rack. Mr. Brunswick rarely spoke to me beyond work-related topics, and never about the dragon. And how did he even know my birthday?

I lifted the bike onto the rack and shrugged. "It's never made a difference in my life," I lied.

I couldn't tell him the truth: that more than anything else in this world, I wanted to kill the dragon. I hated all the dragons, but mostly I hated Viridia, the green dragon that ruled our city and controlled our lives. Just thinking about him made me want to damage something.

Mr. Brunswick wiped his greasy hands on a dirty cloth and eyed me. "I just thought maybe something special happened, what with you being named after him and all."

I gritted my teeth and spun the bike's pedals. My parents named me Beryl, one of the popular "green" names used to honor the dragon. Their generation did stuff like that. I can only imagine what they would think of me now… if they were still alive. They would be appalled, I'm sure.

"Well, you may as well take the rest of the afternoon off," Mr. Brunswick said. "With all the celebratin' going on, I doubt anyone else will come in."

I gestured at the bike on the rack. "Shouldn't I finish this one?"

"It can wait until tomorrow."

I nodded. I began putting away my tools.

"How old are you today?"

This had to be a new record. My boss hadn't spoken this much to me since I took this job seven months ago.

"Seventeen."

Mr. Brunswick nodded. He scratched at his face, his fingers stretching out his chromark, the green facial tattoo that marked him, like all of us, as the dragon's property. "I wonder how old Viridia is today?" he said, not even looking at me anymore.

Too old. If the history they taught us in school were true, Viridia had to be somewhere around a thousand years old. Nothing should live that long.

Once cleaned up, I left the bike shop. I waited in the doorway as a small group of exuberant teens moved up the street, heading for one of the many ongoing celebrations. None of them looked more than two or three years younger than me, yet I felt so separated from them. They chatted and laughed with each other, shoving one another in fun, all without a care in the world.

Had I ever felt that way? Maybe. Three years ago? Before my parents died? No. I had kept to myself most of the time. Even then, I couldn't understand why everyone didn't hate the dragon like I did. Now at least, I was old enough to understand that not everyone had seen the things I had seen. Not everyone had lost what I had lost.

Across the street, some of the green ribbons decorating a clothing store came loose and drifted down the street with the breeze. I rolled my eyes. As if some ribbons could make a difference on any building around here. Every single building looked the same: concrete. Square. Boring. Viridia, both the city and the dragon, had no sense of style.

I pulled my jacket on and moved down the street in the opposite direction. I kept my head down, trying not to be noticed. A few others passed me, walking or biking. When I did glance around, I saw downcast faces, each decorated with the green chromark, the sole markings anyone was allowed to have here. Teens would celebrate, and the elite citizens who lived in the nicer parts of the city would have a good time. But those of us who held jobs knew how things worked. We had nothing to celebrate.

I might have been halfway home when I heard a yell. Looking up, I caught a brief glimpse of dark hair and a black leather jacket before someone plowed right into me. Both of us went sprawling onto the sidewalk.

I scrambled to my feet prepared to unleash some choice words at the stranger when I saw several other figures hurrying toward us from the same direction. Tall and muscular, they wore brilliant green jumpsuits decked out with all kinds of accessories, and carried shockspears. Wonderful. The Viridian Guard.

The stranger jumped up, and I faced a split-second decision. For all I knew, this guy could be some kind of thief or something. But the Viridian Guard represented the dragon. They deserved my hatred and in a moment like this… my resistance.

"This way!" I grabbed the stranger's arm and yanked him down the alley to my right. I had no clear plan in mind, other than to help this guy, whatever it took. The choice of this particular alley might not have been the best way to start. Dead end.

I checked the nearest door. Locked. Deadbolt, most likely. No time to run back to the next door; the Guard would be rounding the corner any second now. "I'm going to regret this," I muttered. I concentrated and mentally triggered a boost in my right leg.

"What—" the stranger began. He broke off as I kicked. The lock shattered, and the door exploded open.

"Come on, come on!" We hurried through the door and found ourselves in the kitchen of some fancy restaurant, one of those reserved for the most elite of the dragon's servants. They must be closed: I didn't see any signs of activity.

Unfortunately, the way across the kitchen led through a maze of tables and workstations. We almost reached the doors into the dining room when one of the Viridian Guard burst in behind us and threw his shockspear.

The spear narrowly slashed the stranger's left thigh, but it was enough to trigger the electric charge it contained. His body contorted as the electricity arced through his central nervous system. Without thinking, I grabbed the nearest pan and hurled it back at the Guard. He ducked, giving me the moment I needed.

I seized the back of the stranger's jacket and half-pulled him to his feet. I yanked him forward through the swinging doors into the dining room.

Then I understood why the restaurant was closed. They were remodeling the entire dining area. Tables and chairs were piled in several unorganized groups, plastic tarps hid the front windows and glass doors from outside onlookers, piles of new ceramic tile waited by the back wall, and the entire stairway to the second-floor balcony area had been torn out.

Time for more split-second decisions. My new friend needed time to recover from the shockspear before he could do any more running, but a quick hiding place wasn't feasible, unless…

I half-dragged him out into the dining area. The chairs and tables were solid wood. Perfect. I let my companion slip to the ground again. I took a deep breath, grabbed one of the chairs, and threw it as hard as I could at the front doors. The result was better than I expected: the chair turned in mid-air and all four legs impacted the glass door at the same time, shattering it and tearing into the outdoor tarp. I guess the owners cheaped out when buying the glass.

Even as the glass shattered, I bent over and began hauling the stranger up onto my back. I looked up at what I needed to do and winced. My legs would kill me in the morning.

I channeled all the boost energy I could into both legs as I clambered up onto the nearest table. Gritting my teeth, I leaped with everything I had. We barely cleared the balcony's railing and tumbled onto the floor beyond it.

Just in time. The Viridian Guard exploded from the kitchen into the dining room below us. The stranger started to roll over, and his dark eyes locked onto mine. I made a shushing motion. We both lay still. Below us, I could hear quick commands being yelled. The Guards, four of them, seemed to take my bait and hurried to the front door.

I eased myself to the balcony's edge and peered over. The Guards pushed their way through the tarps and started to spread out. Then a second group emerged from the kitchen and stopped almost right below me.

One figure in this new group, surrounded by four more Guards, dominated the entire room. Clad in dark green robes with purple edging, it stood at least seven feet tall, bulkier than most men. It reached up and pulled back the hood obscuring its face.

I stifled a gasp. Under the hood, the tall figure was not a man. A reptilian snout with iridescent jade scales turned left and right, peering into the shadows.

I pulled back from the edge. "Fewmets!" I cursed under my breath. I looked at the stranger. "Who are you?" I wanted to demand. How did he attract the attention of a draconic? And on the dragon's birthday! The draconics should all be honored guests at the celebrations. For the first time since the collision on the sidewalk, I felt a stab of absolute fear. Running from the Viridian Guard was one thing, but this…

"He can't have gone far," I heard from below.

Fighting the trembling, I inched forward and looked over the edge again. The draconic moved toward the front door, urged on by the soldiers around him. At the entrance, it paused, and its gaze examined the chair. As if tracing the trajectory, it turned and looked back. Its eyes rested on the pile of furniture and seemed to settle on the very table I had jumped from. To my horror, its head began to rise, looking upward. I jerked back, heart pounding, body shaking.

A shout came from further outside, followed by another. Quick steps echoed below and then silence. Something or someone else had attracted their attention, and we had been overlooked, for now. I checked to confirm no one remained below and then tried to relax. What was wrong with me? My hands still trembled. I had trouble taking in a full breath. Fear. I had never experienced it so strong. Then again, I had never seen a draconic up close.

"Thank you," my new companion whispered. He pulled himself to his hands and knees. I turned to him, about to demand answers, when a beam of daylight from the setting sun pierced one of the upper floor windows and shone full on his face. I rolled over and sat up. He—I—what? This couldn't be right.

Dark black hair with some brown highlights hung low over deep-set dark eyes, no facial hair. But in a curving line down the left side of his face, beginning above his left eyebrow and continuing down to his neck, a series of jet-black tiny dots reflected the sun, flaring out then fading along with the light.

My hand went to my own face. I knew he saw the same pattern there, but in green, not black. Green, like every single person I knew. The stranger wasn't from this city. He didn't belong to the green dragon.

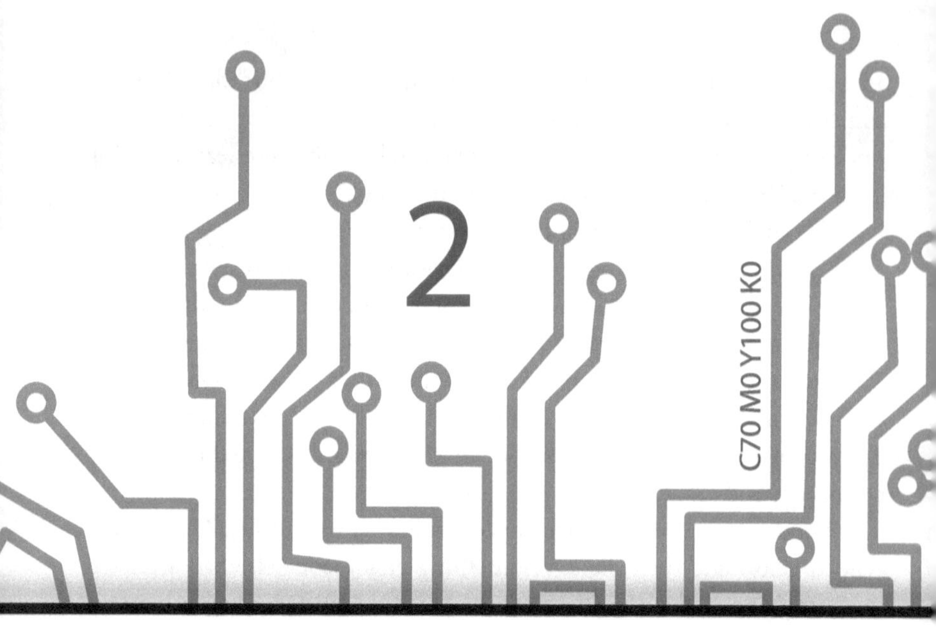

"You're not from Viridia!" The city *or* the dragon.

"Yeah, well, you've got some explaining to do too," the stranger said. He shifted to a sitting position and examined his thigh wound. "Last time I checked, cyb implants are forbidden tech for ordinary guys like us."

A defense rose up in my throat, but I pushed it down. This guy didn't deserve to know anything about me. I saved him, not the other way around. "Who are you?"

"Name's Rick. Richard Onyx. From Atramentous."

Atramentous, ruled by the black dragon. The nearest of the five other cities within The Circle. I almost blurted out that travel between cities without express permission was forbidden, but I suppose we were way beyond "forbidden" now.

I got a better look at Rick now. He appeared to be near my age, maybe a bit older. Those dark eyes aged him, though, almost as if they didn't belong with the rest of the face. He wore black leather gloves, a similar jacket over a dark green shirt, and grayish pants.

"I'm Beryl," I answered. "What are you doing here?"

Rick held out his hand. I stared at him. "What?" he asked. "Don't they shake hands here in your green city?" I blinked and took his hand. His firm grip gave me an immediate respect for his strength.

"There we go. Thanks for the help. Um, things grew too… hot for me in Atramentous, so I decided to try my luck elsewhere." He chuckled and then felt his lip with his tongue. It looked to be swelling, probably from a blow he took in one of our falls. "Looks like green isn't my lucky color."

At that, he started to get to his feet, slipped, and collapsed again. He winced and reached for his thigh. "Ah. I hadn't considered that… I don't suppose your green guardians use poison on their shockspears, do they?"

I pushed his hands away and ripped the hole in his pants wider. The wound showed signs of… something unusual. I could see a bit of green splaying outward through the nearest blood veins. I'm not a doctor, but I did know the Viridian Guard and their tools.

"Yeah, they're poisoned. I was hoping they didn't get a direct enough hit on you, but…"

"Pretty sure it's direct enough." His voice sounded strained.

I thought fast. "Come on." I stood and reached for his hand. "We've got to get you somewhere safe and find a treatment. I could take you to my place, but Kelly's is closer."

Rick allowed me to pull him to his feet. "Okay, but how are we getting down from here? You gonna carry me again, cyber boy?"

"It's not—Never mind." I looked over the balcony edge. "We should be able to hang down and drop easily enough. I'll go first and help break your fall to protect your leg."

Twenty minutes later, after ducking through several alleys and always looking over our shoulders, we made it to the apartment complex where Kelly lived. Like most buildings in Viridia, the complex was a rough concrete-walled building with little outward adornment. By that time, Rick was almost unconscious and leaning on me pretty hard. If the building hadn't had an elevator, I don't think we could have made it to the third floor.

In the hallway, I eased Rick down to the floor and then knocked on Kelly's door. I heard movement inside and figured she might be looking through the peephole. I waved. The deadbolt slid back, and Kelly opened the door.

Kelly was my friend and co-worker, but… I was kind of hoping she would soon become something more. Okay, I hadn't asked her out yet, but I think we both recognized where things were going. I did, anyway. Kelly actually paid attention to me and seemed to enjoy my company, unlike most girls I had been around in my life.

Gorgeous. That's how I saw her. Some people might have thought her somewhat short, and maybe not as thin as current fashion dictated, but her proportions looked good to me. And her hair: soft brown that went on and on, with a few green highlights as her one nod to fashion. She had it pulled back into a ponytail when she opened the door. The shorts and tank top were far more attractive on her than the work clothes I usually saw.

"Beryl? What are you doing here? My—" She interrupted herself with a sharp gasp as she caught sight of Rick.

"Hey, good to see you, too, honey! You don't mind if I drop by with a wounded fugitive from justice, do you?" Actually, I didn't say that. Except in my head. What came out was more like: "Uh… hey."

Kelly glanced up and down the hallway. "Quick, get him inside." She hurried to Rick's side, and together we got him through the doorway and into the apartment. As Kelly shut the door, I eased our fugitive onto her parents' couch. The apartment wasn't spacious by any means, but still larger than mine. Their kitchen was a separate room from the living area; how awesome was that?

"The couch is okay for now, I guess." Kelly turned around and gave a sharp look at the newcomer. "My parents are working tonight because of the parties, but they'll be back in the morning. What in the holy name of Viridia is going on?"

Kelly had been raised by parents who, like my own and many more, revered the dragons as gods. Though neither of us believed it anymore, Kelly's language still sometimes reflected her upbringing.

"Short answer," I said, finding my voice. "I met this guy running from the Guard, I helped him escape, but he got hit with a shockspear. Got any anti-tox?"

She was cute when she twisted her eyebrows. It almost made her chromark look attractive.

"Gods, Beryl. What have you gotten yourself into?" She got a good look at Rick's face. "He's from the black city!"

"Shhh. Yes, I know. Anti-tox?"

With another look at the stranger lying on her couch, Kelly hurried off to search her family's medicine stores. Both her parents worked in the bio-hospital, so I had no doubt she would find what Rick needed. They probably had all kinds of sample drugs lying around here, not that it would be exactly "legal." But everyone had their own tiny acts of defiance, whether they revered the dragon or not. It's basic human nature, right?

"She seems nice…" Rick mumbled.

"You're not allowed to notice that, Onyx." I shot a look to see if Kelly heard any of this. I leaned in closer. "I still have no idea who you are or whether I can trust you, but if you go near Kelly, I swear I'll—"

"I hear ya…" I think he passed out at that point, because his eyes rolled back, and he stopped talking.

Kelly returned with a tube of ointment. "I think this should work," she said, and knelt beside the couch. I helped position Rick's leg so she could see his wound. It had grown uglier since the restaurant, and the greenish tint to the blood vessels appeared more distinct. Kelly frowned and opened the tube.

A few moments later, Kelly and I moved into the kitchen, out of Rick's earshot, even though he seemed to be asleep. As crazy as this whole situation was, I couldn't get over how I was standing there, with her, in her apartment. Before today, we had never interacted outside the bicycle shop. I told her all that had happened, with the exception of the draconic. No need to make things even scarier.

"I guess he can stay here tonight," she said, though I could tell the idea didn't appeal to her. "But what do we do in the morning?"

"I'll stay too," I offered. "Keep an eye on him, just in case. Then, in the morning, I'll drop him off at my place before heading back to work."

Kelly hesitated only a moment before she agreed. Her eyebrows drew together, and she stared off at the couch. "Beryl, I know you hate Viridia, but… actively thwarting the Guard? Isn't that taking things a bit far?" She looked up into my eyes, probably searching for some acknowledgement that I was quite sane, after all.

I closed my own eyes. "No," I said firmly. "It's not enough. If I could figure out how to do it, I would kill him tomorrow."

Kelly's whole face seemed to widen in shock. "But—"

"I know, I know. It's ridiculous and insane. But we weren't meant to live like this, Kelly. It's just… not right."

"Then what is?" When I hesitated, she moved away and poured herself a glass of water.

"I don't know," I admitted. "Freedom. Whatever that means."

After Kelly went back to her room, I stretched myself out as best I could on a large easy chair near the couch. It was far nicer than the one chair I owned. I guess hospital work paid better than the bike shop, though nowhere close to the dragon's elite, of course.

I tried not to think about Kelly getting ready for bed just down the hall. Instead, I looked at Rick and pondered what his arrival meant. The dragon's forces were after him, and that made him my ally. The dragon controlled every part of our lives. People like Kelly might be willing to pretend there was nothing wrong with that arrangement. I wasn't.

Viridia's birthday. What a joke. The dragon had ruled this city for around a thousand years. It was just the way things were. Nothing would ever change that. Nothing could.

And no matter how hard I tried not to think about it, the image of dripping blood forced its way into my mind. It was the image I would never forget, the image that always brought my rage to the surface.

Rage is not conducive to sleep. For the next few hours, I struggled to control my thoughts and emotions. It didn't help that Richard Onyx snored. And sleep would have been a very good thing, considering how fast things fell apart the next day.

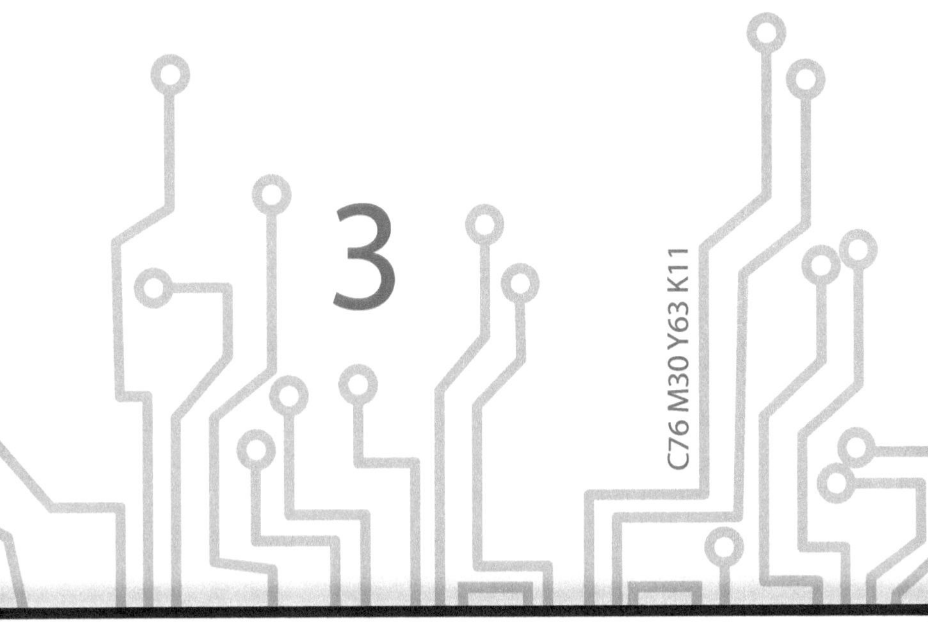

3

The Viridian Guard came for me the next morning. Not an auspicious start to a revolution.

Kelly and I arrived for work as normal at Brunswick's Bicycle Shop. She dealt with customers at the front counter, while I repaired and maintained the bikes. It's a good arrangement. I'd buy a bicycle from her in a second. Except that I already had one, even if I did wreck it last week. If I had time today, maybe I could fix it, but I had paying customers waiting on their bikes.

Mr. Brunswick didn't tolerate any nonsense. He wanted everything to run smooth and efficient. When two members of the Viridian Guard showed up at the front of his store, he was instantly cooperative. Anything less might get someone hauled off to jail for a few days, though Mr. Brunswick would be more upset about the lost work time than he would the jail itself.

"Beryl! You have someone here to see you!"

I emerged from the back, wiping grease off my hands, suspecting nothing. When I saw the Guard, I kept my face stoic, but my insides seized up They weren't carrying shockspears, which was a good sign, but they were fully uniformed in the brilliant green. One had dark hair, while the other had dyed his forest green. He looked ridiculous.

"If you don't mind, Mr. Brunswick, we need to take him with us," the green-haired one said. "My superior very much wants to talk with him about something he might have witnessed last night."

Mr. Brunswick shot me a stern look. Regardless of how things turned out, I wondered if I would have a job after this. He offered our full cooperation with the Guard, suggesting that if the interview were short, I should hurry back. "The bikes aren't going to repair themselves," he ended with a fake chuckle.

I followed the Guard outside where we met two more of their number. These two carried shockspears. So much for optimism. The green-haired guard turned on me. "I don't know who you are, kid, but Troilus Green wants to speak with you. Don't give us any trouble. You don't want me telling a draconic that you resisted arrest."

A draconic? I swallowed. It couldn't have seen me last night. I didn't even see it until Rick and I were both hidden.

My mind ran through different options of conversation with the Guard as we started down the street. I considered acting either confused, rebellious and sarcastic, or facetiously pleasant. In the end, the lead Guard's stern face silenced pretty much anything I might say.

The walk to the Guard station wasn't very far, but felt like it took at least an hour. Being escorted by no less than four Viridian Guard members made me extremely self-conscious. I kept glancing around to see if anyone I knew saw us. I'm not sure if that made me look more suspicious or just nervous. Besides, my legs still ached from yesterday's exertion.

The Guard station had little to distinguish it from the other concrete buildings around it. A bright green awning that matched their uniforms stretched out over the front door. "Viridian Guard Station 4" was inscribed on the large window, tinted to prevent anyone from watching what took place inside.

Once there, they took me to an empty interrogation room and ordered me to sit. I obeyed, sitting on one of the two chairs facing each other across a bare table. I'd seen one of these rooms before, but... the interrogator I would be seeing was something else.

While I waited, I thought about the draconics. No one knew much about them. They were larger than humans and walked upright, but were otherwise like dragons: scales, claws, and teeth. Did they have tails? I couldn't remember. They were said to have the same powers as dragons, to a lesser extent. So with the greens, that meant they had some kind of venom ability, like the dragon himself. Some people called them half-dragons, which was ridiculous. If challenged, old storytellers would trot out some ancient tale about dragons taking on human form and seducing women… Yeah, right. The draconics were just another race. New ones showed up now and then, and you didn't see any human dragons walking around seducing anyone. Fairy tales. Whatever.

The door opened, and the draconic entered. No tail. Huh.

I felt a blast of warm air as it took the seat across from me. None of the stories mentioned that. They also didn't mention the odd smell: kind of a sickly-sweet decay. Death encapsulated in odor form. I blinked and swallowed.

Like yesterday, the draconic wore dark green robes with purple edging. It kept its hood up this time, but I could see the outline of its snout and the gleam of white teeth. It inclined its head to the side and seemed to stare at me. I waited.

"Have we met before?" I jumped. A reaction to the abrupt sound. I'm not sure how to describe the voice. It didn't move its enormous mouth the way we do (no lips, either). The voice came from further down its throat. It added a bit of a rasp to the intonations, but also made it deeper.

"I—think I'd remember that."

The draconic chuckled. "Yes, I suppose you would. It's just… I have a feeling about you. It really seems like we might have encountered one another, perhaps some years ago. Perhaps yesterday."

I shrugged. "Feelings don't change reality."

"Oh, that's where you're wrong." The draconic reached up and pushed its hood back. Despite knowing what to expect, I couldn't stop staring at the face looking down at me. The jade scales glimmered in the light and seemed to ripple as it turned its head. Its teeth were razor sharp, like nothing I'd ever seen before, even in pictures. But its eyes drew my attention most of all. The draconic had jet-black eyes with flecks of green. I couldn't make out a pupil at all, as if its entire eye were the pupil. What kind of vision did that create?

"My name is Troilus Green. I serve the great Viridia, lord and master of us all, god of this city." It leaned forward, placing both clawed hands on the table. "And his feelings do change reality."

Troilus Green stood and towered over me. "When Viridia feels happy, this city prospers. When Viridia feels contentment, the people rejoice." It chuckled again. "And when Viridia feels anger… this city suffers. Feelings are vitally important."

"W-what do you want from me?"

Troilus Green gestured in the air. "As one of Viridia's chosen, I communicate his feelings. Right now… Viridia is annoyed. Do you know why he is annoyed, little man?"

I swallowed again. "I—I would not presume to understand the emotions of one so great as the green dragon."

"Ha! Well said." Troilus Green bent down and leaned on the table again. "But I do understand them. Viridia and I are connected in ways you could never understand. And right now, Viridia is annoyed because things are not as they should be."

I waited. I didn't know whether to say anything else.

"There is a stranger in our city. A wanderer who does not belong. We have heard that he comes from Atramentous, but even that may not be entirely true. He is here, when he should not be here. This is a violation of our laws, and our laws are Viridia's will. Yesterday, on Viridia's very birthday, I pursued this wanderer and nearly caught him."

I tried to look like someone hearing this for the first time. An unsettled feeling roiled my stomach. This thing wanted Rick, wanted him bad. For the first time, I couldn't help wondering if I had done the wrong thing. The thought almost made the unsettled feeling in my stomach rise up.

Troilus Green curled its left hand into a fist. The claws scraped across the metal tabletop, leaving furrows. "Someone spotted you in the vicinity of where this wanderer escaped. Perhaps you saw something?"

"I'm not sure what you're talking about. I haven't seen any strangers."

"Perhaps not." Those massive dark eyes looked down at me, and I tried to look back. The heat radiating off the creature seemed to be growing stronger. The smell grew as well. I resisted the urge to wipe at my nose.

The draconic sat down again. "If you do see him, you must inform us," it said, looking away. "This wanderer seems to incite trouble wherever he goes. He must be found." It waved its right hand in the air. Two of the claws reflected the light. Cybernetic prosthetics? "You are free to go, little man. But we may call you in again at any time."

For a moment, I didn't realize what it had said. Then it struck me and I scrambled to my feet. I might have seemed too eager to get out of the draconic's presence, but I suspected anyone in my position would behave the same, regardless of guilt. I took a step toward the door.

"What was your name again, little man?" The question stopped me. I glanced back, but Troilus Green still looked away.

"Beryl."

"Beryl." Troilus Green said the name as if it were tasting it. "A good name. Honorable to your god. We may meet again, Beryl."

I didn't answer, and the door opened for me. I hurried out. Since the draconic had dismissed me, the rest of the Viridian Guard no longer seemed to care about my presence. I resisted the urge to sprint, but still made it out much faster than I had come in.

What had Rick gotten me into?

I went straight home. I didn't care what Mr. Brunswick would think, but I did feel guilty about not stopping to see Kelly. She would be worried sick. Every step I took reminded me of yesterday's kicking and jumping. Why did it have to ache so much the next day?

I heard an annoying hum when I entered the apartment. The refrigerator door must be open. I had wanted to fix it for months, but didn't have the money.

Rick glanced up from the refrigerator as I entered, but didn't seem surprised to see me. He also didn't seem to be suffering any ill effects from yesterday's poisoning.

"Beryl. Hey. I just woke up a few minutes ago, and I'm starving! Any of this stuff good?"

"We need to talk," I announced.

He looked around the refrigerator door. "Sure, sure. Whatever. Let's chat."

"Who are you, really? Why are you here in Viridia?"

"I thought we covered that already." He held up a bottle of apple juice. "Let me guess: made with only green apples?"

I shoved the refrigerator door shut, making him step back. At least I could silence the hum. "I'm serious!" I said. "I just got interrogated by a fewmetting draconic!"

Rick frowned. "I don't think that's a word. Or if it is, it probably shouldn't be." He mouthed it silently: "Fewmetting."

I glared at him.

Rick sighed, took the lid off the apple juice bottle, and took a quick swallow. "I'm sorry that happened to you, Beryl," he said. "But I'm not surprised. The good news, though, is it didn't actually see us yesterday, or you wouldn't be here now."

"No. It said someone saw me in the vicinity."

Rick nodded and put the juice down. "We lucked out, then. And I owe you again. Thanks."

"You can pay me by giving me some answers."

"What do you want to know? I told you already: my name is Richard Onyx, from Atramentous."

"Why are you here?"

"I told you: things got too hot for me…"

"The truth!" I slammed my fist against the counter. The fridge started humming, even with the door shut. "The draconic told me you were inciting trouble everywhere!"

Rick's eyes narrowed. "And you're a big believer in the words of the draconics, are you?"

"I could have left you to them yesterday!" My hands trembled and I gripped them into fists. My adrenaline was pumped after the draconic encounter.

"But you didn't. Which means that you don't care much for our dragon overlords. And that, my friend, makes us allies."

"Allies in what?"

Rick moved into my tiny living area. "This is a nice apartment for a single guy," he observed. "First floor, even."

I followed, if only to get away from the humming. Pure luck had given me the first floor. My number came up on the housing lottery at just the right time it became available.

"Allies in what?" I repeated.

"Back in Atramentous, I was involved in… let's call it an uprising," Rick explained. He dropped into my favorite (and only) easy chair. I had saved up for over three months to get that chair. I should have spent the money on the fridge. "We thought we had an idea for taking down one of the black draconics and maybe getting a bit more freedom for our part of the city."

He looked at me as if expecting me to sit also. I remained standing, and crossed my arms. It was kind of stupid, but I still wasn't ready to trust him.

Rick looked off into the distance. "We overplayed our hand and got destroyed. I'm the only one who escaped. All of my friends, all of my fellow… rebels… were either killed or captured. Is that enough info for you?"

I lowered my arms, and felt some of my nervous energy begin to drain away. "Sorry," I muttered. I sat down on the loveseat, my only other real piece of furniture, passed down from my parents.

Rick glanced at me. "But you…" He pointed right at me. "You, my friend, think big! Kill the actual green dragon, will you?"

My head snapped up. "You heard that? But you were out."

"Um, mostly out. I was fading in and out of consciousness. But I distinctly heard you say you wanted to kill the dragon."

"Who doesn't?"

Rick snorted. "There are plenty of people who think the dragons are gods, you know. And thousands more who just accept things the way they are." He jerked to his feet and walked around the room. "They never even think about how things could be different. They just follow orders, do what they're told to do, be who they're told to be, and then die like everyone else. I don't even know if they realize how miserable and pathetic they are! Bunch of sheep!"

My eyes widened. I had thought many of the same things, but it was something else to hear someone say it out loud, especially with such fervor.

Rick stopped pacing and looked at me. "Of course, you know why no one entertains those thoughts, right? Why no one in their right mind would try to kill a dragon?"

"Everyone knows." I closed my eyes. It was the only thing that stayed with everyone from history classes. "A city rebelled three hundred years ago and killed their black dragon ruler. The other dragons destroyed them in retaliation." Not just the people. They destroyed the city and everything around it.

"Yeah, the Blasted Lands. There it is, ladies and gentlemen: the visual evidence!" Rick waved at the window. "The constant proof that resistance is futile! Try to fight another dragon and the same thing might happen to you and everyone you love!"

"So let's kill all the dragons." Until I heard myself say it out loud, I hadn't considered that my wild thoughts from the night before might ever go anywhere. But Rick kept saying all the things I already believed.

Rick lowered his chin and smiled. "Now you're talking," he said in a low voice.

Had I really said that out loud? Rick flopped back in the chair. We sat in silence for several minutes, our thoughts full of insanity. Six cities ruled by six dragons. Every dragon had a dozen or more draconics along with a small army of highly trained soldiers. How could we possibly overcome that? Let alone actually kill even one dragon?

"This is crazy," I said aloud. "Even if we had everyone in every city on our side, how would it work? It's impossible."

"We don't need everyone," Rick answered. "In fact, the fewer people we bring into this, the better. We don't need a massive conspiracy. I mean, I'm a… troublemaker, apparently, and you're… what are you, anyway?"

I scoffed. "I work in a bike shop."

Rick's eyes bored into me. "That's not all you are. Come on."

"What do you mean?"

"I saw you. You have some kind of cybernetic implants, don't you? That's fortek. How'd that happen?"

I still wasn't convinced I could trust Rick, but who would he tell about my forbidden tech? I didn't like talking about it, but after demanding the truth from him, I couldn't exactly keep secrets of my own. I closed my eyes.

"Three years ago, there was an accident… I still don't know what it was. Some kind of explosion in one of the factories." I took a deep breath. "My parents and I were walking outside when this entire wall collapsed on us. They were both killed instantly."

"I'm sorry."

I shrugged. "I survived, but the surgeons said I wouldn't be able to walk again."

"That's practically a death sentence in itself." Rick spoke true. If you couldn't work, the dragons had no use for you. Impaired people tended to disappear.

"My parents had a good friend who works in the draconics' cybernetics department. I'm not entirely sure how he pulled it off, but he gave me an implant." My hand went to the small of my back. "Back here, at the base of my spine. I'm told the scar is quite impressive. It lets me walk, obviously.

And if I concentrate just right, I can… boost my leg power. It's like some kind of energy that flows into my legs. I can run faster. Kick harder. Jump higher."

"You can just think it?"

"Sort of." I didn't know how else to explain it.

"That is hue."

"Definitely hue." I found it interesting that someone from Atramentous used the same slang words as we did. "But I pay for it later. My legs are still aching from what I did yesterday."

"Interesting. I've heard of implants to help with walking, of course, but not for the average citizen—"

"Only the elite."

"Exactly. Your friend risked a lot to do that for you. He must be some kind of genius."

I thought about Loden. "Yeah, I guess he really is."

"Just the kind of genius we need to kill dragons?"

I couldn't deny Loden's brilliance, and he might sympathize. Once, he told me the dragons weren't invincible. He seemed to have surprised himself by saying it, and didn't elaborate, but I never forgot it. "I don't know a whole lot of people that can help us," I admitted. "But there might be a few."

"It's better than what I've got." Rick sat up and spread his arms. "I don't know anyone here, and everyone I knew before is gone."

We fell silent again. I thought about the consequences. If we went any further with this at all, I'd probably end up like Rick, with everyone I knew either dead or imprisoned. Thinking about my own death didn't seem like a big deal at the moment. But imagining Kelly and Loden dead or worse gave me pause. I considered telling Rick to forget the whole thing. I could help him get out of the city, but other than that, I would stay out of trouble and go back to my somewhat boring life.

My somewhat boring life of slavery to a giant green dragon that destroyed everything with any value. An image of dripping blood flashed through my mind. I pushed it away and felt the rage within.

No, rage wasn't enough. It couldn't be.

"It's not going to work," I said at last. "I'll help you escape, but that's all."

Rick's face fell. "Are you sure?"

"It's insane. As much as I want him dead… no one can kill a dragon."
Right about then, Troilus Green arrived at my door.

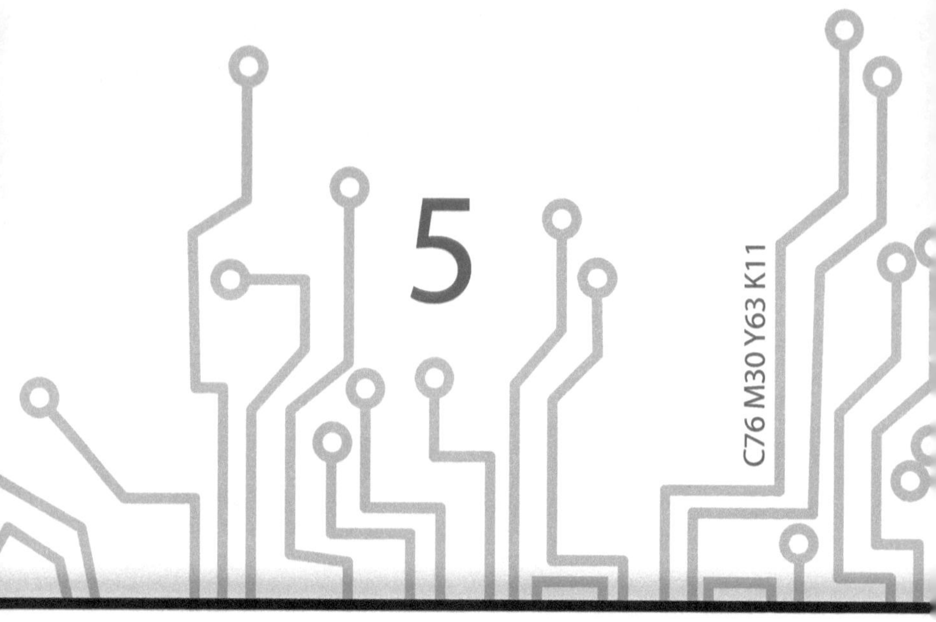

5

A loud bang reverberated against my apartment door, followed by a commanding voice. "Open in the name of the almighty Viridia and his elite Guard!"

Rick and I stared at each other for a split second. "Stall!" Rick hissed and dove for the window.

"Coming!" I called. I got up and started toward the door. I glanced back to see Rick pull the window open and start to climb out. That was a first floor advantage I had never thought about.

Another blow slammed against the door. "NOW!"

I heard the window click as Rick slid it closed behind him. As soon as I turned the deadbolt, the door flew open. I looked up into the eyes of Troilus Green.

"Ah, Beryl. I told you we might meet again." It ducked its head under the door frame and entered the room, its presence filling the space even more than its seven-foot frame. Again, the blast of warm air and the sickly-sweet odor assaulted me. Two Viridian Guards rushed around either side of it and hurried through my small apartment, searching in a controlled rush. At least two more remained outside in the hallway. One of them closed the door behind his master.

The draconic strode into my living area, its gaze glancing on the furniture and moving on. I followed, trying not to tremble. This was bad, very bad. Troilus turned and looked down on me again. It kept its hood up. I could hear the Guard members ransacking my bedroom and bathroom.

Troilus Green wagged a claw at me in warning. "I also told you, if you recall, that I believed we had met before," it said. "You seemed doubtful, but I could tell otherwise. You humans and your pitiful five senses. It's no wonder you're only useful for basic tasks."

I made a show of looking past it to see what the Guards were doing, but also took a quick glance at the window. Closed. No sign of Rick.

"Three years is a long time for young humans, but not for me."

Wait. Three years?

"The explosion." It ran a claw along the top of my easy chair. "You and I were both pulled out of the rubble that day. I remember you, though you were even smaller then. Because of that day, I needed this work done." It held up its right hand to display the two cybernetic claws.

"But you… I'm amazed you're still around. You suffered more damage than I thought a human could survive. Yet here you are. That arouses my curiosity."

I felt something welling up inside. I had already been thinking about that day because of the conversation with Rick, but this was too much. The idea that I shared memories of that day with this thing was repulsive. My breath came in rapid intakes. I gritted my teeth and tried to control it.

"Curiosity is not something I entertain very often," the draconic continued. "There is so little within this city that surprises me. Aside from the petty crimes your people commit, there is hardly anything to attract my attention, to distract me from the mundane tasks of ruling."

"Lord Troilus!" one of the Guard called. "There is definite evidence that another person was here!"

The draconic gestured. "Like that. Not surprising at all. I knew during our interview that you were hiding something. You simple, foolish little man. I will satisfy my curiosity with you, but first, I must ask the obvious, boring question. Where is the wanderer?"

I caught a glimpse of movement outside the window. What was Rick doing out there? Had the Guard found him already? I took a step backward.

"I don't know what you're talking about," I said.

"Ha!" The bellowing laugh echoed through my small home. "You delight me, Beryl. It is rare that I encounter resistance that is so… genuine.

You humans are customarily so pathetic." The laugh's echo ended with a growl. "But make no mistake. I will have what I want, resistance or not. The will of Viridia cannot be denied."

At that moment, the window shattered, and Richard Onyx flew through it, feet first. He must have swung from something to gather enough speed. He rolled through the broken glass and came to his feet. In his right hand, he held a long dagger, a forbidden weapon. "Does this surprise you?" he yelled, using the couch to vault into the air.

Rick plunged the dagger into the side of Troilus Green's face. The draconic's left arm swiped at him, caught him in the chest, and hurled him back across the room. The roar of pain shook the entire room. The Guards started toward us.

"Run, you idiot!" Rick yelled.

I snapped out of my astonishment and gave my legs a quick boost, just enough to get me past a pair of shockspears flying across the room.

"Alive, you fools!" Troilus Green snarled, holding the side of its face with one hand. It spat at me and a cascade of venom struck the floor, hissing and spurting.

Rick scrambled through the window and gestured furiously for me to join him. I almost made it when the draconic raised its other hand and screamed something unintelligible.

A wave of some unknown force rippled through the air and struck me. The power threw me through the window into Rick. We both sprawled onto the concrete, scraping exposed skin. My mind couldn't make sense of what had just happened. It seemed like a moving wall of solid air had slammed into me. I felt bruised all over, even more so on the parts that had struck the ground. My head spun in confusion and pain.

"Go, go, go!" Rick cried, scrambling to his feet.

I followed suit, and we raced down the street. Some of my joints screamed at me from the beating they had taken. Pulses of pain flooded my brain. What was that? I fed another boost into my legs just to keep them moving.

Behind us, I heard loud voices, Troilus Green's loudest of all, and swift footsteps. At any moment, I expected to feel the sharp point of a shockspear pierce my back.

Rick led the way through several turns. He clearly had no idea where to go, but at least we gained some distance on the pursuers. "I'm open to suggestions!" he yelled.

I tried to clear the pain from my head and looked around. "That way!" I pointed down a side street. At mid-day, the streets were almost empty. One lone pedestrian saw us, ducked his head, and hurried out of the way to avoid any involvement. We raced on, the sounds of pursuit still close behind. It wouldn't take long before they brought in reinforcements to cut us off. I could think of only one place to go.

When we turned another corner, I pointed at a large edifice to the right. "In there!"

"Are you bleaking kidding me?" Rick shouted.

If there had been any other option, I would have taken it. Instead, I led Rick through the gates into the courtyard of the Shrine of the Emerald God, the church of green dragon worship.

Early spring weather made the courtyard lush and green (of course). Fountains and iconic dragon statuary waited at every corner. The sacellum lay directly ahead of us, where the worship services took place. But that wasn't my target.

"Quick!" I hissed at Rick. I couldn't be sure whether our pursuers had seen us duck into the courtyard or not. I pushed my way through some greenery and stumbled onto a different pathway. My eyes scanned in all directions to confirm I found the right one.

Every part of my body screamed at me to collapse, my legs most of all.

There. I saw a tiny cottage near the back corner of the courtyard. I looked back to make sure we hadn't been spotted yet. All the trees and bushes should keep us out of sight just long enough.

About thirty feet from the cottage, my left knee gave out. I fell head-long onto the path, despite Rick's best attempt to grab me. I rolled three or four times and came to a stop on my back, the pain worse than ever. I opened my eyes and looked up into the face of my one desperate hope for escape from this situation.

"Bice!" I gasped. "Help us!"

And then I passed out.

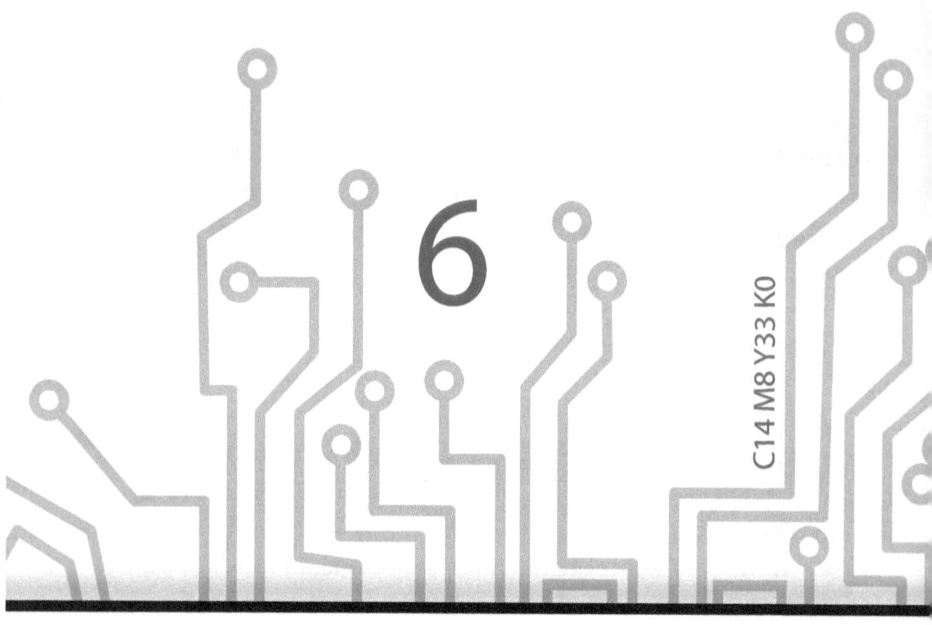

When my consciousness returned, it took its time. I could hear Rick and Bice talking, but for a while, I couldn't make out their words. Bice's calm and soothing voice was the first I could discern.

"…After spending my entire Learning Years training to be a priest, going through the initiation and everything, I realized one important thing," he said.

"What's that?" Rick's voice asked.

"The dragons are not gods."

"Um, isn't that straight out blasphemy for a priest?"

I think Bice chuckled. "Yes, I suppose it is. And that's why I'm no longer a priest. Fortunately for me, I had many friends inside the priesthood, so they didn't have me killed outright. But since I had no other real skills, they put me in charge of the garden here."

I heard Bice get up and move around. "Every day or two, one of the more dedicated priests comes by to try to convince me of the error of my ways. We have good conversations."

"I… can't imagine." I could almost see the baffled look on Rick's face.

"Beryl is awake now," Bice pointed out. "I'll get him some water. Check to see if he's got a fever."

I opened my eyes to see Rick pull the glove off his left hand and reach down to check my forehead. His touch was warm, but even so, I winced.

Bruises on the face too.

"Feels normal to me," Rick said.

I pulled myself into a sitting position on Bice's bed, despite the aches I felt all over. His tiny cottage claimed even less space than my apartment. Bice himself came across the room from the kitchenette with a glass of water. Based on his and Rick's demeanor, I assumed we were out of danger for now.

"What happened?" I asked.

Bice handed me the water and sat down on a rough wooden chair. As always, I marveled at his calm presence. Bice dressed simply in dark colors, but always with a little bit of green to mollify his friends in the priesthood. His skin was far darker than mine, perhaps the darkest I knew. The green chromark was barely visible; as a priest, it split into a V-shape above his eye. I had no idea how old Bice might be, but his short hair had long since started turning gray. Despite that, he seemed as spry as the day I met him as a young teen. He always had a soft smile on his weather-beaten face. Undeterred by my hatred for the dragons and their priesthood, Bice helped me through the dark time after the accident. I owed him a lot, already.

Rick gestured. "Your friend got us hidden in here and sent the Guard in the other direction," he said.

"Please," Bice said. "I didn't send them anywhere. Their own suspicions did that. I merely… made suggestions."

"Whatever you said, it worked. And that's what matters for now."

Bice inclined his head, then looked me over. "I have many questions. First of all, what happened to you? You look as if you had a fight with a brick wall and lost."

"That's what I feel like." I dangled my legs over the side of the bed and closed my eyes. "Rick, have you ever seen that before? That draconic seemed like it… threw some kind of invisible force at me?"

Bice's eyebrows went up.

"Uh, have *you* ever been that close to a draconic?" Rick answered. "I had no idea they had that capability, whatever it was."

"Describe what happened," Bice suggested.

"I'm not sure… It raised its hand and yelled something I couldn't understand. Then it felt like that brick wall you mentioned hit me full force and threw me. But I never saw anything."

"Hmmm."

"You've heard of this?" Rick asked.

Bice took a slow breath. "Among the priesthood, there is a firm belief that the dragon's most loyal, his draconics and high priests, are possessed of great power," he explained. "Some call this power magic, or simply divine."

"Magic. Right." Rick's forehead wrinkled in skepticism.

"Do you believe that?" I asked.

He tapped his fingertips together and sat back. "I've… rarely been near any draconics and had little interaction with high priests. Your encounter lends credence to the idea, but it doesn't have to be magic. It could be some kind of technology that only they possess… what does your generation call that?"

"Fortek."

"Ah, yes. The predilection to condense long words down to a single syllable." Bice chuckled. "In any event, without further evidence, we must conclude that we simply don't know where this power comes from, but at least one draconic seems to possess it. Fascinating."

A long pause reminded me of my injuries. I took a deep breath, testing the soreness of my ribcage. It hurt, but not as bad as I expected. I didn't feel strong enough to put my feet on the ground, and that left knee still throbbed.

Bice shook his head and reached toward me. "I am so sorry. Did you want anything for the pain? You must be aching all over."

"That would be nice," I said.

He jumped to his feet and hurried back to the kitchenette. "Feel free to tell me the rest of the story when you feel up to it," he suggested.

Rick looked at me with an expression that spoke volumes. He wanted to know if Bice could be trusted with all the details. I nodded and began the story from the moment I ran into Rick in the street. Bice returned with some pills that I swallowed. By the time I finished my story, I could feel them working. The pain started to diminish.

Bice looked at Rick. "That was very brave of you to come back for Beryl," he observed. "And attacking a draconic? Some might call that suicide."

Rick shrugged. "If I had aimed better, we might never have to worry about that one again. Instead, I expect we'll just see him with new cyb parts on his face next time." He paused. "I'm going to miss that dagger, though…"

"But you saved my life," I said. "Thanks."

"Hey, you saved me first. We're in this together, pal."

Another long pause waited for someone to say something.

"So what is it exactly that you are in together?" Bice asked. "You think that the two of you youngsters will be able to… what? Overthrow ancient powers that have controlled this land for centuries? Bring down the gods themselves?"

"I thought you didn't believe they were gods!" Rick countered.

"I don't. But their power is unquestionable. To go up against them could be said to be going up against gods by simple comparison."

I felt something stir inside. An image of the shrine flashed in my mind. Rick lowered his head.

"This is what I know," I said slowly. "Viridia is not a god. He's evil and cruel. We… we humans were not meant to live like this. It's wrong. And I will do whatever I can to end it."

Bice applauded. "Well said. There is something within us that yearns for freedom, is there not? That yearning was one of the greatest persuasions I encountered that took me away from the false worship. And that is also why I will help you."

Rick looked up. "How?"

Bice got back to his feet again. "Well, for starters, you need somewhere to hide. This cabin, while suited to my needs, is not sufficient for yours, especially once others join you."

"We can't go back to my place." I felt a tinge of regret. I would miss some things about my little apartment.

"Or anywhere else you normally visit," Bice said. At that, I thought of Kelly. Would the draconic go after her? Did it know she had helped us?

"I know a place that the Church owns," Bice continued, getting some paper and a pen. "As part of my caretaker duties here, I am occasionally given mundane tasks, like cataloging. I found an old sanctuary that is no longer in use. I think it would be perfect for you."

"That's funny." Rick laughed. "To think we'd try to orchestrate a rebellion against the dragons from a center of dragon worship."

"It is somewhat ironic, no? Here is the address." Bice handed me the note he had scribbled. "For now, though, I recommend that Beryl rest a bit longer. You should wait until dark to move again."

I repositioned myself and relaxed back onto the bed. Though reluctant to wait around, I had to admit I did need more rest. Bice's voice faded as he continued speaking.

"In the meanwhile, I will see what I can do about getting some supplies sent there, some food and basic needs..."

As I dozed off, I wondered if maybe this whole idea might actually be going somewhere. Then I thought again of Kelly. I should have told Bice to check on her. But sleep was claiming me, and I could no longer resist.

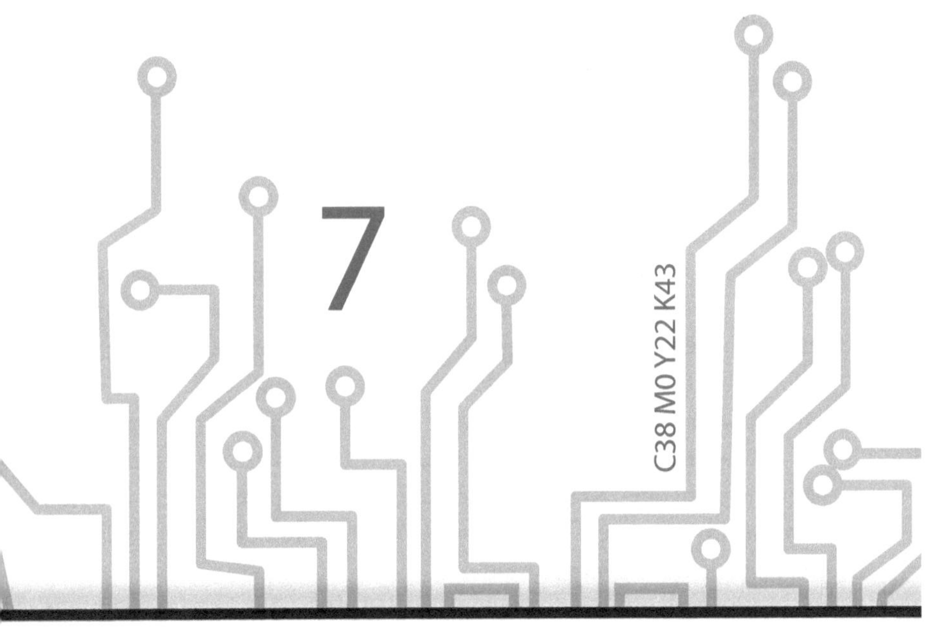

That night, Bice led us to the abandoned sanctuary, an old brick structure in a run-down part of the city. It turned out to be much more than I expected. A foyer greeted us at the opening, with a spiral staircase on the right leading up to a small balcony. The main worship room, overlooked by the balcony, stretched about thirty feet wide and sixty feet long. A few broken pews remained, as well as a broken statue of the green dragon himself, missing one wing and both hands. I glanced at it and looked away. There were memories I did not want to entertain. Branching off from the far side were two small rooms intended for some kind of priest work, I assumed, along with a tiny bathroom.

Rick's excitement added a jitter to his movements. He hurried from room to room, examining everything. "We can use the smaller rooms for sleeping quarters, and do our real work out here in the main sanctuary!"

I found a pile of blankets, food, and other supplies near the front. I looked at Bice, who smiled a little larger than usual. "I'll get you some more, but that was all I could carry by myself for now."

"How can we pay you for this?" I shook my head. He must have made two trips on his own, while I slept.

"Don't worry about it." He laughed. "Because they still hope to win me back, I'm still paid regularly as a priest. But I don't need the money. I'm happy to find a good use for it."

Rick emerged from the back. "Okay, so it doesn't have everything," he admitted. "No kitchen, a tiny bathroom with a broken toilet. But we'll get by. At least we have water."

Bice turned to go. "I will check in on you as often as I can. And bring more supplies."

"Maybe some tools," I suggested. "I might be able to fix that toilet."

Bice soon departed and left the two of us to ponder what kind of insanity we were contemplating. Only after he was gone did I think about asking him to check on Kelly. How could I have forgotten that? So much had happened in one day, but I should have remembered her. Stupid.

We talked far into the night, often repeating what we already knew. I hadn't had anyone to talk to at bedtime since my parents died, and never someone my own age. I had known Rick for barely a day now, but it felt so comfortable having him around.

At some point, we decided we needed sleep. The blankets and wood tile floor were not a match for a soft bed, especially with all my soreness, but it didn't take long until we both drifted off.

Sometime in the early morning hours, Rick woke me with a gentle shake. I looked up to see him holding a finger to his lips. He beckoned me up. We made our way to the door and looked out into the main sanctuary.

A small figure moved around, muttering to himself. He was looking through our supplies in a hurry, glancing around every few moments.

Rick gestured to indicate he would circle around. He slipped out and made his way behind the broken dragon statue. I took a breath, let it out, and stepped out myself. I eased a couple more steps, as close as I thought I could get without alerting the visitor.

"Those are ours," I said out loud.

The small figure vanished before I finished the sentence. He bolted toward the exit, but Rick was already there. His hand snaked out and grabbed the invader's arm before he could get away. With an effort, Rick resisted the small figure's struggles and grabbed his other arm. I lit one of the battery-powered lanterns Bice had left for us and approached.

"Vir'dia-lovin' goons! Lemme go!"

A boy. He couldn't have been more than nine or ten years old. He wore a shirt far too large for him, and his pants were held up by a raggedy pair of light green suspenders. His dirty blonde hair hung in tatters over his muddy face. I held the lantern up close and confirmed what I already suspected.

"He's a street orphan," I told Rick. "No chromark."

"Your mother's an orphan!" the boy snarled at me.

"My mother's dead."

"Good for her! She didn't hafta see your ugliness any more, dragon-lover!"

"Scrappy, isn't he?" Rick observed. "What should we do with him?"

"I think we can just let him go," I said. "There's no way he'll report us to the Viridian Guard. They'd arrest him on sight, and he'd be shipped off to the mines or worse."

"You sure?"

"Yeah, I think so. Listen, kid. We're not dragon-lovers. We hate that green monster more than you do. But you can't take our stuff. Leave us alone, and we'll leave you alone."

Rick let go, and the boy darted several feet away and stopped.

"Where'm I sleep, then?"

"What?"

He looked defiant in the dim light. "This place be mine. You and Blackface there took my room."

"You were living here?"

"What I said."

Rick shrugged and went back to find his blankets for a couple more hours. I looked back at our new acquaintance. "What's your name, kid?"

He snorted. "Sometimes called Lovat."

"Okay, Lovat. I'm Beryl. I'm sorry we took your spot. If you want, I do have an extra blanket here…" Before I finished, he had already grabbed it and headed to a corner.

"Good to meet you," I mumbled, turning away.

"Same to ya, Greenie."

Street orphans were rare, especially one as old as this one. Most didn't survive that long. Either Lovat was enormously resourceful or someone had cared enough to help provide for him. No chromark meant he had been on the streets since he was a toddler.

I looked up and noticed faint sunlight beginning to show through one of the high windows in the sanctuary. Curious to see the sunrise, I made my way up to the balcony. The dirt-caked windows made it impossible to see much. I searched around and found a poorly-hidden ladder that led up to the ceiling.

At its top, I opened a trapdoor and crawled out onto the top of the building. The roof was angled, but not steep, making it easy to find a good seat facing the oncoming sun.

All of the cities—all of my world, really—existed within a ring of mountains known simply as The Circle. Because of that, true sunrise always came late in the morning, while true sunset came in early evening, when the sun sank behind the mountains. While light lingered on a while longer, or cast a faint glow beforehand, like now, it meant our nights were always long. Bice once told me some ancient stories of life outside The Circle, where mountains were far distant, if visible at all, and the sun rose straight out of the ground. In one sense, the concept terrified me. It signified a world without boundaries, without borders.

But at the same time, I rebelled against boundaries. My anger against the dragon and his regime burned forever in the pit of my stomach. I hated his rules, his controls. More than that, I hated him. The mountains formed a natural barrier, and that… was comforting. The dragon created unnatural barriers, and that was wrong.

Just a few short miles from Viridia, the mountains were backlit. The sun would soon ease over the peaks. I watched the light grow. Bice believed since the dragons were not gods, there must be something else more powerful than they were: a real god, perhaps, that controlled things like the sun. I wasn't sure about that, but as I watched it rise, the sun comforted me. There, at least, was something beyond the dragons' power. Troilus Green and his master had no control over the sun. It would rise today, and it would set tonight, and they would have no say in it.

The light expanded, and I saw much of the city laid out before me. So drab and plain. We lived in a realm of concrete. Many of the larger buildings I knew to be apartment complexes, but some were centers of science and engineering. The dragon wanted greater and greater tech advantages for himself and his servants, while specifically limiting what we were allowed to research.

At the heart of the city sat its greatest landmark: the Emerald Ascendancy, built on the highest point. Even though some other buildings grew near it in height, they remained far below. It dominated the skyline from every direction.

If the dragon wasn't flying about somewhere, that's where he would be. The central portion of the complex formed an enormous oval structure dominated by two arches which stretched 400 feet into the air. The other walls were closer to 300 feet tall. The green dragon lived somewhere between those arches. Most citizens considered themselves privileged if they happened to see him ascend from between the arches, or come to a landing within them. Many of the draconics also lived within the Ascendancy, along with several hundred human assistants and staff.

The sun emerged from behind the mountains. Light streamed in all directions for a brief moment. Then something moved between my view and the sun, cutting off the light. A great shadow rose up just outside the city. It drew closer, and I felt a sickening in my stomach. The green dragon. Viridia. Fear warred with hate inside me. He flew overhead, and I felt the wind of his passing. "The skies belong to the dragons," I murmured the old adage. The dragon's green scales shone resplendent in the early light, but his left wing gleamed of silver metal. Rumors said Viridia had more cybernetic enhancements, but the wing was the most obvious.

Unaware of my watch, my hate, or my general existence, the dragon soared higher and then descended in tight circles into the Emerald Ascendancy.

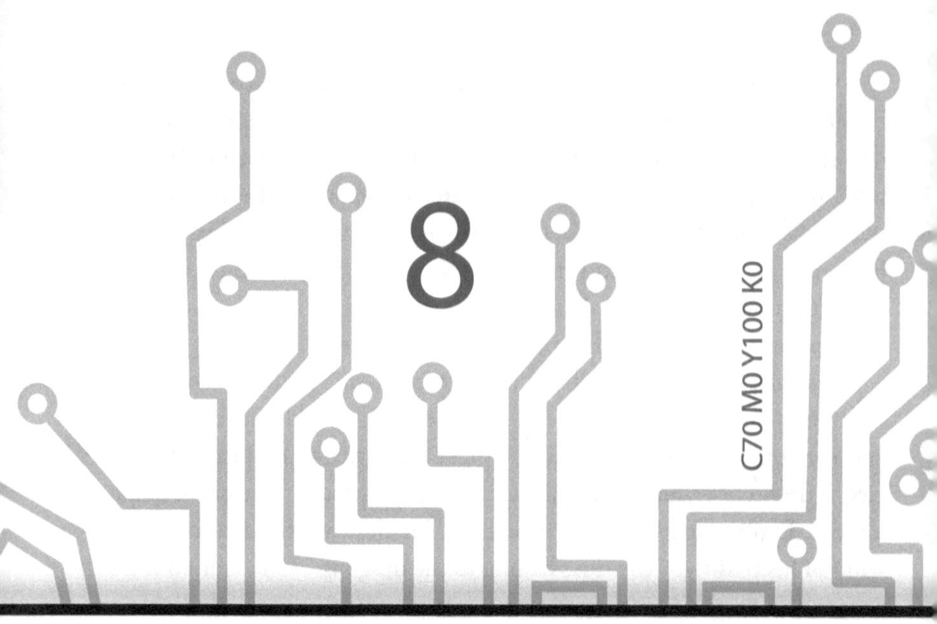

8

The morning light continued to grow, and with it, my concern over Kelly. I had dragged her into this when I brought Rick to her door. Panicked scenarios ran through my head. How could I check on her? Someone told me that some elite units of the Viridian Guard had a method of communication over long distances, another forbidden tech for we ordinary humans. Such a device would sure come in handy right now.

A thought struck me, and I climbed down the ladder back into our new headquarters. I checked on our urchin and found him fast asleep in the loaned blanket. After I relieved myself outside in the alley (we really needed to come up with a better solution to that), I sat down to wait. I kept my back to the broken statue. But it waited there, haunting my thoughts, reminding me of things I did not wish to recall.

Rick came out an hour or so later, yawning. He glanced at me, then headed outside. His movements disturbed Lovat, who came awake and noticed me sitting nearby. "What?" He looked at me through narrowed eyelids.

"I need your help."

Lovat stretched and eyed me with a mixture of curiosity and misgiving. "What I get?"

Expecting this reaction, I spread my hands. "I think we can help each other out here. We have food and other supplies we'd be willing to share with you. You know this city and are probably really good at moving around without being seen."

"Ya?" He clutched the blanket a little harder.

"Yeah. So today, I'd like you to check on a friend of mine and find out what's happening with her."

"She y'girl?"

"Sort of. What do you say?"

He seemed to consider it for a moment, then pointed to our supplies. "Want one of those lights."

"Deal."

I described Kelly for him and explained where he was likely to find her. With a few clarifications, he understood and scampered out the front doors just as Rick returned.

"What's up with the imp?" he asked.

I explained Lovat's errand. Rick nodded. "If he does well on this, he might actually be a good asset. We'll need someone who can run messages and spy on the enemy."

"So what's our next move? We've got big ideas, but the little details that get us there... that we don't have."

"We need more help." Rick tapped the stone dragon with a fingernail. "What about the cybertech guy that helped you? Think we can enlist him?"

"Loden. I think there's a decent chance of that, if I can find him. He's no fan of the dragons. But I'm not sure where he lives or works now."

"Maybe that can be the next job for our little scout. After that, we should have a meeting with him and the priest and anyone else you can think of. We need to establish some specific goals and work toward them. We're not killing a dragon next week."

"If only."

Rick was right. We needed to figure out exactly what we were doing before we tried to do any of it. Overthrowing the dragons would not be an overnight job. For now, I'd settle for getting rid of Troilus Green. I still ached from whatever he had thrown at me.

Lovat returned a few hours later. My anxiety over Kelly drove me to watch for his return, and I couldn't wait any longer to hear what he had learned. Not surprisingly, the little guy demanded his promised lantern before he gave up his information.

"She okay," he told us. "Be here soon."

"Wait, what?" Rick exclaimed.

"You told her where we are?" I shouted simultaneously.

Lovat shrugged. "She want'a know. You did't say not tell her."

"Did you see any sign of Viridian Guard around her? Or the draconic?"

He snorted. "No sign. Think I know that."

"Guess we'll have to be more specific in our instructions," Rick observed, rolling his eyes.

"What should we do?" I asked.

Rick thought for a moment. "I'll get up on the roof. I'll watch out for anyone following her." He headed for the balcony. Lovat retreated to his corner to experiment with his new lantern, while I waited impatiently for Kelly's arrival.

I didn't have long to wait. I figured Lovat would have come back a lot quicker through his own methods, but maybe he did other stuff while he was out. Or maybe Kelly was just in that much of a hurry. She barged into the sanctuary and stopped short when she saw me. Was she trembling?

"Beryl!" Her voice sounded… angry? Or happy? I couldn't tell.

"Kelly. I'm so relieved to see you—" I started to answer.

"What in all the Chromatic Hells have you been up to?" she demanded, rushing forward a few steps then stopping when she got a better look at me. "Your face—what is going on?"

"I'll explain everything," I said, raising my hands. "I'll tell you all about it. Just… are you okay? Did they question you?"

"Question me? You could call it that. I spent five hours at the Guard station getting interrogated by… by…"

"Troilus Green."

What had seemed to be anger in her melted away, and she now looked terrified. "It was a Guard captain at first," she said softly. "And then that… thing came in. Beryl… I have never been more scared in my entire life… I—I—"

I stepped forward, and she fell into my arms. The impact genuinely hurt, but it felt so good at the same time. She didn't cry or anything, but I guess she needed a hug. I felt her trembling start to come under control. "I didn't tell them anything," she whispered.

Rick came down from above and nodded. No followers.

Kelly pulled away and took a deep breath. I hid my disappointment. That hug could have lasted much longer. She nodded at Rick. "Good to see you're here too." She looked back at me. "In fact, he looks to be in a lot better shape than you are. Tell me everything."

I took my own deep breath. "Let's sit down." I started with the moment the Guard took me away from the bicycle shop and related all that had happened since then. As I spoke, I was amazed all of this had happened in less than two days. My life had irrevocably changed in such a short space of time.

"Chroma, Beryl, what are you thinking?" she asked when I was done. She looked at Rick. "You too! How can you two possibly think seriously about rebelling against Viridia and the other dragons? It's insane!"

"Probably," I admitted. "But I don't have much choice now. I'm a fugitive. I can't go back home again."

"You could run away," Kelly said, gesturing wildly. "You could go to… to…"

"Where?" Rick asked. "Should I take him with me back to Atramentous? Maybe we could go to Caesious? Or the Blasted Lands?"

"To the mountains, maybe?" She looked somewhat desperate. "I've heard of people living there, outside the cities—"

"That's a myth," Rick countered. "Nobody lives in the mountains. The dragons like to go there all the time. No one could escape their notice up there."

"We can't run," I repeated. "So we either spend the rest of our lives hiding… or we fight. I know what I want to do."

Kelly closed her eyes and took another deep breath. She let it out slowly.

"Okay." She opened her eyes. "What do you need?"

"Wh—wait. You can't be involved in this. You—"

"You made me involved when you brought him"—she pointed at Rick—"to my door! So whether you like it or not, I'm in this. I already kept your secrets while facing off with… with a monster. I can keep doing that, but you have to let me stay involved. I want to help." She paused. "I need to help."

I looked to Rick. He grinned. "She's got guts. I like her," he said.

"Stop that."

Kelly shot me a strange look. Oops. Maybe I shouldn't warn other guys in front of her when I haven't even said anything to her about my feelings. Smooth.

"Okay, well… um. We're starting to figure out names of people we can recruit. Once we do that, we'll have a planning meeting and decide where to go from here."

Kelly nodded gravely. Then a grin spread over her face.

"Mr. Brunswick said that if I saw you, I should tell you that you're fired." She giggled.

"Yeah, I kind of figured."

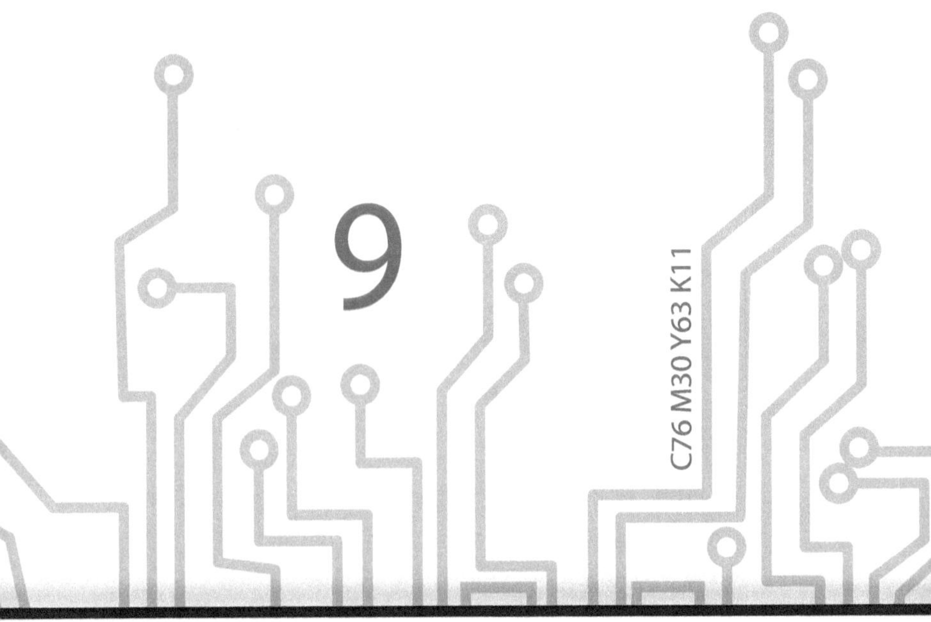

Kelly left a few minutes later. Before she walked out, she gave me another quick hug and shot a look at Rick. "Try not to get yourselves killed for a few days," she said in parting. I watched her go, feeling a confusing mix of emotions.

Relief that she was all right, and pleasure that she had been concerned about me, competed with a new respect for her bravery. At the same time, the thought of Troilus Green looking down at her filled me with rage. Picturing that cruel beast in the same room with her, the kindest girl I had ever met, only strengthened my resolve.

"Where did you get the dagger?" I asked aloud.

"Some crazy guy in Atramentous sold it to me," Rick answered. "Why?"

"We need weapons." I turned to look at him. "The next time I see that draconic, I'm going to kill it."

Rick nodded. He glanced up. "Let's go up on the roof."

I didn't argue, but it seemed like a curious suggestion. Rick led the way up to the balcony and to the trapdoor. We climbed out onto the roof again and looked around at the city of Viridia. The early afternoon sun bathed the city in a dull glow. Only a few small clouds dotted the sky.

Rick pointed to the southeast. "Let's review. Over there is your industrial district, correct?" I nodded. "Not far from the mountains themselves, which are full of mines." He paused. "All the cities are laid out essentially the same, just rotated based on which side is closest to the mountains."

I gestured to the Emerald Ascendancy, toward the center of the city. "I'm guessing you know what that is."

"Of course. The dragons have to have their own place, and it has to be spectacular." Rick took a step toward the edge of the roof and gazed at the massive complex. "Mind you, this one is bigger than most. Viridia has a bigger ego than the others, I think. Caesious has a massive tower, but it's pretty stark. Atramentous, strangely enough, doesn't seem to care. He has a pit. A great, big bleaking pit."

"You've been to Caesious?"

Rick glanced back. "Yeah, I've been to lots of places. I sneak rides on the trains." He pointed northwest. I knew the train station sat on the edge of the city in that direction. The rails traveled in two directions, both of them passing through the vast crops and pastures needed to provide food to the cities. The west line led to the next nearest city, Atramentous. The northwest line led to the center of The Circle, the Hub, where lines connected to all the cities. A northeast line had been almost completed, according to history, right before the destruction of the lost city. The trains traveled at great speeds back and forth, carrying food and trade goods from city to city.

"Green, black, blue, the twin reds, and gold," Rick recited. "All the cities of The Circle. Filled with men and women, boys and girls, living their lives in constant service to the dragons."

"Slavery. Not service."

"Slavery," Rick repeated. He turned in a circle, waving in all directions. "There are somewhere around a hundred thousand people living in this city alone, and it's not the largest one. All told, there has to be close to a million people living in The Circle. Plus maybe a couple hundred or more draconics and six dragons." He stopped and focused on me. "Are we arrogant enough to think that we can make this kind of decision for all of them?"

It was a sobering question, but one for which I already knew the answer.

"Yes." I ticked off the reasons. "First, because it's the right thing to do. Second, as we already observed, we either fight or hide. We don't have any other choices. And third... because I—I hate that... giant lizard, and I want it dead."

"Good enough."

Rick looked back toward the industrial district. "Maybe the secret to killing a dragon is there, or in the mines."

"With work, we could probably find several ways to take out a dragon," I said. "That's not the main problem."

"Right. The main problem is not getting everyone wiped out in retaliation."

"Which is why we need to kill all of them. We've been over this, Onyx."

"But killing all the dragons at once would be… impossible. I don't know if they've even all been in the same place at the same time."

"So how do we kill them one at a time without the others killing everyone?"

We stood in silence for a while.

"A couple of years ago, I saw a play," Rick said. I blinked. A play? "It was the only performance they ever did. The story was about the rebellion that killed the other black dragon."

"Yeah, so?"

"It was only performed once, because everyone involved was killed or thrown in prison. The director, the actors, even the stage hands. Except the writer. They never caught him."

I frowned. I could see why that kind of story wouldn't have been appreciated by the ruling powers, but I didn't know where Rick was going with this.

"Except it had a twist ending." Rick laughed. "In the end, the dragon came back to life."

"That's creepy. What's your point?"

"Wouldn't that be horrible? If we killed them, and they came back? If they were truly immortal?"

I looked at him in confusion. "Are you… I have no idea what you're talking about."

"Sorry. I'm just saying that even when something showed one of the dragons in a more powerful light, they still shut it all down because of the very mention of rebellion."

Silence fell again. I looked northeast, thinking about the Blasted Lands.

"The ideal solution," Rick said slowly, "would be if they killed each other."

I squinted at him against the sunlight. "They've gotten along for centuries, and now all of a sudden, we can convince them to fight?"

"Maybe… maybe if the motivation were strong enough. What if… Oh, Beryl, this might be it." The beginnings of a smile grew on his face. "What if we killed just one dragon, but—"

"But made it look like another dragon had done it!" I exclaimed, snatching onto the same idea.

We had already talked multiple times about killing one or all the dragons, and tossed out dozens of ridiculous ideas, but this one actually made sense. Beautiful.

"So if a dragon were killed and the evidence all pointed to another dragon having done it, then how would the other dragons react?"

"They would band together and hopefully kill the guilty dragon!"

"Two down, four to go. And with the seed of dragon conflict planted, over time we could do the same to the remaining ones. A dragon civil war!"

We debated for a while over which dragon would make the best target and which one would be best to pin it on. Of course, I advocated for the green dragon to die, but Rick thought it was a bad idea since we were based in the green city for now.

A third voice broke into our debate. "You two mean it?"

We turned and saw Lovat sitting on the peak of the roof, watching us. Neither of us had heard him come up. What a pair of secretive conspirators we made!

"Yes, we mean it," I said. "How much did you hear?"

The boy shrugged. "Dunno. A lot. You want to kill Vir'dia."

"How do you feel about that?" Rick asked. I noticed his hand reach toward something in his pocket.

He shrugged again. "Dragon's never done me no good."

I crouched so I could look him in the face. "This is what we're all about, Lovat. We're going to be working on this for however long it takes. It's going to be very dangerous. We want your help, but if you don't—"

"Not scared."

"I'm not saying you are," I reassured him. "Just—"

"Not scared."

"Good. You help us, and we'll help you," Rick put in. His hand moved away from his pocket.

"Just… be careful," I added.

Lovat shrugged again. He turned and scampered down through the trapdoor without a sound.

Rick nodded. "He'll be a good asset," he said again, almost to himself. It didn't feel right to me, using the boy. I could only imagine what the Guard or Troilus Green would do to a street orphan if they caught him working for us. But he wanted to help, didn't he?

"Speaking of assets, I think it's time we found your cyber-tech friend."

I nodded. Finding Loden and setting up a meeting was the next logical step in our campaign. I would write him a note and send it out with Lovat. I looked down at the street and saw Bice approaching, carrying a large bag. "More supplies." I pointed him out.

Rick nodded. "And maybe some tools. We really need to fix that toilet."

I laughed at the absurdity of it all. Here we were, two young men on the run, planning an insurrection that would affect a million people, and we didn't even have a working toilet. The dragons would surely be quaking in fear if they heard of our existence.

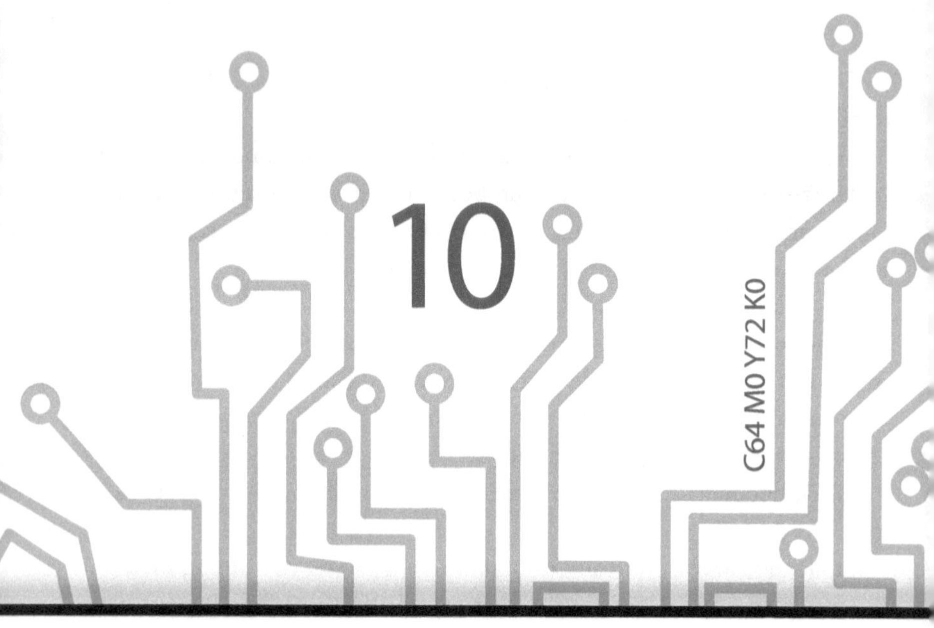

10

"Loden, three years ago, you helped me survive when I should have died. Now, I am asking for your help again. This boy, Lovat, can tell you about my current project. If you agree that this project is a good idea, please send a return message, and we can set up a meeting."

I lowered the note and looked at Rick. "Is that both vague and specific enough?"

"Assuming we can trust this friend of yours, I think so. Is Loden his first or last name?"

"I honestly don't remember. I wasn't in the best of shape when I saw him last."

"Right. The accident." Rick eyed me curiously. "Is that why you hate the dragons so much? The death of your parents?"

I looked away. "My parents were already dead to me long before the accident."

Rick's eyebrows went up. He opened his mouth to ask, but I shot him down. "I'm not talking about it."

He nodded and turned to catalog the new supplies Bice had brought. Sure enough, a set of plumbing tools awaited whichever one of us felt brave enough to tackle the toilet.

My resolve not to talk about the past did not stop my memories from racing back seven years. I saw myself as a ten-year-old, trusting in my parents. I saw myself following them into the Shrine of the Emerald God…

I shut it off there. I would not relive that day. I would not. The fact that it happened was enough, enough to fuel the hatred and rage roiling inside me.

I called Lovat over and explained what I wanted him to do. I described Loden as best as I could. The boy listened to me with an impassive face. Aside from his fierceness when we first caught him, he never seemed to show much emotion at all.

"Do you understand what I'm saying?" I asked.

He nodded. "I'll find him," he said. He stuffed the note into the pocket of his baggy jeans and disappeared through the front door.

Bice sat nearby, observing. I looked at him and almost wanted to rip that calm smile off his face. There were times when I couldn't look past his former profession. If only he weren't so… nice. He got to his feet and stretched.

"Recruitment drive, eh?" Bice knew Loden; in fact, I think Loden was the one who sent him to me. But he also didn't know where to find Loden now.

"Yeah… we can't do this on our own. We have an idea, but we need help."

"If I run into anyone that feels the same way, I'll point them in your direction," he said. He looked toward the door. "Your little friend seems to be coming in handy. I'm glad that worked out."

"Wait… you knew he was here?"

Bice chuckled. "I've kept an eye on Lovat since I hid him here over a year ago. Like yourself, he ran into my garden, trying to hide from the Guard. He was easier to hide. Didn't collapse on my doorstep. How's your pain, by the way?"

"It's a dull ache. Nothing I can't deal with."

Bice peered at my face and put a hand on my shoulder. "Don't let dull aches go on for too long," he said. "If they don't start to fade, they can develop into something worse."

I had a feeling he wasn't talking about my bruises now. Meddling priest.

"I'll be fine."

"Of course you will. See you tomorrow."

After Bice walked out, I wondered how many other strays he had helped relocate or hide. There was so much more to that quiet man than met the eye.

Lovat did not return that night, or even the next morning. As the day progressed, Rick and I tried to pass the time by throwing out ideas on how to kill a dragon. Most of them involved something long and sharp. All of them were impractical. I hoped Loden or Bice or another recruit would come up with a good idea, because ours… weren't.

Rick pleaded complete ignorance on the subject of plumbing and left that job to me. I didn't know much about it either, but boredom and anxiety drove me to see what I could do. Besides, the rodents in the alley were getting a little too bold when I went out there. Where was a cat when you needed one?

I managed to get the toilet disassembled and began investigating the pipes. First I discovered an infiltration of tiny roots that had filled the drain pipe. Cutting and yanking them out took over an hour and was easily the most disgusting job I had ever done. I thought the drain might be okay after that. I ran some water down it, which seemed to work. But there still wasn't any water coming in to the toilet. That would take some investigation or research. I had no idea where to even begin.

When I heard voices back out in the sanctuary, I got to my feet and joined them. Kelly had shown up; it must have been her lunch break. She and Rick were in the middle of an animated conversation, until they saw me. Kelly started my way, wrinkled her nose, and stopped.

"You stink!"

I spread my arms out. "Tell me something I don't know. Apparently, dragon slayers have to be proficient in plumbing." I waved the wrench in the air.

"Which means I failed," Rick added. "I'm not even trying."

Kelly's expression was unreadable. "I guess… I guess I'd rather have you trying to learn plumbing than plotting the end of the world."

"Kelly, I…"

She waved me off. "No, no. I get it. We're committed now. Fight or hide. I know."

I wondered if she was having second thoughts after her commitment the day before.

She laughed a little. "I'll see if I can find a book on plumbing for you."

"Thank you!" Rick's head snapped around. "If we're going to stick around here, it would certainly make it more... pleasant."

A few minutes later, Kelly excused herself and hurried back to the bike shop. There was so much more I wanted to ask her or just talk about with her, but the time never seemed right. I turned toward the back side of the sanctuary and stopped. The broken dragon statue faced me. The image of dripping blood flashed across my mind.

There were so many things I couldn't control right now, so many things I couldn't seem to get done... but I could deal with that. I walked up to the statue, gripped the wrench with both hands, and swung as hard as I could. I smashed through the dragon's head and sent chips of rock flying in every direction.

"Chromatic Hells!" Rick jumped out of the way. "What brought that on?"

I didn't answer and swung the wrench again. I destroyed the remaining dragon wing. With a couple more swings, I made sure what was left didn't resemble a dragon in any way.

I looked over at Rick, my face like stone. "If the Chromatic Hells actually exist, they are reserved for the dragons and their servants. They're the true evil in this world."

Rick folded his arms across his chest. "You aren't going to run off and try to kill them all on your own, are you? Because I think we have the makings of a plan starting here, and if you're going all rage monster on me—"

I cut him off. "You don't have to worry. I can keep it under control."

"If you say so."

"I do."

I turned and tossed the wrench into the back corner. I realized that to him, I might look like some maniac who just lost control and took out his rage on a chunk of rock... Okay, maybe that's it would look like to anyone. But the rage only emerged when I wanted it to. At least, that's what I told myself.

I looked down at the mess of rubble I had created. Part of me felt guilty, and I suppressed the urge to clean it all up. Instead, I bent down and picked up a single shard of rock. Scales carved around in a twist. It looked like it might have been part of the dragon's tail. For some reason I couldn't explain, I put the shard in my pocket. That was it. It would be my reminder and my control. When I felt the rage building, I would hold on to the shard. Maybe it would work. Maybe not. I took a deep breath and went to clean myself up.

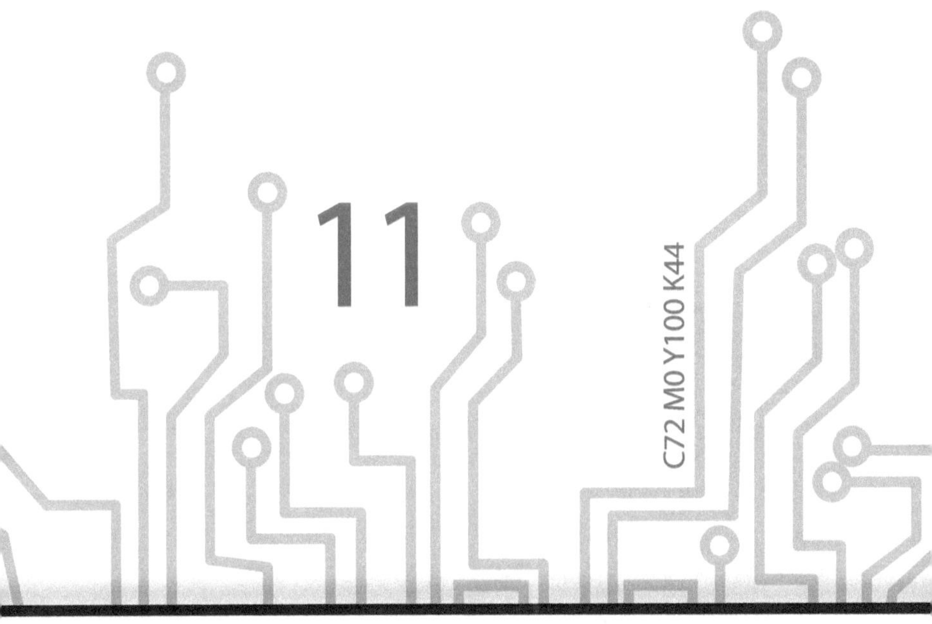

Lovat returned near the end of the day. He reported finding Loden working at the train station, which baffled me somewhat. From cybernetics to trains? At any rate, my old friend said he would join us at noon the next day. I asked Lovat to deliver the message to both Kelly and Bice sometime in the morning, and we would have our first insurrectionist meeting.

Bice arrived a little early with a tall, weathered-looking man in tow. His face had so many cracks and wrinkles, his chromark looked less like a line and more like a cloud. His hand felt rough and scarred when I shook it. Bice introduced him as Celadon, a miner who had walked off his job and ended up here in the city. He had no love for the dragons, either. He didn't have much to say except to ask us to call him Don. After introductions, he took a seat and waited. Bice chatted a little with Lovat.

Kelly showed up right on time, a little out of breath. "Mr. Brunswick hired a new guy, and I had to find a way to give him the slip. He's a little pushy."

I frowned and flexed my fist. "Should I come persuade him to leave you alone?"

"Don't be silly."

I didn't feel silly. Girls are so confusing.

We waited a few more minutes. I began to get anxious. What if Loden wasn't the man I remembered now? What if he had turned us in? The Viridian Guard could be surrounding the place right now. Troilus Green could be at our door.

At that moment, the door did open, but it wasn't Troilus Green who entered. Instead, a familiar older man walked in carrying a long box. A strikingly attractive young woman followed him.

"Sorry to be late," Loden announced. He set the box down; it seemed heavy. He walked up to me and looked me in the eyes. "Beryl. It is… so good to see you again."

Loden looked about how I remembered him: stocky, graying hair cut short almost to his scalp. I seem to remember him being taller, though. As one of the elite upper class, his chromark was much narrower than mine. He put out his hand and took mine in a solid grip. Though I hadn't seen him in years, I couldn't help but feel a lump in my throat. With this man on our side, we would surely have a chance.

Loden turned to look around. "And the rest of you! I have dreamed of a day like this, but never thought I'd see it. I want to know all of you."

I swallowed and began the introductions. Loden embraced Bice as an old friend, then greeted Rick, Kelly, and Don with gusto. He waved at Lovat, who had settled down on top of the growing pile of our supplies.

Then Loden brought his guest forward. "And this is Stacy Moss," he announced. "Some of you may recognize her…"

I didn't, but Kelly's eyes widened. "Holy Viridia! I loved you in Anyone But Jade!"

Oh. An actress. I didn't really pay attention to that kind of thing, but Kelly went to all the plays. Sometimes I wondered if she might be a little obsessed.

Stacy's chromark was barely visible against her dark skin. I think performers are allowed to hide theirs, due to the various roles they played on stage. She made up for it with hair dyed a deep, dark green. Thin, yet curves in all the right places. She must have been quite popular. I wondered how she had met Loden, and why she was here. But I guess none of us had told our full stories. I certainly hadn't.

"Thanks, love," Stacy responded. She sat next to Kelly and patted her leg. I don't think I had ever seen Kelly look that… starstruck.

Rick clapped his hands and suggested we get started. As everyone settled in, he turned to me. "Beryl?"

Was I in charge? I had never thought of it that way, but when it came down to it, I guess I was the one connecting everyone together. I had just never considered myself a leader. These people were looking at me, waiting for me. I took a deep breath.

"Well, I guess you all know why we're here," I began. "Rick and I, as you might have heard, are fugitives. We're wanted by the Viridian Guard. So we…" I paused. That wasn't the way to do it. This kind of gathering needed something more. What could I say? I noticed Kelly's face tensing up, so I took another deep breath and plunged in.

"For as long as anyone can remember, the dragons have ruled The Circle. With their power, their draconic servants, and their human collaborators, they keep everyone else down. They use us. They make us work for them, give them all our best, and follow only their desires. Our technology advances only in the ways that the dragons approve, ways that can benefit them. You've all heard stories of fortek that can do amazing things, but we're not allowed to have it. And if someone is not useful to the dragons, they're… disposed of. Like we're cattle. That's all we are to them: slightly more intelligent cattle, here to serve their needs." I pointed to my face. "They brand us, even, marking us as their property. Even worse, they crave our worship, deceiving people into believing them to be gods, accepting sacrifices. And, and… this is wrong. It's all wrong. And we want to change it." I put a hand in my pocket and gripped the stone shard.

"Well said," Bice murmured.

"How are you going to change it?" Stacy asked. She had an unusual accent. The vowel sounds seemed stronger. It must have been a stage thing.

"The dragons must die," Rick said.

"You have heard of the Blasted Lands, I'm assuming?" she responded.

"We know," I said, taking charge again. "We know the fate that is supposed to befall any who dare rise up against their overlords. That's why just trying to kill one dragon isn't enough. We have to kill all of them. All six dragons must die."

I let the statement sit in the silence that followed.

"Are we… are we absolutely sure that this is the only way?" Kelly finally asked. "I mean, are things really that bad? For the most part, our lives aren't that bad." She looked around the room. "Are they?"

I thought we had already dealt with this. Why was she bringing it up again?

"My wife was pregnant." The deep, craggy voice made us all turn to look at Don. I had forgotten him. When he realized everyone was watching, he shrank back. But he took a deep breath and then continued. "When she lost the baby, she changed. She slept a lot more. She felt like everything was wrong in her life. After she missed a week of work, the Viridian Guard came for her. I've never seen her again."

Don's story was not unusual, but it reminded me of too many things. I gripped the shard in my pocket even tighter. The silence returned. Were they waiting on me to say something?

"The dragons control our lives, and take them when they choose. We want to take those lives back."

Loden spoke up. "This is all well and good, lad," he said. "But do you have an actual plan, or are you just going to give speeches?"

I tried not to react, but that kind of hurt. Maybe he just wanted me to move things along.

"We do have a plan," Rick said. "Well, the beginnings of one, anyway. The first step is to kill one of the dragons and make sure everyone believes that one of the others did it."

"I like that," Stacy declared.

Loden nodded. "I like the concept, and I think killing a dragon is not as impossible as some would think, but how do we place the blame?"

"We spread rumors," Stacy jumped in. "We make sure everyone's already thinking the two dragons hate each other, before we act."

"That's good, but it'll take more than that," I said. "It has to actually look like a dragon did it. Just words won't be enough."

"Digger," Don said.

"Who's Digger?" Stacy asked.

"That's what we called them out at the mines," Don explained. "The big vehicles that we use to tear up the rock. They kind of have teeth, like this." He made a motion with his hands as if they were jaws clamping together.

"Brilliant," Rick said. "So… we kill the dragon somehow and then use a digger to tear its throat out, making it look like it was done by teeth."

"Still not enough," Loden said. "You need more evidence at the scene."

"Then we use blood," Bice said. Now it was his turn to have everyone stare. Unlike Don, he wasn't the least bit uncomfortable at the attention. "In the temples, on the high holy days, the priests use dragon's blood in their ceremonies. I'm sure I can get some."

My own blood went cold. I knew what those ceremonies entailed. I would not think of that. Not. Now. Not here. I gripped the shard in my pocket until my fist shook. Besides, it would be justice if the dragon's own blood could be used against it. Blood that I would always see dripping, pooling...

"That would be fantastic!" Rick exclaimed. "Now we're getting somewhere."

"To really make it work, you would need one more thing," Loden said.

"What's that?"

"A tooth. Plant a dragon's tooth at the scene, as you've described, and there will be no doubt."

"Where would we find a dragon's tooth?" I couldn't imagine we could find one of those just lying around.

Loden pointed to the north. "In the Emerald Ascendancy."

"You think we should break in there and steal a tooth?" I asked, dubious.

"I think if you can do that, I can solve the biggest gap in your plan," Loden said.

"And what's that?" Rick demanded.

"I know how to kill a dragon." The older man smiled, leaned back, and crossed his arms.

Loden would not reveal his plan, no matter how much we pleaded.

"This is something I have been working on for years," he said. "As much as I'm pleased to meet all of you, I don't trust all of you yet. This will be my secret for now."

"Some secret!" Rick snorted. "Just the key to the entire plan."

"If you come up with a better idea, I'm open to it," Loden replied amicably. "In the meantime, shall we figure out who's doing what?"

Bice proposed that he and Lovat assist Don in stealing a digger unit. "But where do we take it?"

"Bring it to me," Loden said. "I'll get it on a train and delivered to where it needs to be."

"Where is that?" I asked.

"You can't kill a dragon here, within the city," Loden pointed out. "You need a little time to plant the evidence before anyone else shows up. The only way to assure that is to do it away from the cities. I'm thinking of somewhere out near the Hub."

Rick agreed with that one. "Makes sense."

Stacy volunteered to start the rumor campaign. "Who are we targeting again?" she asked.

"Green and blue," I answered before anyone else could speak. Rick shot me a look.

"Why them? I mean, I get green, obviously, but why skip over black?" Stacy wanted to know.

"Everyone knows black and green are friends already," I pointed out. "They're neighbors. The rumors will spread easier if we choose a dragon from further away. Blue is far, but not so far that it makes things too complicated." Red was too far away and might be confusing, since there were two of them. Gold was the furthest away, and the one we knew the least about, anyway.

"And we can't kill green, because we'll be using his tooth and blood. So our target is the blue dragon, Caesious," Rick said. The conclusion rankled me, but I knew he was right. Still, I swore to myself that the green dragon would be second in line.

Kelly offered to help Stacy. That left the impossible mission of stealing a tooth for Rick and me.

With the meeting pretty much over, Bice and Don left together to make their own plans. It seemed understood, though, that Don would return later. Apparently, the sanctuary was to be his home, as well. If this kept up, we might have to invest in some bunk beds.

Loden walked to the box he had left on the floor. "I have something for you, now that I know you're serious." Rick and I followed him, naturally curious. I caught a glimpse of Stacy elbowing Kelly and pointing.

"Since the day I helped you, Beryl, I have been thinking about a day like today. For three years, I have been acquiring various items, and preparing. Moving to work on the trains, for example, was my own choice. I convinced my superiors that I had some great ideas for improving their speed and efficiency."

"I don't understand," I said. "Why would helping me make you want to rebel against the dragons?"

Loden pulled something out of the box. At first, I didn't realize what it was. Then he drew the blade from its scabbard, and I knew.

"It's a sword!" Rick exclaimed, before I could.

Loden held the blade up. It was beautiful, even in the dim light of our refuge. He turned it in a slow arc, revealing two edges. The blade itself was about eighteen inches long, with a lengthy handle that could be held with either one hand or two. I had never seen anything like it in my life.

"My great-grandfather told me of a story that was ancient when he was young," Loden said slowly, his eyes on the sword. "In the story, a dragon was killed… by a single man with a sword."

Rick looked skeptical. "That seems…"

"Improbable? I know." Loden chuckled. "Perhaps dragons were smaller back then. Or the man in the story was far stronger and tougher than we are today. I do not expect that we can slay Viridia or Caesious with one of these."

"However…" He turned the blade in his hands and extended the handle to me. "These will come in handy, I believe. Dragons aren't our only enemies."

I took the handle and gripped it tight. I stepped back and slowly moved the sword through the air. For a moment, I stood in awe at the beauty and elegance of the weapon. Almost, I could imagine myself as the dragon slayer in Loden's story. I didn't even notice when he handed a second sword to Rick.

"Other stories tell of whole armies fighting with weapons such as these," Loden said. In my mind, I pictured what that would be like. People once fought with these lengthy blades, cutting into one another, stabbing one another. Hard to imagine. Although… Another image came to mind, and I thrust the blade forward, imagining it stabbing through purple-edged robes and the scaly hide of Troilus Green.

"That's sad." Stacy's voice intruded on my imagination. She jumped to her feet. "Looks like I have my work cut out for me."

Loden laughed. "Indeed. That's the other reason Stacy is here, lads."

I looked at Rick, and he shrugged. Stacy reached into the box and withdrew a third sword. She slid it out and tossed it from hand to hand with ease. "Early last year, we had this show called Against the Crimson Defile," she explained. "I spent four months learning how to use one of these. Our stage manager loves for the props to be as real as possible."

"Show me," I said.

"Not with these." Stacy set the sword down and reached back into the box. This time, she took out wooden practice swords, about the same size. Rick and I exchanged the real ones, though not without a twinge of regret.

Stacy waved her practice sword and indicated for me to come at her. I attempted a swing. Before I realized what had happened, my hand was stinging, and my sword clattered against the floor. Lovat burst out laughing and almost fell off his perch. I retrieved the sword, embarrassed but determined not to let that happen again.

Stacy pointed at Rick. "Now you." He smirked and came toward her, flipping the sword to his left hand. To my surprise, he fared much better than I had. The two of them exchanged several blows, sword on sword, before Stacy managed to spin around the outside of his arm and bring her sword to rest against the back of his neck.

"Not bad," she observed. "You've had some experience."

Rick nodded and stepped away. "Most of it was not with a blade this length," he admitted. "I'm used to daggers."

Stacy nodded. "I can tell. You overcommit some. I can help you get past that. But that's enough for now. I'll work with both of you later."

I picked up one of the real swords again. That same image kept coming back into my head. "Would these blades pierce the hide of a draconic?" At my question, I heard Kelly's sharp intake of breath.

Loden scratched his chin. "I don't see why not," he said. "Draconics are tough, but not to the same degree as actual dragon scales."

Thoughts about the enemy reminded me Loden hadn't answered my question. "The swords are incredible, Loden. Thank you," I said. "But I haven't forgotten that you dodged my question. What made you want to rebel?"

The older man took a seat and sighed. "It's a little hard to explain." He gestured toward me. "Here you were, on the verge of manhood, a victim of a tragic accident. We had the technology to heal you, but we weren't allowed to use it. I had to steal, lie, and break a whole bunch of other laws in order to save your life. Keeping it a secret was the hardest part. It cost me a great deal."

"I'm sorry..."

He waved it away. "I don't regret it, son. Saving life is worth whatever cost I can pay. But it opened my eyes. For the first time in my life, I saw the whole, evil system for what it was. Make no mistake, all of you. To the dragons and draconics, human life is worth no more than that of a rat. They value us only for how we can serve them, and when we can serve them no more, we are nothing more than garbage to be thrown out.

"From that day forward, I began to plan. I soon realized that nothing could ever change unless the dragons themselves were removed from the picture. For a while, I considered whether it would be possible to escape The Circle, find out what was beyond. Surely it had to be better than here."

"There's nothing beyond The Circle," Rick said. It was a mantra we were all taught from childhood.

"The only ones who might know that for sure are the dragons," Loden noted. "And they're not sharing. Regardless, I abandoned that plan. I couldn't just leave and let everyone else suffer. I had to stay. So… I studied everything I could get my hands on related to dragons: their abilities, their habits, their strengths and weaknesses. I came to the same conclusions you did: that they all had to die. But you came up with the best plan I've heard. Pinning the blame on another dragon." He paused and looked at us with a sad smile.

"We're going to start a war, you know."

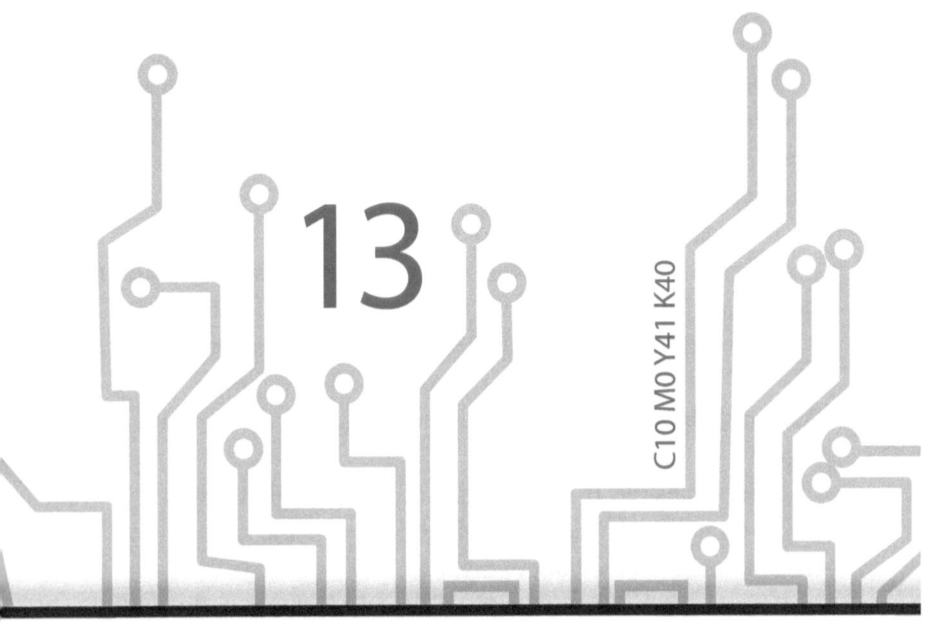

War. What a strange concept. Our history studies, as limited as they were, told very little of war. Around six hundred years ago, the gold dragon had gone to war with the other black dragon (the one that died). The two dragons sent hundreds of their elite guards, led by the draconics, into battle with each other. Neither achieved anything through it, save to kill off scores of their own populace.

"Do you think it will come to that?" Kelly whispered.

"We'll be inviting them to believe that one dragon killed another dragon," Loden answered. "If we succeed, I don't see how it doesn't come to war. We can only hope that this time the dragons fight themselves, rather than using us as their proxies."

I hadn't considered that aspect of the plan. Still, if the Viridian Guard were wiped out in a fight against other dragon forces, I wouldn't shed many tears.

Loden stood and stretched. "Time for me to get back to work," he said. "Beryl. A word outside?"

I followed him out the doors, as Stacy began showing Rick some more techniques using the practice swords. Kelly watched with rapt attention.

Outside, Loden looked around at the deserted street. In our short time here, we had seen very little traffic—foot or cycle—on this particular block. There wasn't much activity at all in this dead part of the city.

Loden took a deep breath. "It really is good to see you again, Beryl. I have thought of you many times in the last few years." He hesitated. "I've meant to check in on you dozens of times, but somehow never got around to it. For that, I'm sorry."

I shrugged. "You had your own life."

"Maybe. But my friendship with your parents was important to me. I should have kept a closer eye on you, for their sake if nothing else."

"I doubt they would have cared one way or the other."

"Ah." At the bitterness in my tone, Loden fell silent for a moment. "You misjudge them, son. They loved you greatly. Their death was truly tragic."

I didn't answer. If Loden didn't accept the ugly truth, why should I bother trying to convince him? My parents were the reason I would never get that image of blood out of my head.

"How is your implant working?" he asked, changing the subject.

"As well as can be expected, I guess." I jogged in place to illustrate.

"And you can access the boosts? How strong are they?"

I shrugged. "I don't know. I can kick pretty hard, run faster than normal." I told him about my jump to the second floor while holding Rick.

He nodded, again scratching his chin. He almost seemed reluctant to say more. In fact, I thought he was about to walk away, when he spoke again.

"You should try pushing your limits. I think it can handle more than you've attempted so far."

Before I could ask more, he turned and strode down the street. "I'll see you again soon," he called over his shoulder.

I re-entered the sanctuary. Everything remained the same. Stacy and Rick continued their swordplay, while Kelly and Lovat watched. A thought entered my head.

"Hey, I want a turn," I said with a wave.

"Sure." Rick wiped his forehead with the back of his glove. "I need a break." He tossed me the wooden practice sword.

I paid close attention as Stacy instructed me in some basic stances and swings. She then moved into actual sparring, showing me both attacks and defenses. It didn't take long for her to deliver a few solid blows against me in various places. Lovat laughed with abandon. Kelly giggled every so often, and apologized every time.

Then my chance came. When a wild swing took me out of Stacy's reach, I turned back, braced myself and then lunged, sending a boost into both legs.

Stacy had already taken a defensive pose to block me, but my burst of speed shocked her. My practice sword slammed into hers with such force they both splintered on impact. Stacy fell backwards. I stumbled, but maintained my own balance. I came to a stop with a wooden stub in my hand.

Rick and Kelly leaped to their feet and rushed forward. Lovat stared, open-mouthed. Rick helped Stacy to her feet, while Kelly stopped short and stared at me.

"Fewmets!" Stacy exclaimed when she caught her breath. "Loden told me you had a cyb implant, but I wasn't expecting that."

I looked at the ruins of the practice swords. "I'm sorry… I just wanted to experiment…"

Stacy laughed and tossed her broken sword into the box. "Don't apologize! That was impressive. You should keep working on that. If that had been a real sword, you might have cut me in half!" The laughter stopped and she regarded me for a moment. "You also could have been killed yourself. Your implant gives you an advantage opponents won't know about until you reveal it. So don't reveal it until the most opportune moment."

I nodded. I had already figured that part out, but it was a good reminder.

"Well, gang, it's been vibrant," Stacy announced, looking around at all of us. "But I need to get back to the stage. Kelly, we'll talk more later about the rumors. You two guys keep practicing. Fortunately, there's another set of practice blades in the box. Enjoy!"

With that, she sauntered out the door. "She's interesting," Rick said, his eyes watching her movements until the door shut behind her.

"You could say that." I glanced at Kelly. "Hey, are you okay with work? It's way past your lunch break."

"No worries," she said. "I told Mr. Brunswick I needed an afternoon off to recover from everything that's been going on. He grumbled, but couldn't argue."

My legs ached a little bit from the boost, so I sat on the steps to the front platform. "It's been quite a day," I said. "And now we have to figure out another impossible job. How do we get into the Emerald Ascendancy?"

"Yeah." Rick paced in a circle. "I have no ideas on that one yet."

"I do," Kelly piped up.

I blinked. "You do?"

"I know someone who works there," she explained.

"Go on."

Was she blushing? "Well, it's this guy… he was in my class during the Learning Years. He, um… We hung out a few times, but it never got very serious. I think he wanted it to be, but… I didn't."

I hated him already.

"So, I was thinking. I could send him a note, tell him I want to see him, catch up, that kind of thing, and then we could, maybe, use him as our way in?"

"We're not likely to find another way," Rick pointed out. "Sounds good to me."

"What's this guy's name?" I wanted to know.

"Mason. Mason Forest."

"Great. We shall infiltrate the Emerald Ascendancy with the help of Mason Forest," Rick declared, striking a pose with his sword. "And it will be the first step toward our victory!"

I noticed Lovat watching all of this with his usual impassivity. The laughter that had consumed him earlier had faded. "Hey, Lovat, you ever been near the Emerald Ascendancy?" I asked.

He looked at me with a blank expression. I pointed in the general direction. "The big place up on the hill? Where the dragon lives?"

He shook his head. "Bad place. Lots death."

"That's one way of putting it." At least Rick and I would be the only ones taking on this job. I didn't like the idea of putting anyone else at that kind of risk.

I leaned back and stared up at the ceiling. Kelly sat down next to me. "What are you thinking?" she asked.

"Lots of things," I said. "Just a few days ago, I was nothing but a bike repair guy. Now I'm sitting around planning a revolution that could start a war and transform our entire world."

"It's crazy, I know. I'm sitting here with you, and I don't even believe it. It all seems… unreal."

The lengthy pause that followed was broken when Kelly shoved my shoulder. "I remember when you first started at the bike shop. You were so confused and cute."

"I was cute?"

"You were! You and your big sad eyes!"

I didn't know what to think of that. On the one hand, cute was good. I think. On the other hand, big sad eyes? "You felt sorry for me?"

She rolled her eyes at me. "Only at first, you goof. You had no idea what you were doing, and it was all so new to you."

"Kind of like now, actually."

"The big difference is that back then, I was the one who could show you around, explain the place to you." That was probably the exact moment that I started to fall for her, come to think of it. "This time around… neither of us know what we're doing."

I had no idea what to say to that.

A few minutes later, Kelly decided she needed to head home. After hugging Rick and me, and attempting to hug Lovat, she left the building.

Rick voiced my thoughts. "Feels empty all of a sudden."

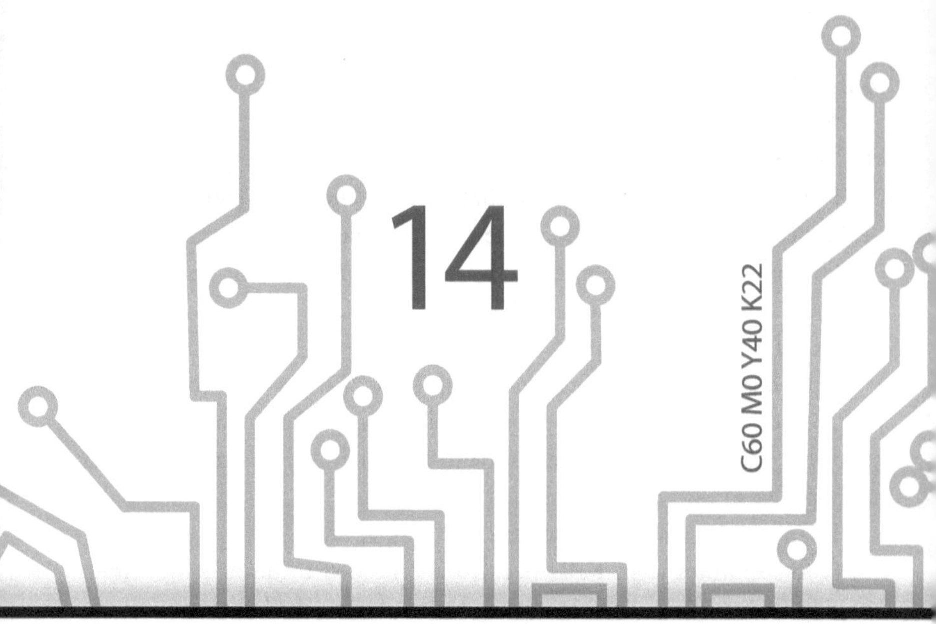

14

Two days passed. Rick and I practiced with the swords. Stacy came by once and spent a couple of hours pointing out our problems. Kelly sent her note to Mason and waited. We all waited. Somehow, Kelly also remembered to find a book on plumbing for me. After I read the entire thing cover to cover, I still had no clue how to solve our pipe problem. It was hard to think about something so mundane while contemplating the end of the world.

Don returned the evening after the meeting. He greeted us, found a place to sleep, and dozed off. When we awoke the next morning, he was already gone. He repeated this process the next evening and morning.

Lovat wandered in and out. I wasn't sure what he did with his time, but he didn't spend much of it in the sanctuary.

When no one else watched, I tried pushing the limits of my boosts. I leaped as high as I could in the center of the sanctuary. I know I got higher than I had while carrying Rick the day we met, but it still didn't seem all that much. Outdoors, I tried sporadic, short boosts to improve my running speed. While I saw some improvement in my control, I didn't think it rose to the level of what Loden hinted at.

On the evening of the second day, Kelly showed us a message from Mason. He sounded happy to hear from her and eager to meet. He arranged a date at a diner on the edge of the city's most upscale regions. I'm not sure if he was trying to impress Kelly or trying to look humble since he knew where she lived. Either way, I found new reasons to dislike him. I would never be able to afford a meal for two in a place like that.

Rick reluctantly agreed that I should be the one to join Kelly at her date. His black chromark made him too conspicuous. Of course, my face was probably plastered all over the place on criminal posters put up by the Viridian Guard. I asked Lovat to find me a hat. He brought me a cap with an Emerald Ascendancy tour logo on it. I didn't think he was mocking me, but I couldn't be sure.

At the appointed hour, Lovat led me to the diner through back roads and alleys. I waited until I knew Kelly and Mason had met and were talking, then I entered. The diner was as I expected: clean and neat, but without any gaudy decorations. Booths lined the walls for intimacy and privacy. Only someone with a serious income, favored by the dragon, could afford to eat here.

"Beryl!" Kelly called from a booth far from the front door. I made a show of looking around, finding her and smiling. I approached with a casual saunter. At least, I think it would be called a saunter. How did one saunter, anyway?

"Mason, this is my best friend, Beryl," she announced. She scooted further into the booth and invited me to join them. Best friend? Well, that was something, I guess, even if it was just for show. "Beryl, this is Mason, the guy I was telling you about."

"Good to meet you," I said, shaking his hand. This guy had been interested in Kelly for years? He wasn't much in the way of competition to my eyes: skinny as a cornstalk, huge glasses, and black hair slicker than grease on a bike chain.

"Likewise," he answered, squinting through his glasses with a perplexed look. Tough luck, buddy.

"Mason was just telling me about his work at the Emerald Ascendancy," Kelly told me. She was really playing this up, making it sound like the most fascinating thing in the world. I thought Stacy was the actress in our group.

"It's nothing, really," he said. "I'm a low level tech worker."

"No kidding? That's gotta be vibrant. How often do you see the dragon?"

He wobbled his head a little bit from side to side and half rolled his eyes. I guess he thought he was communicating humility or something.

Weird. "Oh, not very often," he said. "Viridia comes and goes, but I'm usually inside the lab and don't see him when it happens."

"But to be so close!" Kelly gushed. She inched a little closer toward him.

"I do see draconics almost every day," he said, brightening a little. "They're all over the place."

"That's incredible." I tried to sound enthusiastic. "I saw a draconic last week. I think he works with the Viridian Guard."

"Oh, that must be Troilus Green," Mason said. "He doesn't just 'work' with the Guard. He's in charge of the Guard. Very elite."

I wasn't sure how to feel about that. A waitress came by, and I ordered a drink, something to let Mason know I would be sticking around for a few minutes at least. But I wasn't going to order an entire meal. Let him think his date with Kelly would continue, if he could get rid of me. Also, I couldn't afford it.

"Beryl is such a Viridia fan," Kelly went on. "He collects everything he can get hold of related to him. He even still has his Dragon Action toy collection from when we were kids!"

That… was true, actually, but I had long ago burned the green dragon figures in effigy. Those were some awesome toys. Come to think of it, I guess my old toys were now in the hands of the Viridian Guard, along with all of my other possessions. I felt a tiny ache in my heart.

Mason looked at me and laughed a little. He leaned in. "I actually have one of those on my workstation at the Ascendancy," he confided. "It's the Elite Guard that was mispackaged with a dragon egg instead of a shockspear."

"I have the original Emerald Ascendancy playset," I lied. My parents had never been able to afford that one. "It was always my favorite. That's why I go on the tour any time I can." I pointed at my hat.

Mason's eyes widened. "That playset was the most incredible toy ever made!" he gushed. "I've tried to get one for years!"

"I think Beryl has another kind of collectible he'd like to find now," Kelly said.

"What do you mean?"

"I want the real thing," I said. "No more toys and collectibles. I'm looking for a real piece of the dragon."

Mason wobbled his head again, but this time his eyes darted around.

"What are you saying?"

"You know… a lost scale or tooth. Something like that."

"Oh. Well… uh… yeah. I've heard that dragon scales can be found sometimes, if you know where to look up in the mountains."

I sat back and shrugged. "Yeah, that's the thing. I could never afford a trip to the mountains, even if I knew where to look. But I was thinking… wouldn't there be some of that kind of stuff in the Ascendancy itself?"

"Uh… if you're asking me to get a piece of Viridia for you, then…"

"Oh, could you do that?" Kelly interrupted. "That would be amazing! I'd love to see it too!"

"No, no, no." Mason waved his hands. "I can't do anything like that. You don't understand. They watch us carefully in there. I could lose my job!"

"Awww…" Kelly looked deflated. "Well, I wouldn't want that to happen."

"No, no, of course," I answered. "Still, it would have been… Chroma. I'd give anything for that. I'd trade my entire collection."

Mason's eyebrows went up over his glasses. "Wow. I really wish I could help you out."

"What if… No, never mind. That wouldn't work."

"What?"

"Well, if you could just tell me where to go, maybe I could sneak off from one of the guided tours and try to find it myself. That way, if I got caught, no one would know you had anything to do with it." I threw out the idea as if I had just thought of it.

"That… that wouldn't work. The guided tours only go through areas that are already mostly public," Mason said. "You'd need special access like I have to get into the important areas."

"So you do know where to find them?" Kelly pounced.

"Well, yeah. I mean, I know they sometimes use cast-off dragon scales or teeth for experiments. You know, figuring out how to strengthen them, I think."

I didn't care what the crazy tech guys were doing with the dragon's pieces. I just wanted one of them. Part of me felt a little guilty about how we were going to use Mason. He seemed like a nice guy. Then I remembered he liked Kelly, and my sympathy vanished.

"What if you let Beryl into one of those areas, just long enough for him to grab something and get out?" Kelly asked.

"No, no. That would be as bad as taking something myself," Mason protested. "I'd get fired… or worse!" He looked at me. "You've seen Troilus Green. That thing is terrifying! If one of the draconics knew…"

"No one would know you had anything to do with it," I reassured him. "And like I said… I'm willing to give up my entire collection."

"No… I couldn't. I…"

Kelly leaned in against him. "I told you Beryl was my best friend. We practically grew up together. So if you're helping him, you're helping me. And… I'd be really grateful."

"You… would?" Mason's demeanor changed almost at once. That figured.

"Really grateful," she repeated.

"Um… well… maybe we could work something out…"

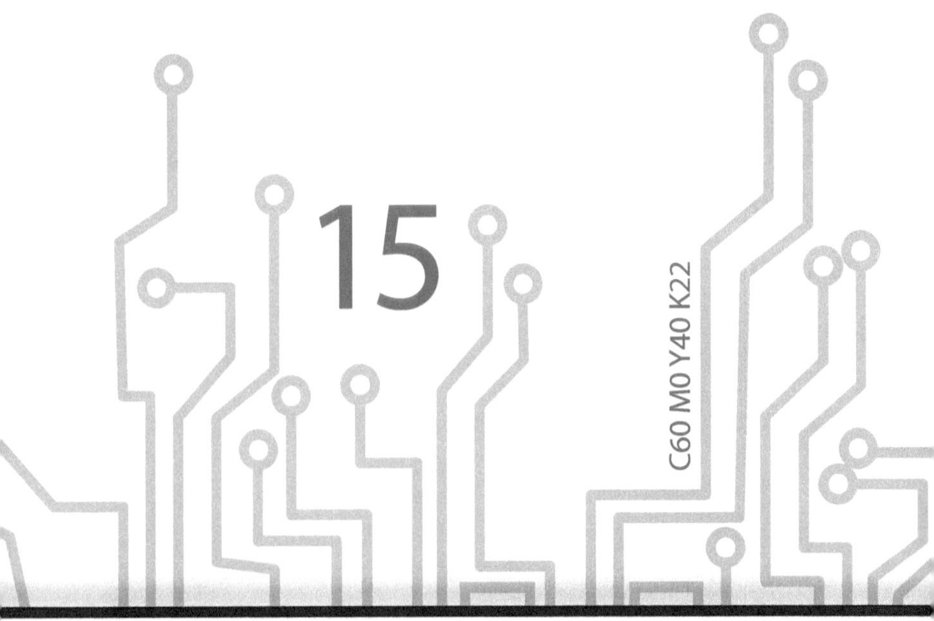

Mason agreed to open a door to let me into the restricted area of the Emerald Ascendancy. From there, he would give me directions to where I would most likely find a dragon's tooth. After we worked out the time for the next day and I thanked him profusely, I left him with Kelly. I hoped she didn't feel the need to show him her gratitude just yet.

I could have had Lovat wait around and guide me back, but I wanted to walk on my own for a change. I pulled my hat down as I moved down the street. A large number of cyclists and walkers moved back and forth in their lanes, far busier than my neighborhood. Yet it was easy to lose myself in the crowd. Living under the dragon and the Viridian Guard meant most people kept their heads down. I didn't need to worry about someone looking directly into my face. Being anonymous turned out to be surprisingly easy.

As I walked, I dealt with the worst part of the plan, in my mind. We were going to kill the blue dragon, not the green one. Even though I knew the logic of it all, even though I knew it was the best plan, I couldn't let it go. I wanted the green dragon dead. My only consolation came from knowing the death of the blue dragon would lead to the death of the green dragon. Eventually. I had to see it as one step on the path. One step at a time.

When I returned to the sanctuary, I told Rick all about the meeting with Mason.

"So this guy gets us in, and we can roam wherever we want!" he said. "Maybe we can get more out of this than just the tooth. You know they have all kinds of fortek in there!"

"You know that place is crawling with draconics, right?" I reminded him. "I don't think we should hang around any longer than we have to."

"I'm just saying that if we see something else, while we're looking for the tooth… that we grab what we can."

"Getting in is one thing. Finding what we want is another. And then there's getting out. Um… how big is a dragon's tooth, anyway?" Maybe we should have thought about that earlier.

"Oh, uh…" Rick held his hands apart about eighteen inches. "I guess it depends on what part of the jaw loses a tooth. It could be from this to, uh… this." He spread his hands to at least twice that length.

"How are we supposed to carry that out without being noticed?"

Rick frowned. "I guess we didn't think about that."

"You guess?"

"Don't worry about it. Something will work out."

"Like what?"

"Well… maybe you could carry the tooth, and I'll create a diversion at one end of the building, then you escape out the other end."

I sighed. "This is crazy. Maybe I should see if Loden can help us somehow."

"He gave this job to us, remember? In fact, his help with killing the dragon was sort of contingent on our accomplishing this. I think we've got to handle this one on our own."

"Yeah, I guess so."

Around an hour later, Kelly showed up. "I think that went pretty well, don't you?" she asked the moment she saw me.

"Yeah, I guess. Did you show him your gratitude?"

She snickered. "Wouldn't you like to know?"

"Great job, Kelly!" Rick exclaimed, giving her a side-hug. "Emerald Ascendancy, here we come!"

"And no plan to go with…" I observed. "What could possibly go wrong?"

The next morning, Rick and I made our way to the Ascendancy. Our barely-existent plan involved entering with a tour group, then breaking off at the point where Mason would meet us. Rick wore my hat to shadow his face. It didn't really go with his black jacket and gloves, but as long as no one tried to look closely, they wouldn't notice his black chromark. Without anything else to rely on, I hoped the week-long growth of facial hair would disguise me enough from anyone who might have seen me on a poster. I had been meaning to shave and never got around to it. Just as well, I suppose.

We gathered at the tourist entrance along with a couple dozen other people ranging from some older couples to a large number of kids still in their Learning Years. Our tour guide, a perky blonde with a permanent grin plastered to her face, came out precisely on time. Her enthusiasm was pretty much sickening.

"Welcome to the Emerald Ascendancy, the home of our lord and master, the majestic dragon Viridia!" she called as we gathered around her. "My name is Fern, and I'll be your guide today. Please stick close and don't wander off. I'll explain everything I can to you, but feel free to ask questions along the way too! Is everyone ready? Let's go!"

With the practiced efficiency of someone who had been doing this for quite a while, she led us through the main lobby up several flights of stairs. "Naturally, the first thing people want to know is whether you can actually see Viridia from inside the building," she narrated. "Let's go up to the third floor, and I'll show you."

At the top of the stairs, we entered a large open room with hallways branching off in multiple directions. On the inner wall, which faced Viridia's dwelling, there were short windows running along at floor level.

"Why are they down on the floor?" a child asked the obvious question Fern was expecting.

"A very insightful question!" she exclaimed, smiling down at the child. "Let me answer it with a question of my own. How would you look through these windows?"

The child obligingly got down on her hands and knees to peer through the window. "Exactly!" Fern clapped. "The windows are designed specifically for this purpose. All those who would desire to gaze upon the glory of Viridia must show true humility. Humility is a big word, but it basically means we recognize how insignificant we are in the face of Viridia's majesty, and we get down low to show this."

I had been through this tour before, of course, but hearing these words again made me want to throw up. Rick noticed the look on my face and leaned in. "Steady," he whispered. "Keep up the act." I scowled and gripped the stone shard in my pocket.

Fern got down beside the little girl, her rear end sticking up. "Come on, everyone," she called.

"And there's her qualification for this job," Rick whispered.

I snickered. After getting a good look at Fern, Rick got down on his knees to join the rest of the tour group. Despite it all, I couldn't bring myself to play that role. Some things were just too much.

"I can't see anything!" another smaller child complained.

"I'm afraid it looks like Viridia is not going to grace us with his presence right now," Fern said, losing her perpetual grin for a few seconds as she got to her feet. "You would be very, very fortunate indeed if he did happen to emerge at this precise moment. But cheer up! There's still much more to see!"

As she led the way down the largest hallway, Fern continued her spiel. "The primary purpose of this part of the Emerald Ascendancy is research! Ever wonder where all the fantastic tech everywhere in our city comes from? Most of it is invented right here…"

I pulled Rick aside, and we hung back. We were supposed to split off right here. As the tour group moved on, we waited around the corner.

"Mason said it was down this hallway," I said, pointing to the opposite direction the group had taken. We hurried down, examining everything we could see.

"Everything in here looks exactly the same," Rick complained. "It's all stark white with green trim. How does anyone find their way around?"

"Third door, third door," I repeated to myself. We reached the third door, and I grabbed the handle. Locked.

"You did tell him the correct time, right?" Rick asked. He glanced over his shoulder.

"This is it. This is what we agreed to." I tried the door again and stepped back, looking up and down the hallway.

Rick checked the next door over, just to be sure. What would we do if Mason didn't show up? Rejoin the tour group? Leave out the main entrance? This plan was pathetic. We were pathetic.

With a click, the door swung open. Mason emerged, glancing around. "Hey, Beryl, I'm really nervous about this… Whoa. Who…?"

Rick shoved Mason against the wall. "Hi, Mason. You can call me Onyx. So glad you could help us."

"What do you want?"

"Beryl already told you. We want a dragon tooth. All you need to do is point us in the right direction and then forget any of this ever happened."

Mason looked at me with narrowed eyebrows. "You don't even have the Ascendancy playset, do you?"

"Sorry, Mason." I did feel bad. "But this is really important."

"This is not what we agreed to!" he huffed. "I'm not helping you!"

"If we get caught now," Rick said softly, "we're pointing the finger straight at you. How long do you think you'll keep your job after that?" He lowered his voice even further. "Or your head?"

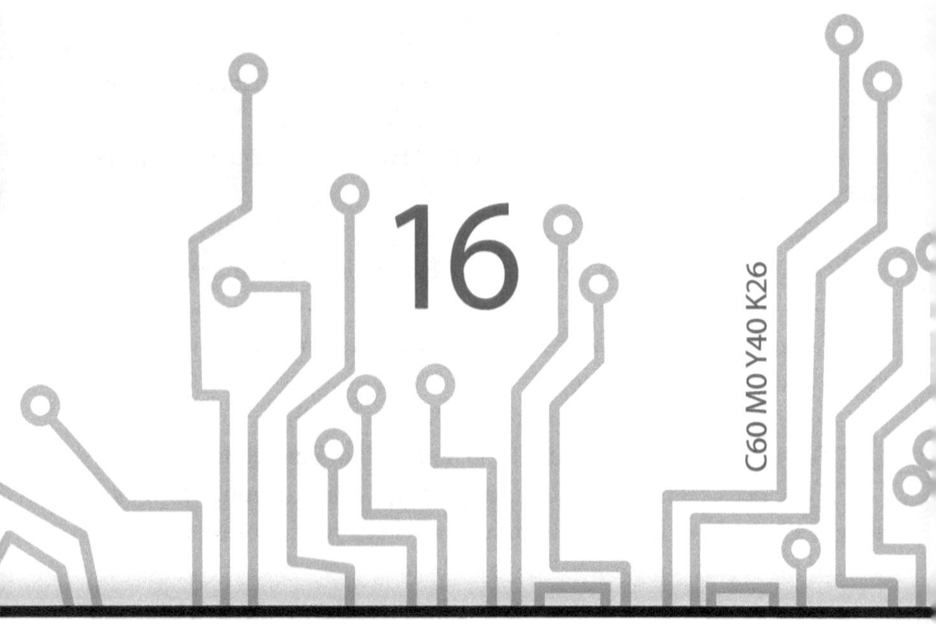

16

Mason actually whimpered. I had never heard that sound from a grown man before. "The research department you're looking for is that way," he whispered, pointing. "Follow this hallway until you find a door labeled 'Research and Development Division Two.' That will take you to a set of labs that might contain what you want. But there will be people there."

"Where can we find a map of this entire place?" Rick demanded.

"Seriously? You think I carry around a map?" I could tell by the way Mason stared at Rick's face that he had now realized Rick's chromark wasn't green. Rick pushed him harder. I glanced around. We had been standing here too long. At any moment, someone might enter the hallway.

Mason wilted. "Okay, fine. There are maps for new workers, but even they don't cover everything. A lot of this place is really secret!"

"Where?" Rick repeated.

Mason gestured weakly. "On your way to the research department, there's a door on the left labeled 'Orientation.' You should be able to find a map there."

"See? That wasn't so hard." Rick let him go and pointed a finger in his face. "Just remember: if you say anything about this, we tell them you were the mastermind."

"I really, really hope I can forget all of this as soon as possible," Mason muttered, pushing past Rick and hurrying away.

"That was a little rough," I said to Rick as we started down the hall.

"I had to scare him." Rick seemed unconcerned. "He'll be okay."

We found the orientation office empty. We shuffled through various new employee information, most of which seemed to be pro-dragon propaganda. It took two or three minutes to find a copy of the map. As Mason had said, huge portions of it were blacked out as secret, much more than I had anticipated.

"How many floors would you say this building has?" I asked.

"From the outside, I would have said somewhere around twenty to thirty," Rick answered.

"That's what I thought. But this map only goes to the twelfth floor. That's at least half the facility that the human workers don't even visit."

"We don't have time to solve mysteries. Let's go."

I handed Rick the map, grabbed one for myself, and followed him out the door.

"What do we do if there's anyone in the lab?" I asked as we hurried along, checking the names over the doors.

"We'll have to make sure they don't sound an alarm."

After passing at least a dozen doors, we found the one we needed. "Research and Development Division Two. I wonder what Division One is?"

"Remember what I said about mysteries?" Rick said. He opened the door and walked right in.

Two lab workers, a man and a woman, looked up from whatever they were doing as we entered. They stared in confusion as Rick strode in like he owned the place.

"I think you gentlemen are lost—" began the man.

"Lost? No, it's your jobs that will be lost when I tell Lord Troilus Green about the pathetic security work in this building!" Rick interrupted in an overbearing voice. He whipped out a badge of some sort and waved it in the air. "I'm Ron Forest, and this is my associate Laurel Jade of Jade Security, Inc. We were hired to test things out here and this, this is just pathetic!"

The lab workers' mouths and eyes got wider and wider as Rick went on. He swept back and forth, always keeping his head moving so they couldn't get a good look at his face. I smiled and nodded when they glanced at me. Laurel Jade? I was amazed they didn't see right through such a ridiculous name.

"Great Viridia above!" Rick cried out. "Within these walls, you work on the divine itself! You experiment with cast offs from the deity, and the bleaking door wasn't even locked!"

As Rick ranted and waved his arms, I walked about the room, trying to locate our target. This room was incredible. I had no idea what anything in here actually did. I saw all kinds of electronic devices, test tubes, and… oh, wait. I recognized a microscope. I wasn't completely ignorant.

"But, but, but, I–" the woman tried to interrupt Rick with little success.

Rick pointed dramatically at one of the tables. "That right there is one of the majestic god's very own scales!" he proclaimed. "Sitting out for anyone to walk by and pick up! Why, I wouldn't be surprised if there was a genuine tooth from the mouth of our divinity's own sacred mouth sitting in a garbage can in here!"

I checked the garbage can. No such luck.

"Don't be ridiculous!" the man finally burst in. "You won't find any teeth in here!"

"Not whole ones, anyway," the woman added.

"I thought that was the kind of work you did in here," I said before Rick could rant some more.

They swiveled to me with looks of relief, perhaps seeing me as the sane partner in this duo. "We do!" the man said. "But they would never deign to give us an entire tooth. Just slivers now and then. Even that scale over there is only half of a full scale."

"That doesn't excuse the lax security!" Rick thundered. "Mr. Jade, do you want me to personally deliver the report to our overlord?"

"The… the door doesn't even have a lock!" the woman cried.

"Mr. Forest," I observed, maintaining my calm demeanor, "I think we are placing too much responsibility where it does not belong. Clearly, these two are not high level supervisors. It is their immediate superiors that we need to address."

"And where would we find them?" Rick demanded. He spun toward the door.

"Ah… our supervisor's office is two doors down on the left." The man pointed. "I really had no idea that security was such a problem. Do you think there's danger?"

"There's always danger," I said. "At Jade Security, we're always keeping an eye out for those who would cause problems for the almighty Viridia."

Rick had already moved out the door. I followed him, shaking my head. "After all, *anyone* could have walked in here."

Outside, I shut the door and leaned against it, letting out a huge breath. "If there really are Chromatic Hells, you're heading to the darkest part of them," I told Rick. "That was... brilliant."

"I've known that for a while." Rick chuckled. "But now what do we do? We didn't find what we needed, and our time is limited. It won't be long before those two either check with their supervisor or tell someone else what just happened."

"I guess we get out while we can." My excitement faded. "We failed."

"No, no, no, no. We can't do that." Rick looked at the map and started down the hall. "Come on."

I hurried after him. "Even if we knew which secret area to check, we don't have a way to get into them," I protested. "We have no idea where to go!"

"Yeah, we do. It's absolutely insane, but at this point, I don't know what else to try."

The hallway opened up into another of the many large rooms facing the interior of the Ascendancy. As usual, the inner wall was lined with the floor-level windows. Rick got down on his hands and knees and peered inside. I followed suit.

I couldn't see much. A great pile of dirt hid our view of the interior of Viridia's actual nesting place. You would have to have a much higher vantage point to be able to see into it.

"We can find a tooth in there," Rick said.

"Did you lose a cyb implant in your brain?" I exclaimed. "We can't sneak into there! Viridia himself is probably down there!"

"I know... but when dragons are actually in their nesting area, they spend most of the time sleeping." Rick tapped on the window with his foot. "He probably won't even notice you."

"He probably won't even... wha—Me?"

Rick glanced at me. "Yeah, it's going to have to be you, Beryl. I need to create the distraction so you'll be able to get out."

"I didn't even want to come here! This is insane!"

"That's what I said. Doesn't mean it doesn't have to be done. Are you backing out on the whole plan now?"

He had me trapped, and he knew it. I knew it. I also knew if I went

down into that nest, odds were I would not be coming back out.
    "How do I get in?"

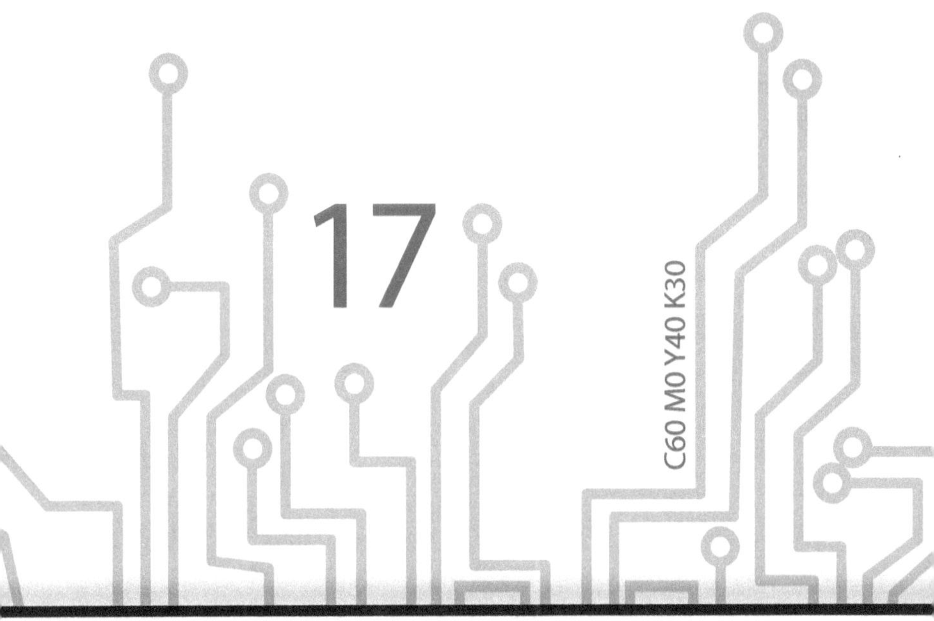

"Let's head down a level and break a window. You should be able to crawl through." Somehow, I wasn't surprised Rick already had an idea. He had probably been thinking about this on the way in.

I followed him as he used the map to navigate down a flight of steps and through some more hallways to another viewing room. We never met anyone along the way. I guess once the Ascendancy workers were at work, they rarely left their stations. At least, that was the way it seemed to work in this area. I couldn't help but wonder about the secret zones.

Rick looked around and then reached behind his neck. To my utter surprise, he grasped the hilt of a sword and pulled it out. He had strapped it to his back and kept it there all morning, hidden by his jacket. I thought he looked a little stiff earlier, come to think of it.

Rick dropped to the ground, tapped on the window, then hit it as hard as he could with the hilt of the sword. The solid thunk wasn't very loud, and the window didn't break. He tried again with equal results.

"Oh, get out of the way," I snarled. I knew I would regret this. I positioned myself and took a deep breath. I channeled the strongest boost I could into my right leg and kicked. The window shattered on impact, and shards tumbled down into the Ascendancy's interior.

We both tensed and looked around. When no one came running, I got down and kicked a few remaining glass shards out of the way. I started to crawl through the window, feet first. My right foot ached. The cyb boost didn't protect it from the actual impact.

"Take this," Rick said, handing me the sword. "You might need it more than I will."

"How will I know when your diversion happens?"

"You'll know." Rick smiled. "I know more than a little bit about electricity. I'll figure something out." With that ominous note, he took off down the hall, leaving me to finish working my way out the window.

The ground waited an entire floor below the window. Once I crawled through, I had to let go and drop. I should have asked to borrow Rick's gloves. I remembered to toss the sword off to the side before I fell. At least I wouldn't impale myself. That would be a great end for a would-be dragon slayer! I landed hard and collapsed on my butt. The ache in my right foot exploded into serious pain.

I retrieved the sword and stood up. Against all my stated beliefs, I could not stop the feeling of awe that swept over me. I stood within the interior of the Emerald Ascendancy, in the midst of a huge oval open space surrounded by sheer walls lined with narrow windows like the one I had broken. High overhead, on either side, the two great arches stretched above the walls.

Somewhere over this pile of dirt in front of me waited the sleeping place of the green dragon himself. The very fact that I had been able to get this far said something. It said the dragon feared no one at all. Who was I, anyway? A fugitive bike shop repairman carrying a sword? It probably couldn't even scratch one of his scales if I ran into him. What was I thinking, anyway? This entire plan, from beginning to end, had to be the greatest bit of insanity conceived in centuries. Was the dragon arrogant? No. I was.

For a moment, I almost turned around and gave up. But then images of my friends flashed through my head. Kelly, Rick, Loden… They were counting on me here. Also unbidden came the faces of my parents and another…

No.

I stifled a curse and climbed the hill. The dirt felt warm to the touch and crumbled when I stepped on it. It had an odd consistency, like burnt bread. My feet sank to my ankles, and an unidentifiable smell rose up with each step. I worked my way as best as I could using one hand to help me, while awkwardly holding the sword out of the way with the other. Oh, this was smooth.

When I reached the summit, I realized I hadn't climbed a simple ridge of dirt surrounding the sleeping dragon. Peeking over the top, I saw the mound I had climbed was merely the outer edge of several such mounds surrounding a deep pit. Apparently, the dragon's resting place lay further down.

Struggling with the uneven and crumbling soil, I made my way to the edge of the pit and looked over the brink. So far, I had not seen any dragon cast-offs like scales or teeth. If any were to be found, it would have to be down below.

I couldn't make out much of anything. A greenish miasma hung over much of the pit, curling and swirling from time to time. It looked like I would be able to climb down the side without too much difficulty. I considered various other ways to hold the sword, but couldn't think of one that worked. Then I realized anyone at the upper floor windows could probably see me. I couldn't stay there any longer.

As carefully as possible, I began my descent. The air grew warmer and somewhat noxious. I struggled to keep from coughing. The miasma grew thicker and thinner in alternating waves as I climbed down, never giving me a clear view of what lay below. The walls of the pit were more solid than the dirt mounds above, though steeper. I waged an ongoing debate in my head about the status of my sanity.

I wasn't sure how much time passed, but both arms and legs grew tired before my feet struck a solid floor. The writhing miasma lifted enough for me to look around. A solid rock floor extended before me, mostly smooth, but scratched here and there with furrows that extended for several yards. I spotted one broken scale resting against the wall nearby, but no other debris. I stood at the base of the hole with no dragon in sight. Instead, a massive cave mouth stretched away to my right. Good thing I hadn't tried to climb down over that. It might not have ended well.

A faint greenish glow came from the cave entrance. With no other options, I took careful steps into the cave, hugging the right wall. As I moved deeper, I lost sight of the opposite wall. I knew Viridia was huge, but did he really need this much room for what amounted to a hallway? After about a hundred yards, the wall changed from rock back to the same brittle earth I had climbed on the surface. It cascaded across the floor, complicating my progress.

I wiped sweat from my brow. An acrid odor filled my nostrils. Between the heat and the smell, I felt sick. I struggled to stay upright.

And then I heard the voice.

First came a low, deep rumble. I felt it in the floor, and a few chunks of the loose earth fell with each intonation. As I inched forward, I realized there were words in the rumble. Viridia, the green dragon, was speaking. An urge to turn and run for my life swept over me, but I pushed past it.

The wall returned to solid rock. The light grew, and I could see enough to move quicker. Soon, I could see the cave opening up into a much larger chamber that seemed to be the source of the lighting.

"…I have felt the loss of power. Someone within the city is draining it." At last, I could make out the distinct words. At least I think I could. The word "power" didn't sound quite right. Another smaller voice replied, but I couldn't understand it.

This sounded like it might be important. I started to pick up my pace, but then staggered and almost fell. The air quality must have been taking its toll on me. My stomach had always been strong, but I felt on the verge of vomiting. With a strong effort, I kept it down. At the same time, my head began feeling somewhat hazy, as if I were getting sleepy. My arms and legs didn't respond like I expected them to. They seemed heavier than usual.

I slogged on until I reached the large chamber. I got down on my knees, crawled to the opening and peered in. My mind struggled to take in all the details.

At first, I couldn't process the vast size of the chamber. The entire Emerald Ascendancy could fit inside it. The opening I knelt in was one of two. A second opening led off to the southeast, I think. My sense of direction didn't feel strong after this underground journey.

The lighting came from dozens of huge electric bulbs mounted on the ceiling. The greenish glow I had seen came not from the lights themselves, but from the reflection they cast off the body of Viridia, the giant green dragon sitting on the floor of the cavern. Two small figures faced the dragon, speaking with him. Draconics. With a sense of absolute certainty, I recognized one.

Troilus Green.

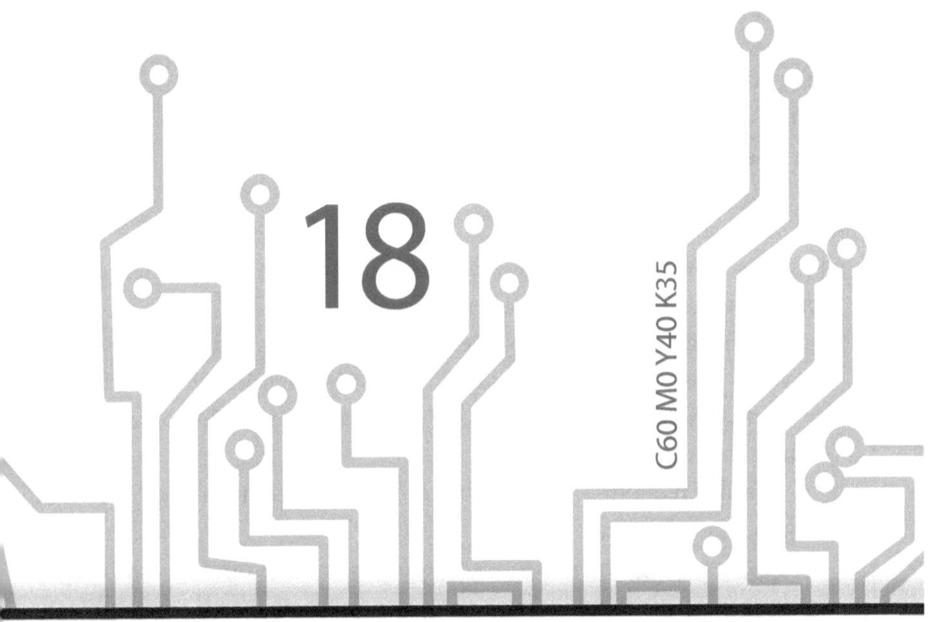

18

The enormity of the dragon stunned my already confused brain. People always spoke in awe of his size, and I knew it as a simple fact. But seeing him fly overhead never conveyed his true magnitude. I was probably closer to the dragon now than most residents of Viridia ever came in their lives. My hazy mind struggled for perspective. I knew Troilus Green was around seven feet tall, and the other draconic with him looked to be even taller. But they were nothing compared to the vast creature before them. In fact, with a quick snap of his jaws, the dragon could have gobbled them both up in less than a mouthful.

As my eyes adjusted to the brightness, I realized the purpose of the lighting, and noticed more refinements to the cavern walls. Large mirror panes had been installed into the walls at various angles. This created a multitude of reflections from the dragon's scales, filling the entire chamber with the green glow I had seen on approach.

The dragon's wings were folded against his body, but the left one gleamed of polished metal. In fact, I could now see that the dragon's central ridge of scales running down his back and down his tail appeared to also be made of metal. That seemed new. I didn't remember seeing it on any of the toys or statues I had been around all my life. I also began to notice a large number of scales had been replaced, including a few on the lengthy neck that held aloft the massive head. The replacement scales were colored green to blend in, but under the bright lights of the cave, I could see the difference. Two horns curved back and up from the top of the head, one of them banded in silver.

My attention turned to the two draconics. The one I didn't know was gesturing and speaking.

"Most dread majesty, your faithful servant Troilus Green here reports some disturbances among the populace."

"There are always disturbances," the dragon intoned. I felt the bass of his voice pass through me. Though the rumble flooded warmth through my body, I couldn't help trembling. "Humans are a troublesome but necessary inconvenience."

"Troilus requests—" began the other draconic but stopped when the dragon shook his head.

"I grant the grace for Troilus Green to speak for himself," the dragon announced. Unbelievable. Even the draconics were forced to treat him as a god?

Troilus Green bowed low. As it did, I noticed a closed doorway behind them, built directly into the rock. I couldn't see a handle on it.

"Lord Viridia, thank you for this unbelievable honor," it began. "I would like to respectfully request permission to use more... forceful methods in dealing with these disturbances. Lies about your greatness are being spoken, and they should not be allowed to propagate further. More critically, the wanderer that Naram-Sin Black warned us about remains at large. We must use stronger tactics to find him."

The dragon's head turned away even while Troilus Green spoke. He seemed almost bored with the request. Was he... looking at himself in one of the mirrors?

"You have whatever authority you desire, subject only to the oversight of Scamandrius Green," the dragon said. "It is nothing. Tell me again of our other progress."

The other draconic, which I assumed to be Scamandrius Green, made a slight bow. "The lab reports are confirmed," it said. "The gene splicing is not as effective as we might have hoped."

Gene splicing? I didn't understand any of this.

"The reds are growing more antagonistic," the dragon observed. He looked back at the draconics. "We must make progress on this. Our very future depends on it."

"There are a number of our scientists who still insist that the cybernetic enhancements are much more effective in the long run," Scamandrius Green answered. "They claim—"

The dragon growled deep in his throat. The tremor that ran through my body added to my overall queasiness and confusion. I let my head rest down on the rock. The cooler surface of the stone felt nice. I could lie here a while, if that big voice would only be quiet.

"I care not for their claims," the dragon snarled. "My will must be done. Cybernetics are useful enough for exterior repairs, if we desire, but unless we are able to overcome the problems with direct brain implantation, we cannot accomplish even the first of our goals. My protection of this city—"

I felt like I was on the verge of hearing something of massive importance. My brain struggled to comprehend it all.

At that moment, the lights within the cavern dimmed and went out. The entire chamber plunged into darkness. As my eyes adjusted, I saw a faint glow: twin green globes moved about. Were those the dragon's eyes? Did they glow in the dark? Could he see in the dark? I scrunched back from the edge.

A secondary set of dimmer lights came on. Scamandrius Green seemed to be consulting with something in its hand. It turned back and announced, "Something has gone wrong, your eminence. The power has gone out within the entire Ascendancy. This is highly unusual."

"And suspicious," Troilus Green added.

That must have been Rick. Worst distraction timing ever.

"Investigate at once," the dragon demanded. "I wish to see this for myself." He began to get to his feet and turn. To my horror, my addled brain realized he would be coming up the tunnel in which I was hiding!

I scrambled to my feet and backed away. My brain cleared somewhat, probably due to panic, and I remembered Troilus Green hinting at other senses possessed by draconics. If that were true, what senses did dragons themselves possess? How could I go undetected?

I hurried back up the passageway, but I knew I couldn't climb out of the pit before the dragon caught up. Already, I could hear his claws scratching on the floor behind me.

I reached the area where the wall had become the brittle dirt. Desperate, I plunged the sword into the wall. It went all the way in. I had a chance. I dug my way into the warm, brittle soil, shoving myself into it as far as I could, letting it fall around me. Only when I was sure the soil covered me did I stop and keep still.

The unusual odor I had experienced before now surrounded me. I tried to keep anything from getting into my mouth or nose. For some reason, I felt even sicker now.

I felt a tremor as Viridia passed by me in the dark. The heat from his presence penetrated my shallow burial and exuded a similar, but far stronger sickly-sweet death smell like that I had experienced in the presence of Troilus Green. I gagged but kept silent. The terror I felt in that moment almost overwhelmed my brain. My head swam, and darkness almost claimed me.

And then he was gone. I continued to lay still for as long as I could. Then I erupted out of the dirt and vomited all over the cavern floor. Again and again, my stomach heaved and emptied itself of everything I had consumed in the past day or more. I continued heaving for another five or six times while nothing came up.

When I could breathe again, I laughed. The dragon would step on this mess when he returned. With any luck, it would make him slip. It was a silly thought, but I couldn't stop thinking it.

Gaining control of myself, I climbed to my feet, staggered, and started back into the large chamber. As hazy as my brain felt, I knew it was pointless to try to climb out the way I had come in. The dragon himself would see me, and even if he didn't, I didn't know how to get back inside the building. My escape route would have to go a different way.

I half-stumbled, half-slid my way down to the floor of the dragon's nest. I made it to the door the draconics had used, but it defied my understanding. A handle didn't magically appear at closer range. I couldn't see any signs of hinges, either. I saw nothing but a solid piece of metal set within a metal frame surrounded by rock.

That left only one way out: the second large cave opening. It would take another lengthy climb to reach it. With my brain barely maintaining control of my limbs, I forced myself into the ascent, my muscles and joints aching all the way. My eyes burned whether I kept them open or not.

After what seemed an unending struggle, I reached the opening and stumbled down into the darkness. Somewhere in the back of my mind, I knew I had lost something or forgotten something, but I couldn't remember what it could be.

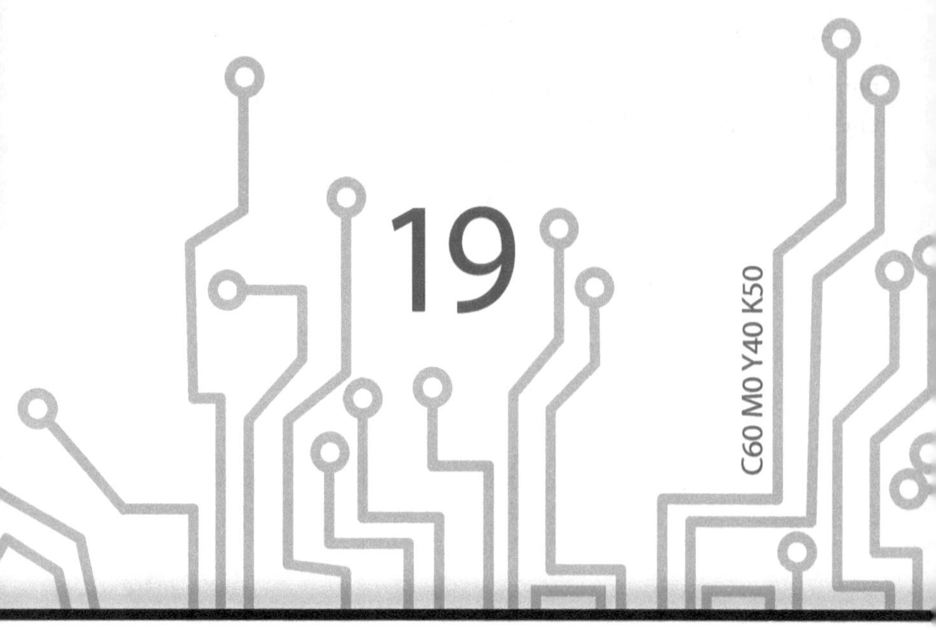

19

The passageway seemed much the same as the one I had entered earlier, but it sloped downward at first. I had no idea where it led, but I had little choice at this point.

Step by slow, awkward step, I stumbled and limped down the passage. My right foot throbbed with pain, but I couldn't remember what had caused it.

The light faded as I left the main chamber behind. I made no effort to follow the wall as I had on entering. I couldn't muster enough concern about being discovered. In fact, part of me felt that being discovered would be a relief. At least then this would all be over.

Time went on. The darkness grew. My pace slowed. Chills began to wrack my body. Somewhere in my brain I knew that meant fever.

Everyone knew the green dragon was poisonous. Did I not even consider the consequences of entering its lair? Who knew how much toxin I had breathed in or absorbed in other ways?

At some point, the tunnel leveled out and stopped descending. I didn't notice when it happened, but once my brain acknowledged it, I recognized it as something good. At least I think I did. My thoughts were dominated by the sheer force of will it took to keep putting one foot in front of the other. I know I used my implant at some point to boost my legs' ability to keep going, but I had no memory of doing so.

My arms hung loosely at my sides, except when they shook from the chills. My eyes could no longer see anything through the darkness, but closing them seemed like such an effort. Tears ran down my cheeks unhindered. My breath came labored and slow.

I tripped over a rock and sprawled onto the ground. For a long time, I didn't move. My joints, my muscles, my entire body pled with me to just stay still. Relax. Get some sleep. But my brain wouldn't let me. I couldn't remember where I was or what I was doing. I could only hold on to two thoughts: something horrible behind me, and the need to reach the end of the tunnel.

So I crawled.

In some ways, it was worse than walking. I now used all four limbs to support my weight, so additional muscles and joints were hurting. But I no longer had to worry about falling. That was good, right?

The tunnel started to slope up. My brain noticed this because it became harder to keep going. My palms and knees were worn raw by the rock floor.

And then the hallucinations started.

I saw Troilus Green. It laughed at me. My brain informed me that I should be angry at this, but I couldn't spare the energy.

I saw Rick. He looked at me, shook his head, and turned away. I guess I disappointed him.

I saw Viridia himself. He seemed indifferent to my struggles and walked right by me. Maybe that one wasn't a hallucination.

I saw a tiny face with curly hair. I knew it was important, but couldn't remember why.

I saw Bice. He looked concerned and reached toward me. His lips moved, and he closed his eyes. Was he talking to me or praying?

Then I saw Kelly. She looked so worried. Maybe she really did care about me. I should tell her how I felt. I wonder how she would feel if I died in this tunnel?

That's when my thoughts turned to death. Was I dying? What was dying? If I died, would all this pain stop?

I collapsed again. My muscles contracted in unusual ways as chills wracked my body. I coughed, and my insides heaved again, though nothing came out. My mouth felt parched. Overwhelming thirst struck me with surprising force.

My thoughts seemed to clear a bit, letting me realize I had been seeing things. I felt somewhat more coherent, but couldn't shake the thoughts of death. For the first time in my life, I wondered what happened afterwards.

The dragons were not gods. They were creatures like anything else. But were there any real gods? Bice believed there had to be some kind of higher power. I didn't know. If there were any gods, they didn't seem very concerned with what took place here. Maybe when I met them, I would tell them I didn't think much of them. Where would that get me in the afterlife, if there was one?

"How is your implant working?"

It took me a moment to realize the voice was Loden's. At first I thought he had found me. Then I heard my own voice replying, "As well as can be expected, I guess."

How disappointing. Just a memory.

"And you can access the boosts? How strong are they?"

"I don't know. I can kick pretty hard, run faster than normal."

That wasn't doing me much good down here.

"You should try pushing your limits. I think it can handle more than you've attempted so far."

"Thanks, Loden. I'll do that. As I'm lying here on the rock floor of a dark tunnel, I'll give my legs a cybernetic boost. Then when the muscle contractions hit, they can be really powerful contractions instead of the smaller ones I'm experiencing now."

Wait, that wasn't how the conversation ended.

My mind wandered off into haze again, and I may have lost consciousness for a while. In a sudden moment, I found myself wide awake again, the urge to escape strong and steady in my head. I pulled myself up to my hands and knees and started moving again. The pain of my raw knees scraping the cave floor helped keep me awake.

Why was it so difficult to think? Something had happened to me, but I couldn't remember. Again with the two thoughts: horror behind, escape ahead. Nothing else mattered.

I crawled.

Time was meaningless to me. Distance was meaningless. Pain, chills, and thirst were my reality. After a while, even the pain grew dull and insubstantial. Only the chills and thirst remained. And the need to keep moving.

I had been seeing light for some time before I realized the significance.

I could see the stone floor below my hands. I pushed myself into a sitting position and looked at my hands. They were shaking, shaking hard for some reason. Maybe if I thought hard enough, I could remember the reason. But then the light distracted me.

Up ahead, in the direction I had been crawling, light beckoned. It streamed in through a huge opening. The light looked kind of green, and that seemed... as it should be. It must be my destination. I needed to reach that light. Nothing else mattered, not even the thirst.

I crawled on some more, until my arms could no longer support my weight. Once again, I lost consciousness. When I regained it, the light still waited, but dimmer. Was it going away? It couldn't go away. I needed to reach it.

I couldn't lift myself up, so I crawled on my stomach. Like a worm or a snake, I slithered my way upward. The ground grew rougher, no longer the smooth stone I had become used to. I dug my hands into dirt and dragged myself.

I don't know how long it took, but I reached the end of the tunnel and rolled out into the light. I ended up on my back, staring into the sky. My vision blurred. I could see nothing but green reaching up toward the dim blue sky. I could not comprehend what the green might be, so I didn't try. The green existed. I knew it existed. And that's all that mattered.

That... and I was dying. The fresh air cleared my mind enough to grasp some things, purging the haze from my thoughts ever so slightly. I was dying. The dragon's poison had been working on me for hours, at least. I had no strength left. My body shook from fever and chills. My brain might not be functional. I was dying. I couldn't deny it.

But... I didn't want to die. I wanted to live. In the stories, true love always kept people alive. Maybe if I thought of Kelly, I could pull through this.

But I couldn't keep her image in my mind. It kept dissolving into Loden looking at me while scratching his chin. Why that scene? Why that conversation? I was dying, and I couldn't even think of the right things to keep myself alive. I needed to stay alive so I could tell the others about what I heard. Or saw. Something about the draconics. Or was it the dragon?

Loden griped at me again. I mentally reached for my implant to satisfy him, so he'd stop interrupting my dying thoughts.

And then the green turned black, along with everything else.

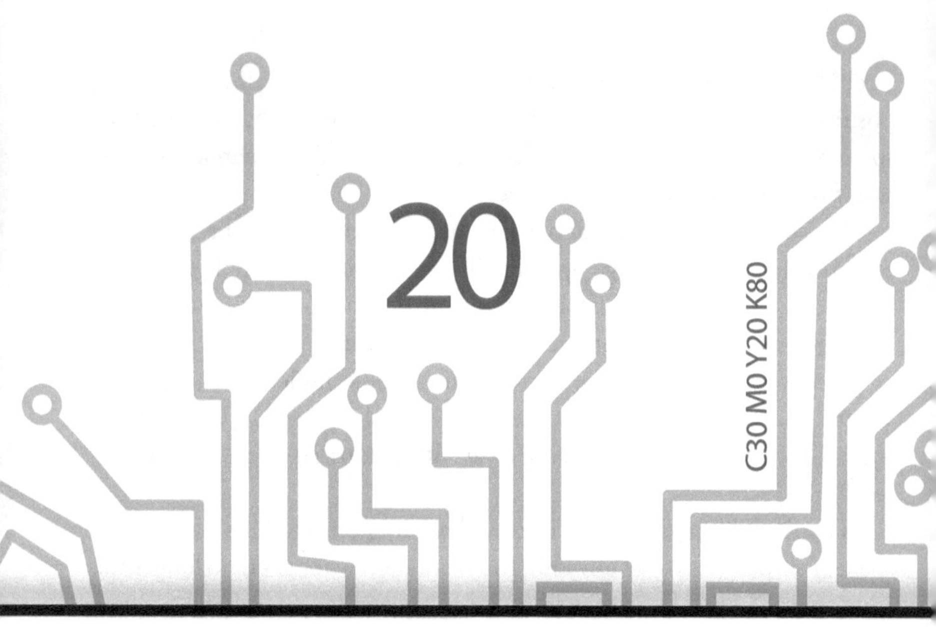

20

I lay awake for at least a minute or two before I could grasp that I was not dead.

I hurt all over. Every joint and muscle seemed to be moaning in pain. My head ached most of all. That must have been what woke me. It was also the strongest evidence that I still lived.

My eyes opened slower than a sunrise. My vision seemed rimmed in blackness and blurred by haze. But I found myself staring up at a bright blue sky. My aching brain recalled it had not been that bright before. Had I been lying there for that long? Almost a day?

The green. The green reaching for the sky was trees! They were enormous, far larger than any trees I had ever seen in the handful of parks and gardens within the city. They were so tall, so straight, so full of life, bristling with bright green needles. I felt a tear in my eye from the sheer beauty of it.

I hated the color green because of the dragon, but this… this was something else. This was green, pure green, untouched and uninfluenced by the dragon. He had nothing to do with it. And that made it glorious.

I don't know how long I lay there, my gaze occupied with the trees. Eventually, the pain and the renewed thirst forced me to contemplate doing something else. I tested my fingers, then rolled my head from side to side. Everything seemed to work, though not without pain. With that knowledge, I closed my eyes, gritted my teeth, and pushed myself into a sitting position.

My head swam in dizziness, and I almost collapsed again. Pain from the rest of my body demanded attention, driving away the dizziness. I coughed and gagged. With no moisture in my throat, each cough caused excruciating pain radiating up and down inside.

After far too long, everything settled enough for me to open my eyes again and look around. I sat on a mixture of grass, open dirt and fallen needles from the trees above me. Somehow, I had crawled about half a dozen feet from the gaping cave entrance from which I had emerged. The trees stood all around me. I couldn't be within the city of Viridia. The dragon had a secret entrance (or exit) to his lair, outside the city.

The dragon. His lair. It started to come back to me. The failure of my mission flooded into my thoughts. I hadn't even looked for a tooth inside the dragon's lair. I had been too sick to even think of it.

My sword. When had I lost it? The last I could remember was jamming it into the mound of dirt to hide it. Had I left it there? I didn't remember taking it with me after that, but I couldn't recall much at all. I knew I had come up this other tunnel, but that was about it.

How long had it been? Judging from the bright sky, more than a day had passed since I first entered the Emerald Ascendancy. What was Rick thinking by now? Had he given up and left the city? What about the others? Our conspiracy might be all over before it really began.

A loud moan startled me until I realized it came from me. I was a mess, but alive. It wasn't over yet.

With a supreme effort, I got to my feet and leaned heavily against one of the tree trunks. The rough bark felt both painful and refreshing. Feeling anything at all felt refreshing.

My eyes wandered around, examining the ground around me. I noted a large open area in front of the cave entrance where the dragon took to the skies. Huge furrows marked the ground from his claws. And then I caught a gleam of something white just beyond that area.

I pushed off from the tree trunk and staggered forward. My legs obeyed my commands, but reluctantly. My right foot made me wince with each step, and I vaguely recalled kicking a window. As I drew nearer to my goal, I kept telling myself I was still hallucinating, imagining things. When I reached it, I collapsed to the ground beside it and reached out in awe.

A dragon's tooth. The foot-long triangular object had a few chips in it, but it had to be a dragon's tooth. Nothing else made sense. It felt cool to the touch and lined with grooves the width of my finger. A larger channel ran along the inside edge, almost the width of my palm. It took both hands to lift it, but it wasn't a burden, far lighter than I expected.

That is, it wouldn't have been a burden if I didn't feel on the verge of death. In addition to the poison's effects, my body kept reminding me I hadn't had anything to eat or drink in hours, if not longer.

Right then, I heard the most beautiful sound imaginable: running water. After I set the tooth back down, I half-crawled and half-staggered my way toward the sound. Everywhere I looked I saw more green. Green grass, green ferns, green bushes, green weeds… all alive. Deep within, I felt an intense desire never to return to the city again.

The ground dropped off beneath me, and I tumbled down a few feet and landed in shallow mud. Surrounded by fallen leaves and a few broken branches, I looked up to see the water in front of me. It looked a little brown from silt, but it moved along at a good clip. A fallen tree trunk lay halfway across the stream, and the water flowed around and under it, creating a tiny rapid. It was the most beautiful thing I had ever seen.

I lunged forward and almost fell in. After rinsing the mud off my hands, I scooped water up to my mouth. It was the finest water I had ever tasted. Some grit lodged in my teeth, but the coldness invigorated me. My throat burned in places where it had been damaged by my earlier struggles, but after a few swallows, the pain diminished. I drank and drank and drank. Then I collapsed back into the mud, letting my hand linger in the water, feeling the current flow over my fingers.

"Thank you," I said out loud through my ragged throat. I didn't know who I was thanking, but it seemed appropriate.

A few minutes passed while I enjoyed the cool water and mud. With a start, I pulled myself back up again and looked around. The banks of the stream were only four or five feet high at most. Huge root systems from trees I did not recognize reached down into the water. The little boy I used to be wanted to climb them. I found myself tempted to just relax and stay there, enjoying the peace. But my hunger and pain reminded me I still had other needs. I took another long drink and then crawled out of the mud.

I climbed up the bank and picked up the dragon tooth. Then I caught another glimpse of something white. Pushing a bush aside, I saw two more teeth partially embedded in the ground. They looked older, not as clean as the first one I had found. Maybe the dragon regularly lost teeth in this spot. I wondered what could cause that.

I felt somewhat strengthened just by taking care of my thirst. I still felt on the verge of complete muscle collapse, and every joint ached, but I decided I had the strength to keep going. I had to try to get back home. My best course led up the hill that housed the dragon's tunnel. From there, I could see more.

I remembered climbing while carrying the sword. Carrying the tooth was just as awkward—actually worse, because of my condition. By the time I reached the top of the hill, I knew I would need another lengthy rest. But I took my stand and looked out in all directions.

I stood closer to the mountains than I'd ever been in my life. How long had that tunnel gone on? The bare slopes of The Circle loomed enormous before me. Though I knew they were still miles away, it seemed as though I could almost reach out and touch them. Someday, I resolved, I would visit the mountains. Their very existence called to me in ways I couldn't understand.

I turned the other direction and saw Viridia. The city looked to be about two or three miles away, at the least. I faced its southeast side, the industrial sector. My heart sank. It would take me hours to reach the city at the meager pace I could manage.

I sat down hard, but barely felt the impact. Somewhere within me, the desire to get back still burned. I knew I would set out, and I knew I would get there. Just… not right this minute.

I lay back on the grass and closed my eyes. A few minutes' rest wouldn't hurt.

When I woke up again, I looked up at the night sky. I felt a chill wash over me, though I wasn't sure whether it was just the night air, or a return of the fever. The city of Viridia gleamed in the distance like a green chunk of concrete pointed at the sky. I would have no trouble navigating, despite the haze over my vision.

I picked up the tooth, got to my feet, and began a slow walk-shuffle down the hill and toward the city.

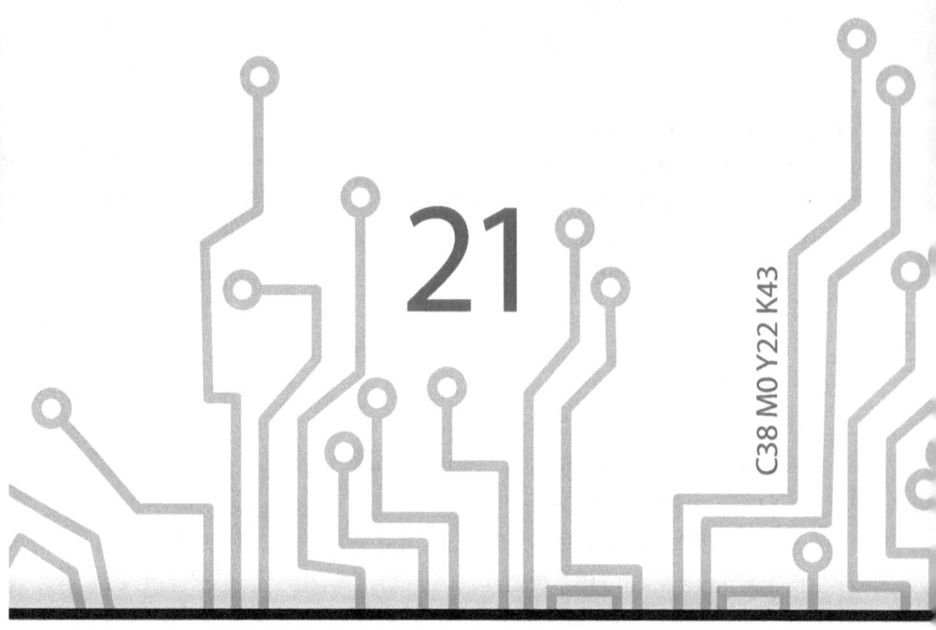

21

Lovat found me. I learned later that he had been roaming the city every minute since Rick had returned without me, searching for any sign or rumor that I still lived. Once I staggered, half-dead, into the city limits, he found me within an hour.

Morning had already broken by then. I had no idea how much of the night I spent asleep, and how much I spent walking. But I made it. Nothing else mattered: whether I could keep my eyes open, or how thick and slow my voice sounded as I tried to explain to Lovat how I felt.

He seemed to grasp my meaning and guided me to a hiding place behind some trash receptacles. "Wait here," he instructed and dashed away. I put the tooth down beside me and curled up around it. "I'm waiting," I said dully to the early morning air which somehow felt cooler than the night. And then I fell asleep again.

I woke when a hand grasped my shoulder. I opened my eyes and rolled over to look up into the concerned face of Bice. That may have been the only time I had ever seen him without at least a half-smile. "Bice," I mumbled. "Good to see you."

"It's very good to see you, as well," he answered. He felt my forehead and looked into my eyes. "We've all been worried."

I nudged the tooth. "Got it."

Bice nodded. "Lovat, would you carry that thing, please?"

The boy picked it up. "This Vir'dia's tooth?" I nodded. He tapped it with a fingernail and shook his head. "Hue." From somewhere inside his baggy clothing, he pulled out a large bag and stuffed the tooth inside it.

Bice seemed to be examining my skin tone or something. "Will I be okay?" I asked, slurring a little.

The smile returned, though it looked tighter than usual. "I believe so," he said. I thought he might be lying, but weren't priests forbidden from doing that? Except he wasn't a priest any more.

"Unfortunately, we can't just carry you through the streets. That would attract too much attention," Bice noted. "I'm going to have to ask you to walk some more, but I'll help you every step of the way."

"I can do it," I mumbled and tried to get up. Bice took my hands and stopped me. "Slowly," he whispered. With gentleness beyond my understanding, he helped guide me to my feet, then slipped an arm around my shoulders.

"Let's go."

I'm not sure that we were any less conspicuous walking that way, but Bice seemed determined. Lovat dodged on ahead, reappearing from time to time to check on our progress. We would walk along a couple of blocks, then stop for me to rest. Each time, I found it harder and harder to get back up. For some reason, this walk seemed even longer than my night's solo struggle to reach the city.

It was late morning before we arrived at the sanctuary. As my head lolled about, I think I saw Rick staring at me and then helping Bice get me inside. After that, I lost myself again. I slept, semi-waking now and then, hearing the voices of my friends, but unable to open my eyes or respond. I heard Bice speaking of dragon poison. I heard Rick swearing with words I had never considered using in that way. He was very creative. I heard Loden saying something about my implant, though that may have been one of those hallucinations again. The one voice I'm absolutely sure I heard was Kelly's. "Come back to me, Beryl," she said. Not "come back to us." She said "Come back to ME." I knew it. I think I must have smiled at that point before drifting off again.

When I finally woke up for real, I knew there had been a change. I still ached all over, but it wasn't the same. The chills were gone. The headache was gone. I felt… relaxed. I took a deep breath, and it felt good.

"Coming back to us, are you?"

Loden's voice. Not the one I expected. I opened my eyes. It took a moment, but my vision cleared, and I could see better than I had since entering the dragon's lair. Loden's wrinkled face and short gray hair looked the same as always. That was comforting.

"Guess I'm alive," I croaked.

"Get him some water," Loden said to someone else. I heard a rustle, and then Kelly was there, holding a cup toward my face. I stared at her and ignored the water. She looked so beautiful, though her eyes were red-rimmed for some reason.

"Drink, you idiot," she said, pushing it at me. Her words were harsh, but the tone... I had always loved the tone of her voice. It sounded so natural and enchanting. Was that the right word?

"I love you too," I wheezed. I pushed up and took the water. It tasted good, but not as good as the water in the stream yesterday... or was it two days ago?

"You've been asleep for three days," Loden said, as if reading my thoughts. "After Bice and Lovat brought you in, they sent for me. I did what I could, but it was Bice's ministrations that really saved you, I think. Without him, we would have lost you for sure."

"I thought I was lost several times," I whispered, still not able to speak at regular volume. I drank more water. Three days? "How long... was I gone before that? Two days?" Five days without food would explain part of why I felt so drained.

"Beryl. You were gone for five days!" Kelly answered. "We were worried sick."

Five days? That didn't make sense. I went to the Emerald Ascendancy in the morning, snuck into the dragon's lair, walked down the escape tunnel, slept a day and a half in the forest, and then walked back to the city. How did that add up to five days? I couldn't figure it out.

"It is a miracle you survived at all," Loden said. "We don't know what you went through, but obviously, the dragon poison, and then your clothes..."

"What about my clothes?" Obviously, someone had changed me into different clothes. But the clothes I had been wearing...

"I burned them," Rick announced, as he stepped into my view. I could now see that I was in the back room of the sanctuary, where Rick and I had been sleeping. "Nothing much else you can do with clothes that are covered in dried fewmets."

"What?"

"Dragon droppings. Really old, dried-out stuff, from the look of it. What did you do - fall into a pile of it?"

I leaned back onto the cot. (I didn't remember having a cot before.) Was Rick saying the brittle dirt I had encountered was actually dragon… poop? Now I felt really stupid.

"We need to get more food into you," Loden said. "You haven't eaten much since we found you, and probably not at all before that." He brought out a box of crackers and offered me a few.

Alternating between the crackers and water, I told them what I remembered. Rick interrupted me at every turn, trying to clarify things. Loden seemed especially interested in the conversation I overheard. Unfortunately, my memory of everything remained hazy. I made it as far as describing what I did when Rick cut the power.

"You breathed in dragon poison for who knows how long, and buried yourself in dragon droppings?" Rick exclaimed. "No wonder you were— you should be dead, man! No one should have been able to survive that! No one!"

"He's right," Loden agreed. "You shouldn't have." He eyed me with one eyebrow down in a curious expression.

"Perhaps there is a higher power," Bice said as he entered the room. "It's good to see you awake, Beryl. How do you feel?"

The other three waited impatiently while Bice examined me and questioned me thoroughly about how I felt. Then he made me start the story over so he could get more insight into what had caused my condition. I described my long, slow escape through the second tunnel and my loss of consciousness when I got out.

"Your body should not have been able to fight this infection on its own," Bice noted. "After all that exposure, there is no way you would have been able to wake up again after that, not without some kind of help."

"What are you saying?" Kelly asked.

Bice looked amused. "I said it when I came in. Perhaps a higher power intervened. I truly do not know." He spread his hands wide. "What I do know is that Beryl is here, he's alive, and he's improving. How he got here, I do not know."

Rick snorted. "Just luck, if you ask me. No need to go looking for anything mystical." His tone sounded derogatory, but there was something else behind it I couldn't quite identify.

Kelly put her hand on mine. "Does it matter?" she said. "Beryl is alive. It's more than I hoped for three days ago."

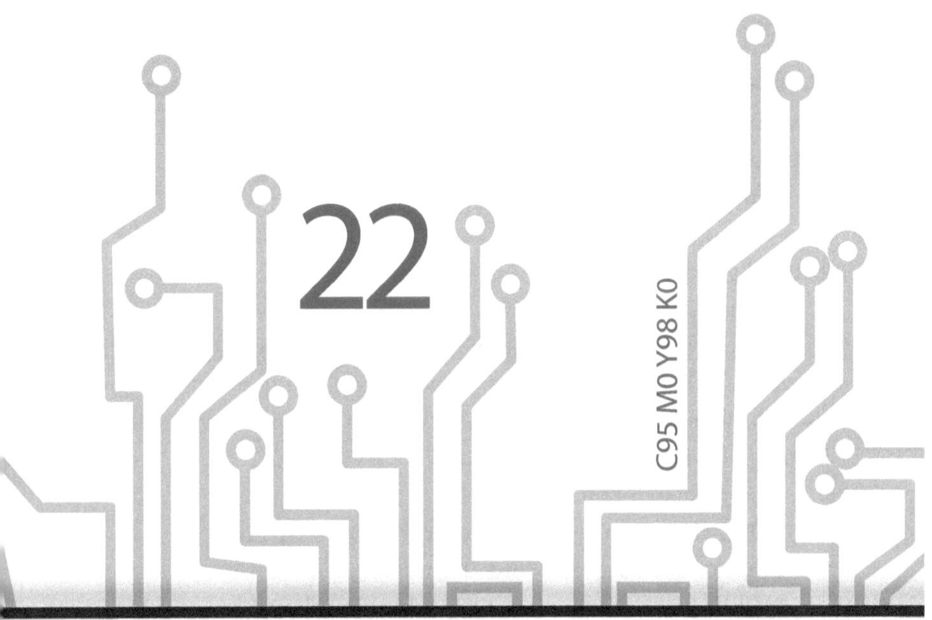

One by one, the others left the room. Bice told me to get some more rest and be patient while my body continued to heal. I apologized to Loden for losing the sword, but he dismissed it. He seemed preoccupied by something else.

At last, only Kelly remained. She acted as if she were going to leave, but I grabbed her hand. "Stay," I whispered.

She stayed. I closed my eyes, basking in the sheer glory of the moment. I had lived, against all odds, and Kelly was here. What else mattered?

"Loden feels so bad about pushing you into that mission," Kelly said. She picked up the cracker box where he had left it. "He blames himself for what happened to you. Rick… he ranted and raged for a while, and then would disappear for hours on end, I guess looking for you. He was the only one convinced you were still alive, I think."

I opened my eyes. "Kelly… while I was in the tunnel, I kept thinking about you," I said. That was sort of true. I had hallucinations of her, along with everyone else. But it sounded more dramatic if I left that part out.

"Beryl…" She stopped and looked away. "I thought about what I might say to you if you came back, but… I still don't know what to say."

"Well, you were worried about me, right? You already said that."

She looked back at me. I could see those red rims around her eyes more now. "I was more worried than I've ever been in my life!" she said.

"And you know what's even worse? I couldn't tell anyone around me why I was upset! My parents, my boss... I couldn't talk to them. I was being torn apart inside and couldn't say a word!"

"I'm sorry." I had no clue how to respond.

"I thought you were dead!" She shoved me in what seemed like anger, but still gentle.

I waited.

"You... you started working at the bike shop right after graduation. I had been there a few months already. I told you a few days ago what I thought about you at the time: you were so sad and confused. I enjoyed helping you learn your way around."

"I appreciated that," I offered.

"Over time, you, you became a really good friend."

Oh, no. She used the word "friend."

"While you were missing, I kept thinking about that, thinking about how much I missed seeing you every day, thinking about how I would feel if you were... were really dead..."

My heart was pounding so loud, I knew that had to be why she paused.

"Beryl..." She gazed at me and seemed almost on the verge of tears. "I... I think I've seen some indications from you, but I'm not sure. Do you think we might be... more than friends?"

I pushed myself up onto an elbow. "I thought you'd never ask," I said, trying to sound suave and on top of things. Instead, I erupted into coughing because I had eaten another cracker and hadn't had any more water while she spoke. Smooth.

After I drank and cleared out my throat, I lay back on the pillow and tried again. "Kelly... I'm trying to say what I feel, but I keep blowing it. The answer is: I've always cared about you."

Her smile looked uncertain. I don't think she believed me. It had never occurred to me she would not believe I liked her, instead of the other way around.

"When we first met, and, and you were showing me how the shop worked, I was starstruck," I went on. "I graduated the Learning Years without a girlfriend, and I wasn't really thinking much about one. You're right: I was confused a lot of the time back then. And then you came along, and you were so kind and pretty and..."

She mouthed the word "pretty" as if she couldn't believe I had said it.

"I fell for you long ago. I've wanted to say something for months, but I… I'm no good with words."

"Liar," she said softly.

I twisted my eyebrows in confusion. "What? No, I'm serious. I…"

She pushed me gently again. "I meant you're a liar about being no good with words."

"Oh."

And then one of my greatest fantasies came true. This awesome, gorgeous girl leaned over me, her green-edged brown hair cascaded around her face and down toward me, and her lips came down to meet mine. It was such a perfect moment, I didn't want it to end.

Then my stomach rumbled, breaking the entire mood.

Later, after filling my stomach with more substantive fare than crackers, I reclined back in my cot. Rick and Bice returned. If they noticed Kelly sat much closer to me, and her hand rested on top of mine, they didn't comment.

"I haven't seen Stacy or Don yet," I noticed. "Is everything going okay with our plans?"

The others exchanged looks. "Don has located a digger that will serve our purposes," Bice reported. "He's keeping an eye on it. Lovat's out checking on him now. He does that regularly. I think the two of them are building a bond."

Somehow, I could see that.

"Stacy's spreading the rumors," Kelly volunteered. "I know it's working, because Frank—that's the new guy at work—told me that he heard there was conflict between the dragons. Somehow, the rumor worked all the way around to him!"

"Yeah, but it needs to get outside our city," I pointed out.

"That's what makes Stacy perfect for the job," Kelly said. "She works in the performing arts. All of them get to travel to other cities all the time, and meet up with actors from all over The Circle. They're probably talking about it even in the red cities by now!"

"That's… great." I could see how that made sense, but somehow I suspected Kelly's optimism might be a little exaggerated.

Rick pointed at me. "But none of it would have been worth anything if you hadn't come back with that tooth! You, my friend, have saved the whole plan."

I attempted a wave, but my hand didn't move far from the cot. "Ah, it was nothing."

"Oh, so you're ready to practice some more sparring with the swords?"

"I did mention losing my sword, right?"

"We have practice swords."

"Okay, you got me. I'll have to pass for now."

Everyone laughed. I relaxed even further. This was so… perfect. Sitting here with good friends, laughing, enjoying each other. This was how life was meant to be, not always worrying about the Viridian Guard, or paying homage to a vile creature that didn't care whether you lived or died. We were meant for so much more, and, in some ways, our relationships were the key to all of that.

Lost in my thoughts, I barely noticed that Bice was telling some sort of ridiculous story about a fellow priest who had an awkward hole in his robe. Kelly and Rick were focused on him, grins on both their faces. Was this what true family should be like? My parents had only been gone three years, but even before that, I had not enjoyed our relationship. For real memories of laughter and fellowship, I had to go back over seven years, when I was so very young. A tear welled up in my eye, an indicator of what I had lost. I wiped it away, letting my melancholy get swallowed in the emotions I had depended on for so long now: anger and hate. The dragons. They kept us from being who we were supposed to be, even from loving one another the way we should.

Kelly noticed I wasn't laughing and looked at me with concern in her eyes. I forced a smile and shook my head. "It's okay," I mouthed. She didn't look convinced.

"So… did anyone ever fix that toilet?" I wanted to know.

"Don't look at me," Rick said, raising his hands. "I told you I didn't understand that stuff."

Our attention was drawn to a knock. Loden stood in the doorway.

"It's time I told you all the rest of the plan."

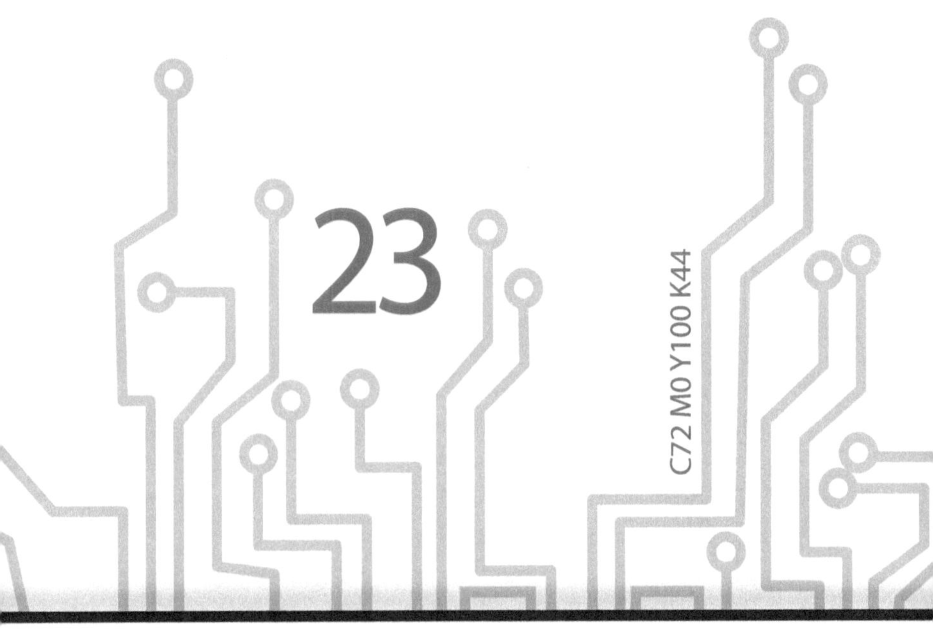

Loden seemed nervous. He paced back and forth for a few moments before he spoke again.

"As you know, I'm an engineer," he began. "Specifically, I used to be a cybernetic engineer, one of the best in all Viridia, if not the entire Circle. My genius was recognized during my Learning Years, and I was put on a fast-track training plan to prepare me for special service."

I had heard of those training plans. Only the very smartest and most specialized students were granted access to them, maybe one out of a thousand.

"After graduation, I was immediately given a job in the Emerald Ascendancy. Over the next few years, my career advanced by leaps and bounds…"

"Wait!" Rick interrupted. "You used to work there, and you didn't give us any advice or help in infiltrating the place?"

Loden bowed his head. "I regret it greatly," he said. "I wanted to test the two of you, see if you were really up to the enormous challenge facing us. But by doing so, I put you both in grave danger, and Beryl paid the price. I am so sorry."

"You should be!" Rick snarled. "If you had just told us what to expect, or where to go…"

"Rick," I called weakly. "Let it go. Let's hear him out."

Loden looked back up. "As it was, Beryl accomplished far more than I could have expected," he pointed out. "I've never been in the dragon's lair or even seen it. The news about the second escape tunnel alone is something that could be used to our advantage in a huge way later on. And then there's what he overheard."

"I don't even understand what I overheard," I said. "You want to explain that?"

"I'll get to it. Let me go back and tell this in order." He paused to collect his thoughts, and then resumed his story.

"As I advanced and gained greater access to the secrets of Viridia, I began to see how much had been kept from us all, from humanity in general. The dragons carefully controlled all that we did and learned, even those of us at the heights of our capabilities.

"Weapons tech was forbidden, of course, as was anything related to the skies. The skies belong to the dragons. It's a mantra everyone knows. But the dragons also fear communications technology. They don't want us to have the ability to communicate over distances. That creates organization. And organized humans are a threat."

"How so?" I asked, not grasping it.

Loden made a vague gesture. "You talked a few minutes ago about the difficulties Stacy was having in spreading the rumors to other cities. Imagine that you could pick up a device, speak into it, and be speaking to a person in Caesious, or any of the other cities, and that person could talk back to you."

"That's crazy," Rick said.

"It exists," Loden declared. "We're just not allowed to build them or try to learn about them. I think the draconics have some. I'm trying to get my hands on some devices that may not be that spectacular, but could help us greatly, anyway."

"It sounds like magic," Kelly said.

"Is it magic when a draconic has his arm completely replaced by metal, and it works just like his old arm?" Loden asked. "We're used to cybernetic technology, because it's become a regular thing. But this 'magic' of communications is actually far beneath our capabilities as scientists. We're just not allowed to work with it."

For a non-scientist like me, I didn't grasp all the implications, but I took Loden at his word. It made sense that the dragons would be so controlling.

"The longer I worked within this system, the more I hated it," Loden went on. "When I broached the subject with my closest friends, they were horrified that I would dare to question anything coming from Viridia."

"You mean my parents." I hoped he wasn't going to go into great detail. There were things I didn't want the others to know. My pain, my rage, belonged to me alone.

Loden nodded. "I can never fully explain it to you, son, but they were closer to me than family. We differed only on the subject of the dragons."

"That's a pretty big difference of opinion," Rick noted.

"Close friendships can endure that kind of thing," Loden argued. "You may not be old enough yet to fully understand that. Give it time."

I never had any friends that close, at least until now. But the friendship Loden spoke of was something different than what I had with anyone here, except maybe Rick… and Kelly, but that was different too, wasn't it?

"At the same time I was inwardly hating the system, I was learning everything I could," Loden continued. "I made breakthroughs that pleased the draconics so well, they gave me further access and independence. They never knew that I didn't tell them everything I discovered. I will take some discoveries with me to the grave rather than let the dragons learn of them.

"Then, three years ago, there was an accident. I was called to the scene because Troilus Green, a prominent draconic, had been injured and would need some cybernetic help to survive. To my horror, I saw the bodies of my closest friends had been pulled from the rubble. And then… even as I was examining the draconic's mangled hand, I saw them pull Beryl out."

Loden paused for a long time. No one said anything. I knew part of what was coming, but it felt strange to hear it told this way, as if it had happened to someone else. Kelly squeezed my hand.

"He was still alive, but only just," Loden said. "I could see that he was badly injured. The draconics would likely deny him medical care, since he would be unable to serve them well in that condition. I had to think fast.

"Pulling in every favor I could, I managed to have Beryl transferred to the Ascendancy where I was working on saving Troilus Green. When some questions were asked, I proffered the excuse that to properly treat the draconic, I needed to test a couple of techniques on someone else, where it wouldn't matter if it went wrong."

I had no idea I had been inside the Ascendancy back then.

"I pretended that the draconic's injuries required much more time to repair than they really did. Most of his enhancements were outward, and I could do that in my sleep by this time," Loden explained. "In reality, I was spending my time implanting Beryl with a highly experimental and highly forbidden piece of cyber technology. It saved his life and let him walk. I arranged to have him transferred back to a hospital where they would discover that he would be all right, after all. And they let him live."

I closed my eyes. I owed this man so much.

"From that day forward, I resolved that something had to change. I began learning everything I could about the dragons, trying to find a weakness to exploit. I studied their physiology, their metabolism, the cybernetic enhancements they've all had done. It was easy for me to do this, as they assumed I was just learning so as to keep helping. I was a good servant, after all. I learned things that I'm not even sure the dragons remember about themselves."

He stopped and laughed softly. "And yet… in one short visit to the Ascendancy, Beryl learned things I never did, including what I think might be one of the most significant things of all."

"What did I learn?" I asked. I still had no idea what he was talking about.

"Well, first, you learned about the exits," Loden pointed out. "I knew there must be a door somewhere from the Ascendancy into the nest, but you actually saw it. You also found Viridia's secret exit in the forest. But most importantly, you overheard a conversation that confirmed some things I've already suspected."

"What's that?"

"First, there is already conflict among the dragons," Loden said. "You heard them talking about a problem with the reds—the red dragons. They're already worried about it, which plays right into our plans. That's fantastic.

"Second, and most importantly, you heard them arguing the benefits of gene splicing versus cybernetics, and Viridia was pushing them hard, wanting instant results. He was upset they weren't making more progress."

"What's gene splicing?" Kelly asked.

Loden frowned. "It's hard for me to explain. Let me put it this way:

you know how Beryl is able to use his implant to boost his leg power? Imagine that we could adjust people—without cybernetics—so they were stronger, faster, and so on."

"To make them better soldiers," Rick observed.

Loden nodded. "Exactly. But also remember that humans are just for experimenting. Once the technique is solid, they'll want to use it on the draconics and even the dragons themselves, because of the most important news we can get from all this."

"And that is…"

"The dragons are dying."

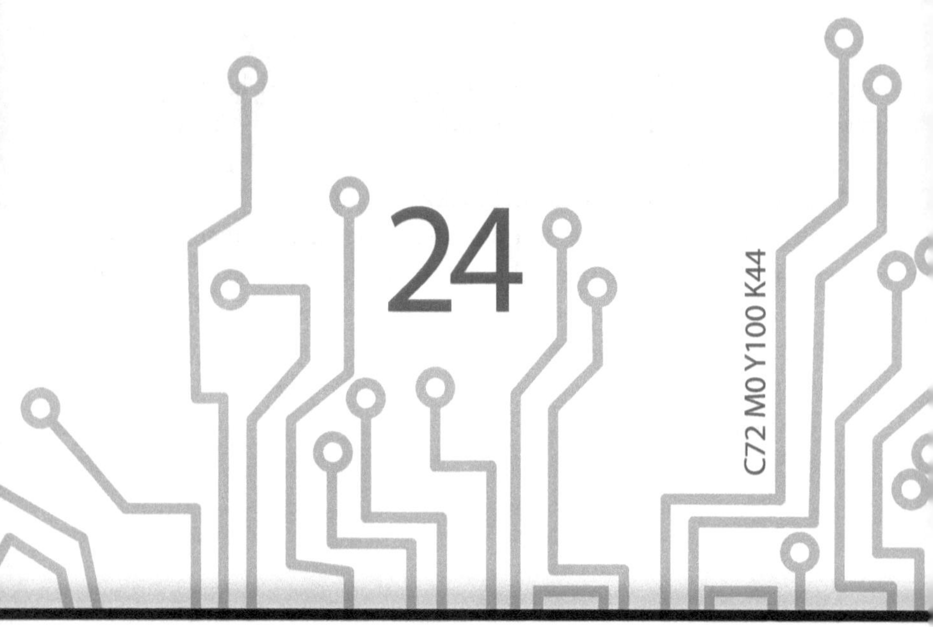

The dragons were dying? That concept just didn't fit with my worldview. The dragons had ruled The Circle for all of recorded history. In fact, recorded history said they were the ones who found The Circle and brought humans to live here. The priests called them immortal. While I hated them, I had never considered that the basic facts I knew to be true might actually be… wrong.

"What evidence do you offer for this?" Bice said quickly. I swear I think he did that to keep Kelly or me from saying something stupid. Two or three stupid things were on the tip of my tongue, at least.

"We all know the entire purpose of cybernetic research is to help the dragons," Loden explained. "The only reason they keep us around is because we can do things for them that they can't do for themselves. I was personally involved in building Viridia's new wing, for example. What if we hadn't done that? What if we never helped them out when they were hurt? Would Viridia still be regarded by the average person as a god if he only had one wing?"

"But you're just talking about them getting injured," Rick pointed out. "How does that translate to them dying?"

"No one questions that the dragons are enormously long-lived," Loden said. "Despite the efforts they've made to suppress our understanding of history, we know all of them are at least a thousand years old, if not older.

However, long-lived does not equal immortal. Based on what I have seen and heard, I believe they are getting old and starting to lose their health."

"Specifically?"

"Why else would they push us harder and harder to find new cybernetic techniques? Why are they desperate to discover the secrets of genetics? All of these technologies are about prolonging life. They're trying to find ways to prolong their own lives, not ours. They don't care a bit for the human lifespan."

Bice nodded. Rick still looked skeptical. I had to admit Loden's conclusions made sense, but… it wasn't hard evidence.

"The scales," I remembered. Loden smiled and nodded. The others looked at me in confusion.

"When I saw the dragon in the cave, I noticed he had dozens of scales that had been replaced," I said. "They weren't the bright metal like other cybernetics, but were colored green to blend in. He's trying to disguise how much he's lost."

"Dragons lose scales all the time," Rick protested.

"But they always grow back," Loden responded. "Viridia's are not. He's getting old."

Silence reigned for a long time as we each pondered what this meant. Earth-shaking might describe it, as if someone had informed us that the sky had become red instead of blue.

"If…" Kelly started and then stopped. She hesitated and then tried again. "If the dragons are dying, then… do we need to do anything? Maybe we should just lay low and wait."

"I don't think so," Loden answered. "The dragons have been around for a thousand years. Even if they are dying, how long will it take? When a human gets old and starts losing their capabilities, it can take some years before they actually die, if they're allowed to live to their natural end. If you extrapolate that out to the dragons' lifespan, we could be talking about another hundred years before they die."

"And how would you know if they did?" Rick broke in. We looked at him. He seemed to be more thoughtful than usual. "Seriously. How would we know? I came here from Atramentous. Do you know how long it's been since anyone's seen him? Most of the dragons keep to themselves. They hide in their shelters and rarely emerge. If one of them died, their draconics and human servants would keep things going and never tell anyone.

It might go on for decades that way before anyone discovered the truth."

"So we still have to act," I said.

"Yes, we do," Loden agreed. "We have no way of knowing how long they'll be around, or, as Rick points out, how long the system will keep going." He hesitated. "I do want to make something clear, however: just because the dragons are getting old does not mean they should not be feared. Even an ancient, dying dragon is a much more powerful creature than we can barely imagine. Look at what shape Beryl is in, just by visiting one's lair.

"They are fearsome, horrifying creatures… but they are not immortal. I was absolutely convinced of this as I kept studying. And that knowledge drove me to find a way to kill one. I explored poisons for a time, but the dragons' unusual physiology makes them virtually impervious to any kind of poison. Fire, of course, will not harm them. It seemed I would have to delve into the absolutely forbidden: weapons research.

"Projectile weaponry has been especially forbidden. Did you know that one of our technicians developed a door that slid open and shut on its own, but he was banned from doing any more work on it, because the draconics feared it could be adapted to throw something? They guard that kind of technology extra carefully. The more I tried to look into that, the more roadblocks I hit, to the point that I grew fearful of exploring it any further."

"What does that leave?" Rick wondered. "The swords?"

"I already said I didn't believe one of them could kill a dragon," Loden answered. "No, I decided I would have to come up with something completely unconventional, something no one would expect. Once I figured out where I wanted to be, I had to figure out how to get myself transferred.

"So I started by making a few notable, but mostly harmless errors in my cybernetics work. I was demoted out of the most elite labs, but was still highly regarded. When I went to my superiors and announced that I had discovered a surprising application to some of my previous work, they were skeptical, to say the least. What could a cybernetics engineer have to offer to train engineering?"

"It does sound like a stretch." Bice chuckled.

"But I made my case. I showed them plans for a new rail-and-engine system that would improve the speed of our trains by four times. They couldn't pass that up. Plus, I had made those mistakes. Maybe I was losing my touch. And if I messed up with the trains, that wouldn't be as bad, right? They approved my transfer.

"I've spent the past year carefully supervising the rebuilding of our tracks, and the meticulous construction of a new engine. I made sure the workers involved only saw the parts they were personally working on, that none of them saw the whole thing. And I built some of the parts personally."

"Are you saying the weapon is in the train?" Rick asked.

"Yes… and no." Loden's playful smile looked out of place on his rough face. "The weapon is the train."

"How does that work?"

He cocked his head. "Sorry, that's all for now. I'm not telling you all the details at this point."

Rick started to protest, but Loden cut him off. "It's not because of trust this time. I just want to keep the technical details to as few people as possible, just in case…"

"Just in case one of us gets captured," I said. "You've probably told us too much already, then."

"Perhaps. But I wanted you to know. I've kept too much secret for too long." Loden contemplated me. "If I have time and opportunity, Beryl, I will pass on everything I know to you."

"I'm a bicycle mechanic. What do I know of cybernetic engineering?"

"In time, you can be much more," Loden said without a smile. "In time…"

Silence again. I could feel fatigue take hold of me, and I think Kelly noticed.

"We should let Beryl get some more rest," she announced.

Loden stirred, as if he had been in deep thought. "Yes… yes, we should. We can talk more later." He said goodbye and left, followed by Rick. Bice checked me over again, and then he also left.

"I have to get back," Kelly said. "I have to keep up appearances, you know. Keep pretending like my life is still the same…"

"But now you don't have to worry so much," I pointed out.

"Are you kidding? I have to worry twice as much. The plan is still the same. We're still going to try to kill a dragon, remember? And whatever my role ends up being, I know you'll be right in the middle of it!"

"But…"

"And now we've been honest about our feelings. There's even more to lose!"

"Did you… I mean, are you sorry about that?"

"No." She folded her arms across her chest and stood there for a moment, looking away. "But it was a little easier when I didn't know that you cared too." She leaned over, gave me a quick kiss on the cheek and hurried out.

I was so confused.

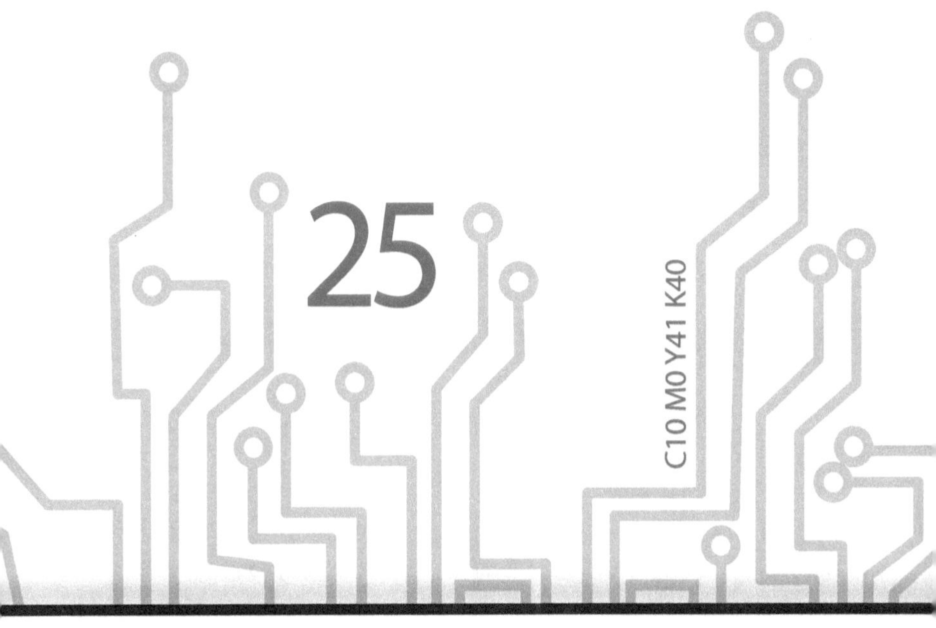

"Again!" Stacy snapped.

Rick wiped the sweat from his brow and took his stance with the practice sword for the fifth time, facing off with our trainer, the actress. Upon arriving this morning, she had stripped off her outer clothes, wearing only shorts and a tank top as she dueled. It was hard not to stare at her as the sweat ran down her dark skin and…

Kelly nudged me hard. How did she know what I was thinking? Three days had gone by since I woke up and Loden told us his story. I was recovering fairly well, I thought, and could get around all right. I didn't think I could do what Stacy and Rick were doing right now, though.

"I thought she was your favorite actress," I protested.

"She's *one* of my favorites," Kelly clarified, "and that doesn't mean you get to stare at her that way."

"I was just trying to pay attention to her technique!"

"Right. And I'm a draconic's mother."

We both continued to watch the duel, and I tried to focus my eyes on Rick. It was really difficult, though. Stacy's movements were so sinuous… Okay, make that sensuous. That's the word. But I wasn't going to admit that to Kelly. I tried to change my focus again, and change the subject too.

"What do you think of Rick?" I asked.

"Rick? Um, he's... uh..."

Was she blushing? "Wait... you're griping at me for watching Stacy and you're..."

"No! It's not like that!"

"Uh-huh."

"It's not!"

"Right."

She punched my shoulder. That actually hurt.

"Still waiting for an answer," I said.

Kelly frowned. "Rick is a mystery," she said. "I guess that's what makes him kind of intriguing."

Intriguing. Okay.

"He's got this whole *rebel* thing down almost too well," she went on. "Gods, look at him. At least he took off his jacket for this, but he still keeps the gloves on! Does he think it makes him look all hue and everything? All he's missing is sunglasses!"

I waited.

"But... it works. I don't know why, but that look really appeals to girls right now. If he didn't have the wrong chromark and wasn't wanted by the Guard, he would probably have girls flocking to him."

"Remind me to find a jacket and some sunglasses."

She frowned. I had done it again. "I'm kidding," I said. "I don't need a flock of girls."

"That's for sure!" Rick had approached while I wasn't looking. He knelt and leaned on the practice sword, sweat running down his face as he tried to catch his breath. "Between the two we have in here, we don't need any more."

Stacy also approached and plopped down on the other side, her legs stretched out right in front of me. This wasn't awkward at all. "So you don't like girls, Rick?"

"That's not what I said!" Rick protested. "I only meant that there are two girls here, both of them equally delightful and beautiful, and two guys. Why do we need any more?"

Kelly colored again, but Stacy was not impressed. "And since Beryl and Kelly seem to be a thing now, you think I'm open to be targeted? Think again, love." She looked at me. "Beryl! You've been off your feet long enough. Let's have a go!"

I was dubious, but got to my feet. Rick handed me the practice sword and sat beside Kelly. "You heard her call me 'love,' right?" Kelly rolled her eyes.

"I feel weak just standing up," I told Stacy. "I'm not sure how I can do anything worthwhile here."

"Loden said you would say that," she answered. "So he told me to tell you to give your legs a boost… but not how you usually do it."

"Huh?"

"When you trigger the boost, you do it as a single action, right? I want you to concentrate and try doing it as a slow, prolonged action, where you're feeding the boost in a very little at a time."

That sounded strange to me, but it couldn't hurt to try. Loden seemed to be implying my implant could do much more than I expected it to. I concentrated, and tried to do what Stacy had described. At first, I felt nothing. Then a little bit of strength seemed to flow into my legs.

"Wow."

"Okay, defend yourself." She launched an attack at me, swinging her sword in a broad arc I managed to duck under at the last second.

"Hey, just because my legs feel better doesn't mean my arms do!" I complained.

"And they won't, if you don't exercise them!" she shot back, swinging again. "You survived something that no one had any right surviving! I think you're recovering faster than you believe too." I managed a couple of parries before she smacked me in the ribs. Even so, I knew she had been taking it easy on me. It hurt to use my muscles again, but I had to admit it felt good.

A few minutes later, I felt much better than I had in days. The slow boost seemed to have made a significant difference. I hoped it wouldn't end all at once and leave me exhausted. Practicing the various moves Stacy showed me felt good, and not just because she had to move in close to demonstrate how I should stand and hold the sword.

I glanced over at Kelly and saw her wide-eyed at something Rick was telling her. I frowned and opened my mouth to interrupt, when the door to the sanctuary flew open. Lovat came barreling in, tripping over a loose blanket, rolling into a flip, and coming back to his feet. Before I could even react, he had grabbed my arm and looked anxiously up into my face.

"Bice i'trouble!"

Through Lovat's broken slang, we were able to pierce together that Bice had been confronted by some of the priesthood. He wasn't clear on exactly what was happening, but it seemed serious enough to terrify the boy.

Rick slung his sword onto his back. "Let's get moving!"

"Wait… are you just going to charge in?" Kelly demanded. "Beryl, you can barely walk!"

"He's stronger than you think," Stacy corrected. She walked up and handed me her sword. "Take this. I'd happily go with, but my face is too recognizable."

"Then I'm going," Kelly said, getting to her feet.

"What? No," I answered. "Bad idea. I don't want to…"

"Don't want to what? Risk me getting hurt? You told me we had to fight. Why should I stay out of things?"

Rick shrugged as he pulled on his jacket. "She's got a point."

With no way to argue any further, I called to Lovat. "Let's go, kid. Guide us to the shrine."

Led by the orphan, the four of us set out winding our way through the streets. I glanced back and saw Stacy standing at the front door, watching our departure. I turned back and nearly lost track of Lovat as he raced on ahead.

In a short time, we were back in an area of town I recognized. This put me more on an edge; I was more likely to be noticed here. Then again, we were carrying swords. We were all going to be noticed if Lovat weren't careful about where he guided us. Soon, I could see the Shrine of the Emerald God just ahead.

"Wait," I called to everyone. Lovat scampered back. "We can't just charge in like this. Lovat, run ahead and find out what's going on. Come back and tell us how many there are and where they're at."

He nodded and disappeared. The three of us moved closer and stopped just outside the walls of the shrine. I ran through the layout in my head: most of the shrine consisted of the large garden Bice maintained, almost a full city block. His small cottage rested against the wall in the right rear of the garden, while the large sacellum occupied the center. It was a round structure, surrounded by pillars, enclosed by walls but open to the sky above. Four doors lead inside, one at each compass point.

Rick got down on a knee next to me. "Got a plan?" he asked.

I shook my head. "Depends on where they are, how many…"

Lovat reappeared. "In th' circle," he announced. "Bice. Five others. All priests, think."

I nodded. "Then we come from above. Follow me."

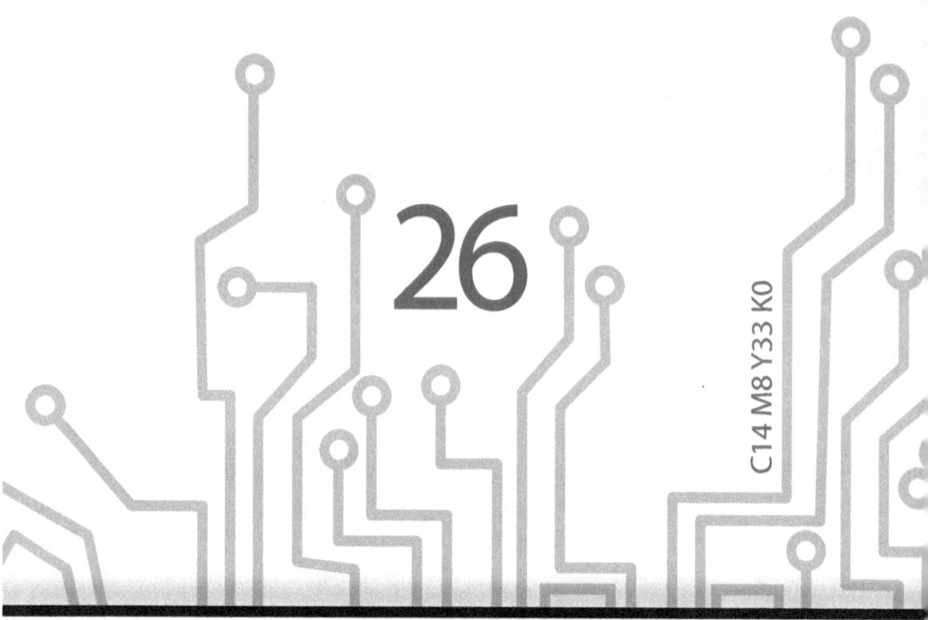

26

I met Bice after my parents' death. He showed up at my bedside during my recovery. He sometimes helped out at the hospital with the hard cases, doing what he could to preserve life. I wanted nothing to do with anyone associated with the church of dragon worship, but when I heard the first hint of his story, I couldn't help but be curious. In time, he won me over and became my friend. He helped me learn to use my implant; Loden must have told him about it and engaged him to advise me. None of the regular doctors could know about it, of course. Through his kindness, Bice became one of my only real friends. If he were in trouble, I was going to help, even if it cost us the entire mission.

I led the way through the main gate and then cut across several flower beds and hedges to circle around to the right of the sacellum. I knew the location of a large oak that could get us to the top. Once there, Lovat scrambled up at once, finding his way much higher than I expected. I gestured to the other two and climbed up myself. Rick and Kelly both followed. I could already hear raised voices coming from inside.

I inched my way out one of the tree's massive branches. From there, I managed to lean across and clamber on to the outer frame of the sacellum, where a three-foot wide parapet connected the ring of pillars. Balancing carefully, I inched across the narrow connecting beam that led to the outer summit of the sacellum. I leaned across the angled roof, barely four feet wide, and peered over the top.

As Lovat had reported, I saw Bice and five priests. Two of them, dressed in unusual white robes trimmed in dark green, stood on either side of Bice, holding strange swords with hooks on the end. The other three stood opposite. The one in the center seemed to be haranguing Bice about something. I leaned in closer to listen.

"…So you continue to deny the very basis of our priesthood!"

"I have always been open about my doubts," Bice responded. "That is why I am not a priest, just a gardener."

The lead priest gestured at one of the white robes, who struck Bice across the face. I clenched the roof edge harder. Rick and Kelly scrambled up next to me. "You could have helped us," Kelly reproved me in a whisper. I didn't answer.

"There are new orders coming down almost daily," the lead priest said. "Purity within the ranks is a necessity."

"Garland, I have worked quietly here for years," Bice protested. "If my work is no longer satisfactory, I will find new employment elsewhere."

"No."

The priest, Garland, stepped up to a point where he could look down on Bice. "You don't seem to understand," he snarled. "Heresy cannot be tolerated within Viridia's borders, even more so here within these holy walls. The word has been given. You will be made an example of those who would betray our emerald lord."

"But why? I have worked here quietly, never…"

Garland gestured again, and the white-robed guard punched Bice in the face this time.

"Five against three?" Rick whispered. "Think we can take them?"

I lifted my hands that had been clenching the roof's edge and noticed some of the wide slate shingles had come loose. I had an idea.

I leaned over to Kelly and whispered, "Rick and I will work our way around to the other side. When I wave at you, shove these shingles over the edge. That will give us a distraction to jump down and attack." She nodded. I glanced back at Lovat and couldn't think of a way he could help. I gestured for him to stay put. He scowled at me.

Rick followed me as we scooted around the outer edge of the sacellum. Below, I could hear the priest ranting on and on about the purity of the religion and how Bice was spreading his corrupting influence among other believers or something like that. Rick grabbed my arm without warning. I looked back.

"He just said a draconic is coming!" Rick hissed. My head jerked and I sped up the pace. We had no time to lose now.

We reached the point I had indicated and stopped to draw our swords. I looked at Rick, and he nodded. I looked across and waved at Kelly. She nodded and shoved the shingles over the edge. Rick and I waited until they crashed to the ground, and then we both flipped over the edge and dropped inside.

I gave my legs a tiny boost to help absorb the impact of landing. Rick somehow landed just fine on his own. We were right behind Bice and the white-robed guards who whirled to face us. "Time to see if Stacy taught us anything worthwhile," Rick noted, leaping forward.

I followed him at a rush. Bice's eyes widened as we engaged the guards. Their eyes darted in every direction before settling on the two of us, but they swung their swords to defensive positions in unison. This wouldn't be easy.

"Get them!" the lead priest shouted, just before another slate shingle landed directly on top of his head. Kelly kept breaking them off and tossing them down.

The guard in front of me sneered and swung his hook-sword at my head. I parried it, but narrowly pulled my sword back without losing it. If I weren't careful, he might wrench my sword out of my hands.

We exchanged a few more blows, and I realized I was outmatched. This guard knew moves that I'd never seen. Funny how that worked. The priesthood apparently had access to fortek weaponry, just like the Viridian Guard, and trained their guards in its use.

I would have to use my only advantage to get out of this, and better to do so fast. I swung in to parry a strike from my opponent, then spun my sword toward him and activated a hard boost. I lunged much faster than he expected, and my sword struck right through his stomach. I looked up at his face and saw his eyes get huge. He dropped his own sword and reached toward my blade. I yanked it out with a gush of blood. His hands did nothing to hold it back as he collapsed to the ground.

I had never intentionally hurt someone like that. I stared down at the guard's face as he choked and gasped. He wasn't dead yet. I opened my mouth, but what could I say? I felt a wash of emotions: sadness at causing pain, sympathy remembering how I had come close to dying myself recently, and then anger at someone who served the dragon so fully that he deserved what happened to him.

At that moment, one of the unarmed priests hit me in a tackle that knocked me off my feet and sent my sword flying. As I struggled to break free, I caught a glimpse of Rick still fighting his opponent, swords clanging. I twisted around, maneuvered my knee in the right position and gave my leg a quick boost. My knee cracked against the priest's jaw and knocked him senseless. It didn't feel so great on my knee, either.

In the back of my mind, I reminded myself I hadn't even been on my feet much before today. I was doing amazingly well, considering.

I got to my feet and looked around in a hurry. Rick stood over his opponent, pulling his sword free. Bice was trying to help the guard I had stabbed. He glanced at me with desperate eyes. The other two priests had retreated under the roof and stared at us.

"You have profaned this sacred place!" the lead priest screamed.

"Yeah, whatever," Rick responded. He started toward the priests.

"No, wait…" Bice protested.

"Drake! Drake!" The voice from above was Lovat's, and at first, I couldn't make out what he was saying.

Then the north doors blew open. One of them snapped off its hinges and flipped multiple times across the ground before coming to a rest only a foot away from me.

A huge figure strode through the broken door into the sacellum. I already knew, before it stepped into the light. It couldn't be anyone else.

Troilus Green had arrived.

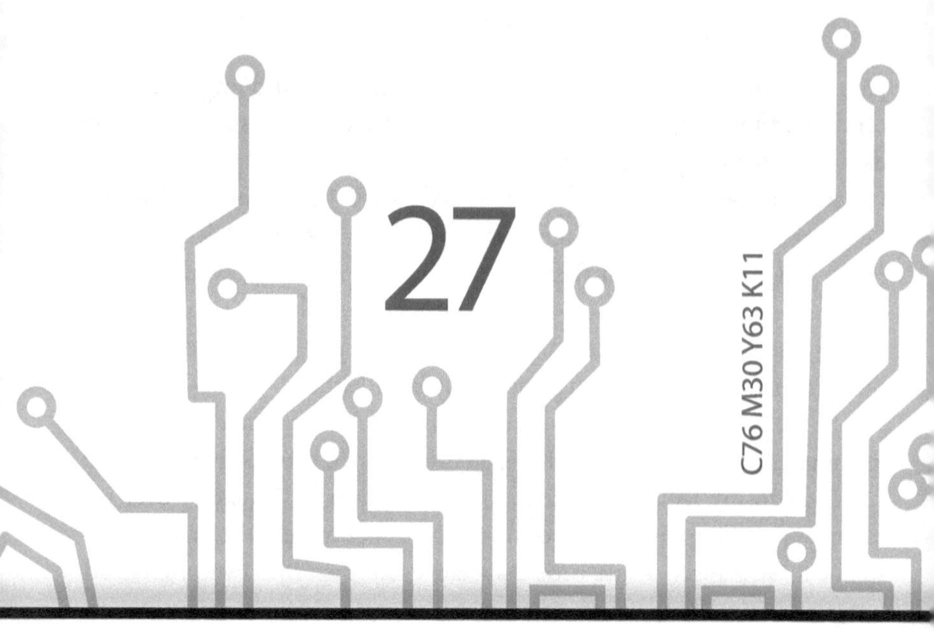

The draconic's eyes swept over the scene. The left side of its face sported a gleaming new metal plate where Rick had stabbed it. I guess the technicians hadn't had enough time yet to shape it to match its snout. The warm air and sickly-sweet odor swept out before it.

"What is this?" Troilus Green roared. Its eyes locked on me. "I come in search of a heretic, and I find you? Beryl?"

"I've been looking forward to our rematch, draconic! Prepare to die!" Actually, I didn't say that. My response sounded more like "uhhh…."

"We missed you too." Rick's words always came faster than mine.

The draconic tapped the faceplate with a metal claw. "I haven't forgotten you, either, Wanderer. I've been searching for you for a long time. Viridia smiles upon me this day."

I scrambled across the floor to pick up my sword. Troilus Green merely watched. Of course it could afford to be calm and patient. We had barely escaped it the last time. How could we stand against it now? I gripped my sword hilt and kept my eyes fixed on Troilus Green. Kelly was now almost directly over it, and I didn't want to give away her position. The two priests hurried behind the draconic, as if taking shelter behind its power.

"I admit to being curious," Troilus Green said. "I never expected to see either of you again after our last encounter. Most rebels, after their first taste of trouble, flee the city and never return. Yet you're still here. Why is that, I wonder?"

"This is my home," I answered. "How about you leave instead?"

"HA!" The laugh was a roar. "I told you before, boy. We are linked. This city is home to both of us. We were even both injured in the same accident." His tone darkened. "And Viridia is god to us both."

"Viridia is no god," I growled. "And in time, he will fall too."

"Impressive. Few would dare to think so high. So you plot against our dread majesty himself, do you? Thank you for telling me why you are still here. Even so, it is the height of arrogance and ignorance for you to think you had a chance to defeat even me, one of our god's lowest servants."

With a snarl, Troilus Green whipped its hand upward and screamed something. The roof exploded upward, hurling Kelly into the air. Rick and I both screamed and lunged forward. We didn't have a chance to reach her in time. Troilus Green caught her falling body with one arm, as if she were nothing more than a ball it had tossed in the air for play. In a flash, it had claws at her neck.

"Shall I tear out her throat?" it growled at us. Rick and I both stopped only a couple of feet away. I looked at Kelly, shifting my stance back and forth. She looked unconscious, bleeding from a few cuts caused by the shattered slate shingles. I didn't see any major injuries, though.

"Drop the weapons."

I looked to Rick. He didn't seem to know what to do, either. I couldn't think of any other option. I knelt and set the sword on the ground. Rick followed suit. He had his left hand out, palm forward, as if to show its emptiness to the draconic.

"Excellent. You can be taught, I see." It chuckled. "This female is important to you, but I know of no crime she has committed. Surrender yourselves and I will show mercy to her."

"You bleaking pile of fewmets," Rick growled.

I bowed my head. "You win," I said. "I surrender."

"Wait!"

I whirled and saw Bice getting to his feet. His attempts to save the guard I had stabbed had been in vain. He lay unmoving with closed eyes. I felt a strange sinking in my stomach. I had killed a man, ended his life. What did that make me?

"Ah, you must be the heretic," Troilus Green observed. "Interesting, though not surprising, that these two came for you. I will require your surrender as well, of course."

"My name is Bice," the older man declared, taking a step forward. His hands dripped with blood. "You have named me heretic, and I take that name as a point of pride from this moment onward." I had never heard him speak so forcefully. His face looked like stone, so different from his usual smile.

"Blood has been shed in this place," Bice went on. He gestured behind him at the bodies. "Sacred life has been ended. I will not allow any further bloodshed to take place."

Troilus Green opened and closed its mouth before finding its voice. "You will not allow? What can you possibly do to stop me, tiny man? Do you not understand who stands before you?"

Bice raised his chin and lifted his hands, displaying the blood. "It is you who do not understand. Today, I am Bice the Heretic, but before that, I was Bice the Gardener and before that, Bice the Priest. I have had years to learn all that I can from your false priests. I know where your power comes from."

"You know nothing!" Troilus Green snarled. It took its claws from Kelly's neck and pointed at Bice. "You are nothing, pathetic heretic!"

Bice pointed back, blood weeping from his finger. "A moment ago, you used the power beneath this location to blast the roof," he went on in the same firm and forceful voice. "You are not the only one who can access it."

Troilus Green's jaw dropped for a split-second, and then he started to scream something. But Bice had already lifted his other hand and began shouting himself. Their imprecations overlapped, both of their voices seeming to change, becoming stronger, louder and more resonant. Rick and I covered our ears. Troilus Green dropped Kelly and pointed both hands at Bice. Their voices continued expanding, and I felt the floor vibrating. Broken shards fell from the shattered roof. I caught a glimpse of Lovat scrambling back away from the edge. The air itself seemed thick, as though it were solidifying. I pushed against it and rushed to Kelly's side, ignoring the draconic. With Rick's help, I lifted her, and we hastened out of the way.

I looked back at an unbelievable sight. Bice and Troilus Green faced each other, expressions twisted in concentration, mouths agape in continuous screaming. And then... I know of no other way to describe it than that I could momentarily see the air. It looked like thin fog in motion. Time seemed to slow. The roof shards drifted rather than fell. The blood running down Bice's hands stopped moving. The air congealed between the two opponents and then inexorably began sweeping back at the draconic. Its arms were forced back, back away from Bice. The air wrapped itself around both arms and lifted Troilus Green up off the ground several inches. He stopped screaming and glared in fury at the minuscule ex-priest.

Bice dropped his hands, and drops of blood sprinkled across the ground. Everything seemed to snap back to normal, except for the enraged draconic held in mid-air by an invisible force. Bice staggered.

"Help him!" I shouted at Rick. He jumped to the older man's side and supported him.

Lovat reappeared at the roof's edge. "Le's go!" he shouted.

Rick glared at Troilus Green, and I could tell what he was considering. Now was the chance. One of us could stab that foul creature through its heart and it would never trouble us again. But to do so, we would have to abandon Kelly or Bice.

"He's right," Bice said, a tremor in his voice. "That won't hold it for long. We need to get out of here."

I looked helplessly down. I didn't have the strength to carry Kelly. I could already feel my energy sapping, draining away after this sudden exertion. "Trade me," I reluctantly told Rick. He nodded and let Bice lean against the wall for a minute while I helped him lift Kelly. Rick staggered a little, but steadied himself. "I've got her."

I went to Bice, and we supported each other as we left Troilus Green behind.

"We'll meet again, rebels!" it shouted. "Be sure of it!"

"No question there," I muttered.

Lovat scrambled down the tree and met us outside. "Guards at gate!" he informed us. "Other way?"

Bice nodded. "There's a hidden gate behind my cottage," he said.

Lovat led the way, and we followed as quick as we could. As we passed the cottage, Bice took a long look. I knew what he had to be thinking. He had lived there for years and was leaving for the last time.

A triumphant roar behind us gave speed to our feet. Troilus Green had broken free. We hurried out the small gate and down the street. We had escaped once more, but yet again, lives were changed forever. Bice and Kelly could never go home.

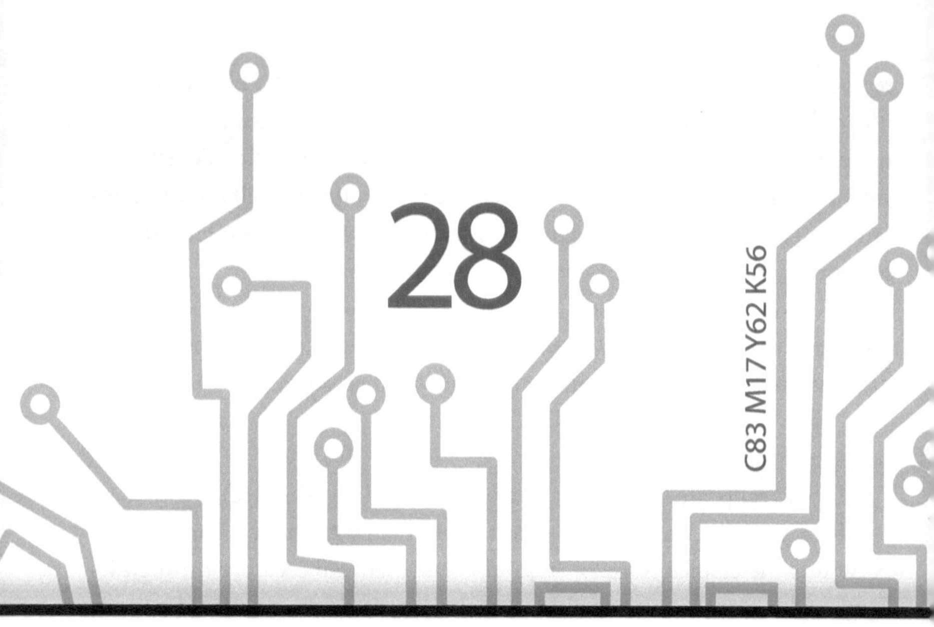

28

Without Lovat to guide us, Troilus Green and its guards would have caught us. Even so, I think we narrowly escaped. I could hear them spreading out in every direction from the shrine, searching every street and alley.

"Come, come!" Lovat urged. He rushed ahead and then back to us, frustrated by our inability to keep up with him.

"You try carrying someone and moving that fast," Rick grumbled through his teeth. I looked anxiously at Kelly; she still hadn't stirred.

"She'll be all right," Bice said, breathing hard.

"You can read my mind now too?" I asked. "What else can you do?"

He shook his head. "No mind reading," he managed.

I growled and kept moving. Explanations would have to wait.

Lovat must have taken us on a more circuitous route, because it seemed a lot longer before we reached the sanctuary. Stacy still waited at the door, as if she hadn't moved from that spot. At first sight, she hurried to meet us and helped Rick carry Kelly the last few feet.

Inside, we put Kelly on my cot. Bice washed his hands and knelt over her. He listened to her breathing, checked her pulse, and examined her injuries. "She might have a concussion," he announced. "I think she'll be fine. Just give her some time and a lot of rest."

I was reluctant to leave her, but there were things that needed to be discussed now. We moved out into the main sanctuary.

"What in the Chromatic Hells happened?" Stacy demanded. "You look like…"

At that moment, I could no longer maintain my own footing. I collapsed onto the ground, but waved away any help. "Sorry, just can't stay up any longer," I said. My muscles ached all over again. Kelly wasn't the only one who needed rest.

"Someone has some explaining to do," Rick declared. He folded his arms and looked at Bice. "That draconic had us dead to rights. We were headed for lockup and execution, and then this guy… did something."

"Magic," I said. "That was magic. And you told us you didn't know what it was!"

Bice sat down as well, gesturing to the others to do likewise. He sat still for a moment, as if collecting his thoughts. It was still strange to see him without a smile.

"When you asked me about the force that the draconic threw at you," he began, "I was honestly surprised. I did not know that the draconics had access to that power. I was not completely honest with you, but at the time, I saw no reason to reveal deep secrets of the dragon priesthood. After all, keeping their secrets is part of what has kept me safe all these years."

"Well, that's out now," Rick observed.

"You're right. But you'll pardon me if I'm still less than completely forthcoming. Some things are hard to explain, and some… it's hard to break a habit that is literally decades old." He paused again.

"Hundreds of years ago, when the worship of Viridia began, he took the earliest priests into his confidence and revealed secrets of The Circle to them. The locations of our cities are not random, nor were they chosen just to be a proportional distance from the others. The cities are built over sources of power."

"Magical power?" I asked.

He shrugged. "Some call it that. As I did tell you, some also call it divine. I don't know for sure what it is. But its very existence is another major factor that convinced me the dragons are not gods."

"How so?"

"The dragons did not create this power. More importantly, they cannot access or use it in any way. It is beyond them," Bice explained. "Thus, they are not gods."

Rick could not sit still. He got back up and paced back and forth.

"This alters everything, even more than Loden's talk about the dragons dying! How could this have been kept such a secret all these centuries?"

"As I said, this was revealed to the earliest priests, and they were extremely cautious about allowing others to learn about it," Bice said. "Until you told me about the draconic using it, I thought that only a handful of the high priests truly understood it."

"And you."

Bice nodded. "Yes, and me. Around twenty years ago, a foolish high priest, who was a friend of mine, told me about it. He thought it would sustain my wavering faith. It did the opposite. Since then, I have studied and practiced and experimented on my own. I'll wager that I know as much now as just about anyone in Viridia."

"You said Viridia revealed this to the priests," Rick said, pointing at him. "Why would he do that? Did he want the priests to have this power? What about the other dragons? Have they told their priests?"

"I'm… not entirely sure." Bice hesitated. "I know that the gold dragon's priests use the power; we have traded information with them. But I have a feeling it's not known in every city. Perhaps there's something about gold and green? Maybe they were instrumental in choosing the city locations? I just don't know."

"There must be a source of this power in the Blasted Lands too," Rick said.

Bice cocked his head, thinking. "I would assume there is. But I don't recall hearing of the power being used in the battle against the humans there… not that it would have helped against the rage of six dragons. Perhaps the black priests didn't know."

"If these sources of power are so important, why make one inaccessible in the Blasted Lands? Why wouldn't they just claim it for themselves?" Rick continued to pace.

I looked at him curiously. "Why are you so upset about this?" I asked.

He waved his arms in the air. "This changes everything! We've been trying to figure out how to survive here, and how to lead an uprising against the dragons themselves… and now we discover that their servants have magical powers? Even more than the fortek they've kept from us?"

"Formag." Stacy chuckled without much humor.

"If it helps, you don't have to think of it as magic," Bice said. "All I can say is that it's some kind of energy, buried in specific spots here in The

Circle. It's only accessible in and around the cities. You can call it science, if you want—just a science we don't fully understand yet."

Every time I turned around, it seemed my understanding of the world changed in radical ways. Keeping up with all of it made my head hurt. But something about it being restricted to the cities set something off within me. A new piece of the plan fell into place in my mind.

"Beryl," Bice said softly. "I think there's something you need to deal with over there." He gestured with his chin toward the back of the room.

I looked where he indicated and saw Lovat curled up in his blanket, facing the wall. His little body was shaking. I could hear faint sounds coming from him and realized that I had been hearing them in the background for some time without noticing. Was he… sobbing?

I looked back at Bice in confusion. "Why me?" I asked. "You would be—"

"You're the leader here," Bice interrupted. "And that's what he needs right now, I think. I believe I know why he's upset."

"Then it really seems like you should be the one going over there." I got to my feet and swayed. I knew better than to argue any further, though. Bice probably knew best. Somehow.

I walked over to the boy and crouched down a few feet away.

"Lovat?"

"Go 'way!" he sniffled.

"What's wrong, man? Can I help you?"

"No. 'M coward."

"What? No, you're not."

"Am so. Too scared. Didn't help."

"You mean back at the shrine? All of us were scared!" I inched a little closer. "I was absolutely terrified."

"You?"

"I was! I thought I was going to die, Kelly was going to die… we were all going to die," I confided. "I didn't see any way out. Bice saved us all."

Lovat only sniffled some more.

I put my hand on his shoulder. He didn't flinch. "If it weren't for you, Lovat, we would have been captured, anyway. You got us out of there. In fact, you're the reason we were there to begin with! You helped save Bice so he could save us, and then you got us all out! What did I do, compared to that?"

He turned his grubby face, now streaked with tears, to face me. "You fought."

"Fighting isn't everything." I shook my head. "Living is what's important. And without you, we probably wouldn't be living right now."

With a rush of clothing and blankets, he hugged my chest, holding me tighter than anything. I awkwardly put my arms around him too, and glanced back at the others. Bice was smiling again.

When Kelly finally woke up, she found me sitting by her side. I guess we had switched roles. I was exhausted myself, but I had to stay awake for her.

She woke with a moan and started to lift up. "Wait, wait," I said, touching her shoulder. "Don't get up."

"My head…"

"It's okay. Lie still. You're going to be all right."

She opened her eyes and looked at me. Disheveled and bruised, she was still beautiful. I almost lost her. The thought killed me. I swallowed hard, then hurried to get her a drink of water and some painkillers.

After she drank, she asked, "What happened?"

I described what had taken place, from the moment Troilus Green had exploded the roof under her. She listened in shock and horror to the strange events, from the draconic holding her hostage to Bice's power. By the end of my story, she was crying softly.

"He saw me; he knows me," she whispered.

"What?"

"The draconic. He knows me now."

I reflected on that. "Yeah, I guess he does."

"I can't go home. I can't see my parents. I can't…" She was breathing harder and harder. I think that's what you call hyperventilating.

I grabbed both her hands. "Stop. Calm down!" I insisted. "You don't know…"

"Yes, I do. You said he recognized you from all the way back at the accident. He's already met me, at the Guard station, when he interrogated me. And now he's seen me again, with you." Her words came faster and faster. "He knows me. He knows where I work. He knows where I live."

She was freaking out. And the worst thing about it: she was absolutely right. Troilus Green knew all of those details by now. She had become a fugitive, like me. It wasn't a big deal when I became one, because I had no family and really no belongings of any value or sentiment. Kelly had a real life, parents who cared about her, a home… and it was all gone now. Troilus Green and the dragon would not ignore her.

"Listen to me, listen!" I tried. I resisted the urge to shake her. Her breaths came out so hard and fast. I took her face in my hands and looked straight into her eyes. They were wild with fear.

"My parents… what if he…"

"Listen. It's not the end. Our plan is coming together. When we succeed, Troilus Green will never bother us again. I promise."

"How do you know? You can't know that! You can't!"

"Yes. I can. Bice just gave me the information I needed."

She looked confused, but it seemed to calm her a little bit. "What do you mean?"

I spoke slowly and firmly. "Troilus Green's power doesn't work outside the cities. And that means it's more vulnerable. I will make sure it's on the train when our plan comes together. And then I will kill it."

"You will?"

"I promise. With him dead, there's nothing to stop you from going home. Trust me. The plan is coming together. It won't be too much longer. And then it'll be over." It would really just be starting, but that wasn't what she needed to hear.

"I… I… My parents, Beryl. My parents. They won't even know what's happened. They'll be worried sick. They…"

"Write them a letter," I urged. "I'll have Lovat deliver it to them. You can tell them whatever you need to."

"A letter," she repeated. I was getting through. "Okay. I can do that."

"But not right now." I let her go. "We're all exhausted. We need more rest. You too. Bice said that's what your head needs most."

"It does hurt a lot."

I spread my blanket out beside her and laid down myself. "Let's just… rest," I said. "Rest is good." I must have been really tired. I sounded like an idiot. But at least Kelly's breath had slowed.

"Goodnight, Beryl," she whispered.

"Goodnight, Kelly."

I drifted off to sleep, but the face that kept coming to my mind wasn't Kelly's. It was the face of the priest-guard as I stabbed him.

When I woke up, I found Kelly awake and waiting. She had already written her letter. I took it to Lovat before doing anything else. Rick sat nearby sharpening the swords as I gave Lovat directions to Kelly's home.

"Did you read it?" he asked.

"What? No. Why would I do that?"

"You should read it and make sure she doesn't give anything away," he answered. He examined the blade and looked back at me with raised eyebrows.

I hesitated. I knew he was right, but somehow I couldn't bring myself to do it. It felt like betraying her, after all I had told her. I needed to give her some trust, didn't I? I handed the envelope to Lovat.

"Only give it to one of them in person. Tell them it's from Kelly. Don't stay, don't answer any questions," I told him.

"Got it." The boy took off.

"I hope we don't regret that," Rick mumbled. I gave him an annoyed look and went to look for a place to relieve myself. Stupid toilet still wouldn't work.

I came back inside and decided to leave Kelly alone for a while. Bice slept in the other side room. I hesitated and then sat down next to Rick.

"Feeling any better?" he asked.

"I think so. Things are moving so fast, though. I keep wondering whether I'll ever have time to completely recover."

He grunted. "And Kelly?"

"She freaked out last night, but I think she's okay this morning."

He grunted again and kept working on the sword.

"Rick… was that the first person you've killed?"

He stopped and looked up. "That's what's bothering you, huh?"

I nodded.

"Not the first for me," he admitted, "but I remember it."

"I keep seeing that guy's face," I told him. "I see the blood. I see Bice trying to save him. I tell myself he deserved it, but…"

"It's normal. The first time I killed someone…" He looked up toward the sun coming through the high windows. "It's been a long time. I remember hating this guy so much. He had mistreated me horribly when I was young, thought he could get away with it. But then I grew up. I got strong. I don't think he ever saw that coming." Rick's eyes gleamed in the sunlight, and his face hardened. "When I cut his throat open, he deserved that and so much more."

He looked back at me. "But I'll never forget the look of shock on his face," he admitted. "It was… satisfying and horrible at the same time." Satisfying and horrible. I only had the horrible part. I'm not sure I wanted it to be satisfying.

"Have you gotten used to it?"

"Used to it?" He shrugged. "I don't know if I'd say that. But I live with it."

It wasn't the answer I wanted, but I didn't know what else to say. Our goal was to kill the dragons, but they had human servants that would try to stop us. What else could we do?

"On another topic," Rick said, sheathing his sword, "we're now going to have six people sleeping here, at least for a while, five guys and one girl. Do we give Kelly a room of her own, or are you going to be sleeping in there with her?"

"I hadn't even thought of that."

"Liar."

Okay, yes, I had thought of it. Kelly and I were "together," and while our kisses were getting more passionate, I didn't think she'd be okay with us jumping straight to sleeping together. While we didn't have to depend on the dragons to give us permission for that kind of thing, it still wasn't… I don't know. Some traditions went beyond dragon law.

"I'd go for it, if I were you."

"Oh, yeah?"

He shrugged. "Why not? You've got nothing to lose. And we know that any day now, one of us could die. Why waste time?"

That was a fair point, but I was reluctant to use it. Somehow, it seemed like coercion, like I was saying, "You'd better sleep with me now, because I might die tomorrow, and you'll regret it." I don't know what exactly made me feel that way, but… there it was. Maybe I was just too much of a nice guy.

Not like Rick. Sometimes he said things that disturbed me, but I didn't want to argue with him. It felt so good having a friend my own age. I didn't want to jeopardize that in any way.

"Also…" Rick said. "We're going to have some supply issues pretty soon. Since Bice can't bring us anything else, we're going to run out of food."

"You're just full of happy thoughts, aren't you?"

He shrugged. "Someone's got to think of these things, and since you're the leader…"

"Why does everyone keep saying that? I never asked to be the leader."

"Whether you asked for it or not, everyone looks to you. You keep proving it, leading the charge to rescue Bice, comforting that kid last night…" Rick stood and started to walk away. "It's part of your nature. I suggest you take it and go for it, as far as you can."

30

"Not there."

I looked at Lovat in confusion as he handed me Kelly's letter back. "You mean they weren't home? You didn't wait for them?"

He shook his head. "Vir'dian Guard trashing place. No one else."

Oh. That was bad. Very bad. It meant Kelly's parents had been taken in, probably arrested. I glanced toward the back room where she rested again. I put the letter into my pocket.

"Don't tell anyone else about this, Lovat, okay? I'll deal with it." I couldn't tell Kelly about this in her current condition. It would destroy her. This whole leadership thing wasn't much fun.

Over the next few days, we settled into somewhat of a routine. Don returned from his mission, having procured the digger and stashed it somewhere on Loden's instructions. Then, to my great relief, the miner fixed that stupid toilet.

"That's so hue!" I exclaimed. Don looked at me funny. Guess he wasn't up on modern slang. "What was the problem?"

"Some of the old pipes were rusted shut," he said. "I replaced them."

I told him about the roots I had cleaned out of the drain. He nodded. "That's actually pretty common," he said. "Happens all over the city."

That's weird. It's not like the city was full of plant life to generate the roots. Where did they come from?

Bice revealed he had already procured the green dragon's blood and that too, was safely in Loden's hands. He set about doing all that he could to help out around the sanctuary, cleaning, organizing and generally serving us far more than we needed.

That meant the next step of the plan depended on Loden. The rest of us just had to wait. I had no problem with this; we all needed some rest and recovery.

Aware of Kelly's plight, Stacy showed up with some extra clothes for her, along with other things I didn't want to know anything about. The two of them conferred frequently in private.

I sent Lovat to check out the bike shop, which he found closed. He checked Kelly's home twice more and even hung around the nearest Guard station a while, but could find no more information about her parents. I kept the letter. The longer I went without telling her, the more I realized I was only making things worse for when I finally did tell her… which made it harder than ever to think about telling her.

Rick and I practiced daily with the swords. He usually beat me in any serious sparring. Not only had he practiced more with Stacy, he could switch from right to left hand with ease. We also took turns on guard duty from the roof. With Bice's exile, we couldn't be sure our sanctuary would remain a safe place. Troilus Green or the priests would work out his connection to this place eventually.

When I wasn't practicing or on guard duty, I spent time with Kelly. With Stacy's help, she seemed to have recovered, for the most part, from the shock of our last encounter's consequences, but an aura of sadness followed her around sometimes. Nothing I said or did could dispel it. I felt even guiltier about not telling her the news.

Rick tried to press Bice for more information about the strange energy source, but the Heretic, as he now referred to himself, stayed tight-lipped. He didn't want to reveal any more, and nothing seemed to persuade him.

After four days of this, Loden showed up unannounced, Stacy in tow. I sent Lovat to the roof to relieve Rick and we all gathered in the sanctuary for another planning meeting.

"The train work is coming along and should be completed in a week or so," Loden explained. "I've chosen the location of our attack and started work on the trap, as well."

"So far, so good," I said. "What's next?"

"Well, here's the one big, gaping hole in our plan," Loden admitted. "I know how to trap and kill a dragon. You've worked out the perfect way to disguise it, so as to pin the blame on another dragon. So… how do we get the dragon, in this case Caesious, to walk into our trap?"

We all sat in silence for a moment. It was a rather massive hole in the plan. Why hadn't this occurred to us?

"I guess we can't just send him an invitation," Stacy broke the silence. "Dear Mr. Dragon, an assassination has been planned in your honor. Your presence is requested at the following date and time."

Don and Kelly chuckled, but they were the only ones. This was a serious conundrum.

"We can plant stories, rumors, something that would get his attention and draw him out," Rick suggested.

"Possible, but why wouldn't he just send humans or draconics to check it out?" Loden said. "It would have to be something that would require his personal attention. And we would have to pinpoint a fairly exact time range for him to show up. We can't just sit around and wait. Timing is important with this plan."

"It would help if you told us the rest of the details," Rick grumbled just loud enough to be heard.

"So we do need to send him a specific invitation," Kelly said. "Stacy's right… sort of. But how do we do that?"

Bice tapped his fingertips together. "I think there may be a way," he said slowly. Everyone looked at him.

"Rick and Stacy are both right," he observed. "Our rumor campaign is going well, from all reports. Word is spreading about a difference of opinion between Viridia and Caesious. Everyone is talking about how they're angry with each other. What if we use that to our advantage?"

"How so?" I asked.

"What we need is a message from Viridia himself, asking Caesious to meet him," Rick jumped in. "Is that what you're saying?"

Bice inclined his head. "Something like that. The problem is that dragons no longer communicate that way. I'm told they meet in person from time to time in the mountains, but it's not a regular occurrence. I've also read and heard some indications that they communicate to each other mentally, from mind to mind… or at least they used to. I'm inclined to think they've lost that ability."

"I ran across that too, in my studies," Loden confirmed. "I think they've lost it too. Or they're at least out of practice. I get the idea that over the centuries, the dragons have become more and more isolated from each other. They don't really need each other, and rely on their servants to handle the trade between the cities, for example."

"Yes, but these rumors are enough to convince them to speak to one another, I think," Bice pointed out. "I think it would make sense for one to contact the other. We just need to do it for them."

"That puts more of an urgency on the plan," Rick said. "We need to send this message before a real one gets sent."

"Good point," I agreed. "Loden, you might have to speed up that train work. Bice, do you have an idea of the form this message would take?"

He closed his eyes and continued tapping his fingertips together. "It's all about history," he said. "We need to appeal to Caesious based on ancient traditions, traditions that pre-date The Circle itself. We can have Viridia offer to meet him in a neutral location—our location—to… no, wait… wait…" He paused and cocked his head to one side.

"I'll need to send Lovat to, ah, borrow a book for me, to get this exactly right, but I think it can be done," he said at last. "We don't have Viridia offer to meet. We have Viridia offer an ancient apology, delivered by one of his fairest virgin daughters, as of old."

Everyone else looked at the girls. Stacy lifted her hands. "Don't look at me," she protested. "I work in show business. That train left the station long ago."

Kelly blushed and looked away. "I am," she whispered. Rick nudged me, but I felt better about not pressuring her over the past few days.

Stacy looked at me with a raised eyebrow. "Either you're too nice for your own good, or you work way too slow, boy."

Bice opened his eyes. "Oh… OH. No, no, no. I didn't mean that literally, necessarily. But now that you mention it, maybe dragons have a sense about that kind of thing. I don't know. That was the way it was done in ancient times."

"The apology?" Loden pressed.

"Right. If someone were making an appeal or an apology to a dragon, whether that someone were another dragon or a town full of people, they would send out one of their... virgin daughters to meet the dragon at a designated time and place," Bice explained. "The girl would present the appeal and then, uh... she would sing to the dragon."

"Sing?" Kelly turned to Stacy. "This is sounding much more like something you should do!"

Stacy looked thoughtful. "It would be the performance of a lifetime," she admitted. "My career's going to be over when all this erupts, anyway. May as well go out with something fantastic. Um... these appeals didn't end with the dragon eating the 'virgin daughter,' did they?"

"Not unless the dragon was unhappy with the message," Bice answered.

"But in our case, the dragon will be dead," Rick said. "It doesn't really matter what he thinks of the performance."

"To some extent it does," Loden said. "We'll need to get him in position and keep him there just long enough."

"As I said, I'll find the proper protocol, and I believe this will work," Bice concluded. "We just have to be sure Caesious gets the message."

31

Bice explained what he needed to Lovat and sent him out. Since the boy couldn't read, Bice had to describe how the book looked in some detail. I hoped it would work out.

Bice sat for quite some time with Stacy and Kelly and discussed dragon etiquette. Apparently, once upon a time, it was very important. From what I heard of their discussion, it sounded nothing like what I had overheard in the Emerald Ascendancy. Times had changed. Bice hoped this ancient appeal would arouse Caesious' curiosity enough to bring him in person. I had to admit it sounded like a good plan. The only part that sounded off was the delivery system. Loden had a vague idea of sending the message on a train, but that didn't seem direct enough.

Every time I thought we had a great plan, someone (like me) would find another problem in it. It gave me a headache. Of course, even when we had plans, they didn't work out very well, like the Emerald Ascendancy adventure. I had a fleeting thought about Mason. I wondered if he kept his mouth shut. Well, at least Kelly wouldn't feel obligated to meet up with him again. She could stay safe here with us.

Two days later, Stacy was running me through a workout when we heard an urgent banging on the roof. We looked up and saw Rick scrambling through the trapdoor as fast as he could. "Viridian Guard!" he yelled. "They're moving this way in a systematic fashion!"

A look of shock and desperation swept over Stacy's face. "Now? But I…"

"Let's go, let's go!!" I yelled. I took a swift look around. We couldn't just run and hide and come back. There were too many supplies lying around here. Too much evidence. They would know we had been here. We needed to grab what we could and run.

"I can't be seen. I can't. I—"

I grabbed Stacy by both arms as Kelly, Bice, Don and Lovat all came on the run. "Stacy! It's okay. Get your stuff and we'll get out of here!"

Rick rushed down the balcony stairs. "They'll be here in a couple of minutes! I saw at least two squads and two draconics!"

"How did—?" Kelly began.

"It's the Viridian Guard! It doesn't matter!" I said. "Gather up essentials, whatever you can carry, and let's get out of here! Lovat, lead us through the back ways!"

He nodded and watched while we ran around grabbing things. Unconcerned, he found his favorite blanket, rolled it up, and stuffed it inside his shirt. Then he picked up the electric lantern I had given him.

Through it all, Stacy seemed in a state of shock. She put the practice sword down and pulled on her hoodie, her movements slow and deliberate. I sympathized, but there wasn't time to worry about her career. Now was the time to worry about lives.

I grabbed my sword and gave her a gentle push. The others were already moving out of the doors. "Come on, Stace. If we hurry, no one will ever know you were here."

"Time's up!" Rick called from the doorway. "We have to leave NOW!"

I urged Stacy outside only to remember one of the most crucial things. "The tooth!" I turned and rushed back inside. The backpack holding the precious dragon tooth had been overlooked in our rush. I grabbed it and slung it on my back. I spared a parting glance around our old home. The sanctuary, while it had once been used for evil, had been a good shelter for us. I wouldn't miss that stupid toilet, though.

"Spread out!" I heard from the front foyer. They were already here! I turned toward the back, only to hear more voices. They were coming in from both sides! I spun around in a circle. Where could I go?

"Hey! Stop where you are!" The first Viridian Guard had entered the sanctuary and raised his shockspear to throw.

I looked up, triggered an enormous boost, and jumped. This balcony was a good bit higher than the one in the restaurant from weeks earlier, and had a taller railing. To my surprise, I made the jump with room to spare. Loden had been right about my capabilities, it seems.

"He's on the balcony!"

"Hurry!"

Above the scattered cries of the Viridian Guard as they yelled at each other, I heard another voice. It started low, but built up into a massive roar. I took a quick glance over the railing and once again saw Troilus Green march in below me.

I had no time to consider. The guards would reach the top of the stairs at any moment. I took a quick running start and leaped through one of the sanctuary's high windows.

I exploded through the glass, shielding my eyes with one arm. As I emerged into open air, I saw everything with amazing clarity. The ground waited for me over thirty feet below. The rest of the team moved down an alley up ahead, with two hanging back. Bice and Rick, I think. One lone Viridian Guard had already rounded the front corner, pointing and yelling.

As I fell, two more of the high windows exploded above me. Troilus Green was lashing out with its power.

I gave my legs as much of a boost as I could, hoping to diminish the impact. As I hit the ground, I let go of the sword to keep from cutting myself in half. I rolled forward, banging my knees, elbows and head. The backpack's straps ripped, and it tumbled away from me.

For a brief moment, I lost my bearings and maybe even consciousness. Rick skidded to a stop next to me. "You all right, cyber boy?"

I shook my head to clear it. With Rick's hand to steady me, I got to my feet. Noticing the sword nearby, I stooped to pick it up.

At that moment, a strange feeling swept over me. The ground seemed to vibrate and the air thicken, exactly as it had in the shrine. The voice of Troilus Green grew louder and louder from within the sanctuary.

"Move, move, move!" Bice's voice urged.

I turned to look for the backpack. A rumble swept over us, followed by a creaking and straining sound. The backpack lay on the ground behind me, about ten feet away. Rick sprinted toward it.

Troilus Green's voice reached a sound level that hurt my ears. And that's when it happened.

The entire side wall of the sanctuary ripped apart from the rest of the building and toppled toward us.

My brain refused to let my body react. I was in two places, two times, all at once. In one, my mother screamed and my father shoved me as hard as he could. In the other, Rick grabbed the backpack and spun back, moving as fast as he could, losing his balance. In both, a massive wall of bricks fell toward me.

I snapped out of it and focused on the present. The guard that had come around the corner backpedaled and ran. Bice stepped beside me and screamed something I couldn't hear, thrusting his arms upward. Rick stared into my eyes as he ran toward us, still a couple of yards away.

A thunderous roar echoed through the streets as the wall crashed down around us. Whatever Bice did shielded the two of us somehow. A hailstorm of bricks rained down around us. Kelly screamed. A massive dust cloud erupted all around.

"Rick!" I yelled. I lunged toward him. He lifted his head and shook the dust off, but I could see his lower half buried under a pile of bricks.

Bice beat me there and pushed debris aside. Mocking laughter rippled out from the sanctuary. Even as I grabbed a brick and tossed it aside, the roof of the sanctuary collapsed inward. A fearsome shadow moved through the dust cloud.

Rick shoved the backpack containing the dragon's tooth at me. His dust-caked face locked onto mine with an intensity I'd never seen. "GO!" he snarled through clenched teeth.

I grabbed the backpack and ran. Bice followed me, and the words I heard coming from his mouth were not very priest-like.

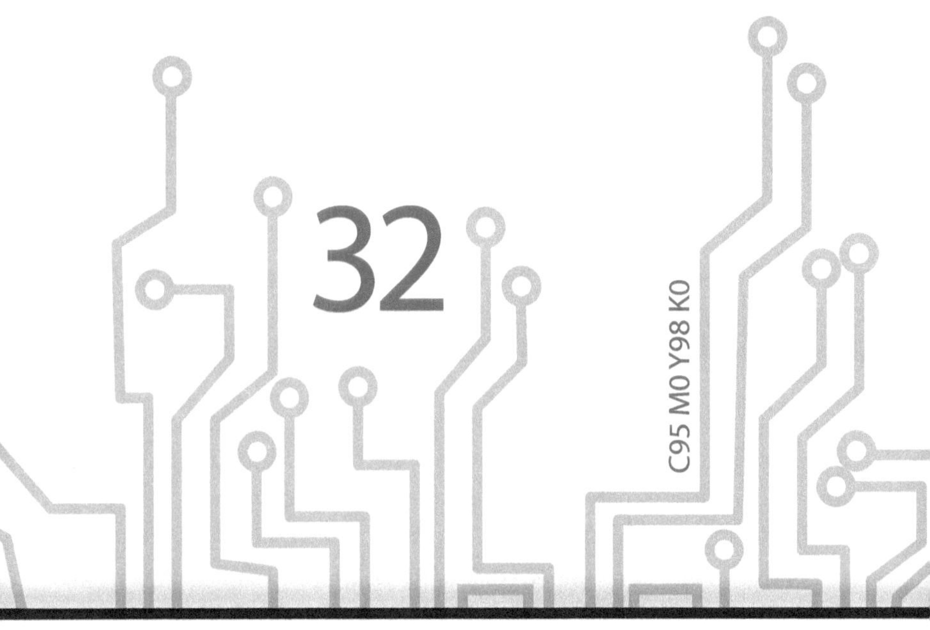

The other four stared in horror as Bice and I joined them. "Let's move!" I ordered. "Come on!"

"But Rick—"

"We can't help him, Kelly. Lovat, lead the way!"

The boy raced down the alley, trusting us to keep up with him. I spared a quick glance backward and saw Troilus Green bending over the spot where I knew Rick still lay. A crowd of guards joined him. Everything in me wanted to run back and fight, to defend my friend. But the odds were too high, and he had wanted me to go. I fought the lump in my throat and coughed dust.

Lovat turned another corner, then backpedaled. We all caught up with him and saw several Viridian Guard members moving in our direction. One of them let out a shout.

"Keep moving, keep moving!" Don urged.

Lovat took us down a different alley, climbed over a pile of garbage and ducked under a low-hanging fire escape. He pointed ahead and turned on to another street, almost colliding with a cyclist.

We had gone about thirty feet in the new direction before someone yelled, "There they are!" Lovat dodged down the nearest left, but it would be clear to our pursuers which way we had gone.

"We need to split up!" Bice said. "There's too many of us! Makes it easy for them to spot us!"

"We need a destination to meet at," I said. "And a second guide."

"I can do it," Bice said. "I know the streets well enough."

"The train station," Don suggested, repositioning the bag of tools on his back.

"Right. I hope Loden can hide us." Before I could say anything else, Bice had grabbed Kelly's sleeve and pulled her down an alley to the right. I was about to follow when a shockspear bounced off the wall in front of me.

I spun and found a Guard right in my face. Instinctively, I swung my sword and slammed the hilt against his forehead. I guess he had been moving too fast to defend himself. He collapsed against me.

Two more Viridian Guards ran around a corner right in front of us. Before they could react, Don stepped up and swung his wrench at the nearest one's head. He went down hard. The second brought up his shockspear in time to parry a second blow from the big miner.

I didn't want to risk cutting anyone, so I tackled the Guard and took him to the ground. Another blow from Don's wrench put him to sleep. As I climbed to my feet, I took a moment to sheath the sword and put it on my back.

"C'mon! C'mon!" Lovat begged, hurrying ahead of us. On a whim, I grabbed one of the dropped shockspears as I followed.

I knew Lovat could move faster than any of us, but Don surprised me with his speed. The two of them weren't making it easy for us to keep up. I could have boosted myself faster, but I didn't want to leave Stacy lagging behind.

"There!" The voice came from behind us, but not too close.

Lovat made the mistake of glancing back as he rounded the next corner and collided with a large food cart. The owner, a bearded man in a whitish apron, seemed unfazed.

"Ho, Lovat, what's happening?" He knelt and helped the boy to his feet. Lovat looked around and grabbed his fallen lantern. "Pursuit?" the vendor asked. Lovat nodded.

"Go." The vendor moved to push his cart again. "I'll do what I can."

"Thanks, Lance," Lovat mumbled. He grabbed a sausage sandwich from the cart as he took off again.

I heard the sausage vendor chuckling as we ran on past several more food carts. A few moments later, I heard a loud crash and a cry of annoyance. "My cart! Watch where you're going! Viridia take you!"

Eating as he ran, Lovat guided us straight through a crowded shopping district. Exclamations of surprise and outrage followed us as we barreled through.

"Gods! What do you think you're doing?"

"Someone's in a hurry."

"Chromatic hells!"

"I paid for that sandwich!"

The only real difficulty came from keeping the shockspear to myself as I pushed through the crowd. When people caught a glimpse of me coming, they backed off. Even so, at one point, I couldn't stop, and a middle-aged man who didn't move fast enough got a jolt, sending him to the concrete. I leaped over him and kept going.

Stacy, however, wasn't prepared for a body lying in her way. She tried to avoid stepping on the man, spun to the side, and tumbled with an anguished cry.

I stopped, turned, and rushed back to her side. She sat up, but stared in horror at her foot.

"Are you all right? Can you stand?"

"It's my ankle," she answered. "I think—oooh, I broke it last year in a stage accident. It might—agh—be broken again!"

Don appeared next to me. He handed me his wrench. "Uh, why do I—" I started to say, then realized he was bending down to pick Stacy up. Lovat came back and hopped from one foot to the other while he waited. Don lifted Stacy with surprising ease. "Let's go," he said.

We escaped the shopping district and entered another residential area. The streets were lined with apartment buildings, but very few people moved about the roads at this time of day. Lovat weaved in and out of the buildings, taking us on a confusing route that would leave any pursuit far behind. Don seemed to have no trouble keeping up while carrying Stacy. For her part, she bit her lip and tried to keep from crying out in pain. After a few minutes of this, we slowed our pace to a walk.

"Think we lost 'em," Don observed.

"Yeah, I hope the others did as well." I worried about Kelly, but she had Bice with her. If things got desperate, he had a few tricks of his own.

We still weren't very inconspicuous, or at least I wasn't. It wouldn't be hard to notice someone carrying a large wrench and a stolen shockspear with a sword strapped on his back. I couldn't look normal anywhere in Viridia right now.

After some discussion, Don and I decided to find a place to hide until dark, at which point we would make the rest of our way to the train station. We had at least another ten miles to go, and carrying Stacy that far would be wearing, even on our amazing miner. Fortunately, finding an empty building was never much of a problem in Viridia. When buildings were abandoned, for whatever reason, they often remained that way. Since the dragon maintained the city's population at a precise level, no one new would be moving in.

Once inside one of those buildings, Don lowered Stacy to the ground. I knelt down beside her ankle, which looked horribly swollen, turning several shades of blue and purple. I wasn't sure what one did for a broken ankle. Should we bind it up?

"Just leave it, Beryl," Stacy said with a grimace. "I need real medical attention, and quick." She gritted her teeth and a high-pitched groan escaped her lips.

"What can we do?"

"We? Nothing. Don and I will handle it."

"I will?" Don jerked his head back.

Stacy looked up and give him a tight smile. "Yeah, big guy. You will." She took a deep breath. "You're going to carry me to the theater district. It's closer than the train station. I'll find a friend to help me get to a doctor."

"What will you tell them?" I wondered.

"Beryl, love, I'm an actress. I make stuff up all the time."

"I don't know if I can find my way back," Don said, rubbing the back of his neck.

"Lovat, go with them," I said. "I'll wait here until you get back."

I took Stacy's hand. "It'll be okay. Loden can hide the rest of us and the plan will continue. Just… take care of yourself for now."

She looked back, sympathy in her eyes. "Don't give up on Rick," she whispered. "After all, I haven't given up on—agh!" She reached for her ankle and then pulled back and ran her hand through her hair, grimacing.

Don knelt back down and lifted her again. The three of them left the building and hurried down the twilit street.

I wondered who Stacy had been about to mention. She had lost someone to the dragon too, it seemed. I had been curious as to why she joined us. Out of everyone in our group, she had the best life, after all.

My thoughts turned back to Rick. Troilus Green had been after him even before we met. What was happening to him now? I didn't think he would tell anyone about Loden and our plan, but what if they tortured him? What if they just executed him?

For the first time in my life, I had a good friend my own age, and now he was gone. Inwardly, I made a promise. No matter what it took, I would get Rick back.

While I waited, I took some time to examine the shockspear I had appropriated. The normal length appeared around two feet, but it had an extension that could slide out and snap in place, adding another eight or nine inches. The "shocking" part of the spear was only contained in the first foot or so. I chuckled in delight when I discovered the switch that turned the power on and off.

About an hour later, Lovat and Don returned. Don said Stacy would be okay, but he didn't say much else. We left the building, and Lovat led the way again. We took a much more direct route now, though we kept an eye out for any enemies along the way.

We spotted a single Viridian Guard on patrol. At first we bypassed him, but then I got an idea and motioned for the other two to follow me back. I crouched behind a garbage can and got a good look at the Guard. He looked about my exact size, which is precisely what I wanted. This might be the way to get Rick back.

Following my instructions, Lovat "accidentally" dashed around a corner right in front of the Guard, stopped short, and then ran back. The Guard yelled and followed him, of course, into a blind alley where Lovat pretended to be trapped. As the Guard moved toward his prey, I snuck up behind him.

"Bleaking orphan brat," the Guard snarled. "Time to say goodnight."

"My thoughts, exactly," I said as I tapped him with the shockspear. He spun around and looked at me. I checked the switch. The power was on. Why hadn't he...?

"Uhm. I guess your uniforms are insulated against your own shock-spears." Idiot. It made perfect sense, of course. Otherwise, how often would they be accidentally electrocuting each other or themselves? I had been carrying one for a few hours, feeling paranoid the whole time.

He grinned at me. "Something like that." And then he swung his own shockspear.

I wasn't insulated. As the shock passed through my body, all of my muscles stiffened. I lost all control over my body as pain erupted everywhere. I think I screamed something obscene. Then I fell. The pain already wracking my body prevented me from feeling the impact when I hit the ground.

I could see the Guard looking at me, still grinning. Then Lovat landed on his back, and pounded at his head with tiny fists. The Guard yelled something, but before he could do anything else, Don stepped over my body and punched him in the face. Lovat leaped clear as the Guard slumped to the ground.

They both knelt over me. Soreness blossomed everywhere, but the pain faded, and I regained control of myself. I pulled myself up on an elbow and pointed at the Guard.

"Take his uniform off."

The train station was a long, low building, newer than most in the city, but definitely not built with aesthetics in mind. Aside from some windows and signs directing people around, it was mostly a big chunk of concrete. Typical for Viridia.

We avoided the busy parts of the station, where people were loading and unloading cargo, even at this time of night. Don and I waited in the shadows while Lovat snuck in to see if he could find Loden. He emerged victorious a few minutes later, followed by the technician. Loden's eyes widened at seeing us and got even bigger when he understood what had happened. Bice and Kelly had not arrived.

Loden brought us inside to his workshop. "Everyone else has gone home already," he explained. Lovat, sensing my concern, announced he would look for the other two. After dropping off his blanket and lantern, he went back out into the streets.

"This is troublesome." Loden paced back and forth. "I don't know where you can stay, the new engine isn't ready, and we haven't even sent the message yet. Plus, if Rick tells them anything…"

He went on, but I didn't really listen. I stared in awe at everything around me. Don set down his bag of tools and whistled as he looked around too.

Loden's "workshop" was far larger than any I had seen in the Emerald Ascendancy. You could have fit a dozen bike shops inside it… and then stack another dozen on top of that! I guess it had to be that large considering the size of the projects they worked on in here. At the west end of the room, three huge sliding doors admitted railroad tracks that spanned the length of the workshop. Sitting on those three tracks were two older train engines, three boxcars, Loden's new engine and a pair of bright new passenger cars. Another engine hung from cables high enough for workers to walk underneath it. There were tools and devices all over the place, some I recognized and some I couldn't comprehend at all.

Loden's new engine looked spectacular. Unlike the older engines that looked blocky and ugly, this new car defined sleek and streamlined. I marveled at the smoothness of its curves and reached out to touch it. "It's a beauty," I said. Of course, the color scheme could be better. Shades of green were getting so old. The blue stripes were a nice touch, though.

"Had to make it look attractive," Loden observed, coming up beside me. "But it's what's inside that matters."

"The weapon?"

"Oh, that too. But I was talking about the motor. The speed of this thing is amazing. I've already had some pushback from a few more close-minded technicians telling me man wasn't meant to travel that fast."

"What did you tell them?"

Loden chuckled. "I told them that if Viridia himself approved this method of travel, who were they to question it?"

Don had walked around the room and came back. "I have an idea," he offered.

It was so rare for him to speak without being addressed, I was almost too surprised to answer. "What is it?"

He pointed over his shoulder at a boxcar set further away from everything else. "Are you doing anything with that one?"

"No, the axles on it got twisted somehow. It's just sitting there and waiting until someone has time to make new ones," Loden said. "It's very low priority."

"Why don't we stay in there?"

"You mean during working hours?" Loden scratched his chin. "It wouldn't be very comfortable, and you'd have to keep quiet. We get pretty noisy in here, so it would hard to sleep. When everyone leaves, you could come out here, but even then, you'd have to keep things low-key to avoid attracting attention from outside. Other than that… sure, why not?"

Don and I went around behind the boxcar and opened the large sliding door on the opposite side. The boxcar had plenty of room inside for those of us who would need space to hide during the day. Loden's list of short-comings was accurate, but for lack of a better plan, I supposed it would have to work. At least the workshop had a fully operational restroom.

Loden prepared to shut down for the night. He was showing me how to operate all the lights in the workshop when we heard a knock at the door. Before I could hide, the door flew open and Bice appeared, followed by Kelly and Lovat.

We rushed to greet each other, talking over one another, exchanging stories and expressing concern. Kelly hugged me until I had to push her away so I could hear their story. They had never been in any real danger of discovery, but had been forced to swing around a pretty far distance before they could make their way back here. Both were exhausted.

With the current situation resolved, Lovat found a ladder on the side of the engine and climbed on top of it in seconds. As we talked, he wan-dered here and there, examining everything with wide eyes.

Loden put a hand on my shoulder. "Beryl, I have to leave, but tomor-row I'll—" He broke off and looked away. "Tomorrow, I'll help you get Rick back. It's… We'll get him back."

When Loden said it, I believed it.

34

With Loden gone, we turned off most of the lights. I explained our new sleeping arrangements to the rest of the crew. After some exploration and discussion, everyone agreed the first priority now was sleep. Lovat moved from the roof of the engine to the roof of the boxcar. When I suggested he join the rest of us inside, he turned me down. I realized he could go undetected up there just as well as we could inside, so I left him alone.

Loden returned early in the morning. He woke me and then Bice, gesturing for us to follow him and let the others sleep on. The three of us gathered at his workbench.

"First of all, I checked on Stacy," Loden said in a low voice. "She's in the hospital getting the best of care, due to her status. The ankle is definitely broken again, but she should be okay otherwise.

"Now, we have to decide some things quickly. The other workers will be here in about half an hour. The train is not ready, so we have a few days. We need to decide: is it worth going after Rick right now?"

"Of course it is!" I insisted. Bice nodded.

"Okay, then." Loden scratched his chin. "We'll see what we can do. Bice, I'll need you to stay with the others and keep things quiet. I'll give my workers their orders for the day and tell them to go home when they're done. Keep an eye on them but don't attract attention."

"We'll be fine," Bice answered. "I need to work on the letter to

Caesious."

"Beryl and I will see what can be done about Rick. If all goes well, we should be back by tonight, probably before the workers even leave." He hesitated. "If it doesn't go well… I'm not sure what to tell you."

"We'll flee the city," Bice said. "There won't be any other choice."

"Wait, wait," I broke in. "I don't want to risk the entire plan. Loden, I'll go alone. I stole a Viridian Guard uniform last night, and I can use it to—"

"To what?" he interrupted me. "Are you just going to walk in to the guard station and ask if any dangerous refugees have been brought in?"

"I… hadn't really thought it through yet."

"Exactly. And don't worry. I'm coming with you, but if there's anything too risky, we pull out. The plan is bigger than any one of us. Even Rick."

I took a deep breath. Loden was right, of course. I just wasn't ready to give up. Rick had crashed into my life and transformed it forever. I couldn't abandon him.

Bice rejoined the others. We found a place outside where I could wait for Loden. Once he welcomed all of his work crew and got them busy, he joined me and we set out. It felt a little odd not to have Lovat with us, but this mission wasn't about stealth and we knew the way well enough.

We walked with the rest of the pedestrians and cyclists on their early morning commutes. As always, no one scrutinised anyone else on the streets. On Loden's advice, I had left behind my sword and shockspear. He claimed the large bag slung over his shoulder held everything we needed. My curiosity about the bag's contents warred with my concern over Rick.

After about an hour, we approached the same Guard station I had visited when all this began. Troilus Green appeared to operate from here, making it the best place to look for Rick. We stopped about a block away and secluded ourselves behind some debris in an alley.

Loden opened the bag and removed an odd-looking rectangular metal box with several dials and buttons on it. He extended what looked like a tiny metallic pipe from the top. "They call this a 'talker,'" he explained. "It's for communicating over distance."

I had heard rumors of these devices all my life, but had never seen one. I found it hard to accept such a thing could work.

He fiddled with a dial. I heard a kind of metallic hissing and crackling from the talker, but nothing else. "We won't hear anything unless they use theirs, and I've tuned it to the right channel." He frowned and adjusted a dial again. The odd noise continued. "I'm pretty sure I have the right Guard channel. All we can do now is wait."

We waited. I tried not to be too impatient. My mind wandered, going back a day to watch that wall collapse again. It had literally looked the same as the falling wall that had taken my parents. Was the strange magic the priests and draconics commanded the cause of their death? Had I encountered it that far back?

I jolted out of my reverie as a voice came out of the talker. It was somewhat distorted and broken up by the strange crackling sounds, but I could make it out. "Station Four here. The high priest needs an escort from the Ascendancy back to his home. Anyone available at Station Three?"

Another voice responded almost immediately. "Station Four, we've got it covered. Thanks for the alert."

"Most of what we hear will probably be like that," Loden said. "We'll just have to hope we hear something about Rick."

"They can't hear us talking?"

"No, the talker doesn't pick up my voice unless I'm holding this button." He pointed.

We fell silent and waited. Two hours passed. From time to time, I got up and stretched my legs. Loden scribbled in a notebook, muttering to himself. I craned my neck for a quick glance once, but couldn't make any sense out of the drawing I saw. It looked like a lot of random shapes and lines thrown together.

I shifted and felt pressure on my leg. I moved and discovered the stone shard in my pocket. I had almost forgotten about it. I took it out and examined it. It seemed petty, somehow, to keep this. The image of the dripping blood flashed across my mind again. I closed my eyes and gripped the shard. This was why we were here. The dragon and his followers were evil.

The talker spoke again, this time discussing a dispute between some workers at the bio-hospital. Three guards were dispatched to take care of it. I thought of Kelly's parents again. How long could I keep that news from her? The longer I waited, the worse it made things. I shoved the shard back into my pocket.

Loden rummaged in his bag. "Here, let me show you something," he offered, holding an object up. It looked like a metallic cylinder sealed on both ends. "We may be able to use this if the timing is right."

"What is it?"

Loden smiled. "The Viridian Guard use these all the time. They're smoke canisters. You pull this handle"—he showed me—"and throw it. Smoke comes pouring out. It's irritating too. Makes people tear up and cough."

I hefted the canister and considered how far I could throw it. While the canister had possibilities, I couldn't help but feel annoyed at yet another example of technology only available to the dragon's chosen.

Over the next three hours, we overheard several more boring conversations on the talker, but nothing that seemed to reference Rick. Loden's bag held some water bottles and sandwiches that we consumed as the sun climbed higher. Why hadn't I brought the Guard uniform? It might be crazy to walk into the station, but at least it was action of some sort. I could walk in, toss the gas canister, and… the plan stalled about there.

Sometime after noon, we finally heard what we had been waiting for: "Station One, this is Station Four. Is the truck on its way? Troilus Green is nearly finished with the wanderer."

"That's him!" I exclaimed. "That's what Troilus Green called Rick: the wanderer."

"That's odd," Loden murmured, turning up the volume on the talker.

"Station Four, the truck's on the way," came the answer. "The driver and two guards will be ready to move the prisoner. What's the destination?"

"Station One, the destination is the Emerald Ascendancy, level seven."

"Hmp. I've never been on level seven," Loden observed. "Always wondered about that one."

"But now we know something!"

"Indeed we do. It appears they'll be moving Rick by truck. This will probably be the only chance we have to rescue him. Got any ideas?"

I smiled. "I'll need a bicycle."

35

As a child, I was in awe of the dragon's trucks. Bicycles were the primary method of travel on Viridia's streets, but the occasional truck drove by a few times a day. My young mind saw them like trains without rails: loud, dirty, and amazing. Motorized vehicles of any kind were reserved for the Viridian Guard and "cargo transportation as deemed vital to the city's needs." I underlined that phrase in a workbook one day and never forgot it, especially once I learned that "vital" meant "whatever the elite want."

I watched the truck stop in front of Guard station. It had a basic four-wheeled configuration, a front cab where two people could sit, and an enclosed rear area for prisoners or other cargo. Painted green, of course. If we heard right, Rick was about to be loaded into the back of that truck and taken away to the Ascendancy.

I looked down at the bicycle Loden and I had appropriated. I had deliberately looked for one much tougher-looking than my own. The last time I tried what I was about to attempt, I had wrecked my old bike. The remains of it were probably gathering dust in the back storage room of Brunswick's Bicycle Shop.

The driver and his companion were discussing something about one of the truck's front tires. The driver threw his head back, laughing. At that moment, his companion noticed the Guard station's doors opening. He pointed and the two of them straightened up, looking serious.

Rick came out of the station, escorted by two more guards. His hands were tied behind his back, but he looked otherwise all right, from what I could see. The two guards took him around to the back of the truck. As one opened the door, Troilus Green also emerged from the station.

I gripped the handlebars tighter. If the draconic came along, that might ruin the plan. Loden and I could deal with the guards, or at least I hoped we could, but Troilus Green was another matter. I didn't even have my sword.

The draconic talked to Rick while the guards waited. I saw Rick's head turn up toward the beast and could almost hear him respond with something sarcastic. Troilus Green didn't like his response. It lashed out with a quick blow that sent Rick tumbling to the street, unable to stop himself because of his tied hands. I winced.

I wondered what it would be like to control that strange power like Bice. I imagined myself throwing a wall of air right now, knocking the guards and Troilus Green back. It would certainly make things easier.

The draconic went back inside and the guards hustled Rick into the back of the truck. Both of them climbed in with him. With the driver and passenger, that meant four guards total.

As the truck started up, I began pedaling. The truck presented our best chance for rescuing Rick, but we couldn't do it right out in front of the Guard station. We needed to wait until they rounded a corner or two. Loden waited a few blocks away along the route we assumed they would take. We couldn't be sure about that route, however, which is why I got the bike.

The truck began moving with a jerk and a loud pop. I pedaled harder. I had almost reached the Guard station myself by the time the truck really got moving. I had no idea how fast the trucks were allowed to travel, but it was much faster than bicycles typically ran.

At this point, anyone else on a bicycle might be in trouble. I wasn't anyone else. A quick boost into my legs got them moving faster and faster. For the moment, I just needed to keep up with the truck, not overtake it.

We turned a corner, and I poured on the speed. I was gaining on them now. One more turn and we'd be at the right spot. I wondered if the driver or passenger could see me in a mirror, and if so, what they were thinking.

The second turn came up sooner than I had expected. They were taking a slightly different route than we had guessed. Loden would have to run to get to the new street.

I boosted my legs even further and began to overtake the truck. The bicycle protested, shaking and rattling. It had not been built for this kind of sustained speed.

From my back pocket, I pulled one of the gas canisters. "Please stay together," I whispered to the bike. If it gave out now… I pedaled as fast as I could and came up right beside the truck.

Keeping one hand on the handlebars, I brought the canister to my mouth and ripped the handle loose with my teeth. I caught a quick glimpse of the driver's stunned face gaping at me with open mouth before I tossed the canister right past him into the cab of the truck.

I stopped pedaling. Momentum kept the bike going for some time, but it wasn't enough to save it. I could feel the front tire coming apart. With one last quick boost, I leaped free and landed running on the street.

Ahead of me now, I saw smoke erupt out of the windows of the truck. A loud screeching sound drowned out any yells from within as it came to an abrupt stop. The rear tires lifted off the ground almost a foot before slamming back down.

I continued rushing forward, leaving the ruins of the bicycle behind. The doors of the truck's cab flew open, and the driver and passenger tumbled out, coughing and gagging. I let my momentum carry me straight at the driver, who managed to get his head up just in time for me to punch it. He slammed back against the truck's door and collapsed on the ground.

I came to a stop, but grabbed my fist with my other hand. That really hurt! My knuckles might be bruised. I always thought punching someone would hurt them, not me.

My eyes began watering, and I coughed a little. Great. I guess I ran through some of the smoke. From the other side of the truck, I heard a loud thump. I ran around the front and saw the passenger on the ground. Loden stood over him, holding what looked like an extendable baton of some sort. He had one hand over his face in an effort to protect it from the gas.

Loden gestured and we both ran to the back of the truck. I heard a commotion taking place inside. I didn't think much of the gas would have gotten into the back, but I couldn't be sure. There were still two guards to deal with, and they would have shockspears. I grabbed the door handle and looked to Loden, who had another gas canister at the ready. He nodded.

I yanked the door open. Loden lunged forward to throw the canister and then stopped himself.

Rick stood there with his back to us, pulling on his gloves. Both guards lay unconscious beside him.

"Umm. We're here to rescue you," I said, feeling stupid.

Rick turned around. He grinned through a mass of bruises and cuts. "Thanks, Beryl. I knew I could count on you." He leaped down beside us, stumbled and gave me a quick embrace. His clothes were torn in several places and I saw bloodstains at each tear. Both knees looked bruised and bloody from getting knocked to the street.

Loden looked in at the guards. "Impressive. How'd you pull that off?"

Rick shrugged. "When the draconic was knocking me around back at the station, it helped loosen the ropes around my wrists. By the time you guys got the truck to stop, I was free." He thumbed back at the unconscious guards. "They were facing the back, ready for anything. Except for me to come up behind them and knock their heads together. Got my gloves back, too." He held up his hands and wiggled his fingers.

"We'd better go before any more guards show up," Loden said. He turned away.

"Should we take the truck?" Rick asked. He looked like a small child asking to keep a pet.

"I think that would be a little difficult to hide." Loden chuckled and gestured for us to follow him.

Rick obeyed, but almost collapsed after three steps. I hurried to his side. For all his bravado, he was human like the rest of us. No one could go through what he had experienced in the last day and just saunter off.

"Guess I need more help than I thought," he admitted. With Rick leaning heavily against me, we hurried down the streets.

Getting Rick back to the train station without being noticed turned out to be much harder than anticipated. A fugitive refugee with the wrong chromark was much more noticeable when he couldn't walk without help and his face was covered in bruises. After a few attempts, Loden left us hiding in an alley again while he went back to his job. I tried to make Rick comfortable as we waited for evening. At least the team was back together now.

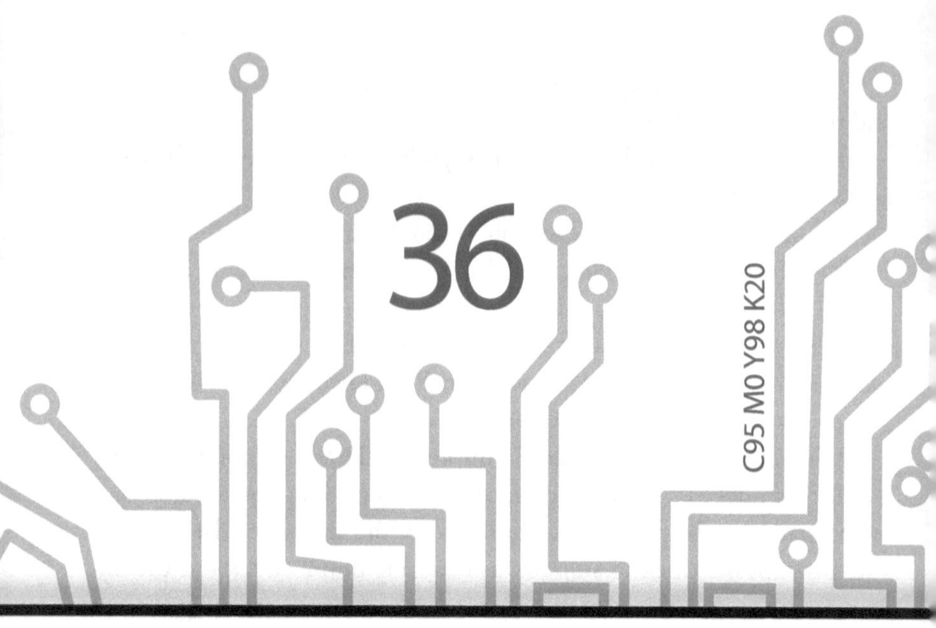

36

Rick needed rest, so I left him alone. He slept fitfully, muttering in his sleep. At one point, he began listing names, mine included. I wondered what he was dreaming, or if Troilus Green had coerced him into giving up those particular names. We could be in big trouble if he gave up Stacy or Loden. Then he said some other names I didn't recognize. Daub? Tinge? I couldn't tell for sure. Maybe those were some of the friends he'd lost in Atramentous. I realized how little I really knew about Rick's story. It seemed every time we talked, the focus was on the present, not the past.

As twilight drew near, Lovat showed up. He led us through some back ways, but took it slow for Rick. When we reached the train station, all the workers had gone and the rest of our team waited. Loden had already told them what had happened, but they were all still relieved to see Rick alive.

Kelly seemed more relieved to see me in one piece. We hadn't had any real time together since the sanctuary had been attacked. While Bice looked over Rick's injuries, we moved off to the side and found a quiet place to be alone. I kissed her until she finally broke us apart.

"Do you think Stacy will be okay?" she asked.

My brain took a few moments to adjust. "Stacy? She should be okay, except for the ankle."

"I mean, do you think she'll still be able to sing for the dragon?"

"Oh. I hadn't thought of that. I guess it depends on whether she can walk on it. Do you think there's another problem?"

"No, no. Her singing voice is amazing!" Kelly paused, then added lower, "Not like mine."

"I've never heard you sing, but I enjoy your speaking voice," I said. "You're probably better at singing than you think you are."

She snuggled a little closer. "You have to say things like that. You're my boyfriend."

"Does that make it less true?"

"Sort of. I don't know."

If I were really her boyfriend, shouldn't I have told her about her parents? Instead, I changed the subject.

"Did Bice finish the message?"

"I think so. He was working on it almost all day in the boxcar."

"I have an idea for getting the message to Caesious."

"Oh?"

I told her about ambushing the Viridian Guard and taking his uniform. "So I was thinking… I could deliver the message dressed in the uniform."

"That sounds crazy dangerous!" She pulled away. "Go to another city? In disguise? Haven't you done enough dangerous things already?"

"We have to do something. I think this is our best bet."

"Then… let Rick go. Or Bice."

"Rick has the wrong chromark, not to mention his injuries. And I suspect that Bice is now far more well-known and wanted than I am, after what he did at the shrine. The word has probably been spread about him." I didn't know that for sure, but to be honest, I really wanted this mission. Visiting another city would be an incredible experience, regardless of why I went.

"I just… I want you to live through all this," Kelly said slowly. "From what we talked about earlier, it didn't sound like you would have a whole lot left to do, and I was hoping… I was just hoping you would stay safe."

"Because you care about me?"

"Of course, you idiot!" She punched my shoulder lightly. "And… to keep myself from being absolutely terrified over what we're doing, I've been trying to think about after all this."

"After the dragons are gone?"

"Yeah. Do you ever think about it?"

I shook my head. "Not a lot. I've been so focused on right now that I haven't spared much thought for the future."

"What will we do if we win?"

What would we do? I had no idea. I just wanted to kill the dragons, setting free a million humans… after that? Who knows? "I dunno. I guess people will still need their bikes repaired."

"Could you go back to that?"

"I don't know." It would be strange, that's for sure. Acting like nothing had ever happened.

"When the dragons are gone, we'll need new leaders," Kelly pointed out. "Not rulers like they are, but leaders to help guide the people as we, you know, change everything. You would be one of those leaders, Beryl. You should be one of them."

Leading a small rebel band, a handful of people, was one thing. Being a leader of a city? I couldn't comprehend that. But what if Kelly was right? What if I had a real future after the dragons?

"I'm going to try the uniform," I told her, getting up.

Inside the boxcar, I stripped down and pulled on the Viridian Guard uniform. It fit pretty well. I had to cuff the sleeves a bit, but it still looked right, from what I could tell. There was one way to find out, of course. I picked up the shockspear and walked out into the open.

Rick was the only one who didn't know about the uniform. He charged halfway across the room to attack me before he recognized my face. "What in The Circle do you think you're doing?"

Kelly came up and checked the fit of the uniform. "I don't like it," she announced. "You need a different uniform."

"Maybe someday," I said with a grin. "For now, this one will have to do."

"What are you thinking now, lad?" Loden asked.

"I'm going to deliver Bice's message to Caesious. Does anyone see a better way?"

Loden and Bice both looked like they wanted to raise an objection, but couldn't think of one. "You already know my opinion," Kelly said. "I think it's an unnecessary risk."

"It's a great idea," Rick admitted. "I just wish I could go, instead."

"All right, then," I said. "What's our timetable?"

"The message is ready," Bice said. He brought out the document he'd been working on, a large sheet of parchment-style paper with very elaborate calligraphy. It looked impressive, to say the least.

"I have a hard time reading this," I admitted. "I didn't learn this kind of writing."

"It's only taught to the priests," Bice explained. "But the message is precisely what we agreed on. In simple terms, it speaks of regret over the nasty rumors that are circulating, a reminder of ancient agreements and alliances, and an offer to send a virgin daughter to meet him at a neutral location. This blank spot"—he pointed—"is for the date and time. Loden?"

The engineer scratched his chin, as usual. "The train is almost ready. Let's say Beryl leaves on the first train out tomorrow morning. He would be able to deliver the message and be back here tomorrow night, barring any trouble. We could ask Caesious to meet at noon three days later. I can arrange for the train's 'test drive' to take place then."

"If that's the best we can do, let's go for it." Bice took the document to fill in the information.

"This is really happening," Kelly said. "Four days from now—"

"We kill a dragon!" Rick exclaimed.

Loden tapped on a notepad. "I've already had the digger delivered to a pick-up location," he said. "I've been planning to arrange for the rest of you to travel there. I guess that'll have to be the day after tomorrow, after Beryl gets back. Then it'll just be up to Stacy at the meeting. And this baby." He patted the train engine again.

"So… your train *will* kill it, right?" I asked.

"Yes, I have little doubt of that. And then Don will use the digger to rip it up like teeth. Speaking of which, you did bring the tooth, right?"

"We've got it," I said. Rick snorted.

"So we plant that and the blood, and…"

"Then what?" Don asked.

"We find a place to hide and see what happens," Bice said, returning.

"We will need somewhere to go," Rick agreed. "Has anyone thought of that?"

"I have a place," Loden said. "Give me tomorrow and I should be able to explain."

It occurred to me that Loden was the absolute central key to this entire plan. Any of the rest of us were expendable, but if something happened to him… the whole plan would be gone, along with any chance of any of us surviving for very long. We had put our lives and everything else into his hands.

A loud knock rattled the workshop's side door. Loden shot a look that way, then motioned for the rest of us to hide. By the time he reached the door, we were all out of sight. I couldn't resist a peek around the side of the boxcar.

Loden looked outside. "Oh, my," he exclaimed and stood back, holding the door open.

Stacy entered the room on crutches.

"Everyone calm down!" she called, waving one hand as we all rushed out of hiding.

A flurry of discussion erupted as Stacy played up her stay in the hospital and the broken ankle. She insisted she could still go through with the plan.

"What do you think?" I asked Loden.

"I… I think it's a problem," Loden admitted. "When meeting the dragon, she has to stand in the right place, and then probably lure it to follow her into our trap. Plus, with all our fancy writing, I think Caesious would be insulted if our 'beautiful virgin daughter' turned up with an injury."

"You mean I can't face a dragon? I'm so disappointed." She didn't look like it.

"What do we do?" I wondered.

"There's a simple answer," Stacy said. "Don't worry about it. Kelly will take my place."

"What? No, I can't!"

Stacy swung herself over to Kelly's side. "Don't stress, love, you've got this," she soothed. "You've been with me practicing. You've heard it all."

"I can't sing!"

"Oh, yes. You can. I've heard you, when you didn't think I was listening." Stacy re-arranged herself next to Kelly with some difficulty. "Girl, you've got the voice for it. You just need a little instruction—which I can provide—and a whole lot of self-confidence."

"But I, I can't face a dragon!"

I wanted to say something, anything, to encourage her, but I felt sick about the whole thing. Kelly would have to stand in front of the dragon? If he got angry, he could bite her in half. If the train weapon failed, he would tear her to pieces. All sorts of horrible scenarios ran through my mind. And I still hadn't even told her about her parents. She looked at me, expecting something.

"You can do this." It wasn't me; it was Rick. He stood directly in front of Kelly, took her hand, and looked into her eyes. "I have absolute confidence that you can handle it. I've seen your courage and heard your voice. You have all that you need. I believe in you, and I think everyone else here does too."

We all murmured agreement. I felt a twinge of jealousy.

"It's settled, then." Stacy clapped her hands, then grabbed for her crutches again before she lost balance.

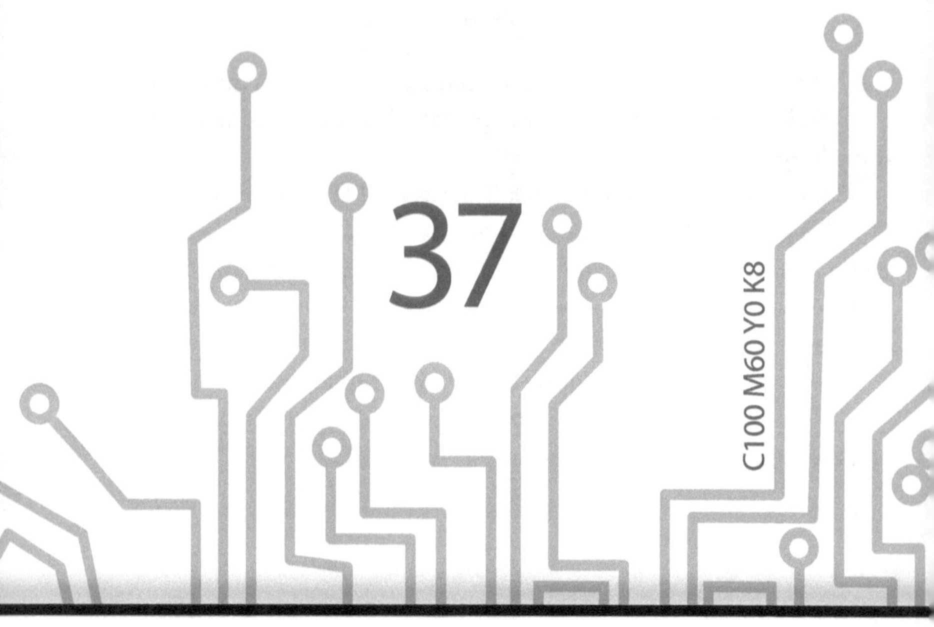

"This is your first train ride, isn't it?" Loden had asked.

I had simply nodded. No one got to travel to other cities simply for fun. You had to be involved in specific forms of trade, or be an entertainer like Stacy. I heard the dragons used to take part in science exchanges, letting researchers visit other cities, but that didn't happen much now. The dragons were becoming selfish of their scientific breakthroughs.

When the train first started moving with a jerk, I held back the urge to gasp. The sensation of motion shook me for a moment. I could feel the rumble of the engine and the movement of the wheels on the tracks.

Before now, the fastest speed I had traveled happened when I boosted my legs while biking. The speed I achieved in those moments had been exhilarating. I couldn't feel the wind while inside the train, so the sensation wasn't the same, but I knew we were traveling much faster than I had managed on the bike.

I couldn't stop staring out the windows. I was probably the most goggle-eyed passenger on board, not that there were very many. Aside from me, I saw a couple of trade representatives in fancy suits, and another Viridian Guard member, assigned to train duty on a regular basis. At first, he smiled to see me and tried to be a little chatty, but I told him I was on an important mission and couldn't share anything. I assumed an engineer, at least, worked up front, but I never saw him.

I did see parts of The Circle I had never seen before, at least in person. During my Learning Years, I had looked at plenty of pictures of the fields, forests and pastures that filled all the lands outside the cities. But I had never seen them in person, beyond the little you could see from a tall building. Now I saw so much life, so much growth. It wasn't as awe-inspiring as my awakening in the pine grove, but I felt almost the same as I had then. Green was still everywhere, but so were other colors, like yellow and brown. I knew some of the vast fields were wheat and corn, but I knew little else. Once again, I felt that strange desire to leave the cities for good, to stay away from all the metal and concrete, and enjoy the pureness of this outdoor world.

"We're approaching Caesious," one of the merchants observed. I shook my head. Had we been traveling that long already? I strained my eyes to get a glimpse of the blue city.

"Over here," the other merchant told me. I shifted to the other side of the passenger car and looked.

Up ahead, the train turned just before it crossed a large river and entered the city of Caesious. Stacy had told me the river encircled the entire city, which I found fascinating—almost as if it were a moat around an ancient castle. The bridge and the river itself were both lit up by blue spotlights. The effect appeared somewhat muted here in the late morning hours, but I'm sure it looked quite dramatic in the evening. Maybe I would get a better look at it when I left. Beyond the river lay the city itself: a gleaming metropolis of blue-tinted glass and metal everywhere I looked. While Viridia consisted primarily of drab concrete with occasional green flourishes, designed for functionality above all, Caesious seemed to be designed more with beauty in mind. The massive tower Rick had mentioned dominated the skyline. He had called it "stark," and I had to admit it looked somewhat bland compared to most of the smaller buildings. The strength of the structure dictated it have less glass. And somewhere up there at the top lived the blue dragon.

I felt a twinge of guilt. We were going to kill the ruler of this city, to set its people free. What if they didn't want to be free? What if the dragon was actually a good and kind ruler here? Then my mind jumped to the dragon worship as practiced in Viridia, and I remembered that Bice had told me the practices were the same or worse in all the other cities. No creature who accepted that kind of worship could be good and kind.

The train crossed the river and entered the city. In Viridia, the train station lay right at the edge of the city. Here, the station lay within the city, a few blocks from the central tower. I wondered if there was any meaning behind that.

The first thing I saw when I stepped off the train was a massive poster showing off the blue dragon in all of his glory. I noticed one back leg at least partially cybernetic, and the gleam of metal showed itself in a few other places. Before I could study it further, a uniformed worker directed me to a desk where a bored-looking controller waited to greet me. He sat sandwiched by a pair of impressive-looking members of the Cerulean Corps, the blue city's equivalent to our Viridian Guard.

Like their city, the Cerulean Corps stood out. While the Guard jumpsuit I wore sported only one shade of green, the Corps uniform was composed of multiple shades of blue, ranging from a very light cyan to a dark indigo. They also wore helmets fitted with blue-tinted (of course) visors. Neither of these two had their visors down. In place of the shockspear I carried attached to my back, they wore some kind of projectile hand weapon at their hips and carried a simple baton that appeared to be made of some kind of hardened plastic.

The controller's eyes narrowed as I walked up, and he lost his bored expression. It looked like the rumors had been doing their work. "What are you doing here, Green Guard?" he demanded. I tried not to focus on his bald head. Apparently after losing his hair, he had gotten his chromark extended over his entire head. Unless… all of our chromarks were really like that, only hidden by our hair. I had an urge to examine my scalp in a mirror.

"Viridian Guard," I corrected. "I bear a message that I can only deliver to a high priest of the Sapphire Robes." Bice had told me to insist on that. The quickest way to the dragon here went through the priests. Working my way through the police forces and upward would take much longer.

"A high priest, eh? Let me see this message." His voice had the most annoying, whiny tone I had ever heard.

I showed the rolled parchment, now bound by twin green and blue ribbons, but I didn't hand it to him. "The message comes directly from the Emerald Ascendancy. I am under strict orders not to show it to anyone else."

"Direct from the big Emerald, eh?" The controller eyed the parchment and then looked to the guard on his right. "Can't hurt to humor him, I guess. Send a runner to the high temple. Should be one or two high priests hanging around this time of day." The guard nodded and left.

The controller looked back down at his desk and scribbled something on a notepad. I waited. After about a minute of nothing happening, I spoke up again. "Is there… somewhere I can wait?"

He looked back up, as if surprised to see me. "Oh, you're good where you're at."

"Could I have a drink of water?"

"A drink of water." He said the words as if they were the strangest thing he had ever heard. He glanced at the other guard, then looked back at me and sighed.

"Fine, there's a waiting room over there," he said, waving to his right. "You'll find what you need, I'm sure."

Another train pulled out behind me as I walked in the direction indicated. I found a small room with an open door. Inside were a handful of (blue) chairs, a table with a variety of snacks, and a water fountain with a stack of plastic cups. I got a drink and settled in to wait.

Though I had put it out of my mind for the trip, I couldn't help thinking back to early this morning and my last talk with Kelly. It had not gone well.

"Why were you okay with putting yourself in danger, but not okay with me doing it?" she had demanded.

"I'm not okay with any of it!" I insisted. "I just want to keep you safe." Since I hadn't said anything about her being in danger, I had no idea where this was coming from.

"Keeping me safe would have meant never getting involved in any of this!"

"Well, it's a little late for that."

"You're right on that." She folded her arms across her chest. "I'm not just some little girl for you to always protect, you know."

"I never said you were!"

"You just let your actions speak for you, and they're speaking loud and clear."

I was baffled. I had no idea—wait. Maybe I did. Was this because Rick had supported her in front of everyone, and I hadn't?

"I guess this is our first fight, huh?"

"And maybe our last." She marched away.

What had I done?

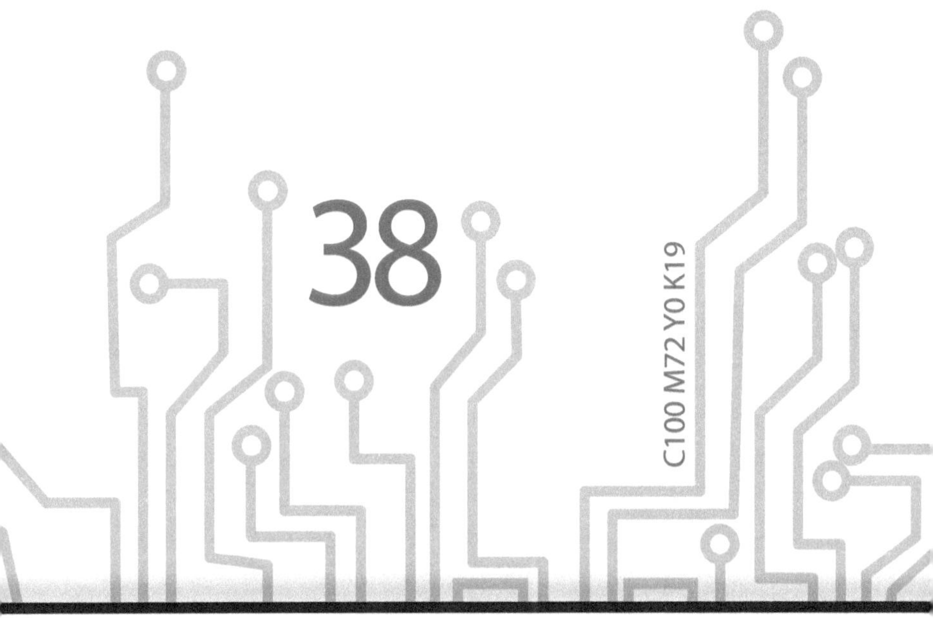

38

Mazarine Chalybeous, High Priest of the Sapphire Robes, Guardian of the Cerulean Books of Lore, and Luminary of the Azure Hue, swept into the waiting room, preceded by a lesser priest, who announced his name and title. Two more of the Cerulean Corps guards followed close behind.

I bowed briefly with, I hoped, the proper respect. Like the controller, the high priest's chromark continued over his shaved head, but did not split into a V-shape like our priests. His skin might be the palest white I had ever seen. He wore gorgeous dark blue robes trimmed in cyan, and a circlet set with a massive sapphire on his forehead. His facial muscles were so tight with annoyance, I worried the sapphire might pop loose.

"Why have you come?" he demanded without any other pleasantries.

"I bring a message to your lord and master, directly from my lord and master," I answered, holding out the parchment and trying not to stare. If the sapphire did pop loose, would it be proper etiquette to dive forward and catch it for him?

Mazarine Chalybeous snatched the parchment from my hands and unrolled it. As he read, his facial expression changed dramatically. The muscles loosened, but his eyes widened more and more as he approached the end. He looked up at me with a snap.

"Do you know what this says?"

I shook my head. "I was only told to deliver it to a high priest. I have not opened it or looked inside." The sapphire would not be falling. I felt strangely disappointed.

He looked at the parchment again. "This is unprecedented. Well," he corrected himself, "the precedent is hundreds of years old, I suppose. Astounding. And considering the rumors that have been flying, this is likely extremely good news."

"Should I wait for a reply?"

"No, no, this is not that kind of message." He shook his head and rolled the parchment back up. "What is your name, young man?"

"Beryl," I replied before thinking to lie.

"Beryl," he repeated. "A fine name. A jewel that is primarily, of course, green in color, making it a popular name in Viridia. What is generally not known, however, is that it can also be blue. Or even red or gold."

I did not know that. "Thank you, sir," I answered, bowing again.

The high priest appeared about to leave, then paused. A look seemed to pass between him and one of his escorts. "Caedan," he said, "Stay with the young man until he gets on the train back to Viridia. I don't want him to feel we mistreated him here. I'll deal with that ridiculous controller myself."

"Of course, sir."

Mazarine Chalybeous swept out of the room as imperiously as he had entered, perhaps more so. I remained alone with the Cerulean Corps guard he had called Caedan.

He surveyed me for a moment and then removed his helmet, revealing a young face, a few years older than me perhaps. His skin was a light olive tone, while his black hair had been cropped very short. His eyes were a striking shade of iridescent blue—that seemed off, somehow. Maybe they had a procedure here for altering eye color?

"Your eyes go well with your uniform," I observed.

"Yours don't." He set the helmet down on the snack table.

"Sorry… I don't know your culture. Did I offend?" I tried again.

He seemed tense, watching me without blinking. "Why are you here?"

I rubbed my forehead. "To, uh, deliver that message. That's done now, so I'll get on the first train back to Viridia."

He glanced out into the main train station and then focused back on me. His hand rested near his projectile weapon. That couldn't be good.

"You are not a soldier," he declared.

"What?"

"During my Learning Years, my aptitude for combat was quickly recognized. From that point on, I have been in training. It took a lot of effort for me to get into the Cerulean Corps. I assume it's the same for the Viridian Guard."

"Yes, it is," I agreed. "Years of training."

"You're lying."

"Wh-why do you say that?" Alarm bells went off in my head, but maybe I could still talk my way out.

He paced deliberately to his left, cutting me off from the door.

"Trained soldiers have a bearing to them. We can recognize one another, regardless of city. You are not a real soldier."

I spread my arms. "Look, I think we're getting off—"

"I have been bodyguard to the High Priest for five months!" he interrupted with vehemence. "I will not allow you to harm him or betray him in any way!"

"Is that why he left you here?"

"He did not see what I saw. But do not think that will matter. Whoever you are, you have no way out here. Tell me the truth: why are you here?"

My mind raced. What was the right play here? Should I keep trying to convince him I was Viridian Guard? My persuasion skills hadn't been very hot so far. But if not… what? Did I fight him? Then what? I couldn't risk him telling anyone anything. The whole plan hinged on this.

"I see this may take more inducement," Caedan said, his hand straying from the projectile weapon to his baton.

"Do you love the dragons?" I blurted.

He paused and an odd expression swept over his face. "What do you mean?"

"Do you love the dragons?" I repeated. "How much do you adore Caesious?"

"If you question my loyalty—"

"I'm asking you as a fellow human being," I said. "I understand your loyalty and your service to the Corps and all that. I'm asking if you genuinely love the dragons."

"Caesious is… beyond such things. I fail to see what that—"

"Do you worship him?"

"This is pointless." He gripped the handle of his baton. "You are stalling me for some reason, but you have said enough to convince me I was right. You are a threat to my master and I will inform him, once I deal with you."

So much for diplomacy. This guy was better armed and far better trained than I was. I had no sword this time, just a shockspear, which wasn't easily accessible (or even turned on). I had only one option now.

I sighed. "I didn't want to do this," I mumbled. His expression of slight confusion transformed into wide-eyed incredulity as I triggered my implant and charged him. I put a huge burst into my legs, figuring the strongest and fastest charge possible would be needed to take this guy down.

I aimed my tackle right at his gut, hoping to knock the wind out of him. It worked. Unfortunately, he wasn't far from the wall, so I didn't take him to the ground. We slammed against the wall and stopped. I stepped back and grabbed at the shockspear on my back. I struggled with the strange connection it had with the uniform. By the time I had it in my hands, Caedan had recovered and pulled out his own baton with his left hand. He reached for his projectile weapon with his right.

Above all, I had to keep him from getting to that, as I had no idea what it could do. Without turning on the shockspear, I swung it as a club and smacked his right hand hard on the knuckles. I didn't even get a short exclamation of pain in response. Instead, he swung his baton upward in an arc that caught the tip of my chin as I tried to pull back. My jaw slammed together, and for an instant, I saw stars.

"That's some trick," Caedan growled. "But it's clearly not enough."

He might be right. Now that I had exposed my one trick, I probably didn't stand a chance.

He came at me hard, swinging his baton in rapid arcs. I managed to block a few of them with the shockspear, but he still landed blows against my right leg and side. It hurt, but the Viridian Guard uniform absorbed some of the impact. That's why it had so many layers, I guess.

It seemed pointless to use my implant, but I kept triggering it, anyway. I needed more strength and speed in my upper body, not my legs, but at least it helped keep me moving. I pivoted off one foot and then the other, boosting my speed each time to throw him off. It worked for a few minutes, but I couldn't keep it up forever. Already, I could feel the ache.

The boosts let me strike back a time or two, but my blows against his uniform seemed even less effective than his against mine. Eventually, his skill won out. I boosted myself hard and he dodged, expecting it. He spun around behind me and jerked his baton up under my chin, grabbing it with both hands. It pressed hard against my windpipe, cutting off my air.

"I still don't know who you are or what you want," he whispered as he tightened his grip, "but I'm taking you down."

In leaving my hands free, Caedan made a big mistake. I slid one hand up the shockspear until I found the activation button. Even as I felt my world starting to go black, I twisted the spear and tagged him on the leg. His muscles went rigid, and the baton slammed even harder against my neck. That might not have been the smartest move I could make.

39

I dropped the shockspear as we both went down. Straining, I pushed the baton away from my neck and rolled free. I coughed and gasped for air. Everything spun, and darkness tried to push into my vision from all sides. In the midst of that darkness, I saw Caedan start to move again.

I scrambled, grabbed the shockspear and jolted him again. I needed time to recover. To my relief, he slumped unconscious after the shock this time. I collapsed onto my back and worked to control my breathing. My neck felt seriously bruised. Deep breaths were painful, but I kept pushing it.

Once my breathing stabilized, I took the guard's baton and projectile weapon. The latter was a curious thing, but I didn't have time to examine it. I needed to decide what to do with this guy. I stood and looked down at him.

The logical thing would be to kill him and hide the body. I could almost hear Rick's voice in my head saying, "You'll live with it." After all, if he got loose, the message to Caesious would fall under suspicion. The entire plan would be ruined. Right now, this Cerulean Corps guard—Caedan—stood in the way of our plan. What was his life compared to the million we were going to set free?

He was a servant of the dragon. More than that, he was a member of the dragon's enforcement arm. More than that, he worked for the dragon religion! Outside of the draconics, it would be hard to find someone more tied to the system we wanted to overthrow. He represented everything wrong with our world.

But looking down at his unconscious form, I couldn't help but think of the other man I'd killed. I could see the face of the priest-guard at the shrine, his eyes expanding in shock as I drove my sword through his torso. I saw Bice's hands soaked in blood as he tried desperately to save the guard's life. And I saw his empty face, devoid of life, as he lay dead on the ground.

I also remembered my own brush with death, and the wonder of that moment when I looked up at the trees, alive. Life was something to celebrate, not destroy.

I leveled the shockspear and rested the point against the guard's chest. I could not allow him to destroy our plan. Rick would not even hesitate in a situation like this, I knew.

But…

The priest called him Caedan. He had a name. He was a person. He had hopes and dreams like me. Like the guard I had killed. I never knew his name.

What other options did I have? If I didn't kill him, I had to prevent him from telling what he knew. Unless I could convince him to keep quiet on his own, there were only two ways to handle it. I could bind him and hide him where he wouldn't be found until it was too late. But the assassination of Caesious was still three days away. Was that even feasible? Could I find a way to keep him restrained that long? And where would I hide him? We were in the train station, crawling with guards and officials!

The other way would be even more complicated. But it might be the only solution if I didn't want to kill him.

His head rolled to the side. He was about to wake up. I had to make a decision.

"Don't move," I told him as soon as I was sure he could hear me. He didn't answer, and glared at me in return.

"I don't want to kill you. But I will, if I have to. One quick thrust of this thing and you're dead. The Viridian Guard fills the tips with poison, you know."

"Then why don't you kill me?" he asked hoarsely. "I will not stand by while you… do whatever it is you're here to do."

"I delivered the message. That was all I came for," I said. "And like I told you: I'm leaving on the next train back. My only problem now is what to do with you. I can't just leave you here."

"Because I will report you immediately."

"Exactly. So either I kill you, which means I'd then have to hide your body, or I tie you up and hide you somewhere for a couple of days… or you give me your solemn promise to keep quiet about all this."

He shook his head. "That's not happening. If you let me go, I'll go straight to the High Priest." He hesitated. "But I… I don't want to die."

"Then we're kind of stuck. I can think of only one other solution, but you're not going to like it."

"What's that?"

"I take you with me, back to Viridia. You stay with me for three days, and then I let you go." The blanket pass Loden had obtained for me would cover this, I assumed. I also doubted anyone would question my being accompanied by a Cerulean Corps member. It might cause some talk, but that would be okay.

"You want to take me hostage?"

"No, I want to let you go, but I can't trust you to keep quiet. So the only thing I can think of is to take you with me."

"Why three days?"

My turn to shake my head. "I'm not telling you anything more."

The sneering condescension had disappeared from his face. He was thinking through everything I had said, looking for some way out.

"This is it," I said. "I either have to kill you, or you come with me. And I'll need your word that you won't try to escape or cause problems for me along the way. Once we get to Viridia, I'm not worried. With the rumors right now, no one there would trust you if you ran away from me."

He shifted his legs. I pressed the spear point a little harder. "Don't try anything. It would only take a flick of my wrist to shock you again, and then a quick jab and you'd be dead."

"I don't think you have it in you to kill me," he said, but his voice lacked conviction.

"You wouldn't be my first kill. I'm a desperate man. You were right that I'm not Viridian Guard. So how do you think I got one of their uniforms?"

That seemed to give him a little pause.

"If I don't return to my post, they'll look for me," he said. "They'll discover that I left with you. They won't know what to think of that."

"I'd rather them be confused than be convinced the message is a fake." His eyes widened, and I realized I had said too much again. I wasn't very good at keeping secrets.

"What's your name?" I asked him, changing tactics.

"Caedan Teal. Why?"

"Caedan, my name is Beryl. You and I have something in common." I leaned closer. "We're both human. And humans should be free of the dragons."

"You're insane."

"Maybe. But that's my goal. Give me the three days, and you'll see what I mean. After that, you're free to go, free to return to your job and tell them you were held hostage by a madman, or whatever you want. I don't care."

I think I convinced him I was totally unpredictable and dangerous, especially talking about being free of the dragons. At any rate, he didn't argue any more. He glanced around and seemed to be thinking it over.

"Fine. Three days," he said at last. Then he closed his eyes. I think he felt ashamed for choosing his life over his duty. That was his problem. I took a deep breath. I didn't have to kill him.

"Your word?"

"You have my word. I won't try to escape."

I lifted the shockspear away and braced myself, in case of betrayal. Caedan climbed to his feet, watching me the entire time. He didn't make any moves to attack me again. I looked him over and thought of something.

"Give me your projectile weapon holder," I said, pointing to his belt.

He rolled his eyes as he began to unhook it. "It's called a holster," he grumbled. "Are all greenies are ignorant as you?"

"No, some of them are worse." I took the holster. Keeping an eye on him, I hooked it onto my belt and put the projectile weapon into it.

I picked up Caedan's baton and offered it to him. "Can I trust you with this?"

He took it cautiously. "Yes. I guess it would look awkward if I had no weapons, huh?"

I nodded, turned off my shockspear, and attached it to my back.

"Welcome to the resistance, Caedan Teal. I hope you survive."

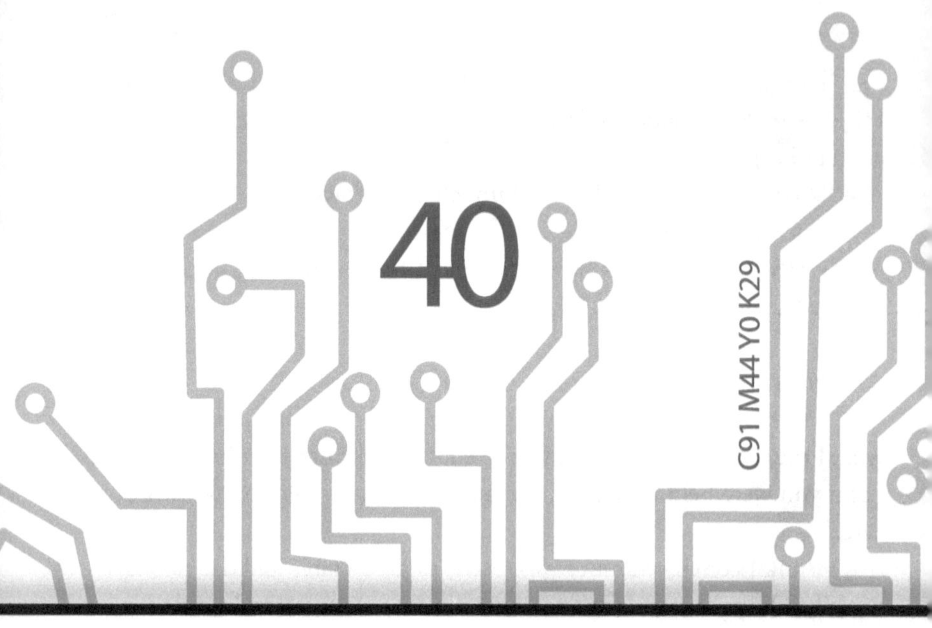

We had no trouble getting on the train the next time one arrived. I waved my pass at the attendant, who didn't even spare a glance for Caedan. After a short wait, the train got underway, and we found seats in a dining car, facing one another. We were alone. It made me wonder why they even bothered with passenger and dining cars when they were used so little. I guess when someone important *did* travel, they wanted something nice ready for them.

"What did you mean by 'resistance'?" Caedan asked.

"It's sort of a description of what I do," I said. "I resist the dragons and want them gone. It's not an official title or anything."

"Okay." He paused. "I'll concede that life isn't perfect under the dragons, but… it's the way things are. The way they've always been. The dragons are immortal, invincible. How can you even think it could change?"

I sighed. "I can't explain it all to you, even if I trusted you, which I don't. Just wait three days and you'll see. Either things will be changed forever, or, or I guess I'll be dead. And things will keep going 'the way they've always been.'"

He fell silent, which relieved me. I didn't know what to tell him or how much. Plus, I needed to figure out what to tell the rest of the team when we got back.

I grew distracted again by the rapidly moving scenery outside. I wondered about the lucky few who got to live outside the cities and work the farms and fields. Did the Viridian Guard and other forces check up on them all the time? I assumed they had to do a certain amount of work to produce the crops and herds. If they didn't… well, I guess it was about the same for them as it was for us. Except they got to live outside. That had to count for something.

I toyed with the projectile weapon in its holster. I pulled it out and examined it. I located the trigger mechanism underneath the sleek, light body of the weapon.

"What does this do?" I asked.

Caedan rolled his eyes. "We call them stunners. It actually does pretty much the same thing as your shockspears, just in a different way." He pointed at the end. "When you pull the trigger, two wires launch out and latch on to the target. Then electricity is channeled through the wires."

I nodded. The principle made sense. I could see how, in some situations, this might be a superior weapon than the shockspear. For one thing, it wouldn't kill someone. I think.

Caedan looked away, and left me alone with my thoughts again. I thought about the final train ride three days from now. I wondered who would be on that ride, apart from Loden. And how would the train help kill the dragon? Maybe Loden would turn the entire thing into a stunner or shockspear.

The return trip seemed so much faster. Twilight arrived as we approached Viridia. The drab architecture looked so boring after Caesious. But Caedan found it all interesting and asked too many questions. He especially wanted to know more about the Emerald Ascendancy.

"It's not so great inside," I told him.

He whirled back at me. "You've been inside it?"

"Yeah. I've even been in the dragon's lair." I probably shouldn't have said that, but I was still annoyed by the condescension he'd shown me earlier.

"No one goes in Caesious' tower," he murmured, looking back at the city.

The train came to a stop, and I scanned the area. I spotted Loden approaching and breathed a sigh of relief. Somehow, I had been sure some real Viridian Guard members would be waiting to take us into custody.

Loden also looked relieved when I stepped out and waved at him. He lifted his hand to wave back and then froze as Caedan stepped out behind me, carrying his helmet. The expressions that ran across Loden's face were almost comical.

As we approached each other, I smiled, trying to show everything was all right. "Loden!" I greeted him. "I want you to meet someone. This is Caedan Teal. He's, um…" I hit a loss of words. I kept thinking I knew how to do this, but when it came down to it, I never had the right thing to say.

"I'm his hostage," Caedan chimed in. "You must be the brains behind this. I knew this guy"—he thumbed at me—"couldn't have done it on his own."

"Hostage. Okay." Loden looked at me, lifted a hand to scratch his chin, but stopped. "Let's get back to the workshop, and you can explain."

He led the way. I glanced about and noticed no one in sight. Loden must have arranged it. Good decision, since I had brought a visitor. I check on Caedan. His crazy eyes seemed to latch on to every detail as he examined everything around us. Was he looking for a way out? Memorizing our descriptions so he could turn us in?

Loden opened the door to the workshop, and a surprising melody fell on our ears. I froze as I realized it was Kelly singing. She didn't have a powerful voice and sounded a little hesitant, but the music contained warmth and brightness. Neither breathy nor nasal, it was just… Agh. Why couldn't I find the right words? I wanted to stop and listen to that voice forever. I felt an ache inside, thinking about the strain in our relationship.

I didn't even notice the lyrics at first. Then I heard, "Who can stand before your majestic power?" before she stopped.

"Good, good," Stacy's voice said. "Your voice is very lyric, and I love it, but you're still not convincing me."

"Probably because I don't believe the words," Kelly answered.

"That doesn't matter. Do you think I believe the things I say on stage? Acting is convincing people that you believe things, that you are things, when you may not be."

"Beryl's back!" Lovat called out.

"Who was that singing?" Caedan whispered to me.

"My girlfriend," I shot back, hoping that was still true.

We entered the workshop behind Loden, and the rest of the team came running to meet us, eager to hear of my mission. Kelly and Stacy came last, but everyone slowed upon seeing Caedan. The unknown had entered our home.

"I'm guessing things didn't go quite as planned," Rick said first. His bruised face looked even more colorful than when I left.

"The plan went very well," I announced. "The message was delivered. I just ran into a… complication afterward."

"Yes, tell us about your complication," Loden said with arms folded.

I gestured beside me. "This is Caedan Teal. He's going to be joining us for a few days. Caedan, these are my friends. You may as well get to know them—"

"You managed to recruit someone from Caesious?" Don asked.

"Not… exactly."

"You called him a hostage," Loden pointed out.

"A what?" Kelly exclaimed.

I sighed as several people talked at once. Caedan seemed highly amused by it all, keeping a half-smirk on his face the entire time.

I lifted my hand for silence and waited. Then I explained what had happened and how I had been forced to resolve it. Caedan kept silent, to my relief.

"You should have killed him," Rick said bluntly. I heard a couple of murmurs of agreement, but didn't notice where they came from. Loden stalked away.

"And what? Hid his body in the snack room?" I snapped. "That wouldn't have caused any suspicion, I'm sure! Use your brain, Onyx!"

"Then you should have thrown him in front of a train!"

"Then maybe you should have gone!"

"Maybe I should have!"

Bice stepped in front of everyone and extended a hand to Caedan. "Caedan, I'd like to welcome you to Viridia," he said in his calm, measured tones. Caedan took his hand. "Things are a bit crazy here, but give it time. I'm sure you'll understand us better and fit right in. My name is Bice."

The half-smirk disappeared from Caedan's face and his eyes widened. "Bice the Heretic?" he gasped, releasing the handshake and taking a step back.

Bice's eyebrows rose. "Well, that's interesting. It seems my reputation is spreading among the clergy, even in other cities."

"You can't just welcome him here," Rick protested. "He's a soldier, a servant of the dragons. He even works for their priesthood!"

Bice looked at him. "And who are you? We have only your word about your past in Atramentous. Should we kill this man because he was raised in a different city? Has a different color chromark?"

"That's different," Kelly protested. "Rick has proven himself. This guy doesn't even claim to have changed."

"I agree," Don said.

"Then we kill him because of his upbringing? Because he hasn't had a chance to even consider a different way?" Bice argued. I found myself relaxing somewhat while letting Bice take the lead. He always knew what to say.

"It doesn't matter," Loden said. I hadn't even noticed him walking back up to us. "We can't risk the plan at this stage."

With that, he swung a shockspear from behind his back and plunged it straight at Caedan's chest.

In a fluid motion, Caedan's left arm swept up. His forearm blocked the shockspear, diverting it up, while his right arm whipped out his baton. He took a half-step backward and dropped into a defensive stance.

"He's got a weapon!" Rick exclaimed. "Beryl, are you insane?"

Loden held the shockspear across both hands. He had counted on the success of his first strike and now didn't know what to do.

"Want me to take him?" Don asked.

"Stop it, all of you!" Bice commanded.

"I've planned this for three years," Loden responded, his voice shaking with rage (or was that fear?). "I will not have it all destroyed by this… this… dragon-lover!"

"Who are you to decide who lives and who dies?" Bice demanded. "In trying to overthrow the false gods, do you make yourself one instead?" He looked around at the others. "Listen to us! Life and death are not abstract, insignificant things! The life this man possesses is a thing of immeasurable glory!" He looked back at Loden. "Would you take that from him? You believe you have that right?"

I stepped up between them. "This was my decision!" I announced. "I made it, and I take responsibility for it. This fighting is pointless."

"But Beryl," Stacy said softly, "Can you make a decision for the entire group? Doesn't that put you in the place of the dragon?"

"You asked me to be the leader here," I shot back. "Being a leader is about making decisions for the entire group! But if you don't like my decisions, you have the right to leave." I looked around. "Any of you."

No one moved. Loden still shook, but he had lowered the shockspear.

"Caedan stays," I said firmly. "I gave him my word that he would be free to go in three days. In return, he gave me his word that he would not try to escape. My word, my promise, will not be broken. I hate the dragons and their servants with every part of my being. I want nothing more than to destroy them! They are pure evil. And I will fight them to my dying moment. But if I do not keep my word, if my promises mean nothing, then, then I am no better than a draconic. I have to hold on to something, something that makes me different from them!" My voice cracked as something welled up in my throat. "Kelly, we spoke the other night about what life would be like when all this is over. You, you had dreams about what it could be, and even what I might be. So what kind of man am I? Am I a man who just, just kills anyone who opposes him? Or am I a man that saves life and keeps his word?"

I faced Caedan, who still stood in his defensive stance, but stared at me with his mouth ajar.

"I don't know what kind of man you are," I told him. "But I know what kind of man I want to be. Can we stick together for now?"

Caedan lowered his baton and straightened up. He shook his head and snorted. He looked past me at everyone else and chuckled.

"You people…" He paused. "I don't fully grasp what it is you're trying to do, and whatever it is, I think you're all insane for doing it." He pointed at me. "But this guy's insanity is something else. I want to see what he does next." He laughed. "I gave my word too. And if keeping that is a sign of manhood, I can't let this lunatic be a better man than me."

I took a deep, long breath to push down the lump in my throat. I turned around to see Bice nodding in approval. Loden looked at the floor, still holding the shockspear, but no longer shaking. Rick's eyes were narrowed and his brow furrowed, as if a number of different scenarios were running through his mind. Lovat started to wander away. Don looked down and scratched at his cheek. Stacy and Kelly both had sad little smiles on their faces. I'm not sure what that meant.

A long silence followed.

"Well!" Stacy exclaimed. "I guess we'd better get back to it, then.

Come on, Kelly. Let's sing." Kelly rolled her eyes and followed as Stacy hobbled back in the direction of our boxcar.

"You sounded great, by the way!" I called. She didn't respond.

"Girlfriend, huh?" Caedan observed quietly.

Rick and Don wandered off as well, leaving me with Caedan and the two older men. Loden raised his eyes and looked at me. "If he ruins everything, I will never forgive you," he told me. He tossed the shockspear off to the side and walked back to his engine.

"Come on," Bice said. "We don't have much in the way of food, but I can offer you a little, if you're hungry."

"We ate on the train—" I began, but Caedan interrupted me. "Sure. I'm starving."

Bice led us to a work table he had appropriated for our group's meals. He scavenged a sandwich for Caedan, but I turned down anything but water. While he ate, we listened to Kelly and Stacy practicing. I continued to feel the ache in my chest. I still didn't understand what had happened between Kelly and me. I hoped we would get a chance to talk again soon.

Caedan gestured to the engine. "That looks streak," he said. "What kind of train engine is that?"

"Loden built it," I answered. "He says it's four times faster than existing engines."

Caedan whistled.

"So…" Bice began. "I can't help but ask: what have you heard about me?"

Caedan took another bite and waved the half-eaten sandwich in the air. "Oh, yeah," he said around his mouthful. "The priests are freaked over you. They were saying something about you running off with all the secrets. I didn't hear much more than that."

"Fascinating."

"Is it true? You got all their secrets?"

"I have… some secrets," Bice answered with his characteristic smile.

Caedan raised an eyebrow, but didn't press it. He finished off the sandwich. "Thanks for sticking up for me back there," he offered. "I don't remember being in a tighter spot."

"I told you," I said. "I gave my word."

"As did I," Bice answered. "I have promised not to kill another human being."

"Who did you promise?" I wondered.

"Whatever powers there be beyond the dragons," he replied, getting up. He walked away as Caedan and I glanced at each other. "I don't know what he means, either," I offered. Caedan chuckled.

"You're all crazy in different ways, I guess."

Rick approached the table, practice swords in his hands. He set them down and looked Caedan in the eyes.

"I've changed my mind," he announced. "Welcome to the team, Caedan. I think you'll be helping us out before this is over."

That was a huge relief. I didn't want anything threatening my friendship with Rick. I hated to think of us being opposed to each other on anything serious.

"I'm just a hostage," Caedan answered, his eyes straying to the practice swords.

"Any good with a blade?"

"I've had a lot of combat training. While none of it focused on blades like these, I think the principles are applicable." Caedan took one of the swords and held it up.

"Let's find out," Rick said, grabbing the other sword and gesturing for him to follow. Caedan jumped up, then slowed. Maybe he didn't want to seem too eager.

They moved out into open space, and I followed to watch. Lovat joined me, munching on an apple.

Rick took his usual stance, holding the sword in front of him with both hands. Caedan flipped the sword and held it so that the blade shielded his forearm, then took a more defensive stance, leaning on his back foot. Rick frowned at the unorthodox approach.

I had fought Caedan and knew he was highly skilled, but Rick's prowess with the sword had been growing by leaps and bounds. He already beat Stacy more times than not—before her accident, that is. This would be interesting.

Rick launched a basic attack, which Caedan deflected with ease. His style, with the blade pointed down, might be difficult to counter. I could see how it worked well for defense, but I couldn't tell how he would ever be able to make any attacks of his own. Rick continued to attack, weaving back and forth, trying different methods. He took advantage of his ambidexterity to switch up a couple of times, hoping to throw Caedan off balance. It didn't work.

The expression on Caedan's face confirmed what I had already suspected: he loved the action, the fight. I wondered if that was what had convinced him to give up and come with me: the chance for more fighting.

Caedan waited until Rick tried an overhand blow. He blocked it with a solid blow upward, then spun inside and stabbed his blade straight back between his own left arm and side. The tip poked Rick in the stomach hard enough to make him jump back a step.

Rick glared at me. "How'd *you* beat this guy?" he demanded.

Caedan looked back at me with a smirk. "That's what I'd like to know," he agreed.

"Secrets," I replied. "We all have them."

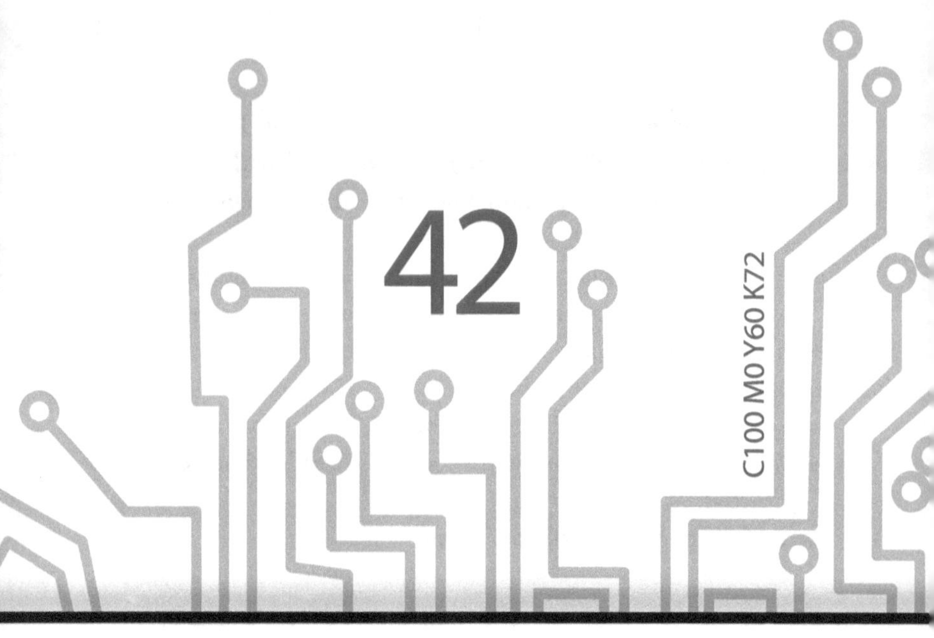

"I need to talk to you. Come here!" After his duel with Caedan, Rick pulled me aside and led me over to Loden's workbench where the older man stood tinkering with one of the talkers.

"What now?" I asked warily.

Rick pushed his hair out of his face and glanced around. Loden put down the talker and gave him his full attention.

"While I was a prisoner, I overheard some things," he began. "They were trying to get information from me, but I was listening every minute."

"Did you tell them anything?" Loden asked.

"What? No! Of course not!"

"He needed to ask, Rick," I said. "It's not an insult."

"Yeah, well, there wasn't much I could tell them if I had wanted to. That stupid draconic already knows most of us."

"Except Stacy and Loden."

"Ahhh… that's why we need to talk." Rick looked at Loden. "I think he knows about you."

"What?"

"That is… I don't think he knows you're with us." Rick gestured at himself and me. "I think he knows you're not loyal. He was talking about an engineer."

"That could be anyone," I protested.

"An engineer that has developed a new train?"

When neither of us responded, Rick went on. "He was talking to someone about the demonstration coming up. He said he'd be riding on the new train and learning everything he needed to know about it. Then, uh, he said he'd get rid of the engineer."

"Why?" I said. "What has he done?"

"I've attracted too much attention over the years," Loden said, tight-lipped. "They were bound to get suspicious eventually."

"I'm not going to let it happen," I said. "I'll kill that monster."

Loden frowned. "We'll deal with it later."

"But—"

"Later, I said. Now get the others over here. We need to finalize our plans."

Once the others had gathered, Loden announced, "What I'm about to show you is one of the draconics' most closely guarded techs." Caedan stayed on the outskirts of the group, but listened intently.

Loden held up the device we'd used to listen to the police. "We call this a 'talker,'" he explained. "And with it, we can communicate over distance."

"How much distance?" Bice asked.

Loden shrugged. "We've tested them up to a mile apart, but the sound isn't always good," he said. "Out where we're going, it should work well enough for our purposes. Unfortunately, I can't show you right now how they work; someone within the city would probably overhear us. Once you're out in the open, you should try them out yourselves. I'll teach you all how to do it. I'm going to keep one on the train, and we can double check our final status when it's time.

"Now. Let's go over the final details of our plan." He shot an annoyed look at Caedan and then pulled up a large chalkboard the engineers used for scribbling down calculations and ideas. As he began to draw a make-shift map, he went on:

"In a few hours, all of you will be taken to the staging area. I've arranged for that passenger car over there"—he gestured—"to be delivered to the spot I've chosen. Don and I have been covering the windows, and no one has any reason to check inside it, so you all should be safe as long as you don't draw any attention to yourselves."

"Gotta be better than the boxcar," Rick said.

"Once the train delivers the passenger car and leaves, you can exit and move to this spot." Loden had been drawing a long line I assumed repre-sented the train track. Now he drew a small circle near the center of the board. "It's about a hundred yards to the right of the tracks. All of this area is covered with hills, and this spot is not visible from the track. I've set up a shelter there, along with plenty of supplies. I've been working on this place for over a year. The digger is already there and waiting. It's sheltered under some trees, so it shouldn't be easily visible from the air when the dragon flies over. Don, you should probably test-drive it to make sure everything's in order.

"Tomorrow and the next day, you should all familiarize yourselves with the landscape and everything in the area. But keep out of sight when trains are going by. That should be the only danger. This area is primarily used for herding sheep, but it's time for shearing. They won't be around for a few days, at least."

"You've timed all this so perfectly," I observed.

"I told you I've been thinking about it a long time," he replied. "So… all that's left is to talk about the last day. Beryl, do you want to take over here?"

Loden and I had already discussed this, so I knew what he wanted me to say. He could have done it himself, but it was that "Beryl's the leader" thing again. At least I looked more "in charge" now with the Viridian Guard uniform I still wore.

I jumped up and stood beside him. "Okay, so most of you know what's going to happen. Loden will be on the train. Don, of course, will be man-ning the digger. Lovat, I want you with him in case he needs anything." They both nodded. "Kelly, you've got the biggest job of all. Loden's briefed me on where you'll need to be. I'll show you everything when we get there. And then… you'll be standing out there in the open by yourself."

I searched her face, knowing that what she would be doing was the most terrifying thing any of us would ever do. "But I will be only a few feet away," I said. "And so will the rest of us."

"If anything goes wrong, I will distract the dragon," Bice spoke up. "That will give Beryl and Rick a chance to get you out of the way."

"But… he knows about you," Kelly said. She shot a glance at Caedan.

"That's what I'm counting on."

"He'll kill you!"

"If anything goes wrong, we're likely all going to be dead," Rick said.

"Except Stacy, of course, since she's staying back here in Viridia, where it's nice and safe."

"I can't abandon my fans," Stacy said.

"Everything about this plan has to go just right or we're all dead," I said. "If we manage to escape the dragon somehow, then we'll be hunted down soon thereafter. I don't want there to be any doubts about this. It's astonishing victory… or death. And, and—if you want to back out now, that's okay. I never expected our group to get this large, anyway."

"None of us are backing out." Rick dismissed it with a casual gesture. "You spelled it out a long time ago: either we fight, or run and hide. I'll go out fighting."

There were murmurs of agreement from the others. I hadn't expected any of them to quit, but I wanted them to have the option.

"That settles it, then," Loden broke in. "Now let me show you all how to use the talkers."

I watched with interest as Loden showed how to turn the devices on and then tune them to the proper "channel," which apparently meant one of the numbers on a dial. After that, it was as simple as holding a button down and talking.

While Loden answered questions from the others, I glanced outward at Caedan. He didn't notice me watching him, and I wondered what he was thinking. He looked pensive, as if he were thinking hard about all that we were doing. In a sense, Caedan's reaction to our plan would give us some idea of how most of the rest of the humans would react. He had been raised all his life to serve and worship the dragons, like the rest of us. Unlike the rest of us, he had not come to a point where he hated it and wanted to change it.

Lost in thought, I moved away from the others.

Rick followed me and gestured with his chin at Caedan. "We can't trust him, you know."

"I know."

"Then why keep him around?" Rick tried to look me in the face, but I turned away.

"I told you: I don't want to kill him."

"Let's tie him up and leave him in the boxcar," he suggested. "Loden can keep an eye on him. Then we can set him free when this is all over."

I shook my head. "He's my responsibility. I'm not dumping that off on anyone else." As soon as I said it, I realized that might be a problem later on. Why did everything have to be so complicated?

"So he's your new best friend now, I guess."

I shot Rick a look. "Don't be ridiculous. I've known him for less than a day."

"You knew me for less than a day before you were talking about killing a dragon."

"That's different. I knew I could trust you."

"How?"

"How? Because you were on the run from them! This guy, he's—he's—"

"He's one of them."

That wasn't what I was going to say, but he was right. Caedan even wore the uniform of our enemy. I couldn't forget that.

Rick sighed. "Look, I know I was pretty harsh when you brought him in, but I don't really regret it. You need to keep focused. We have to do… whatever we need to do to win. If Caedan gets in our way at all, I'll kill him without a debate."

"I know." It was time to change the subject. "Listen, we can't let Loden die. And I think I know how to save him."

He narrowed his eyes. "How?"

"It will actually help the overall plan. Loden thinks that the blood and the tooth will be enough to convince everyone that the green dragon killed the blue." I lowered my voice. "But I think we need something more. Loden is going to use this train as a weapon, right? What if more evidence was found on the train?"

"Like what?"

"Like the body of Troilus Green."

"I like this plan." Rick grinned and glanced back at the others. "Though I do understand why you didn't share it with everyone."

I nodded. "After we get to the staging area and get everything ready, I'm coming back. We know Troilus Green is going to be on the train—"

"And you'll kill it? How?"

"That's the part I haven't quite figured out yet."

"Kind of a crucial piece of the plan, don't you think?"

"Look, we'll be away from the city, so its powers won't work. We'll be in a narrow train car. I'm hoping that I'll be able to use the same technique I used on the guard at the shrine. In all of our encounters, it's never seen me use my implant. I'm hoping I can catch it off-guard."

Rick cocked an eyebrow. "It saw you leap out of the sanctuary. I think it has a good idea that you're different."

He had a point.

"You don't even know if your sword will penetrate its skin."

"Even if I fail… well, maybe just keeping it busy on the train will be enough. It'll probably still die."

"Not if it stops Loden and ruins the whole plan. Or it kills you. And how are you going to get off?"

"Thanks for the encouragement."

Rick spread his arms wide. "Hey, I'm on your side on this! I think it's a great idea. But you need to think it through. Come up with a plan that works. You've got two days."

Loden clapped his hands for attention. "All right, everyone! We've got less than an hour before the morning crew arrives. Let's get everything moved into the passenger car."

"Time for me to say goodbye, everyone," Stacy said. "And… good luck!"

We all echoed each other in saying goodbye to her. She turned to Kelly. "Kelly, girl—you can do this! I believe in you!"

"We all do," I added, which earned me a quick look.

Loden opened the door for Stacy as she shuffled through on her crutches. The rest of us turned to the job at hand. We took everything we had from the boxcar, along with some new supplies Loden had procured, and loaded it up inside the darkened passenger car. Then the goodbyes were repeated, this time with Loden, and everyone climbed in. I was about to follow the others when Loden grasped my shoulder.

"Beryl, I…" He didn't meet my eyes. "You were right. About the blue kid. If we're not defending human life, then we're wasting our time. Tell him I'm sorry."

"I can do that." I tried to look him in the face. "Loden, do you have a plan for getting off the train? Before the end, I mean."

His hesitation was brief but noticeable. "Yes, I have a plan," he answered. He took a step away, then hesitated again. He glanced at the clock then hurried to his desk and retrieved an envelope. He returned and thrust it into my hands. "Take this." His voice sounded even gruffer than usual. "I always meant for you to have it. But don't open it until the dragon is dead."

"Loden. I'm coming back."

"Of course you are."

"I mean tomorrow. I'm coming back tomorrow. I'll be with you on the train."

"Don't be an idiot."

"I—Thanks for everything." I felt that big lump in my throat again. "I, that is, you've—"

He nodded, looked as if he were going to hug me, then turned away. "Get on the car," he said. "Workers will be here any second now."

I felt like there was too much left unsaid between us. This man had done everything for me. He had saved my life and now was risking his own in so many ways. I wanted to say so much more. Well, I would be coming back, so… yeah. I'd find the time. After I killed the draconic.

Inside the passenger car, everyone found a comfortable spot and began discussing the trip. So much nicer than the boxcar. Everyone could have an entire seat to himself, even stretch out and rest. We'd need some of that. I'd only gotten a two-hour nap in the middle of the night myself. I glanced around and chose a seat behind Kelly.

"Can we talk?" I asked her.

"I suppose."

"I'm sorry for not supporting you when Stacy got hurt," I said, repeating the words I'd gone over in my head several times. "I should have. You're going to do an amazing job. I've heard you, and it's fantastic."

She grunted. That was it? What else was I supposed to say?

"Um… I feel like there's still a problem between us, but I don't know what it is."

She rolled her eyes. "I don't understand you, Beryl."

"That's okay. I don't understand myself half the time, either."

"I mean it. You started all… this. You dragged me into it. You dragged all of us into it. But you… you give speeches about being committed and stuff, but what about you? Are you committed?"

"Me?" How could she say that?

"You brought one of the enemy in here, risking everything!"

Oh. Him.

"And if that weren't enough…" She stopped. Something else was going on here, but I didn't know what it was yet. Her eyes welled up with tears. Oh, no. Oh, no.

"How long have you known? About my parents?" she choked out.

Fewmets. Somehow she found out. Honestly, I had pushed that to the back of my head. I hadn't even thought about it since yesterday. What could I say?

"I, I asked Stacy… to check on them…" she whispered between sobs.

The back of the seat separated us. Should I get up and go around it? Try to hug her? I was devastated, but she had to be feeling worse. There might not be a way to fix things after blowing it this bad.

"Kelly, I—"

"You were trying to protect me!" she snapped, wiping her eyes with her sleeve.

"Well, yeah. You were so upset after the fight at the shrine… I didn't think—"

"You never think! You just act! That's all you do!"

"No, I—"

"You think that you're thinking about me, but you aren't. You're thinking about yourself! You and your deluded plans!"

My chest felt the deepest ache I had ever experienced. The passenger car was silent now. I guess everyone could hear us.

"Gods, I hope you're happy now. Your plans are going to happen. And we're all going to die. You know that, right? We're all going to die!"

"Kelly, I never meant to hurt you. I love you—"

"You don't know what that means!" She got up and moved to a different seat at the far end of the car. I turned around and slumped back in my seat. The others pretended they weren't looking at me. Silence dominated for a very long time.

A few minutes later, we heard the workers arrive and go about their business. We heard engines roaring, doors opening, and scattered yelling. After half an hour or so, the passenger car experienced a jolt as they hooked it up to another car. Then we started moving.

I glanced back at Kelly from time to time. She never met my gaze or acknowledged me. The ache in my chest felt like my rib cage was going to implode. At this point, I would have given up every plan against the dragons if I could get her back. What good was revenge and freedom if Kelly and I weren't together?

Rick moved to the seat across from me. "Give her time, man," he whispered. The train began to pick up speed. We must have moved outside the city by now.

I shook my head. "I don't think so. I really messed things up."

He shifted a little closer. "You can't let this mess you up, Beryl. As hard as it is, you need to put it aside and focus."

I knew he was right. That didn't make it any easier. My brain could tell my heart to go away, but that didn't mean it would.

"We don't even need dragons to ruin everything," I muttered. "We can do that all on our own."

Rick snorted. "What? Did you think humans were perfect? That if we overthrow the dragons, everything will be peace and harmony? This is real bleaking life, man."

"Then what are we fighting for?"

He thought for a moment, searching for the right words. "The chance to make our own mistakes, I guess. At least it'll be us that makes them, and not some stupid overgrown lizards."

"Is that what your friends back in Atramentous thought?"

He nodded. "And they all died for it. But at least they died on their own terms, fighting for something they believed in."

I looked around the passenger car. Kelly had curled up on her seat, face hidden. Lovat lifted up one of the window covers, so he could peer out at the passing countryside. Don and Bice were discussing something between them. Caedan sat alone, sullen and lost in his own thoughts.

"How do we compare to that group?" I wondered.

Rick raised his eyebrows. "This group is far less trained in fighting, and far more… diverse in ages, that's for sure. But it's got one great big thing going for it that my last group didn't have."

"What's that?"

"A guy named Beryl."

44

My brain knew Rick was trying to make me feel better. But it was still my heart that reacted to his words, and that's what it needed right now. I smiled and sat back to wait.

After a couple of hours, the train slowed and came to a stop. We heard loud voices as the workers unhooked the passenger car. I know I heard at least one person complaining about why this car needed to be delivered to the middle of nowhere. They pushed the car off to the side, and a few minutes later we heard the train leaving. I waited a moment longer and then looked outside. The train was out of sight.

"All right, we're here," I announced. "Let's see what we need to see."

We all climbed out, blinking in the bright sunshine. The passenger car had been pushed off the main tracks onto a short rail segment next to an open-walled shed. A number of rusting tools were scattered about. I could see why the workers had wondered about this. It had to be an odd place to leave any kind of train car. Rolling hills surrounded us on every side, dotted with occasional trees. In the distance, I could see glimpses of the train track.

I pointed east. "About a hundred yards that way, Loden said!" I led the way over the nearest hill and back down the other side. As promised, we found the "shelter" Loden had talked about, though it took some searching: a cave opening with a roof built over the entrance. All of it had been carefully shrouded with bushes and long grass, to keep it hidden from above.

"Digger," Don grunted, pointing. I looked and saw a large construction vehicle of some kind tucked under a grove of trees.

I got Bice and Don busy moving our supplies from the passenger car into the cave. I would have sent Lovat to help them, but he had undergone an amusing transformation. The orphan boy ran up and down the hills, sometimes falling and rolling, occasionally laughing out loud. Like most Viridians, he had never been outside the city itself and now was delighted with the wonder of nature. I left him to his enjoyment. Work could come later.

Rick, Kelly and I needed to check out the final staging point. Caedan followed, uninvited.

We crossed two more hills, following the rails. Walking on the grass among the scattered trees reminded me of when I woke up outside the dragon's lair. The sense of awe at the green of nature remained, but not as strong. I glanced back at Caedan. No blue out here, though. Except the sky. The skies belong to the dragons, but I suspected that meant more to Caesious' followers. Did they think of their dragon every time they looked at the sky?

We reached a wide open plain nestled among the hills. I glanced back at the rails that led to Viridia. From the map Loden had drawn, I knew the track here wove back and forth between the tallest of the hills. It made a very circuitous route, but I guess the original builders didn't much care about straight lines. There was a double set of tracks, of course, to allow for trains going and coming at the same time, but the outward rails had all been replaced with Loden's new design to work with his new engine.

We followed the track out into the plain. Rick pointed out a spot where one of the crossbeams had been splashed with dark green paint. "That's where you'll stand, Kelly," he said.

I looked up. "So the dragon will fly overhead and hopefully land… over here." I ran ahead and examined the area. This space looked like the widest open spot, which made it easiest for landing. I hoped It made sense to the dragon too.

Kelly examined the ground. "And here is where I need to lure him." She pointed to an unusual configuration on the tracks. To the casual eye, it might look like a split in the tracks, where a new branch line might be built later. But we knew better. This was the trap. A dragon's weight would trigger it, and the rails would snap up, binding it in place long enough for the train weapon to arrive. At least, that was the plan. Loden said it would work.

I looked down. A heaviness settled into my limbs. Right around forty-eight hours from now, we would be trying to trap and kill a dragon in this spot. If anything went wrong, Kelly would die here. And Bice. And Rick, most likely. Me too, if I made it back in time. Maybe Don and Lovat could get away. I hoped so, anyway.

We stood in silence, each thinking our own thoughts. Despite the moment and the location, I couldn't help but think about Kelly and our broken relationship. I looked at her in time to see the wind catch her hair and whip it up and around her face. She caught it and pulled it out of the way. Her hair had almost no trace of green left. Either it had all grown out, or she had cut those strands. I reproached myself for not noticing that earlier. She had probably expected me to comment on it. Too late now.

"What about the trap?" Kelly asked, breaking the silence. "Won't they be able to find it, after everything?"

"I wouldn't worry about it," Rick said. "There won't be much left of it in the debris, and if there is, we'll clean it up when we bring in the digger."

"Let's head back," I said.

We returned to the cave and helped the others sort and arrange our supplies. Loden said he had already stocked "a little bit" here, but he was the master of understatement. We had enough non-perishable food here to feed our group for a month, at least. I had spotted a creek nearby, so we would have no lack of water, either.

Don and Lovat went to check out the digger. I heard its engine start up with a loud roar. I knew Loden had chosen this spot for its seclusion, but still I worried someone might hear. I walked out of the cave and watched as Don drove the vehicle out of the grove.

It looked somewhat like some of the larger devices I had seen at the train station, but still unique. Most city dwellers, myself included, would never see a vehicle like this in action. It didn't run on wheels like every other vehicle I knew; instead, it had a pair of continuous tracks made up of a bunch of strips of metal. It crawled rather than rolled. The driver sat inside a windowed shelter from which he could control the massive claw-like arm that stretched up and then down. The end of it, the claw itself, did look like the jaws of a dragon or some other creature. It looked much smaller than an actual dragon's mouth, but I figured it would serve our purposes.

Don seemed satisfied with the digger's condition after a couple of minutes, backed it up into the grove again, and shut it down. Everything appeared ready.

We all took some much-needed naps in the cave, except Lovat, who spent his time exploring. The cave's interior felt cool, away from the sun, but not too cold. We were amply provided with blankets, in any case. I expected it would get a lot colder during the night.

Evening approached and Don built a fire. While the twilight lingered, he sent all of us to gather as many fallen branches as we could find. We returned, arms laden, to find him breaking up some old wooden crates. He created a small cone-shaped pile with some of the wood, filled it with smaller sticks and some paper and ignited it with a lighter he carried in his pocket. He fed the blaze until he had a fire the size of a small table. We gathered around it for warmth and enjoyment. We had all seen fire before, of course, but never like this. Despite Don's careful ministrations, it seemed a wild thing, unfettered by anyone's control. It reached toward the sky, straining as if to escape into the air above.

Don stretched out on the ground, putting his hands behind his head. He gazed up at the sky. "I could get used to this," he said.

I looked up too. Wispy clouds stretched across the star-studded black canvas. It took my breath away.

"So many many," Lovat said.

"We never see the stars like this in the city," Kelly whispered.

"There is so *much* the dragons have kept from us," I said.

Only the sound of the fire crackling filled the silence that followed.

"There's something I don't get," Caedan announced without warning. I looked back at him, across the fire. The glow lit up the brighter parts of his uniform in an odd pattern. He had a grim twist to his mouth.

"What is it?"

"It's not hard to understand that you all are trying to kill a dragon," he said. "And you think you've even got a plan to do it. But you didn't kill me. You're focused on the dragons, not their servants. You"—he pointed at me—"seem especially obsessed with this. Like you really, really hate them. Why?"

Rick snorted and lay back to star-gaze. The others all looked at me.

"We all hate them," I said. "They oppress us, treat us like their property, and, and keep us from being all that we could be, what we *should* be. They're monsters who would just as soon eat you or step on you."

Caedan shook his head. "No, for you it's personal. I can tell. What is it?"

Bice leaned closer to me. "If you truly want to win him over, Beryl," he said so that only I could hear, "this might be a good time to tell that story."

He made sense. We had to shine a light on the depths of the dragons' depravity, if we wanted to win anyone else to our side. But it hurt so much. I wasn't sure I could do it.

I took a deep breath and let it out slowly.

"I had a baby sister."

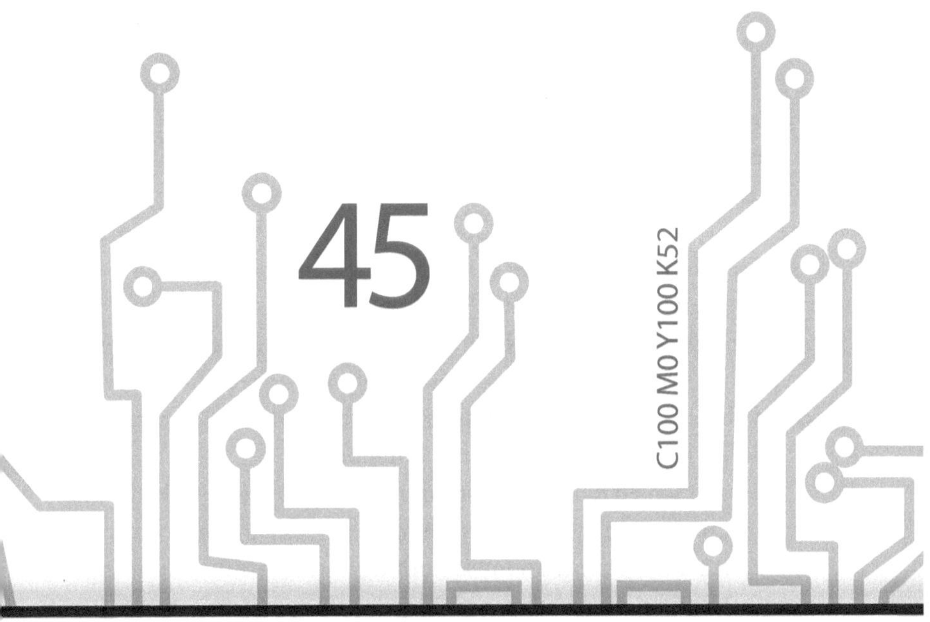

45

Kelly let out a little gasp. She knew what it meant. Bice lowered his head. Rick sat up, interested. Caedan looked on, waiting for the rest of the story.

"Seven years ago, my parents had a second child," I said, forcing each word out past the growing anger in my heart. "She was a beautiful little girl with… with wispy curls of golden hair. My parents were… overjoyed. And I, I fell in love with her from the very beginning. I had been alone for so long. I had no real friends, and my parents worked such long hours. Having a baby sister was like a dream, a dream come true. My mom could stay home with both of us for a while, and we could play and…" I trailed off and swallowed hard.

"And then… when she was only a month old, my parents said we needed to go to the Shrine for her, her dedication." My throat constricted, but I had to go on. "They were so excited, so happy… so I was too. They told me about my dedication and how wonderful it was."

I put my head down, my chin resting on my chest. The warmth of the fire pulsed against my forehead. But inside, I felt nothing but cold. Cold rage. And sorrow. As angry as I felt, I couldn't lose the grief.

"Only three of us came back home."

A long silence followed, broken only by my deep breaths and a few quiet sobs from Kelly.

"I'm… sorry," Caedan said. "Our customs aren't the same, so… I don't quite know what that means."

"In Viridia," Bice took over, "the dragon mandates that every child must be dedicated to him. Only the worthy are allowed to live and serve him. The dedication ensures their worthiness. If children are not dedicated, they never receive their chromark and can never be a part of regular society, like Lovat here." He tossed a stick into the fire. "In an elaborate ceremony, a priest lowers the infant into a large basin filled with the dragon's blood. The baby is completely immersed. In this way, the dragon's blood touches everything, guaranteeing the child's worthiness.

"Unless they do not survive the ceremony."

Caedan seemed reluctant to speak again, but he finally asked, "How?"

"It is all a lie!" Bice said with such force I expected to see the fire move away from him. "The ceremony is nothing and determines nothing. The priests already know whether a child will be allowed to survive. Viridia must have a stable population, and some children are more desired than others.

"Beryl's parents already had one child. And they were not highly-educated or skilled in their fields. Thus, it was already decided that they would not be allowed to have another child."

"In Caesious, couples are allowed only one child, regardless," Caedan said. "After a woman has her child, the doctors do something to her so that she can't do it any more."

"Viridia is more interested in the ceremony, the religious connection to it all," Bice said. "The children are sacrifices, no matter what they call it. The parents are sometimes told that it is an honor for their child to be taken by the dragon's blood, that… Viridia wanted the child for himself. And that the children will serve him forever in the afterlife."

"She never even had a name!" I groaned through gritted teeth. "Children are named after the dedication ceremony. My parents… they were so… shocked that, that they wouldn't even tell me what they were going to name her!"

A wall had gone up between my parents and I that day, a wall that only strengthened as I grew older and fully understood what had happened. At ten years old, however, it was enough to know that my baby sister was gone and the ones responsible were the priests of the green dragon. Hatred conceived in me that day and grew to its present form over seven years of anger and sorrow.

I climbed to my feet and walked away from the fire. Why had they even taken me to the ceremony? They knew there was a possibility! They knew! Were they so blinded by their devotion to the dragon that they didn't even consider it? That must have been it. They believed the dragon to be a god. Their faith assured them they were doing the right thing.

But in my mind, all I could see were tiny golden curls dripping with dragon's blood. Nothing would ever erase that image from my head.

I took the stone shard of the dragon statue out of my pocket and fingered it. I wanted to throw it as far as I could, but instead I just rubbed the carved scales with my thumb. I wasn't ready to get rid of it just yet.

I heard footsteps behind me. "Go away, Bice," I growled. Over a year ago, the former priest had pulled the story out of me. He had tried to comfort and counsel me a number of times, but I wouldn't listen to him. He said the dedication ceremony was one of the things that drove him from the priesthood, but I didn't care.

"Good thing I'm not him," Rick answered. "He'd probably be trying to make you feel better."

"And you're not?" I put the stone shard back in my pocket.

"No. I finally understand you, my friend. And that's a good thing."

I snorted. I had reached the top of the hill and looked out over the countryside. In the distance, I saw the lights of a train moving along at a sluggish pace.

Rick put a hand on my shoulder. "I told you that everyone I knew in Atramentous had been killed or captured. You and I—we've both lost loved ones to the dragons. And Kelly now—she's lost her parents. Don lost his wife."

"Yeah? So?"

"So I'm saying we're connected. We all have reason to hate the dragons, you most of all, maybe. So we use that."

"Use it?"

"The anger and hate—let it drive you. It gives you strength." He removed his hand from my shoulder and looked out over the hills. "It does for me."

I knew what he said was true to some extent, but also... not completely true. If I leaned solely on my hate, I would have killed

Caedan for sure. And I still knew that would have been wrong. At the same time, there was no denying the strength that anger seemed to give me at the right times.

I also knew the rage burning inside of Rick seemed to dwarf mine sometimes. He kept it hidden most of the time, but it was always there, behind those aged eyes of his. If I lost all of the team and somehow survived alone, I guess my rage would be pretty crazy too. But... also sorrow. If Kelly, Bice, and the others died and I lived, I would mourn for them for... forever, really. I didn't see sorrow in Rick. Just the rage.

We were all shaped by events in our lives, turning points that helped define who we were going to become. And yet, we had a choice on how they would define us, didn't we? Rick could have let the loss of his friends lead him into despair, to giving up. But instead he chose to fight on, to honor their memories by trying again and again. Loden could have let my parents' death be just another sorrowful moment in life, but he used it as motivation to construct an elaborate plan to kill a dragon.

I resolved right then that no matter what happened in two days, I would keep on. If we succeeded or failed, I would never give up. The cause was greater than any of us.

Rick had moved away from me while I was lost in my thoughts. I took a deep breath and shuffled back toward the fire. I should not avoid my friends right now. I would be leaving them in the morning, after all.

As I approached the fire, Bice came out to meet me. "The others are getting ready to sleep," he said. He searched my face in the flickering light. "Are you all right?"

"I will be."

"I think you will too," he agreed. "But not just because you finally told the story. Beryl... on that day, you lost more than you know. By losing your sister and the connection to your parents, you lost your entire family. It is not good for a man to be alone. For seven years, you've been searching, even if you didn't know it, for community, for relationships to replace those you lost." He gestured back toward everyone else. "I think you've finally found that now. You needed people to care for you as you cared for them. That's what you have, whether you realize it or not."

I gave him a slow nod, smiled and moved on. Don and Lovat had made their beds near the fire. I could see the appeal of that, but I don't think I could sleep out in the open that way. I needed the security of some walls. I headed to the cave entrance and saw a figure standing there, waiting for me.

Kelly.

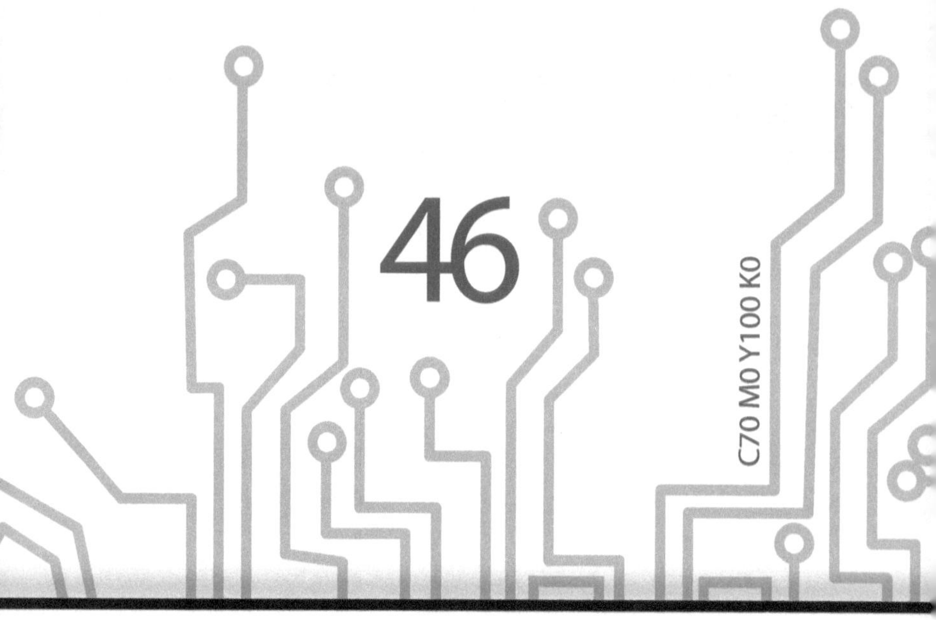

As I neared her, I opened my mouth to say something, but she stopped me. "Shhh."

Taking my hand, Kelly led me back into the cave. We passed Caedan, who gave us a curious look but didn't say anything. We left the range of the lanterns and found a spot where Kelly had laid out our blankets. My heart was racing faster than the train that brought us here. Kelly sat next to me on the blankets and leaned against my shoulder. What was happening here?

"Beryl, I'm so sorry," she whispered. "I didn't know."

"It's not your fault."

"I know, but I feel horrible about how I treated you earlier." She snuggled a little closer. "I understand you better now, I think."

"Uh… that's good?" I had no idea how we had gone from her screaming at me to this. My emotions and hormones both were running around in circles, bumping into each other, trying to figure out what to do.

"But. I was still right. I told you that you didn't know what love means. And that's true, but not for the reason I was thinking then."

"Oh?"

"No, it's because for years, you haven't had anyone show you what love means. You've been so alone."

"Are you going to show me?" I swallowed hard.

"I am showing you, silly."

She lifted her face and our lips met. I held her tight and reveled in the moment. I still didn't understand why this was happening, but I was going to enjoy every second of it. We slowly slid down on the blankets. And then I felt something wet touch my lips. Our kiss had a salty taste.

I gently pushed her away and looked up at her face. Why was she crying? "What's wrong?"

Kelly put her head down on my chest. I wiggled my shoulders and found a somewhat comfortable position to be able to keep her there. I hoped my rapid heartbeat wouldn't scare her.

"You lost your sister," she said softly. "And then your parents. I've lost my parents now… I don't know if they're alive or dead. I just don't know." She sniffed and the tears continued to flow.

My life really did not make sense sometimes. How did we go from passionate kissing to this? A very strong part of me told me to kiss her again, anyway. She was in a highly emotional state. I could easily take advantage of that. I could almost hear Rick urging me. And why not? We might all die in less than thirty-six hours. Why not grab this opportunity while I had it?

Because… I knew deep down it would be wrong. I would be taking advantage of her. It would be awesome and exciting, but she might regret it later.

"But there might not be a 'later!'" the other side of me screamed in my head.

"Shut up!" I said aloud.

"Mm?" Kelly murmured.

"Nothing. It's okay. Everything's okay now," I told her. She clung to me tighter, her tears wetting my shirt.

Just as I knew that killing Caedan was wrong, I knew that using Kelly's fragile emotional state to get what I wanted from her would be wrong. Stacy said I was too nice for my own good. I wondered what that meant at the time. Now I knew, I guess. I continued to whisper comforting words to Kelly until her tears stopped and she fell asleep.

There was also that whole "virgin daughter" thing. Bice said it wasn't necessarily literal, but what if dragons really could sense something like that? I sighed. Why couldn't anything in my life be simple? I settled back and tried to get to sleep myself.

I woke to the faint sound of Kelly singing. Daylight streamed into the cave, showing it to be empty. I got up, stretched and moved to the entrance. Kelly sat there, practicing her song. As I approached, I heard something about "humble beauty" but she sang so quietly, I couldn't make out the other words.

She heard me coming and stopped, turning with a smile.

"Good morning, sleepyhead." She greeted me with a quick kiss.

"Good morning," I muttered. It still baffled me that she had forgiven my earlier mistakes.

"I didn't see any reason to wake you up. We've all needed a good night's sleep."

I nodded, then shook my head. It dawned on me how much of the morning had already passed. "Oh, no. I need to get moving!" I ran back into the cave and began grabbing a few things.

Kelly followed. "What are you talking about? We don't have any plans for today. It's all about tomorrow."

I stopped and took her hand. "Kelly, thank you for last night, and… and I do love you. But I have to get back to Viridia today."

She jerked away. "What? Why?"

"I can't let Loden be on that train alone. He's going to need my help."

"That wasn't part of the plan," she protested. "What are you talking about?"

"Troilus Green is going to be on the train. He's going to kill Loden after the demonstration."

"What? I don't understand."

"I can't leave him alone. Plus, killing the draconic will help the plan. It's another guarantee that the green dragon will be blamed. When they find the draconic's body, it—"

"No. No, no, no. You can't do this. You can't!"

"I already told you I was going to do this. Remember?" She had been pretty upset when I told her the first time, so I guess I shouldn't be surprised it had slipped her mind.

"Does Loden know?"

"Yes, he—"

"Then don't you think he has a plan to deal with it? Why do you need to go? We had a day to ourselves, Beryl! One last day! Why would you take that away?"

"Because that thing hurt you!" I shouted.

She stopped.

"Because it hurt you," I repeated. "And it took your parents. And now it wants to take Loden. I have to do something."

Emotions warred on her face. I could see she still wanted me to stay, but understood why I needed to go. At least, I hoped that's what I was seeing. My record on identifying her thoughts and moods hadn't been very good lately.

"Then you can't go alone," she said. "Take Rick with you."

"I need him here to help you, in case I don't make it back in time."

"He's not going alone," Caedan announced, walking up from further back in the cave. "I'm going with him."

"Uhhh. I don't think so," I said.

"I'm your hostage, remember?" Caedan hooked his baton into his belt. "I have to follow you around. Besides, fighting a draconic sounds like fun."

I didn't like this idea, but as I considered it, I realized he was right. I couldn't leave him behind and trust that he and Rick wouldn't get into some kind of fight. My own conscience trapped me.

"Him?" Kelly asked. "You—this is crazy, Beryl!"

"What about our lives isn't crazy?" I said, slinging my sword onto my back. I considered the shockspear, but opted to take Caedan's stunner instead. I grabbed a couple of protein bars and a canteen of water. "Let's go, Caedan."

We left the cave, Kelly still behind me, still unsure. To be honest, I wasn't so sure myself. But at this point, I felt committed. I couldn't back down now and still claim to be a leader here, could I? Did leaders change their minds?

Rick met us at the exit. "Taking the blue man with you?"

I nodded. Rick frowned, but nodded back. Good. I needed his approval. "Take care of things here," I said, and grasped his hand. "When I get back, we're killing a dragon."

He looked me in the eyes and smiled. "That's what we've been about since we met. Now go kill a draconic first!" With those words, my resolve settled. No turning back now.

I looked back at Kelly. "I will be back. Trust me. I'm coming back."

"Nothing ever works out for us, does it?" she whispered. "I know you plan to come back, but I don't think that's up to you."

"I don't—I, uh…" I had no idea what to say.

"Goodbye, Beryl." She leaned up and kissed me, then pulled away quickly.

"Goodbye…" My voice trailed off as she hurried into the cave.

"It'll be okay," Rick said. "I'll be watching her."

"Yeah, I know. Tell Bice where I've gone… but, uh, not until I've been gone a little while."

"Will do."

I started walking, heading southeast. We would cut across and meet the train tracks after a mile or so. I hoped we could maybe catch a ride somehow. Otherwise, well, we'd have to walk all day and most of the night. I could do it, and I knew Caedan would have no trouble. Either way, we'd be in Viridia in plenty of time. I hoped.

This was it. Everything was falling into place.

So why did I feel like everything was falling apart?

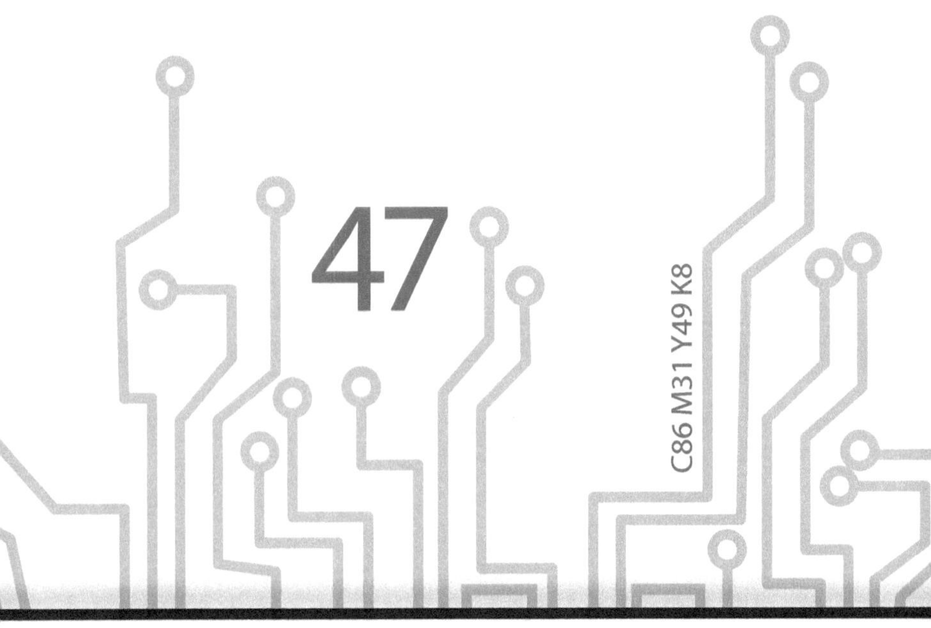

When we reached the top of the hill, Caedan stopped and pointed to the east. "What's that?"

I looked off in the indicated direction. The hills came to an end not far away, and the plains stretched away as far as the eye could see. But in the distance, it looked like a brownish mist hung over the plains. It was ugly and unnatural, the only thing I had seen out here that clearly did not belong. I felt a sadness settle into my gut.

"It's the Blasted Lands. I didn't know it was that close."

"In Caesious, they say the Blasted Lands are growing. Every year, they get larger."

"Huh. I wonder if that's true." If so, then someday the Blasted Lands would consume everything within The Circle. Our plans and wars wouldn't even matter in the long run. Everything here would die.

"We have to go beyond The Circle," I said, the thought just occurring to me.

"Seriously?"

I blinked and looked back toward the southeast. "I don't know. I just thought... I don't know."

Caedan kept up with me as we went downhill. "You don't ever think small, do you? Kill a dragon, leave The Circle..."

I ignored him.

"Even at a pace like this, we won't reach Viridia tonight," he said a few minutes later. "I don't think you realize how far out we are."

I stopped and looked down at the train tracks just below us. "I know exactly what I'm doing," I answered him. "About ten miles down the track from here is a farming station. Trains aren't stopping there this time of year, but they do slow down as they pass through, because there are sharp turns both before and after it. We should be able to board one and ride the rest of the way in to the city."

"For someone who took his first train ride two days ago, you've become quite the expert."

"I studied Loden's maps and notes," I said. Thinking of Loden reminded me of the envelope he had given me. I had stashed it with the rest of my gear back in the cave. Because of everything that had been happening with Kelly, I hadn't even been tempted to open it yet. Now I wished I had brought it along.

Caedan let us walk on in silence for another half-hour before he had to speak again.

"Listen, about last night—" he began.

"Watch it," I growled.

Both of his hands went up. "No, no, I'm not—I'm not going to say anything, uh, I'm not going to question you, or, um, anything bad. I just, uh…"

"What?"

"I wanted you to know that, uh, I guess I understand you a little better now."

I grunted. People kept saying that.

"I mean, I still think you're crazy, and this will never work, but, uh… I get why you're doing it, at least."

I acknowledged him with a quick nod and kept walking. The silence lasted a couple of minutes this time.

"So what happens if you win?"

"What?"

"If, if somehow you pull this whole thing off, if you actually kill a dragon… then what?"

"Then the dragons fight each other, and we kill whichever ones survive that. We don't stop until they're all dead."

"You'll need a lot more help for that," Caedan said, almost to himself.

"You'll need uprisings in all the cities."

"I haven't thought much about it yet. I'm just trying to get through tomorrow alive."

"In the face."

I had no idea what he meant by that phrase. It must have been some blue city idiom that only made sense to them. It was another reminder that even though we had so much in common, the people of the cities had been segregated for generations. There were probably many differences we hadn't even thought about yet. Stacy hadn't seemed all that worried about it, though, and she had traveled to the other cities. Rick came from Atramentous and we didn't seem to have any major differences. I hoped that meant we had enough to bind us all together; that once people saw the dragons could be defeated, they would band together throughout all the cities.

"It's a hope," I said aloud.

"What?"

"Never mind." Of course, by pinning the blame for the dragon's death on another dragon, we weren't really showing them that, were we? We were making it look like the only thing that could kill a dragon was another dragon. We would definitely need a new plan after this one. Maybe Stacy could spread the true story, but as a rumor? I don't know. We needed to talk about this.

A couple of hours later, we reached the end of the hills and came down to the farming station. We approached cautiously, just in case anyone else happened to be around, but no one appeared, as I expected. The various storage buildings didn't interest me. I focused on the tracks. At one point, they ran underneath a flat roof—I guessed it was there to shield workers from the weather while loading. I pointed it out to Caedan.

"We'll climb on there and wait," I said. "When the train goes under us, we'll get a running start and then jump on top of a boxcar."

"You make it sound so easy."

I knew it was a risky move. But I also knew my implant would help erase any risk for me. Caedan… well, I hoped his training had him in good enough shape that he could pull this off. Otherwise, it might be a lonely ride after all.

One train had gone by while we were walking. I didn't know when the next one would come along, but I knew there had to be more than just the one per day. We might have to wait a few hours, but it would be worth it.

We climbed on top of the roof in short order and settled in to wait. We munched on protein bars and drank our water. The sun moved overhead, and the heat began to build. I loosened the Viridian Guard tunic around my neck.

"These uniforms weren't really made for sitting out in the sun," Caedan observed. At least he had left the helmet behind.

We waited. And sweated. The sun moved across the sky. A day like today wouldn't be that hot under any other circumstances. It might be quite nice if you weren't wearing a hot uniform. On a roof. With no shade.

"What if another train doesn't come?" Caedan asked for the third time. I ignored him for the second time. If it didn't come, it didn't come. My plan would be ruined. Loden would face Troilus Green alone. I saw no need to discuss it.

Sometime around the middle of the afternoon, we heard the sound of a train approaching. Without a word, we both ducked low and waited. In a few minutes, the train came around the final sharp turn, slowing as it did so. I knew it wouldn't speed up because of the oncoming turn after the station.

As the engine came under our hiding place, we both jumped to our feet. I watched as a number of boxcars went under us. "Now!" We spun and ran as fast we could. I gave myself a slight boost to get a little edge and outdistance Caedan. The end of the roof came up way too fast, and I leaped through the air. Another quick boost to my legs helped with the landing, but not much. I rolled and slid and grabbed at anything I could reach. I managed to find something to hold just in time to prevent myself from sliding off the side of the car.

I took a deep breath and calmed my nerves. Only then did I look back to see how Caedan had fared. He lay on top of the next boxcar, also holding on for dear life. He grinned and waved.

Regaining a sense of balance, I maneuvered myself to a more secure position. Once I felt more confident, I moved to the back of the car and then jumped to the next one. Caedan helped stop my progress, and we knelt side-by-side.

"We should probably move to the last car," I yelled over the sound of the wind. "It'll be easier to drop off from there when we get close to the station."

Caedan nodded. "I hope you've got a better plan for catching the next train," he said.

"Loden will help us."

Of course, Loden had been against my returning. He might actually have a plan of his own. With any luck, our plans would work together. But when had luck been on my side lately?

Loden was not pleased to see us. But he wasn't surprised.

"I knew you wouldn't let this go," he grumbled. "I received notice that Troilus Green would be accompanying me on the test drive, along with two of its guards. Supposedly, they want a first-hand look at this new tech. But we know the real reason."

"We'll kill it," I said with more confidence than I felt. "A draconic's body will only add to the overall plan, right?"

Loden snorted. "And do you have a plan for how to kill it?"

"Sort of. I didn't really plan for the two guards, but I'll have to make it work. One against three aren't the best odds—"

"Do all greenies have trouble with counting or is it just you?" Caedan interrupted. "I count three against three."

I shot him a look. "You're going to help me?"

He shrugged. "The opportunity to test my skills against the Viridian Guard and a draconic? Sounds totally streak. I should be thanking you."

I honestly didn't see that coming. At least not yet.

Loden rolled his eyes. "Fine. Let's get you hidden, then."

The test run for the speed train, as Loden called it, would only involve the engine, a special passenger car linked to it with no gap, and a flat car holding some basic equipment for repair work in case anything went wrong. With our help, Loden added another large crate to the flat car, attached it firmly, and then told us to get inside.

"When you feel the train start moving, wait about thirty seconds for us to clear the station, and then get out quickly. You'll have to get over to the main car before we reach top speed, or the wind will tear you off."

"Listen," I said, "There are things I wanted to say to you. I owe you so—"

"Stop." He cut me off. "Beryl, you don't owe me a thing. I was blinded for too many years, and that blindness cost you everything—your sister, your parents. I could have changed things. I could have saved them. And I didn't. Let me finish the job now."

"If I could have chosen my own father…"

He snorted. "That's a nice sentiment, but you don't mean that."

"Yes, I do! Loden, you—I'd be nowhere without you. I'd be dead without you!"

"Yes, well, there's still a good chance of that happening in the next two hours, as things stand. I'll see you shortly."

He closed the crate, and Caedan and I waited in darkness. My hand found the release cord for the lid. I made sure I knew its location and then let go. No use holding on to it for what might be an hour or so.

We waited. Most of this trip had been waiting. We waited to jump on to a train. When we arrived at Viridia, we had to wait almost all night for Loden to return. We had taken turns getting some rest then. Now, here we were waiting again, only this was the last time. Within a very short time, we would be fighting for our lives.

"At least it's cooler than being on top of that roof," Caedan said.

"Why are you helping me?" I asked. "I mean, I wanted to win you over, but this is abrupt."

"You haven't won me over," he said. "I'm just waiting for the moment you promised to let me go. In the meantime, it doesn't matter what I do, really. So I could sit around and be bored, or… enjoy a good battle. I've always wanted to fight a draconic. How strong are they, really?"

"What if we lose and you're captured? Your life will be over."

I could almost see him shrug in the darkness. "The only way you're really going to let me go is if you do win, so I guess I need to make sure that happens. I gave you my word, and I'm sticking with it."

"You're an honorable man, Caedan Teal."

"Thanks. I'd say the same for you, except for that whole kill-all-the-dragons thing. I have a hard time seeing honor and insanity in the same place."

I didn't know what to say to that, so I didn't answer.

We waited.

After about half an hour, we heard more voices. Though I strained, I couldn't make them out. I did think I heard the deeper tones of a draconic voice now and then.

More time passed. The voices drew closer and then went out of range again. I heard the engine start up. I grabbed the release cord and waited. It took at least another five minutes before we started moving.

I counted out the thirty seconds and yanked the cord. The lid of the crate snapped open; the wind ripped it away. Caedan followed close behind me as I scrambled out and jumped across to the back door of the passenger car. We looked through the door's window and saw the two guards. Beyond them, the imposing figure of Troilus Green hid any view of Loden. All of them had their backs to us.

Caedan had his baton at ready. I drew my sword and pulled out my stone shard with the other hand. The train was picking up speed now, already moving faster than the regular trains, from what I could tell. I looked at Caedan. He nodded. We positioned ourselves on either side of the door. With a grunt, I smashed the stone shard into the window and braced myself.

The first guard emerged from the door and Caedan dispatched him with a vicious blow to the temple just as he reacted to seeing us. Caedan yanked him forward and threw him off the train.

As the second guard appeared, I attempted the same trick, hitting him with the hilt of my sword, but he managed to stay conscious and swung his shockspear. In a swift motion, I drew the stunner from its holster and pulled the trigger. The wires shot out and latched on to his chest. After a few seconds of electricity, he went down, twitching. Caedan and I grabbed him by the armpits and slung him off the train too. I figured both guards would be injured by the impact, possibly breaking some bones, but at least they wouldn't die.

Without hesitation, we charged into the passenger car.

"Ah, there you are, Beryl." Troilus Green towered over us, the sickly-sweet smell permeating the air. The deep, raspy voice chuckled. "I was wondering when you'd show up."

"Chroma! You didn't say how big it was!" Caedan muttered. He had swept up the fallen shockspear and had it ready to stab. The two of us could stand side-by-side in the wide walkway between the seats. The draconic, on the other hand, dominated the entire thing. His head nearly touched the ceiling.

"You keep such interesting company," Troilus Green observed. "First a black, now a blue. Oh, and the heretic. What an odd conglomeration you are! Where is the wanderer? Has he abandoned you?" It raised a hand, palm outward, toward us.

"Your powers don't work here, outside the city!" I snarled.

The draconic tilted its head and seemed to grin even more. "Just as well, then." It flexed its claws. "I will enjoy spilling your blood."

"Yours first!" Loden cried, stabbing from behind with another shockspear. He thrust up through the back of Troilus Green's right knee.

At the startled roar that shook the passenger car, I lunged forward, triggering my implant with a solid boost into my legs. I aimed my sword at the draconic's chest and leaped into the air. Behind me, Caedan rushed forward too.

My sword slammed into Troilus Green's chest—and I lost my grip. The sword slid across something incredibly solid and tumbled to the floor. I bounced off the draconic and fell myself, scrambling to stay on my feet. A massive fist slammed into my chest and sent me flying back the way I had come. I hit one of the seats and cartwheeled over it before I slid to the floor.

Caedan didn't stand a chance. Troilus Green caught his shockspear in mid-air and snapped it like a twig. Before Caedan could even look surprised, the draconic backhanded him into the air. He slammed into the wall of the train and slumped down, unconscious.

With lightning speed, the monster whirled and slashed. I couldn't see, but I heard a cry of pain from Loden. The draconic twisted back toward me, its claws glistening with blood. Chuckling again, it ripped the robe from its body, exposing a chest criss-crossed with strips of gleaming metal that pulsed with an electric green glow.

"I told you we were in the same accident together three years ago. I just didn't tell you how much they had to do to keep me alive!"

The train rushed on toward its deadly encounter. Loden and Caedan were down. I had no weapons.

We had lost.

Troilus Green took two steps and seized me by the front of my chest. Its claws, metal and organic, cut furrows as they grasped my Viridian Guard tunic and lifted me into the air. I found myself staring back into those green-flecked obsidian eyes. The metal plate on the left side of its face had been refined since last I saw it, blending smoothly with its jade scales.

"You pathetic little human. You fancy yourself some kind of rebel leader, gathering followers, causing minor disruptions, taunting me—me, Troilus Green, deadliest servant of the almighty Viridia!"

"But here you are," I growled. I tried grabbing its claws and prying them loose, but I couldn't move even one. "Maybe you're more worried… about me than you admit."

"You are nothing but an annoyance, an insect to be crushed beneath my feet. Do you think you are the first to rebel against us? You are not. You are not even the strongest or smartest, by far. Why, you do not even know the first things about the world around you. We live in a world of science and magic intertwined, where one becomes another and few can tell the difference." It raised its other hand and I saw a strange spark pass between two of the claws. "I have stood in the presence of gods! I have walked in the burning coals of their fury. I have seen what lies beyond The Circle. I have felt the very life-pulse of this world. You… are nothing."

"Well, you're a big lizard!" Except I didn't really say that. I think I made a little noise in my throat.

"Let me show you how little you know."

The monster switched to holding me by the neck and held its palm flat out against my chest. "Like this." Again it spoke one of those strange words I couldn't comprehend. Invisible power slammed into my chest as if I had been punched by a railroad tie. I felt several ribs crack and lost my breath for a moment.

How was that possible? Was Bice wrong? Or had he not told the whole story again?

Troilus Green regarded me for a long moment.

"Your only possible value is in helping me find the wanderer. But you have brought me others from which to pry that information. As I said, you are nothing at all." Its jaws seemed to loosen and become wider. In that instant, I genuinely believed it was going to eat my face. Razor-sharp teeth approached me. The acrid smell of the draconic's breath enveloped my nostrils. I could see greenish saliva dripping from the upper jaw, striking the massive tongue and running down into the blackness of the beast's gullet. I closed my eyes, thinking of Kelly and hoping Rick could save her.

"Wait…" a feeble voice called. Loden. I opened my eyes and twisted my head to see him. He lay on the floor behind Troilus Green. He looked horrible. The draconic's claws had ripped across his torso, cutting deep. At the rate blood was pumping out of him, he wouldn't last long.

"What do you want, dead man?" the draconic snarled, its jaw popping as it resumed normal shape.

"Don't kill him," Loden said. "He has the tech your master is desperately seeking."

What?

"What are you talking about?" Troilus Green pulled back from my face and looked down at Loden.

"In your master's… world…"—Loden struggled with every word, but drew himself up—"he was worthless. He was… nothing, like you say. But you… and your master are wrong. Life, his life, is valuable. Didn't you… see him move? It's cybernetics."

"Is this true?" the draconic demanded, shaking me.

"Yes," I answered. I didn't see any point in lying now. "After that accident, he gave me an implant. Base of my spine. It's how I can move so fast."

"That's not very impressive, though it does explain some things. I must see this for myself." It flipped me in the air and hurled me down, face-first onto the floor. The pain of my ribs striking the floor almost made me lose consciousness. Claws scraped my back and ripped what was left of the tunic away. A heavy foot slammed onto my upper back, pinning me down. I struggled to catch a breath.

"You are both full of lies," Troilus Green said. "I see no implant. No scar."

Wait. What? I reached back with my left hand to try to feel the small of my back. Of course there was a scar there! That's what… Loden… had always told me…

"I didn't put the implant in his spine," Loden whispered. "I put it in his brain."

Dead silence settled on the passenger car, broken only by the sound of the train's wheels turning faster and faster. If Loden told the truth, he had discovered something the dragons coveted most of all. I heard the green dragon himself talking about cybernetic brain implantation. But if it was in my brain, that meant…

"It is not possible." Troilus Green finally spoke again.

Loden coughed violently. "Think about it. He boosts his legs to make those runs and jumps…" He coughed again. "But he does that with his brain! He only boosts the legs because…" He choked and coughed again, but he didn't need to finish the sentence. Because that's all he had ever told me. Because I never even thought of trying anything else.

"He *was* very badly damaged in that accident," the draconic mused. "Perhaps…"

I closed my eyes and concentrated. I aimed a light boost into both of my arms, instead of my legs. I immediately felt them strengthen. I positioned both hands flat on the floor, took a deep breath and focused. Power flooded into my arms. I pushed down as hard as I could.

I erupted off the floor, throwing Troilus Green backward with a startled roar. Strength like I never knew filled my upper body. I channeled some down into my legs for good measure. My heart raced. Spots appeared before my eyes for a moment. I felt indestructible.

But I still faced a seven-foot-tall draconic with cybernetic enhancements of its own. Troilus Green regained its composure and balance far quicker than I might have hoped. With guttural snarls, it leaped forward, claws outstretched.

I blocked one of the clawed hands with ease, but the other slipped in past my defenses and grabbed my neck. For a second time, it lifted me off my feet. The claws began to tighten.

But this time was different. Pouring more boosts into my hands and even fingers, I reached up, grasped two of the claws around my neck and snapped them backward. The bones shattered with loud pops. Troilus Green howled in pain and anger, and I dropped to the floor again. I ducked a ferocious swing from its other hand and searched the floor around me. I spotted the sword and dove for it.

I wasn't fast enough. Troilus Green grabbed my ankle and slung me into the air. I slammed into the roof and bounced across several seats before coming to a rest, battered and gasping for breath. The boosts helped me ignore the pain, but like always, using them would leave me drained, especially if I kept this up much longer. There was a limit, even to these new abilities. I just didn't know exactly how far I could go.

"I do not require you to be alive when our scientists rip this technology out of you," the draconic growled. "You have hurt me, and that is more—"

I poured a huge boost into my arms and yanked one of the seats free from the floor. I spun and hurled it into Troilus Green's face. It smashed the seat away, but it gave me the chance I wanted. I lunged across the floor, again diving for the sword. Again the draconic was too fast. It kicked me in mid-leap, halting my progress and knocking me hard against another row of chairs. Stars danced in my vision.

"Beryl!" Caedan's voice. I glanced his way and saw that he had crawled, unnoticed in the chaos, to pick up the sword himself. He hefted it and gestured with his chin.

I looked back at Troilus Green just in time to dodge another punch that might have taken off my head if it had connected. The draconic entered absolute feral territory now. As its arm slid past me, I could see individual jade scales standing up. Venomous spittle flew from its mouth, open in a perpetual snarl of rage. This was a monster. Monsters need slaying.

"Now!" I yelled. The draconic whirled to see Caedan, ducking low to reach for him.

I boosted my legs and leaped upward, kicking off one of the seats and twisting in the air as Caedan tossed the sword up and over Troilus Green's head. The draconic spun back to meet me. With perfect timing, my hand closed over the hilt with the blade aiming down. Putting every bit of cybernetic boost into my arms as I could, I brought the sword straight down into Troilus Green's open maw. The entire blade went in, piercing through its open lower jaw and into its neck, ripping open scales and cybernetic coverings alike. Venom burned its way across both my hands and wrists. I let go and collapsed to the floor.

Troilus Green fumbled for the sword embedded in its jaw and throat, but its hand never managed to connect. I scrambled backward on all fours. With a deep and rasping moan, the draconic staggered, wavered, and fell. Its wounded head landed right in front of me. As I looked into those strange eyes, the green flecks faded and disappeared. Only blackness remained.

Troilus Green was dead.

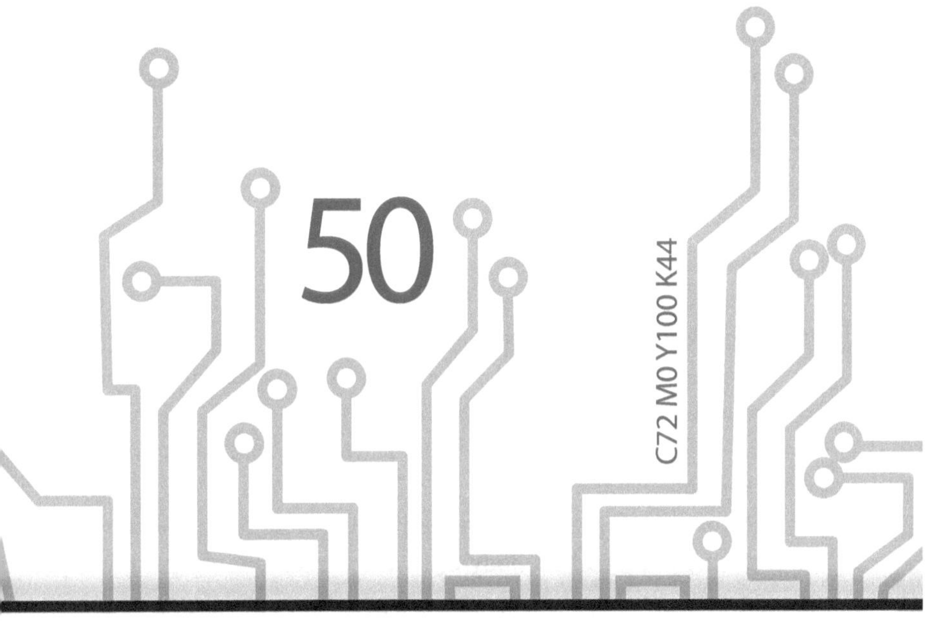

50

"Wow." Caedan's open-mouthed stare caught my attention, but only for a moment. I scrambled past him, slipping on blood and venom. Loden lay still at the far end of the passenger car.

I crouched at the older man's side and pressed against one of his chest wounds, trying to stop the bleeding. I didn't know a lot about injuries, but I could tell I wasn't doing much good.

Loden coughed. His hand came up and grasped mine. "Don't bother," he whispered. "It's too late for me."

"No, no…"

"It's… okay, Beryl. I didn't expect… to survive today."

"But—but you can't… I need you."

"Listen, son, the train is going to do… what it's supposed to do. I've taken care of that." His voice was so low, I had to lean in close to hear him. "You need to get off. There's a backpack on the last seat." I glanced toward the back of the car. Caedan got to his feet, still staring at the draconic's body. "Put it on. And then… go out and… pull the left cord. When you… want… come down… right cord…"

I didn't know what he meant. Come down?

"Loden, please… hang on. Caedan probably knows how to— Caedan!" I yelled at him.

The blue-clad soldier snapped out of it and hurried to my side. He knelt and looked over Loden's wounds. His face grew pained, and he shook his head. "There's nothing I can do, Beryl."

Loden was saying something else. I leaned back down next to his lips. "Don' forget… envelope." He closed his eyes and stopped breathing. I thought he was gone, until he drew in another breath. "Be… proud… if you… were… m'son."

Loden took a deep, ragged breath and then let it all out. His head lolled back, and he stopped moving.

Three years earlier, when I woke up in the hospital and Bice told me my parents were dead, I didn't cry. I didn't mourn them. They were dead to me after they killed my sister. I had felt only a cold anger deep inside that never quite went away.

But now… a sob wracked my aching body. While Caedan watched helplessly, I pulled Loden's body close and vented my sorrow, my anger, my loneliness, and my despair into that passenger car. I didn't even know I was capable of that kind of weeping. My sobs exploded into the air, each one a strain of lament and anguish. My entire body shook over and over. I felt depleted inside and out. The boosts exhausted me, but this took it to another level. Caedan got to his feet and left me there while he gathered up our weapons.

The sobs were only beginning to subside when a loud crackle came from the front of the car. Rick's voice, muddled by a low buzz, could be heard. "Is this working? If you can hear me, let me know. The dragon is coming! Did you hear me? The dragon is coming!"

My eyes met Caedan's. Loden's talkers had slipped my mind. As I took a few deep breaths to control myself, Caedan stepped past and found the talker near the engine's controls. He picked it up and pushed the talk button.

"We hear you. Uh… the draconic is down. The train is on schedule." Caedan looked at me with raised eyebrows. He let go of the talk button and asked, "Do we tell them anything else?"

I shook my head. "No." I took another ragged breath. "Not yet. We've got to get off of this train."

The talker squawked again. "Got it," Rick's voice answered. "The dragon is circling. Should be landing soon. The singer is waiting."

I let Loden's body down onto the floor with care. I wanted to do more for him, but it would be pointless. I whispered "goodbye" and got to my feet. I staggered and leaned against the wall, which didn't provide a lot of support as it rocked. My whole body, drained and exhausted, did not want to respond to my commands. Bruised and battered all over, multiple ribs cracked or broken inside my chest, stinging gashes across my chest and back… My hands, though… the draconic's venom had coated them from fingertip to just past my wrists. They burned as if fire ran up and down each finger. I kept triggering boosts to keep myself from screaming in pain.

Loden had talked about a backpack. I careened to the back of the car and found it on the last seat, somehow undamaged. I picked it up and looked it over. Two cords with plastic handles hung down over the straps, one on each side. I assumed it had been designed with one person in mind. Should we attempt to make it two, or…

I had no time to worry about it. Kelly was about to face a dragon.

I noticed my stone shard lying on the floor just inside the door. I considered leaving it, but once again, couldn't quite do so. I picked it up and stuffed it back into my pocket.

"Come on." I opened the back door, stepped out onto the platform, and felt the wind whipping by.

Caedan paused long enough to yank my sword out of the body of Troilus Green. He tucked it into his belt and then joined me. He eyed the backpack warily. "How is this going to work?"

"Put it on and let's see."

"Me?"

"Yeah, you. I can jump off and survive. You can't."

Caedan looked skeptical, but he pulled the backpack on. "Now what?"

"Loden said to pull the left cord to go up and the right cord to go down, I think."

"You think?"

I yanked the left cord. I heard the hiss of air exploding through a tube of some kind, and Caedan erupted off the train and into the air. He yelled something, but I couldn't hear it over the wind and the train. The hiss I had heard came from some kind of canister that inflated a huge balloon over Caedan's head. He was… flying.

"The skies belong to the dragons," I murmured. "But not any more."

The train flew along on its predetermined route. In a matter of minutes, it would reach the hills, wind to and fro through them and arrive at the staging point where Caesious the blue dragon had already landed. I would be there in moments.

I spared one more look up at Caedan floating through the air. He was almost out of sight. I hoped he could figure out how to get down. If nothing else, that balloon would deflate eventually, right?

I looked to the side at the ladder that led to the car's roof. I needed to be up there, where I'd be able to see ahead of the train. I gripped the first rung.

The burning feeling on my hands continued to get worse. The implant couldn't shut down all the pain. At least it could strengthen my hands now. I took a deep breath and concentrated on my fingers and holding on tight. I kept expecting all the flesh to tear off my fingers with each grip.

Rung by rung, I climbed up the ladder and emerged on top of the train. The wind tore at me like hundreds of eager hands, trying to throw me back to the ground where I belonged. I had to strain just to focus my eyes to look ahead. Maybe I was somehow boosting my eyelids to help me squint against the constant force of air. The thought made me chuckle a bit, which I immediately regretted. Those ribs, broken or not, hurt.

I saw a set of hand-holds running the length of the car, down its center. I focused, boosted what I thought I needed, and lunged against the wind. I would have screamed, but if I opened my mouth, the wind might tear off my lower jaw. I landed hard and grabbed for the hand-holds. My burning fingers wrapped around one of them and latched on with a death-grip. The wind lifted the rest of my body into the air and ripped a small cry from behind my clenched teeth.

I continued feeding a boost into my hand to hold on. I pulled myself down and hooked one foot under a hand-hold, while I grabbed another with my other hand.

The train took a sharp turn, almost breaking my new hold. We had entered the hills. Only a few moments remained before the end.

51

My only problem now was hanging on until the right time. It didn't help that my implant and my entire body had already been strained to the breaking point, if not beyond. I didn't understand everything about my new abilities, but I could tell I was pushing way past the safe zone. The consequences for abusing my body like this might be severe.

But at that point, I didn't care. I almost couldn't feel my hands now, but I held on. Only one final turn remained. The staging point waited just past the next hill.

That's when my right arm gave out. One moment, I was holding tight. The next moment my hand released and my arm dangled uselessly at my side.

Desperate, I channeled more boost energy into my left arm and held on. I had to see what was happening. But how? Maybe… The implant was in my brain. I could use it to strengthen the muscles in my arms, legs… What if I tried to strengthen the muscles and nerves around my eyes? Could I improve my vision?

I tried, focusing my thoughts on my eyes and the muscles related to them. The train jerked and my chest slammed against the roof, threatening to knock me out with the pain.

The train rounded the final corner. My eyes zoomed ahead, farther than I'd ever seen before. Or maybe I saw things only in my imagination.

Regardless, I had no power to influence events as they unfolded before me.

Kelly was there. Alive! And singing! From this distance, I couldn't make out the sound of her voice, let alone the words. But I saw her, live or in my mind's eye, wearing an old-style peasant's dress that Stacy had obtained for her. Her arms were spread, and she backed away from the dragon step by step. I could almost make out Bice and Rick's hiding place within a cluster of bushes about two dozen feet away.

Caesious, the blue dragon, appeared every bit as imposing as the green dragon, if not more so. He looked larger, a truly majestic figure, straddling the train track, wings still spread into the air. The scales on his upper body were a bluish-gray tone, not as bright as the painting in the train station. On his underbody, the scales lost the blue and became almost slate gray. His limbs were thicker than the green dragon's, but as the poster had shown, his entire back left leg was either metal or encased in metal. I also caught a glimpse of some metal on his right front leg. I could see a few other gleams, but given the color of his scales, he could have replaced far more of them without it being noticed. The magnificent head, far broader and larger than the green, sported a bright blue beard of some kind below his lower jaw, and one massive horn extended forward.

One more step is all it would take. One more step and… the dragon lifted both front legs up in the air and roared. With his wings still spread out, it was an awe-inspiring sight. He had certainly spotted the train by now. Was he angry or pleased? I couldn't tell. I strained my vision to see more. Caesious came down… and his right leg landed on the rigged branch line.

The trap activated. With a clang that resounded through the hills, the fake rails sprang up and snapped into place around the dragon's leg, trapping him in position where we wanted him. Kelly turned, stumbled, and ran. My vision snapped back to normal, and I blinked several times.

Beneath me, the train underwent a remarkable transformation. Whole sections of the engine's exterior ripped apart, swept away behind the onrushing train. I stared in disbelief at the front of the train, now an eight-foot-long massive blade. I flew toward the dragon at unbelievable speeds, riding on top of what was essentially a giant sword! Loden was a genius.

Caesious screamed in rage and pulled at the trap. He unleashed a fury of electrical fire from his mouth. It enveloped the tracks and raced up the rails to meet the oncoming train. Electrical bursts wrapped themselves around the train, and I winced as it passed over me, though without any pain. The bursts did nothing to slow the train's approach.

I had stayed on board too long already. I needed to get off. I gritted my teeth, channeled everything I could into my legs, and leaped into the air.

For a moment, I hung suspended, looking down as the train consumed the final few feet of track. The dragon pulled hard, and the trap moved. "NO!" I screamed. Caesious rolled onto his side just as the train arrived. I saw the blade strike him, but I couldn't tell what happened next. I began to fall. As the engine came to an abrupt halt, the passenger car and flatcar both launched into the air, narrowly missing me. Everything came back down just as quickly and collided in a spectacular impact. A cloud of smoke erupted as I fell into it.

I hit the ground and lost consciousness for a moment. I had kept boosting my legs to control the impact, but it wasn't enough. The boosts were fading, almost gone. The overwhelming pain brought me back awake almost at once. Smoke surrounded me. I couldn't see.

Desperate, I concentrated on putting something, anything into my legs. When I felt a bit of strength, I pushed myself up onto my feet and staggered toward the wreck. The smoke began to dissipate.

Caesious lived. His last-minute roll had saved him. The blade had ripped into his underbelly, spilling his guts, but hadn't pierced his heart. Unless something happened and quick, he would be able to pull himself out of the wreckage and escape. His head reared up and unleashed another blast of electrical fire. It struck the ground behind Kelly's running feet, launching her into the air.

I screamed. There was no way I could get there in time to do anything. I saw Kelly hit the ground and lay still. I tried everything I could think, straining my link to the implant to its limits, but I could only lurch forward one step at a time.

Then Rick appeared. He flew out of his hiding place, sword unsheathed, moving faster than I thought possible. He dashed through the wreckage, vaulted on top of a piece of the flatcar and launched himself through the air into the dragon's chest. His scream of rage and pain was drowned out by the death-scream of Caesious, the blue dragon.

The dragon rolled away, still screaming. Its legs, tail and head writhed in the air. I saw no sign of Rick.

I looked back to Kelly. Bice was there, helping her to her feet. She looked all right.

The dragon continued to writhe, but his movements were slowing. Had Rick done it? Had he survived?

"Beryl!"

I looked behind me to see Caedan hurrying down the hill. Before he got to me, he stopped and stared at the dragon. Until that moment, I don't think he believed our plan had any hope of success. And this dragon ruled his city. He was literally watching his god die. He pressed a fist to his mouth, wide-eyed, shaking his head in denial.

The writhing slowed further. I stared at the mighty face as it descended and came to rest on the ground. Its eyes seemed to find Caedan and me as we watched. "The Circle…" it whispered. "The Circle will… fall. Auric…"

A crackle of electricity swept over the dragon's head, and its eyes turned glassy. It grew still.

Caesious, the blue dragon, ruler and master of a hundred thousand or more, was dead. We had killed an ancient creature of unbelievable power, a god of this world.

No, not a god. It was a monster. And monsters needed to die. With that thought, I collapsed.

Caedan's arms came about my shoulders and lifted me up. "Technically, I guess I'm no longer a hostage," he muttered. "But I suppose I'll see this through now."

Even with his help, I could barely move. We approached the wreckage with halting steps. I saw Bice and Kelly approaching from the other side. I would have waved if I could. My right arm remained dead and my left wasn't much better.

I caught a glimpse of movement in the debris. A blackened figure stood shakily to his feet. "Rick?" Bice called. The figure turned to meet them. Kelly broke away from Bice and ran forward to embrace Rick. I felt a stab in my heart.

Bice noticed our approach then. "Beryl? Beryl!" He came running to meet us. He looked at me with such concern, and took Caedan's position holding me up. "I'd ask if you're all right, but you clearly aren't," he said.

"Were you actually on the train? How did you survive that?" I shook my head, unable to answer for the moment.

Kelly and Rick came next. Kelly looked fine, though a little disheveled. Rick, on the other hand… I couldn't tell how much of his body had been burned, and how much had been blackened by ash. Not a hair remained on his head. I stared at his right hand. Metal fingers flexed and curled. It was cybernetic. All this time and he… He noticed me staring and shrugged.

"Secrets," he said with a raspy voice. "We all have them."

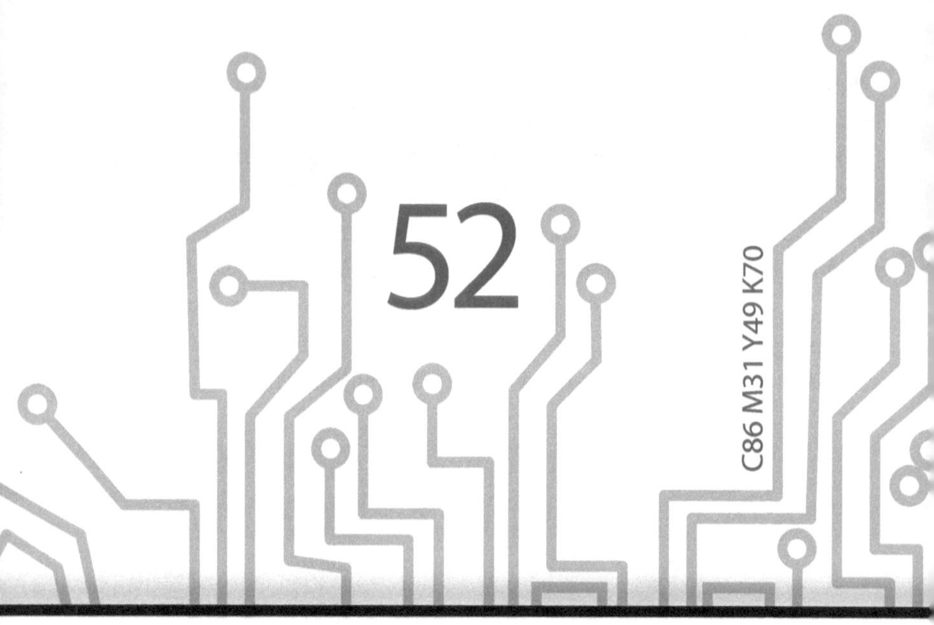

52

Kelly peered at me. "What happened to you?" she asked.

My energy was failing so fast, I couldn't even get the words out. "He discovered new things about himself and then killed a draconic," Caedan answered for me. "I've never seen anything like it. But even that..." He shook his head and looked at the dragon's corpse. He stumbled forward another step and then fell to his knees. I wondered what was going through his mind.

"Loden?" Bice asked softly.

I shook my head again. I wanted to say more, but I had no strength.

"But he saved us all," Rick said. His voice sounded like it hurt a lot. Maybe as much as the pain that was starting to re-enter my consciousness from all parts of my body. Rick stared at the dragon's face with a look of intense concentration, though I couldn't tell much else from his blackened face. He had been working toward this victory longer than most of us.

An engine roar broke into the silence that followed. We turned to see Don and Lovat riding the digger over the hilltop.

"Time to plant the evidence," Bice said with a tight face. "Kelly, Caedan, get these two back to the cave. I'll be there to help as soon as I can."

Kelly and Rick could have gotten there far quicker than I could, but they moved slow to accommodate us. Caedan had to practically carry me the rest of the way.

"I want to hear all about it," Rick said with that painful voice. "But maybe after we recover a bit."

"We did it," Kelly said. "We really did it. We killed a dragon."

"That was impossible," Caedan said. "But… you did it."

"We," I whispered, nudging him. I think I had to boost my vocal cords.

"Yeah." He didn't seem altogether thrilled by that.

I felt myself losing consciousness at this point. I managed to catch Kelly's eye. "You were amazing," I murmured.

She nodded gravely. "I guess I was."

I tried to chuckle, but couldn't muster up the strength. Blackness seeped into the edges of my vision. "Loden…" I groaned. That was it for me.

I didn't wake up for three days. When I finally did, the pain roused me. I hurt all over. The strongest agony came from my ribs and my hands. I groaned. Or did I scream?

"Your body is going to take a while to heal." I heard Bice's voice. "Give it time."

I shifted and mercifully fell asleep again.

The next day, I didn't feel much better when I woke up again. Rick sat beside me this time. Almost the first thing I saw when my eyes opened was his cybernetic hand. It was the most sophisticated-looking piece of cyber-tech I had ever seen. No wonder he hid it with gloves. Cybernetics were not given to common humans.

"Where'd that come from?" I asked in a gravelly voice, then coughed.

"You're awake!" Rick's head jerked back. I noticed he also sported bandages all up his arm and the entire right side of his face. He glanced down at his hand. "It's a long story," he said. "But it's the only reason Caesious is dead now. Without it, my arm would have burned away long before the sword reached his heart." His voice still sounded ragged, but not as bad as before.

I would have to get Rick to tell me that "long story" later. I suspected it was the reason Troilus Green had been so intent on his capture.

He leaned in toward me. "We did it, Beryl. We actually did it."

I closed my eyes and nodded. I listened to him go on for a while about how amazing everyone had been, including me. But when he mentioned Loden, I made a pained noise in my throat. He fell silent. A moment later, I felt his hand pat me on the shoulder.

"He, uh, he was kind of like a dad to you, huh?"

I nodded again and fought the lump in my throat. "Do you... do you remember your father, Rick?"

"I remember far too much. My dad was a monster."

"My dad... really wasn't. Neither was my mom." For some reason, memories of both of them flooded my thoughts. Good memories, from before I started to hate them. Memories of Dad getting down on the floor and playing Dragon Action toys with me. Memories of Mom holding me when I cried over the mean kids making fun of me. Memories of Loden laughing with both of them at our dinner table. All three were gone now, and... I missed them all. My anger and hatred faded in grief.

I could hear Rick continue talking, but couldn't quite make out his words. Even the sound of his voice faded away.

A day later, I managed to sit up. Bice fed me oatmeal and answered some of my questions.

Don had ripped out Caesious's neck with the digger and also tore away at his torso some more. Lovat crawled up on the dragon's body and planted Viridia's tooth. Bice sprinkled Viridia's blood around it and then poured the rest out in a visible damp spot nearby.

After that, the team went into hiding. Don drove the digger all the way to the Blasted Lands to hide it. It took him over two days to walk back. In the meantime, everyone else hid all traces of our presence and hunkered down in the cave to wait.

Things got tense when the investigators arrived. First on the scene came the Cerulean Corps, followed by a handful of blue draconics. Lovat, despite warnings to the contrary, snuck out and watched everything. He reported that the Viridian Guard had shown up shortly afterward, leading to loud arguments and even a few blows between the two groups.

The Viridian Guard fled. A train arrived from the city of Caesious, and with a great deal of effort, they managed to take the body of their fallen god away. A few soldiers and one draconic remained behind and continued to search the area. They found the body of Troilus Green, whatever remained of it, and it too was taken away.

Bice and Caedan had worked to conceal the entrance to the cave, even going so far as to partially block it with some large stones. In spite of it all, they had been almost forced to fight when the Cerulean Corps came within a few yards of us. In the end, the cave remained undiscovered and our presence undetected.

When I told Bice about how Troilus Green had used his power outside the city, his face went grave. "I honestly did not think that was possible," he said. "Things have been altered somehow." He left me alone, saying he needed to think about it.

Kelly came to see me and talked for quite a while. She wanted to hear about Loden, of course, and the battle on the train. She told me enthusiastically about how she pushed past her fear to sing those first few words of the dragon anthem. After that, it flowed easily, and she amazed herself with her own courage. Left unsaid was anything about us, our relationship. When I tried to direct the conversation that way, she deflected it to another topic, and then told me to get more rest. I wondered if things would ever be the same with us. Even though she had welcomed me back after I lied to her, I left her to go fight Troilus Green. And then I wasn't back in time to save her. Rick did that. Even if Kelly forgave me, I'm not sure I could forgive myself. I didn't deserve her. And my heart ached with that knowledge.

Most of all, I mourned for Loden. I would give up everything to get him back. It was my fault, anyway. I had started the fight with Troilus Green on the train. If I hadn't, Loden might be here now. The dragon would have still died. Everything would be better. The loss and guilt ate away at me. I had achieved an impossible goal, but it felt empty. What was the point?

A few hours later, I remembered the envelope. At first, I didn't want to find it. Reading Loden's last words to me might be too much to handle. I didn't want to sob again like I had on the train.

I gave in after another hour of indecision. I searched through my gear and found it. My bandaged hands were too clumsy to open it, so I sought out Bice. He took one look at the envelope and nodded. He opened it for me, removed the single sheet of paper inside, and spread it out where I could see.

We both read the five words scrawled on the page, looked at each other and laughed.

"Typical Loden." Bice chuckled.

The page read: "Cave back wall. Finger. Boost."

"Do you know what it means?"

I nodded. "I'm pretty sure."

Bice and I walked to the very back of the cavern. When we first explored this place, I examined this wall and noticed its unusual smoothness. I assumed it had been carved that way. Now I suspected something more.

At my instruction, Bice unwound the bandages from one of my fingers. It had an unhealthy green tint to the skin, but I ignored that. I placed my finger against the cold surface of the rock and closed my eyes. Concentrating, I channeled a quick boost into the finger. I wasn't sure what to expect, but just feeling the familiar internal fluctuation of the implant made me smile. In a way, Loden would always be with me.

We heard a metallic hum. The wall started to vibrate. I stepped back. A loud crack echoed through the cave. The wall shifted backwards a few inches. Then it gradually slid to the left. Light spilled out, blinding us momentarily.

I blinked several times to adjust my eyes. A hidden chamber of the cave lay in front of us. I stepped inside, followed by Bice, who muttered something about the Chromatic Hells.

We entered a long, low room. Smooth walls and floor indicated careful construction, not a natural cavern. Electric lights hummed on the ceiling, operating off a generator that had to be somewhere among all the other tech littering the floors and tables throughout the chamber. Some pieces reminded me of things I knew, while some were totally unfamiliar.

I saw devices resembling shockspears. The boxes on one table looked like talkers. One extra-large piece of strange tech hung from the ceiling. It almost looked like... a pair of wings?

Bice moved to a set of shelves near the door, packed with a bunch of unorganized notebooks. He picked one up and flipped it open.

"These are all his notes," he said. "All of his inventions. Everything he ever created on his own." Bice looked up at me. "Do you realize what this means? Even the secret to your implant could be in here!"

I nodded, turning in a circle. Loden had left me everything. His inventions had been the keys to taking down the dragon. Now he had left us an entire room full of keys that might unlock more secrets than we had even begun to imagine.

I always wanted to kill a dragon, as I said earlier. Maybe everyone has had the same thought at some point in their miserable lives. The thoughts never go anywhere, of course, because trying to kill a dragon is insane.

But we did it. We killed a dragon. As unbelievable as that seems, it was only the first step. Five more dragons still ruled The Circle. One million people remained under their power. We had changed nothing yet. But at the same time... we had changed everything.

Two days later, the war of the dragons began.

For more information on the Dragontek Lore series,
and other upcoming books,
visit timfrankovich.com

Joining the mailing list is the best way to stay informed,
plus you get free stories!
(including Rick's story before he arrived in Viridia!)

If you enjoyed this book, please post a review
on Amazon, B&N, Goodreads, etc.
There's no better way to spread the word.

Acknowledgements

This book leapt almost full-formed into my brain about four years ago. The first draft came a few months later. I set it aside after some feedback, and moved on to my epic fantasy series (*Heart of Fire*) instead. After getting through two books of that, I needed to take a break and do something different. I pulled this manuscript out and began re-working it. I've learned a lot in four years, and I think the result is far stronger than it would have been back then.

Special thanks to my beta readers Stephen Tallman, Allen Perkins, and Monica Zwikstra. Continued appreciation to David Farland and the Apex Writers Group for education, enlightenment and encouragement.

If you want to keep track of my progress on all my writing, you can connect on timfrankovich.com, my Facebook author page, Twitter, etc. But the best way, which keeps you informed and gives you exclusive previews, is to join the mailing list. Sign up on the website. (You'll get free stories too!)

Tim Frankovich has been exploring fantastic worlds since third grade, when he cut up a grocery sack and drew a Godzilla-meets-superheroes story. Since then, he's gotten a little bit better at the writing part (not so much with the drawing).

His goal as a writer is to transport readers to another world, make them care deeply about characters in dire situations, and guide them deeply into life itself.

At the moment, he is probably suitably conscious somewhere in Texas with his beloved wife, awesome four kids, and a fool of a pup named Pippin.

www.ingramcontent.com/pod-product-compliance
Lightning Source LLC
Chambersburg PA
CBHW021139110726
47900CB00002B/416